凡事預則立，
成功是給有準備的人。

No pain, no gain.
No cross, no crown.
No pressure, no diamonds.

* * *

沒有辛苦，就沒有獲得；不勞則無獲。

沒有十字架，就沒有皇冠；吃得苦中苦，為人上人。

沒有壓力，就沒有鑽石；沒有壓力，就沒有動力。

No risk, no reward.
No guts, no glory.
No work, no pay.

* * *

沒有風險，就沒有回報；不入虎穴，焉得虎子。
沒有勇氣，就沒有榮耀；不入虎穴，焉得虎子。
沒有工作，就沒有薪水；無功不受祿。

No smoke, no fire.
No harm, no foul.
No money, no honey.

* * *

沒有煙，就沒有火；無風不起浪；事出必有因。

【籃球】沒有傷害，就不算犯規；小事情，沒關係。

沒有錢，就沒愛情。

如何準備英語口試

我年輕的時候，參加 IBM 公司的智力測驗。考試前我到了書店，買了所有智力測驗的原文書，全部做過一遍，結果輕易通過考試，別人誤以為我很聰明，那些平常很厲害的人，反而沒有通過。從此，我就知道，**無論參加什麼活動都要準備**，成功是給有準備的人。

參加英語口試，一定要有自信，要練到覺得自己英文是全世界最好的，**自信來自於充分準備**。這本「**英語口試寶典**」，你要背得滾瓜爛熟，題目和答案一起背，自己問、自己答。全書按內容難易度分成：初級 (Elementary)、中級 (Intermediate)、中高級 (High-Intermediate)、高級 (Advanced)，及優級 (Superior)。即使你英文已經很好，建議你還是按部就班從**初級 → 中級 → 中高級 → 高級 → 優級**，分階段準備。

為什麼要「問一答二」？

如果別人問你："***What's your name?***" 你只回答："***Alex Smith***." 這樣不夠熱情。如果你回答："***I'm Alex Smith***." 別人聽起來就舒服多了。再加上一句："***Just call me Alex***."，**你就在散發溫暖了**，人人喜歡你。

為什麼題目和答案要一起背？

養成「自問自答」的習慣，會讓你的英文快速進步。祕訣是，一定要短句，**句子越短越好背，只有短句才能背得下來**。全書共有 810 組問與答，2,430 個句子，無人能背得下來。但是**分組有助於記憶**，連問題一起背，以「一口氣英語」的方式，三句一組，九句一段，背起來就容易多了。

劉毅

目 錄
CONTENTS

英語口試 — 初級

Elementary

英語口試「初級」Oral Test 1~14

1. 所謂「初級」，是最基本的，也是最重要的。

2. 背的時候，題目和答案要一起背，所以美籍老師錄音也是同一人。

3. 要練習自問自答，背到變成直覺，才能應付考試。

4. Elementary Oral Tests的錄音QR碼只有唸問題，保留足夠的時間讓你練習回答。

Elementary

Oral Test 1

用手機掃瞄聽錄音

【問與答一起背】

□ 1. ***What's your name?***	你叫什麼名字？
I'm Alex Smith.	我是艾力克斯•史密斯。
Just call me Alex.	叫我艾力克斯就好。
□ 2. ***How old are you?***	你今年幾歲？
Fifteen.	十五歲。
I'll be sixteen next month.	我下個月就十六歲了。
□ 3. ***How are you doing?***	你好嗎？
I'm doing good.	我很好。
Couldn't be better.	好極了。

I'm doing good.

**

Alex Smith (ˈæləks ˈsmɪθ) *n.* 艾力克斯•史密斯【Alex 這個名字男女通用】

I'm doing good. 我很好。(= *I'm doing fine.* = *I'm doing well.* = *I'm doing great.*)

Couldn't be better. 字面的意思是「沒辦法更好。」表示「好極了。」(= *I couldn't be better.*) 不可說成：*Can't be better.* (誤)

□ 4. ***Where are you from?***	你來自哪裡？
Taiwan.	台灣。
My hometown is Hsinchu.	我的故鄉是新竹。
□ 5. ***Where do you live?***	你住在哪裡？
Now I live in Taipei.	現在我住在台北。
We moved there five years ago.	我們五年前搬去那裡。
□ 6. ***Are you a student?***	你是學生嗎？
Yes, I'm a student.	是的，我是學生。
I'm in high school.	我就讀高中。

**

hometown〔'hom'taʊn〕*n.* 故鄉；家鄉
Hsinchu〔'ʃɪn'tʃu〕*n.* 新竹
move〔muv〕*v.* 搬家
high school 高中

move

□ 7. ***What grade are you in?***	你是幾年級？
I'm in tenth grade.	我是十年級。
I'm a sophomore in high school.	我是高二學生。
□ 8. ***Do you have a nickname?***	你有綽號嗎？
I have an English nickname.	我有個英文綽號。
It's Alex.	就是艾力克斯。
□ 9. ***Tell me a little about yourself.***	告訴我一些關於你自己的事。
I like to make friends.	我喜歡交朋友。
I enjoy being around people.	我喜歡和人在一起。

** ——————————

grade (gred) *n.* 年級

I'm in tenth grade. 可説成：The tenth.（十年級。）

I'm in the tenth.（我是十年級。）

sophomore ('sɑfm̩,or) *n.* 高二學生；大二學生

nickname ('nɪk,nem) *n.* 綽號

make friends 交朋友

around (ə'raund) *prep.* 環繞；在…周圍

around

【背景説明】

Oral Test 1

3. ***How are you doing?***（你好嗎？）不要和 What are you doing?（你正在做什麼？）弄混。***How are you doing?***（你好嗎？）常簡化成：How you doing? 就和 How are you? 一樣，非常普遍。可回答：***I'm doing good.***（我很好。）一般說來，good 可當形容詞用或名詞，有些字典把這種情況當副詞，這是文法的盲點，最簡單的方法，是把 ***I'm doing good.*** 當作慣用句來背。也可說成：I'm doing fine. 或 I'm doing well. 或 I'm doing great. 意思都相同。***Couldn't be better.***（好極了。）源自 ***I couldn't be better.*** 這是現在式的用法，過去式就要用 Couldn't have been better.（好極了。）

【比較】 A：How's your new teacher?
（你的新老師如何？）
B：***Couldn't be better.***（好極了。）

A：How was your weekend?
（你的週末如何？）
B：***Couldn't have been better.***（好極了。）

9. ***I enjoy being around people.***（我喜歡和人在一起。）可說成：***I*** really ***enjoy being around*** lots of ***people.***（我眞的很喜歡和很多人在一起。）I enjoy having many people around me.（我喜歡我周圍有很多人。）I like having many friends around me.（我喜歡周圍有很多朋友。）

Oral Test 2

Elementary

【問與答一起背】

□ 1. ***Who do you live with?***	你和誰住在一起？
My parents.	我的父母。
I also have a younger sister.	我也有個妹妹。
□ 2. ***How big is your family?***	你們家有多少人？
There are five of us.	我們家有五個人。
My older brother lives in Australia.	我的哥哥住在澳洲。
□ 3. ***Do you have any siblings?***	你有任何兄弟姊妹嗎？
Yes, two.	有，兩個。
My little sister and my brother.	我妹妹和我哥哥。

** ___

younger sister 妹妹（= *little sister*）（↔ *elder sister* 姐姐）

big〔bɪg〕*adj.*（數量、規模）大的

How big is your family? 你們家有多少人？

older brother 哥哥（= *elder brother*）

Australia〔ɔ'streljə〕*n.* 澳洲

siblings〔'sɪblɪŋz〕*n. pl.* 兄弟姐妹

siblings

□ 4. ***What's her name?***	她叫什麼名字？
Ally.	艾莉。
Her name is Ally.	她的名字是艾莉。
□ 5. ***How old is she?***	她今年幾歲？
She's three years younger than me.	她比我小三歲。
She's twelve.	她今年十二歲。
□ 6. ***What grade is she in?***	她是幾年級？
6th grade.	六年級。
She's still in elementary school.	她還在唸小學。

** ________________

Ally (ˈælɪ) *n.* 艾莉　　year (jɪr) *n.* 年；歲

young (jʌŋ) *adj.* 年少的；年幼的

be three years younger than 比…小三歲

grade (gred) *n.* 年級　　still (stɪl) *adv.* 仍然；還

elementary (ˌɛləˈmɛntərɪ) *adj.* 基本的；初等的

elementary school 小學（= *primary school*）

□ 7. ***What's your sister like?***	你的妹妹是個什麼樣的人？
She's awesome.	她很棒。
She's really smart.	她真的很聰明。
□ 8. ***Are you guys close?***	你們很親近嗎？
Super close.	超級親近。
We spend a lot of time together.	我們很多時間都在一起。
□ 9. ***What do you like to do together?***	你們喜歡一起做什麼？
Watch movies.	看電影。
We also play badminton.	我們也會打羽毛球。

**

like (laɪk) *prep.* 像　***What is she like?*** 她是個什麼樣的人？

awesome (ˈɔsəm) *adj.* 很棒的　smart (smɑrt) *adj.* 聰明的

guy (gaɪ) *n.* 人；傢伙

you guys 你們

close (klos) *adj.* 親近的

close

super (ˈsupɚ) *adv.* 非常

spend (spɛnd) *v.* 花費；度過　together (təˈgɛðɚ) *adv.* 一起

badminton (ˈbædmɪntən) *n.* 羽毛球

play badminton 打羽毛球

Oral Test 3

【問與答一起背】

□ 1. ***Do you have any interests in common?***	你們有任何共同的興趣嗎？
Sure.	當然。
We like the same movies.	我們喜歡同樣的電影。
□ 2. ***Do you ever argue or disagree?***	你們曾經爭論或意見不合嗎？
Of course.	當然。
We fight once in a while.	我們偶爾會吵架。
□ 3. ***What do you fight about?***	你們會爲了什麼吵架？
Small things.	小事。
Like who has to wash the dishes.	像是誰必須洗碗。

**

interest〔ˈɪntrɪst〕*n.* 興趣　***in common*** 共同的
sure〔ʃʊr〕*adv.* 當然　same〔sem〕*adj.* 相同的
ever〔ˈɛvɚ〕*adv.* 曾經　argue〔ˈɑrgjʊ〕*v.* 爭論
disagree〔ˌdɪsəˈgri〕*v.* 意見不合　***of course*** 當然
fight〔faɪt〕*v.* 打架；吵架　***once in a while*** 偶爾；有時候
like〔laɪk〕*prep.* 像是　dish〔dɪʃ〕*n.* 盤子；(*pl.*) 餐桌用盤碟
wash the dishes 洗碗（= *do the dishes*）

argue

□ 4. ***What are your parents' names?***	你的父母叫什麼名字？
My father's name is John.	我父親的名字是約翰。
My mother's name is Carol.	我母親的名字是卡蘿。
□ 5. ***May I ask what your parents do?***	我可以問你的父母是做什麼的嗎？
My dad's an engineer.	我爸爸是工程師。
My mom is an accountant.	我媽媽是會計。
□ 6. ***How old are they?***	他們今年幾歲？
He's 45.	我爸爸 45 歲。
She's 43.	我媽媽 43 歲。

**

Carol〔'kærəl〕*n.* 卡蘿

dad〔dæd〕*n.* 爸爸

engineer〔,ɛndʒə'nɪr〕*n.* 工程師

mom〔mɑm〕*n.* 媽媽

accountant〔ə'kaʊntənt〕*n.* 會計；會計師

engineer

□ 7. ***Do you get along with your parents?*** 你和你的父母相處融洽嗎？

Yeah, we get along. 是的，我們相處得很好。

Most of the time. 大部份的時候。

□ 8. ***What's your dad like?*** 你爸爸是個什麼樣的人？

He's very patient. 他很有耐心。

He's a friendly person. 他是個友善的人。

□ 9. ***What's your mom like?*** 你媽媽是個什麼樣的人？

She's a bit strict. 她有一點嚴格。

But she's kind, too. 但她也很親切。

** ──────────

get along 處得好　　yeah〔jɛ〕*adv.* 是的（= *yes*）

most of the time 大部份的時候

patient〔ˈpeʃənt〕*adj.* 有耐心的

friendly〔ˈfrɛndlɪ〕*adj.* 友善的

a bit 有一點　　strict〔strɪkt〕*adj.* 嚴格的

kind〔kaɪnd〕*adj.* 親切的；好心的

kind

Oral Test 4

【問與答一起背】

□ 1. ***Who are you more like?***	你比較像誰？
I'm more like my dad.	我比較像我爸爸。
We have the same sense of humor.	我們有同樣的幽默感。
□ 2. ***Do you have any aunts or uncles?***	你有任何阿姨或叔叔嗎？
Oh yeah, several.	喔，有，有幾個。
Both of my parents come from big families.	我的父母兩人都來自大家庭。
□ 3. ***Do you have many cousins?***	你有很多表兄弟姊妹嗎？
Yes, I have many.	是的，我有很多。
I have over 20 cousins.	我有超過二十個表兄弟姊妹。

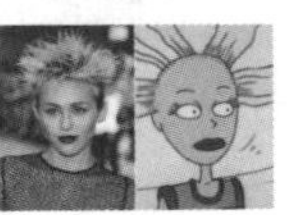

like

** ______________________

like〔laɪk〕*prep.* 像　　sense〔sɛns〕*n.* 感覺
humor〔ˈhjumɚ〕*n.* 幽默　　***sense of humor*** 幽默感
aunt〔ænt〕*n.* 阿姨；姑姑　　uncle〔ˈʌŋkl̩〕*n.* 叔叔；舅舅
yeah〔jɛ〕*adv.* 是的（= *yes*）
cousin〔ˈkʌzn̩〕*n.* 表（堂）兄弟姊妹

□ 4. ***Do you see your grandparents often?*** 你常去看你的祖父母嗎？

My dad's parents passed away. 我爸爸的父母去世了。

But we visit my mom's parents often. 但我們常去探望我媽媽的父母。

□ 5. ***How old are your grandparents?*** 你的祖父母今年幾歲？

My grandpa is 70. 我的祖父 70 歲。

My grandma is 65. 我的祖母 65 歲。

□ 6. ***Where do they live?*** 他們住在哪裡？

In the countryside. 在鄉下。

They don't like the city. 他們不喜歡都市。

**

grandparents〔ˈgrændˌpɛrənts〕*n. pl.* 祖父母

pass away 去世　visit〔ˈvɪzɪt〕*v.* 拜訪；探望

grandpa〔ˈgrændpɑ〕*n.*（外）祖父

grandma〔ˈgrændmə〕*n.*（外）祖母

countryside〔ˈkʌntrɪˌsaɪd〕*n.* 鄉村地區

city〔ˈsɪtɪ〕*n.* 城市；都市

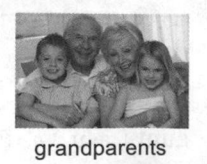

grandparents

□ 7. ***How often does your entire family get together?***	你們全家人多久聚在一起一次？
Not so often.	不是很常。
Once or twice a year.	一年一或兩次。
□ 8. ***When do you have family reunions?***	你們全家人何時會團聚？
On holidays.	在假日。
We always meet during Chinese New Year.	我們在農曆年期間總是會見面。
□ 9. ***When you're all together, what do you do?***	當你們全都聚在一起時，會做什麼？
We enjoy a big meal.	我們會享用大餐。
We chat and watch TV.	我們會聊天和看電視。

** ___________________________

entire (ɪn'taɪr) *adj.* 整個的；全部的　***get together*** 聚集；聚會
so (so) *adv.* 非常 (= *very*)　once (wʌns) *adv.* 一次
twice (twaɪs) *adv.* 兩次　reunion (ri'junjən) *n.* 團聚；團圓
holiday ('hɑlə,de) *n.* 節日；假日　meet (mit) *v.* 會面
Chinese New Year 農曆新年　together (tə'gɛðɚ) *adv.* 一起
enjoy (ɪn'dʒɔɪ) *v.* 享受　big (bɪg) *adj.* 豐盛的
meal (mil) *n.* 一餐　chat (tʃæt) *v.* 聊天

【背景説明】

Oral Test 2

2. ***How big is your family?*** 字面的意思是「你們家有多大？」引申為「你們家有多少人？」(= *How big is the number of people in your family?*) 可説成：How many are there in your family?（你們家有多少人？）(= *How many people are there in your family?*)

7. ***What's your sister like?***（你的妹妹是個什麼樣的人？）可客氣地説：Please tell me what your sister is really like.（請告訴我，你的妹妹究竟是什麼樣的人。）也可説成：Tell me about your sister.（告訴我關於你妹妹的事。）What kind of person is your sister?（你妹妹是什麼樣的人？）【kind〔kaɪnd〕*n.* 種類】

Oral Test 3

1. ***Do you have any interests in common?***（你們有任何共同的興趣嗎？）Do you and your sister have interests in common?（你和你的妹妹有共同的興趣嗎？）Are you two alike?（你們兩個像不像？）(= *Are you two similar?*) Do you two like the same things?（你們兩個喜歡同樣的事物嗎？）【alike〔əˈlaɪk〕*adj.* 相像的】

Oral Test 4

1. ***We have the same sense of humor.***（我們有同樣的幽默感。）(= *We are similar when it comes to humor.*) We laugh at the same things.（我們會為了同樣的事情笑。）We both have a good sense of humor.（我們兩個都很有幽默感。）

Elementary

Oral Test 5

【問與答一起背】

□ 1. ***Where were you born?***	你在哪裡出生？
In Kaohsiung.	在高雄。
It's Taiwan's second biggest city.	它是台灣第二大城市。
□ 2. ***When were you born?***	你是什麼時候出生的？
In October.	在10月。
October 6th to be exact.	精確地說，是10月6日。
□ 3. ***What year were you born?***	你是哪一年出生的？
In 2004.	在2004年。
I'm part of Generation Z.	我是Z世代。

Kaohsiung

**

be born 出生

Kaohsiung (ˈkauˈʃjuŋ) *n.* 高雄

second biggest 第二大的　birthday (ˈbɝθ,de) *n.* 生日

October (ɑkˈtobɚ) *n.* 十月　exact (ɪgˈzækt) *adj.* 準確的；精確的

to be exact 精確地說　part (pɑrt) *n.* 部分

generation (ˌdʒɛnəˈreʃən) *n.* 世代　***Generation Z*** Z世代

□ **4.** ***What's your sign?*** 你是什麼星座？

I'm a Libra. 我是天秤座。

It's the sign of justice and harmony. 它是公平正義與和諧的星座。

□ **5.** ***What's your middle name?*** 你的中間名是什麼？

I don't have one. 我沒有中間名。

Most Chinese don't. 大部份的中國人都沒有。

□ **6.** ***Where did you grow up?*** 你在哪裡長大？

In Tainan. 在台南。

I moved to Taipei last year. 我去年搬到台北。

**

sign〔saɪn〕*n.* 星座

Libra〔'librə〕*n.* 天秤座；屬天秤座的人

justice〔'dʒʌstɪs〕*n.* 公平；正義

harmony〔'hɑrmənɪ〕*n.* 和諧　　middle〔'mɪdḷ〕*adj.* 中間的

middle name 中間名【如 George Bernard Shaw 的 Bernard】

grow up 長大　　Tainan〔'taɪ'nɑn〕*n.* 台南

move〔muv〕*v.* 搬家　　Taipei〔'taɪ'pe〕*n.* 台北

□ **7.** ***Did you like the neighborhood where you grew up?***	你喜歡你成長的地區嗎？
I loved it.	我很愛。
It was a nice neighborhood.	它是個很好的地區。
□ **8.** ***What was your childhood like?***	你的童年生活如何？
It was carefree and happy.	無憂無慮而且快樂。
My childhood was fun.	我的童年很有趣。
□ **9.** ***What do you miss most about being a kid?***	你最想念小時候的什麼？
I miss the games we played.	我想念我們玩的遊戲。
I miss the friends I had.	我想念我的朋友。

** ————————————

neighborhood〔ˈnebɚ,hʊd〕*n.* 鄰近地區
nice〔naɪs〕*adj.* 好的
childhood〔ˈtʃaɪld,hʊd〕*n.* 童年時期
carefree〔ˈkɛr,fri〕*adj.* 無憂無慮的
fun〔fʌn〕*adj.* 有趣的　　miss〔mɪs〕*v.* 想念
kid〔kɪd〕*n.* 小孩　　game〔gem〕*n.* 遊戲

neighborhood

Elementary

Oral Test 6

【問與答一起背】

□ 1. ***When's your birthday?***	你的生日是什麼時候？
It's June 13th.	六月十三日。
My birthday's in the summer.	我的生日是在夏天。
□ 2. ***How old will you be?***	你快要幾歲了？
I'm turning 18.	我快要十八歲。
I'm almost old enough to drive.	我年紀差不多大到可以開車了。
□ 3. ***Any birthday plans?***	有任何生日的計劃嗎？
Yes, I've got plans.	是的，我有計劃。
I'm going out to have dinner.	我要出去吃晚餐。

**

birthday〔ˈbɝθˌde〕*n.* 生日

June〔dʒun〕*n.* 六月　　turn〔tɝn〕*v.* 變成

summer〔ˈsʌmɚ〕*n.* 夏天

plan〔plæn〕*n. v.* 計劃

I've got 我有（= *I have*）　　have〔hæv〕*v.* 吃

birthday

□ 4. ***Will you have a party?***
I probably won't.
Everyone is busy with exams right now.

我可能不會。
現在大家都在忙著考試。

□ 5. ***Do you like birthday parties?***
I think they're ok.
Just not for myself.

你喜歡生日派對嗎？
我認爲還不錯。
只是不要爲我舉辦。

□ 6. ***Describe a typical party.***
We all eat together.
People give gifts.

描述一個典型的派對。
我們全都
會一起吃東西。
大家會送禮物。

** ——————————

你會舉辦派對嗎？

have〔hæv〕*v.* 舉辦　***have a party*** 舉辦派對
probably〔ˈprɑbəblɪ〕*adv.* 可能
be busy with 忙於　***right now*** 現在
ok〔ˈoˈke〕*adj.* 好的；可以的
describe〔dɪˈskraɪb〕*v.* 描述
typical〔ˈtɪpɪkl̩〕*adj.* 典型的
gift〔gɪft〕*n.* 禮物　***give gifts*** 送禮物

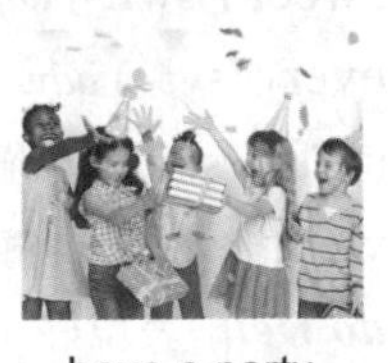
have a party

Elementary

☐ 7. ***What would you like for your birthday?*** 你生日想要什麼？

Nothing much. 不要什麼貴重的東西。

Just a card is enough. 只要一張卡片就足夠了。

☐ 8. ***What's the sweetest gift you've ever received?*** 你曾經收到最可愛的禮物是什麼？

It was a big stuffed animal. 是一隻大型填充玩具動物。

I still have it in my room. 我仍然把它放在我的房間裡。

☐ 9. ***What are your wishes for the upcoming year?*** 未來這一年你有什麼願望？

To do well in school. 要在學校表現良好。

To improve my spoken English. 要改善我的口說英語。

**

would like 想要 card〔kɑrd〕*n.* 卡片

card

sweet〔swit〕*adj.* 令人高興的；討人喜歡的；可愛的

ever〔ˈɛvɚ〕*adv.* 曾經 receive〔rɪˈsiv〕*v.* 收到

stuff〔stʌf〕*v.* 填塞 ***stuffed animal*** 填充玩具動物

wish〔wɪʃ〕*n.* 願望 upcoming〔ˈʌpˌkʌmɪŋ〕*adj.* 即將來臨的

do well 表現好；考得好 improve〔ɪmˈpruv〕*v.* 改善

spoken〔ˈspokən〕*adj.* 口說的；口語的

spoken English 口說英語；英語會話

【背景說明】

Oral Test 5

2. ***October 6th to be exact.***（精確地說，是 10 月 6 日。）(= *To be exact, October 6th.* = *To be exact, it's October 6th.*)

3. ***I'm part of Generation Z.***（我是 Z 世代。）可說成：I'm a member of generation Z.（我是 Z 世代的成員。）***Generation Z***（Z 世代）是指 1990 年中葉至 2000 年後出生的人。

4. ***What's your sign?***（你是什麼星座？）(= *What's your star sign?*)
I'm a Libra.（我是天秤座。）(= *My star sign is Libra.*)

十二星座的名稱

星 座	英 文	星 座 日 期
牡羊座	Aries〔ˈɛriz〕	3 月 21 日～4 月 20 日
金牛座	Taurus〔ˈtɔrəs〕	4 月 21 日～5 月 21 日
雙子座	Gemini〔ˈdʒɛmə,naɪ〕	5 月 22 日～6 月 21 日
巨蟹座	Cancer〔ˈkænsɚ〕	6 月 22 日～7 月 22 日
獅子座	Leo〔ˈlio〕	7 月 23 日～8 月 22 日
處女座	Virgo〔ˈvɝgo〕	8 月 23 日～9 月 23 日
天秤座	Libra〔ˈlibrə〕	9 月 24 日～10 月 23 日
天蠍座	Scorpio〔ˈskɔrpɪ,o〕	10 月 24 日～11 月 22 日
射手座	Sagittarius〔,sædʒɪˈtɛrɪəs〕	11 月 23 日～12 月 21 日
魔羯座	Capricorn〔ˈkæprɪ,kɔrn〕	12 月 22 日～1 月 20 日
水瓶座	Aquarius〔əˈkwɛrɪəs〕	1 月 21 日～2 月 19 日
雙魚座	Pisces〔ˈpɪsiz〕	2 月 20 日～3 月 20 日

8. ***What was your childhood like?***（你的童年生活如何？）可以客氣地說：Please tell me what your childhood was like.（請告訴我，你的童年生活如何。）How was your childhood?（你的童年生活如何？）Did you have a good childhood?（你的童年生活愉快嗎？）（= *Was your childhood OK?*）

Oral Test 6

2. ***I'm turning 18.***（我快要十八歲。）可說成：I'll be eighteen.（我將會是十八歲。）（= *I'll be eighteen years old.*）I'm going to be 18 on my birthday.（到我生日時，我就是十八歲了。）

3. ***Yes, I've got plans.***（是的，我有計劃。）（= *Yes, I have plans.*）可說成：Yes, I've made plans.（是的，我做了一些計劃。）

5. 生日到的時候，別人問你 ***Do you like birthday parties?***（你喜歡生日派對嗎？）你不喜歡，就可以說：***I think they're ok.***（我認爲還不錯。）***Just not for myself.***（只是不要爲我舉辦。）（= *I just don't want one for myself.* = *I just don't want one for me.* = *Just not for me.*）用 myself 加強 me 的語氣。【詳見「文法寶典」p.118】這句話也可說成：No party for me.（不要爲我舉辦派對。）暗示 I don't really like birthday parties.（我不是很喜歡生日派對。）

7. 回答 ***What would you like for your birthday?***（你生日想要什麼？）時，一般都會謙虛地說：***Nothing much.***（不要什麼貴重的東西。）或 ***Nothing much*** at all.（不要什麼貴重的東西。）***Nothing much***, something small.（不要什麼貴重的東西，只要小東西就可以了。）【***not…at all*** 一點也不】

Oral Test 7

Elementary

【問與答一起背】

□ 1. ***What's your home like?***	你的家是什麼樣子的？
It's very comfortable.	它非常舒適。
We have three bedrooms.	我們有三間臥室。
□ 2. ***What type of home do you live in?***	你住的是什麼類型的房子？
It's an apartment.	它是公寓。
But it's in a small building.	但它是在一棟小型的建築物裡。
□ 3. ***What's your neighborhood like?***	你的那一區如何？
It's a nice place.	它是個很不錯的地方。
It's very safe.	它非常安全。

** ______________________

like (laɪk) *prep.* 像　comfortable (ˈkʌmfətəbḷ) *adj.* 舒適的
bedroom (ˈbɛd,rum) *n.* 臥室　type (taɪp) *n.* 類型
apartment (əˈpɑrtmənt) *n.* 公寓
building (ˈbɪldɪŋ) *n.* 建築物；大樓
neighborhood (ˈnebə,hud) *n.* 鄰近地區
nice (naɪs) *adj.* 好的　safe (sef) *adj.* 安全的

apartment

□ 4. ***Do you have any pets?***	你有養任何寵物嗎？
I don't.	我沒有。
I've never had a pet.	我從未養過寵物。
□ 5. ***Why not?***	為什麼不？
Our building doesn't allow pets.	我們的大樓不允許養寵物。
People think they're too noisy.	大家認為牠們太吵了。
□ 6. ***Do you want a pet?***	你想要寵物嗎？
Yes, I want a cat.	是的，我想要一隻貓。
I think they're good pets for apartments.	我認為牠們是很適合公寓的寵物。

** ______________________________

have〔hæv〕*v.* 養（寵物）（= *keep*）

pet〔pɛt〕*n.* 寵物

allow〔əˈlaʊ〕*v.* 允許

noisy〔ˈnɔɪzɪ〕*adj.* 吵鬧的

pets

☐ 7. ***Do you do chores?*** 你做家事嗎？
Yes, I have chores. 是的，我有家事要做。
I take out the garbage every night. 我每天晚上倒垃圾。

☐ 8. ***Do you have an allowance?*** 你有零用錢嗎？
Yes, I do. 是的，我有。
I get 2,000 a month. 我一個月有兩千元。

☐ 9. ***Do you have a curfew?*** 你有門禁時間嗎？
I have to be home by 10. 我十點前必須回家。
But I can stay out later on the weekend. 但在週末我可以在外面待得比較晚。

** ______________________

chores〔tʃorz〕*n. pl.* 雜事；家事（= *household chores*）
take out 把…拿出去　garbage〔ˈgɑrbɪdʒ〕*n.* 垃圾
allowance〔əˈlaʊəns〕*n.* 零用錢（= *pocket money*）
curfew〔ˈkɝfju〕*n.* 宵禁；宵禁時間；關門時間
by〔baɪ〕*prep.* 在…之前　***stay out*** 留在外面
later〔ˈletɚ〕*adv.* 較晚地　weekend〔ˈwikˈɛnd〕*n.* 週末

Oral Test 8

【問與答一起背】

□ 1. ***Do you get enough sleep?***	你有充足的睡眠嗎？
No, I don't.	不，我沒有。
I don't get enough rest.	我沒有得到足夠的休息。
□ 2. ***How many hours do you get?***	你睡幾個小時？
Around six hours.	大約六個小時。
I'd rather get eight.	我寧願睡八個小時。
□ 3. ***Do you sleep well?***	你睡得好嗎？
I don't sleep well.	我睡得不好。
I have trouble sleeping.	我很難入睡。

** ———————————

sleep〔slip〕*n.* 睡眠　*v.* 睡覺　　rest〔rɛst〕*n.* 休息
around〔ə'raʊnd〕*adv.* 大約
would rather 寧願
trouble〔'trʌbl̩〕*n.* 麻煩；困難
have trouble* (*in*) + *V-ing 很難…

I have trouble sleeping.

□ 4. ***What do you do when you have trouble sleeping?***	當你很難入睡時，你會做什麼？
I'll drink warm milk.	我會喝溫牛奶。
I'll read until I fall asleep.	我會閱讀直到我睡著。
□ 5. ***What time do you usually go to bed?***	你通常幾點上床睡覺？
I'm usually in bed by eleven.	我通常十一點以前上床睡覺。
I have to get up early.	我必須早起。
□ 6. ***What time do you usually get up?***	你通常幾點起床？
Around 7 am.	大約早上七點。
I try to be up by 7:15.	我儘量七點十五分以前起床。

**

warm〔wɔrm〕*adj.* 溫熱的　fall〔fɔl〕*v.* 變成（某種狀態）

asleep〔ə'slip〕*adj.* 睡著的　***fall asleep*** 睡著

go to bed 上床睡覺　usually〔'juʒʊəlɪ〕*adv.* 通常

in bed 在床上　by〔baɪ〕*prep.* 在…之前

get up 起床　am *adv.* 上午（= *a.m.*）

up〔ʌp〕*adj.* 起床的

□ 7. ***Do you often dream?*** 你常做夢嗎？

All the time. 一直都會。

I dream a lot. 我常常做夢。

□ 8. ***Do you remember your dreams?*** 你記得你的夢嗎？

Sometimes. 有時候。

They never make sense. 都是一些不合理的夢。

□ 9. ***Did you sleep well?*** 你睡得好嗎？

Yes, I did. 是的，我睡得好。

I slept alright. 我睡得很好。

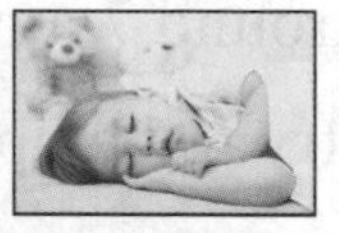
I slept alright.

**

dream〔drim〕*v.* 做夢　*n.* 夢

all the time 一直　***a lot*** 常常（= *often*）

sometimes〔ˈsʌm͵taɪmz〕*adv.* 有時候

make sense 合理

alright〔ɔlˈraɪt〕*adv.* 沒問題地；極好地

Oral Test 9

【問與答一起背】

□ 1. ***What's your daily routine?***	你每天的例行公事是什麼？
I walk my dog every morning.	我每天早上遛狗。
Every night, I recite One Word English.	我每天晚上背誦「英文一字金」。
□ 2. ***What's your weekly routine?***	你每週的例行公事是什麼？
Every day, I go to school.	我每天上學。
I work out every other day.	我每隔一天運動。
□ 3. ***What do you usually do on weekends?***	你在週末通常會做什麼？
I do some reading.	我會看一些書。
I usually go shopping.	我通常會去購物。

** ________________

daily ('delɪ) *adj.* 每天的　routine (ru'tin) *n.* 例行公事
walk (wɔk) *v.* 遛（狗）　recite (rɪ'saɪt) *v.* 背誦
weekly ('wiklɪ) *adj.* 每週的　***work out*** 運動
every other day 每隔一天；每兩天　weekend ('wik'ɛnd) *n.* 週末
do some reading 看一些書　***go shopping*** 去購物

□ 4. ***What are you doing this weekend?***	這個週末你要做什麼？
I'm going out of town.	我要出城去。
I'm going to visit some relatives.	我要去拜訪一些親戚。
□ 5. ***How much free time do you have?***	你有多少空閒時間？
Not much.	不多。
I'm usually free on Sundays.	我通常星期天有空。
□ 6. ***What do you do when you have free time?***	當你有空時你會做什麼？
I watch TV.	我會看電視。
Or I play with my friends.	或是和朋友玩。

**

town〔taʊn〕*n.* 城鎮　***go out of town*** 出城
visit〔ˈvɪzɪt〕*v.* 拜訪；探望
relative〔ˈrɛlətɪv〕*n.* 親戚
free〔fri〕*adj.* 有空的　***free time*** 空閒時間
on Sundays 在每個星期天

visit

□ 7. ***When do you take a break?***	你何時休息？
After lunch.	午餐後。
I relax for 30 minutes.	我會放鬆三十分鐘。
□ 8. ***If you had more free time, what would you do?***	如果你有更多空閒時間，你會做什麼？
I would walk.	我會走路。
I would go for a walk every evening.	我會每天晚上去散步。
□ 9. "***Time is money.***" ***Do you agree or disagree? Why?***	「時間就是金錢。」你同不同意？爲什麼？
I agree with you.	我同意你的說法。
I guess wasting time is wasting money.	我想浪費時間就是浪費金錢。

** ______________________

break (brek) *n.* 休息　***take a break*** 休息一下

relax (rɪ'læks) *v.* 放鬆　***go for a walk*** 去散步

Time is money. 【諺】時間就是金錢。

agree (ə'gri) *v.* 同意　disagree (ˌdɪsə'gri) *v.* 不同意

agree with *sb.* 同意某人；和某人意見一致　waste (west) *v.* 浪費

【背景說明】

Oral Test 7

9. ***Do you have a curfew?***（你有門禁時間嗎？）

可說成：Do you have a curfew on school nights?（隔天要上課的晚上，你有門禁時間嗎？）【***school night*** 隔天要上課的晚上】Do your parents give you a curfew?（你的父母有沒有規定你什麼時間要回家？）（= *Do your parents expect you to be home at a certain hour?*）

Oral Test 8

2. ***How many hours do you get?***（你睡幾個小時？）（= *How many hours do you sleep?*）可說成：About how many hours of sleep do you get every night?（你每天晚上大約睡幾個小時？）***I'd rather get eight.***（我寧願睡八個小時。）（= *I wish I could sleep eight hours.*）I'd prefer eight hours.（我比較喜歡睡八個小時。）可加強語氣說成：Of course, I'd rather get eight hours of sleep.（當然，我寧願能有八個小時的睡眠。）

3. ***I have trouble sleeping.***（我很難入睡。）I'm not a sound sleeper.（我睡得不好。）（= *I'm not a deep sleeper.*）【sound〔saund〕*adj.*（睡眠）充分的】I often toss and turn in my sleep.（我睡覺時常常輾轉難眠。）【***toss and turn*** 輾轉反側；翻來覆去】

6. ***I try to be up by 7:15***.（我儘量七點十五分以前起床。）（= *I try to be out of bed by 7:15.*）My goal is to be awake and on my feet by 7:15.（我的目標是七點十五分之前起床。）【***on one's feet*** 站起來】I try hard to be up by 7:15 am.（我儘量在早上七點十五分之前起床。）

8. ***They never make sense***.（都是一些不合理的夢。）可說成：They never make much sense to me.（都是對我而言沒什麼意義的。）My dreams are confusing.（我的夢令人困惑。）【confusing〔kənˈfjuzɪŋ〕*adj.* 令人困惑的】I never understand my dreams.（我從不了解我的夢。）

9. 在 ***I slept alright***. 中，alright（= *all right*）的意思有：①不錯（= *fairly*）②相當好的（= *very good*）③進展順利（= *going well*）。***I slept alright***. 可能是：①我睡得還好。（= *I slept OK.*）②我睡得很好。（= *I slept fairly well.*）

Oral Test 9

2. ***I work out every other day***.（我每隔一天運動。）（= *I exercise every other day. = I work out every two days.*）

3. ***I do some reading***.（我會看一些書。）（= *I read some.*）I read every weekend.（我每個週末都會看書。）On weekends, I always manage to do some reading.（週末時，我總是會設法看一些書。）【manage〔ˈmænɪdʒ〕*v.* 設法】

Elementary

Oral Test 10

【問與答一起背】

□ 1. ***What's your favorite color?***	你最喜愛的顏色是什麼？
I like blue.	我喜歡藍色。
It's a nice calm color.	它是個很好，能使人平靜的顏色。
□ 2. ***What's your favorite animal?***	你最喜愛的動物是什麼？
I like bears.	我喜歡熊。
Both polar bears and pandas.	北極熊和貓熊。
□ 3. ***What's your favorite hobby?***	你最喜愛的嗜好是什麼？
I like outdoor activities.	我喜歡戶外活動。
I like hiking and biking.	我喜歡健行和騎腳踏車。

polar bear

** ———————————

favorite〔ˈfevərɪt〕*adj.* 最喜愛的　*n.* 最喜愛的人或物
calm〔kɑm〕*adj.* 冷靜的；平靜的　bear〔bɛr〕*n.* 熊
polar〔ˈpolɚ〕*adj.* 極地的　***polar bear*** 北極熊
panda〔ˈpændə〕*n.* 熊貓；貓熊　hobby〔ˈhɑbɪ〕*n.* 嗜好
outdoor〔ˈaʊtˌdor〕*adj.* 戶外的　activity〔ækˈtɪvətɪ〕*n.* 活動
hike〔haɪk〕*v.* 健行　bike〔baɪk〕*v.* 騎腳踏車

□ **4.** ***What's your favorite part of the day?***	你一天之中最喜愛什麼時候？
I like after dinner.	我喜歡晚餐後。
It's my relaxation time.	那是我的放鬆時間。
□ **5.** ***What's your favorite day of the week?***	一星期當中，你最喜愛星期幾？
It's Saturday.	星期六。
I have lots of free time then.	那時我有很多空閒時間。
□ **6.** ***What's your favorite snack?***	你最喜愛的點心是什麼？
I love grapes.	我喜愛葡萄。
I could eat grapes all day.	我可以整天吃葡萄。

** ——————

relaxation (ˌrilækˈseʃən) *n.* 放鬆

lots of 很多的　　***free time*** 空閒時間

snack (snæk) *n.* 點心

grape (grep) *n.* 葡萄　　***all day*** 整天

grapes

□ 7. ***Who is your favorite superhero?***	誰是你最喜愛的超級英雄？
Definitely Batman.	當然是蝙蝠俠。
Superman's fine, too.	超人也不錯。
□ 8. ***What's your favorite season?***	你最喜愛什麼季節？
Autumn.	秋天。
I like the cool fall weather.	我喜歡秋天涼爽的天氣。
□ 9. ***What city do you like the most?***	你最喜歡那個城市？
My home, Taipei.	我的家鄉，台北。
There's so much to do there.	在那裡有很多事情可做。

Batman Superman

** ______________________

superhero〔ˈsupɚˌhɪro〕*n.* 超級英雄
definitely〔ˈdɛfənɪtlɪ〕*adv.* 當然
Batman〔ˈbætˌmæn〕*n.* 蝙蝠俠
Superman〔ˈsupɚˌmæn〕*n.* 超人　fine〔faɪn〕*adj.* 好的
season〔ˈsizn̩〕*n.* 季節　autumn〔ˈɔtəm〕*n.* 秋天（= *fall*）
cool〔kul〕*adj.* 涼爽的　weather〔ˈwɛðɚ〕*n.* 天氣
home〔hom〕*n.* 家；家鄉

【背景説明】

Oral Test 10

1. ***It's a nice calm color.***（它是個很好，能使人平靜的顏色。）可説成：Blue makes people feel calm.（藍色使人覺得平靜。）Blue is a relaxing color.（藍色是能令人放鬆的顏色。）能讓人放鬆的顏色有：blue（藍色）、white（白色）、green（綠色）、pink（粉紅色）等，而讓人不安的顏色（alarming colors）有：orange（橘色）、red（紅色）、black（黑色）等。

4. ***I like after dinner.***（我喜歡晚餐後。）這句話再次證明，學文法反倒成爲學習的障礙，怎麼會 after dinner 當名詞片語用？在「文法寶典」p.21 有介詞片語可以當名詞用，如：A rat rushed out from ***under the bed.***（有一隻老鼠從床底下衝出來。）但這種用法很少，所以要把 ***I like after dinner.*** 當成慣用句來看，等於 I like the time after dinner.（我喜歡晚餐後的時間。）

6. ***I could eat grapes all day.*** 字面的意思是「我可以整天吃葡萄。」引申爲「我非常喜歡吃葡萄。」（= *I really enjoy eating grapes.* = *I'm crazy about grapes.*）【***be crazy about*** 非常喜愛】

9. ***There's so much to do there.***（在那裡有很多事情可做。）（= *There are so many things to do there.*）You can do many different activities there.（你可以在那裡從事很多不同的活動。）There's a lot to do in the city.（在那個城市有很多事情可做。）

Oral Test 11

【問與答一起背】

□ 1. ***What languages do you speak?***	你會說什麼語言？
Mandarin Chinese.	中文。
I can also speak English.	我也會說英文。
□ 2. ***When did you start learning English?***	你何時開始學英文？
It was a long time ago.	很久以前。
I started when I was a kid.	我小時候就開始學。
□ 3. ***How long have you been learning English?***	你學英文學多久了？
It's been many years.	已經很多年了。
Since elementary school.	從小學開始。

**

language (ˈlæŋgwɪdʒ) *n.* 語言
Mandarin (ˈmændərɪn) *n.* 中文；國語
Mandarin Chinese 中文；國語
kid (kɪd) *n.* 小孩
elementary (ˌɛləˈmɛntərɪ) *adj.* 初等的
elementary school 小學（= *primary school*）

elementary school

□ 4. ***How's your English?***	你的英文如何？
My English is alright.	我的英文還不錯。
I'm getting better with practice.	因為練習我變得越來越好。
□ 5. ***Can you read English well?***	你的英文閱讀能力好嗎？
I can read pretty well.	我的閱讀能力相當好。
I can read short stories.	我可以閱讀短篇小說。
□ 6. ***How do you practice speaking?***	你如何練習口說？
I talk as much as possible.	我儘量多說。
I also practice with foreigners.	我也會和外國人練習。

** ———————————

alright〔ɔlˈraɪt〕*adj.* 還不錯的；相當好的

practice〔ˈpræktɪs〕*n. v.* 練習　　pretty〔ˈprɪtɪ〕*adv.* 相當

short story 短篇小說

as…as possible 儘可能…

foreigner〔ˈfɔrɪnɚ〕*n.* 外國人

□ 7. ***Do you take any English classes?***	你有上任何英文課嗎？
Yes, I'm taking two.	是的，我正在上兩種。
Conversation and Reading.	會話和閱讀。
□ 8. ***What's challenging about learning a language?***	學語言最具有挑戰性的是什麼？
Memorizing vocabulary.	背單字。
That's most challenging for me.	那對我而言最有挑戰性。
□ 9. ***What's difficult about learning English?***	學英文困難的是什麼？
The grammar rules.	文法規則。
I have trouble with those.	我對於那些有困難。

**

take〔tek〕*v.* 上（課）　　conversation〔ˌkɑnvəˈseʃən〕*n.* 會話

challenging〔ˈtʃælɪndʒɪŋ〕*adj.* 有挑戰性的

memorize〔ˈmɛməˌraɪz〕*v.* 背誦；記憶

vocabulary〔vəˈkæbjəˌlɛrɪ〕*n.* 字彙

grammar〔ˈgræmɚ〕*n.* 文法

rule〔rul〕*n.* 規則　　trouble〔ˈtrʌbl̩〕*n.* 麻煩；困難

memorize

Elementary

Oral Test 12

【問與答一起背】

□ 1. ***Do you play any sports?***	你有參加任何運動嗎？
Yes, I do.	是的，我有。
I play baseball.	我會打棒球。
□ 2. ***How long have you been playing?***	你打多久了？
Since I was a kid.	從我小時候。
I've been playing for six years.	我已經打了六年了。
□ 3. ***What position do you play?***	你打什麼位置？
I am the pitcher.	我是投手。
I like to throw the ball.	我喜歡投球。

** ——————————

pitcher

play〔 ple 〕*v.* 參加（球賽、比賽等）；打（…球）
sport〔 sport 〕*n.* 運動　　baseball〔ˈbes,bɔl 〕*n.* 棒球
how long 多久　　kid〔 kɪd 〕*n.* 小孩
position〔 pəˈzɪʃən 〕*n.* 位置
pitcher〔ˈpɪtʃɚ 〕*n.* 投手　　throw〔 θro 〕*v.* 投擲

☐ 4. ***What's the objective of the game?*** 比賽的目標是什麼？

To score the most runs. 要得到最多的分數。

It's to score higher than the other team. 得分要比另一隊高。

☐ 5. ***How many players are there?*** 有多少個球員？

There are 9 on a team. 一隊有九個球員。

So we need 18 to play. 所以我們需要十八個球員才能打。

☐ 6. ***Did your team play well this season?*** 你的隊伍這一季打得好嗎？

We did really well. 我們打得很好。

We won many games. 我們贏得許多比賽。

** ——————————

objective〔əbˈdʒɛktɪv〕*n.* 目標　game〔gem〕*n.* 比賽

score〔skor〕*v.* 得（分）　run〔rʌn〕*n.*（棒球）一分

the other（兩者的）另一個　team〔tim〕*n.* 隊

player〔ˈpleɚ〕*n.* 球員　season〔ˈsizn̩〕*n.*（球）季

do well 表現好　win〔wɪn〕*v.* 贏

□ **7**. ***Did you have a good coach?***	你們有好的教練嗎？
Yes, he was excellent.	是的，他很優秀。
He was a fantastic coach.	他是個很棒的教練。
□ **8**. ***What kind of league is it?***	它是什麼聯盟？
It's the college league.	它是大學聯盟。
Each university has a team.	每個大學都有一隊。
□ **9**. ***When's your next game?***	你們的下一場比賽是什麼時候？
It's this Saturday.	是這個星期六。
I think we'll win this one, too.	我認爲我們這一場也會贏。

** ——————————

coach〔kotʃ〕*n.* 教練

excellent〔'ɛksḷənt〕*adj.* 優秀的

fantastic〔fæn'tæstɪk〕*adj.* 很棒的

kind〔kaɪnd〕*n.* 種類　　league〔lig〕*n.* 聯盟

college〔'kɑlɪdʒ〕*n.* 大學；學院

university〔,junə'vɝsətɪ〕*n.* 大學

【背景說明】

Oral Test 11

1. 「中文」可說成：Chinese，或 Mandarin，或 ***Mandarin Chinese***。I speak ***Mandarin Chinese***.（我會說中文。）（= *I speak Chinese.*）***Mandarin Chinese*** is my native language.（中文是我的母語。）【native〔ˈnetɪv〕*adj.* 本國的】

4. ***I'm getting better with practice.***（因爲練習我變得越來越好。）（= *With practice I'm improving.*）【improve〔ɪmˈpruv〕*v.* 進步】

5. ***Can you read English well?***（你的英文閱讀能力好嗎？）（= *Can you read and understand English well?*）可說成：Are you able to read English OK?（你看得懂英文嗎？）（= *Is your English comprehension pretty good?*）【comprehension〔ˌkɑmprɪˈhɛnʃən〕*n.* 理解力】

9. ***I have trouble with those.***（我對於那些有困難。）（= *Those are not easy for me.*）English grammar is difficult for me.（英文文法對我而言很難。）I'm not good at using English grammar.（我不擅長使用英文文法。）【***be good at*** 擅長】

Oral Test 12

1. ***Do you play any sports?***（你有參加任何運動嗎？）（= *Do you play on any sports teams?*）

4. ***To score the most runs.***（要得到最多的分數。）（= *The objective is to score the most runs.*）run 等於 point（一分）。「目標」可用 objective，goal，或 purpose。The team ***that scores the most runs*** wins.（得最多分的隊伍贏。）

6. ***We did really well.***（我們打得很好。）（= *We played very well.*）

Oral Test 13

【問與答一起背】

□ 1. ***How do you make new friends?***	你如何交新朋友？
I ask people questions.	我會問人問題。
I'm a good listener.	我是很好的聽衆。
□ 2. ***Do you make friends easily?***	你很容易交到朋友嗎？
Yes, I do.	是的，我很容易。
I enjoy meeting people.	我喜歡認識人。
□ 3. ***Did you have any childhood friends?***	你有任何小時候的朋友嗎？
I sure did.	我當然有。
I had several good friends.	我有幾個好朋友。

** ___

make friends 交朋友

listener〔ˈlɪsn̩ɚ〕*n.* 聽衆

easily〔ˈizɪlɪ〕*adv.* 容易地　　enjoy〔ɪnˈdʒɔɪ〕*v.* 喜歡

meet〔mit〕*v.* 認識　　childhood〔ˈtʃaɪld,hʊd〕*n.* 童年

sure〔ʃʊr〕*adv.* 當然

make friends

□ **4.** ***Do you have any long-distance friends?***	你有任何遠距離的朋友嗎？
Yes, I have a pen pal.	是的，我有一個筆友。
She lives in California.	她住在加州。
□ **5.** ***How do you keep in touch?***	你們如何保持連絡？
We talk online.	我們會在線上談話。
We Skype each other.	我們會用 Skype 互相連絡。
□ **6.** ***Do you have a close group of friends?***	你有一群親密的朋友嗎？
I have three good friends.	我有三個好朋友。
We're very close.	我們非常親密。

**

distance〔ˈdɪstəns〕*n.* 距離
long-distance *adj.* 長途的；長距離的　pal〔pæl〕*n.* 夥伴；朋友
pen pal 筆友　California〔ˌkæləˈfɔrnjə〕*n.* 加州
keep in touch 保持連絡　online〔ˈɑnˌlaɪn〕*adv.* 在線上；在網路上
Skype〔skaɪp〕*v.* 用 Skype 連絡【Skype 是一種軟體，可以讓你免費打電話給世界各地用 Skype 的人】
close〔klos〕*adj.* 親密的　group〔grup〕*n.* 群；組；團體

□ 7. ***Have you made any friends gaming?***	你在玩線上遊戲時有結交任何朋友嗎？
I've made a lot.	我交了很多朋友。
We have a good time.	我們玩得很愉快。
□ 8. ***Have you ever met them in person?***	你曾經親自和他們見過面嗎？
No, I haven't.	不，我沒有。
Some live very far away.	有些人住得很遠。
□ 9. ***What makes a good friend?***	成為好朋友的必備特質是什麼？
Honesty does.	誠實。
Being loyal does, too.	也要很忠實。

** ————————

game〔gem〕*v.* 玩遊戲

a lot 很多　***have a good time*** 玩得愉快

ever〔ˈɛvɚ〕*adv.* 曾經

meet〔mit〕*v.* 和…會面　***in person*** 親自

far away 遙遠的　make〔mek〕*v.* 構成；造就

honesty〔ˈɑnəstɪ〕*n.* 誠實　loyal〔ˈlɔɪəl〕*adj.* 忠實的

【背景説明】

Oral Test 13

4. ***Do you have any long-distance friends?***（你有任何遠距離的朋友嗎？）可説成：Do you have any friends overseas?（你有沒有任何在海外的朋友？）(= *Do you have any friends in another country?*)【overseas〔′ovɚ′siz〕*adv.* 在海外】Do you have any foreign friends abroad?（你有沒有任何在國外的外國朋友？）（= *Have any foreign friends abroad?*）【abroad〔ə′brɔd〕*adv.* 在國外】

6. ***Do you have a close group of friends?***（你有一群親密的朋友嗎？）（= *Do you have a group of close friends?*）可説成：Do you have a few very good friends?（你有一些非常好的朋友嗎？）

7. ***Have you made any friends gaming?***（你在玩線上遊戲時有結交任何朋友嗎？）（= *Have you made any friends while you are gaming online? = Have you made any friends while playing an online game?*）【online〔′ɑn,laɪn〕*adv.* 在線上；在網路上 *adj.* 線上的】

8. ***Have you ever met them in person?***（你曾經親自和他們見過面嗎？）（= *Have you ever met an online friend in person?*）可簡化爲：Ever met them face to face?（曾經面對面地見過他們嗎？）【***face to face*** 面對面地】

9. ***What makes a good friend?***（成爲好朋友的必備特質是什麼？）（= *What are the qualities of a good friend? = What are the characteristics of a good friend?*）【quality〔′kwɑlətɪ〕*n.* 特質 characteristic〔,kærɪktə′rɪstɪk〕*n.* 特性】

Oral Test 14

【問與答一起背】

□ 1. ***Tell me about your closest friends. What are they like?***	告訴我關於你最要好的朋友的事。他們是怎樣的人？
They're great.	他們很棒。
They're a lot of fun.	他們非常有趣。
□ 2. ***What do you and your friends like to do?***	你和你的朋友喜歡做什麼？
We like to go out for fun.	我們喜歡出去玩。
We like to have dinner together.	我們喜歡一起吃晚餐。
□ 3. ***How often do you get together?***	你們多久聚會一次？
We get together every week.	我們每週都會聚會。
We meet up every weekend.	我們每個週末都會見面。

** ―――――――――――

close〔klos〕*adj.* 親密的　　fun〔fʌn〕*n.* 樂趣；有趣的人或事物

be fun 有趣

They're a lot of fun. 他們很有趣。(= *They're great fun.*)

for fun 爲了樂趣　　have〔hæv〕*v.* 吃

get together 聚會；相聚　　***meet up*** 遇見；見面

weekend〔ˈwikˈɛnd〕*n.* 週末

□ 4. ***Where do you like to go?*** 你們喜歡去哪裡？

We like KTVs. 我們喜歡 KTV。

We also like to eat out. 我們也喜歡去外面吃飯。

□ 5. ***Do you have a best friend?*** 你有最要好的朋友嗎？

Yes. 有。

My best friend's name is Josh. 我最好的朋友名字叫喬許。

□ 6. ***What is he like?*** 他是個怎樣的人？

Josh is hilarious. 喬許很好笑。

He can always make me laugh. 他總是能讓我笑。

** ___

eat out 去外面吃飯
Josh (dʒɑʃ) *n.* 喬許
hilarious (həˈlɛrɪəs) *adj.* 很好笑的
laugh (læf) *v.* 笑

eat out

□ **7.** ***Where did you meet him?***	你是在哪裡認識他的？
We met in kindergarten.	我們幼稚園就認識了。
We were in the same class.	我們在同一班。
□ **8.** ***How long have you known each other?***	你們彼此認識多久了？
9 years.	九年。
He's my oldest friend.	他是我認識最久的朋友。
□ **9.** ***Do you have more guy friends or girl friends?***	你的男性朋友還是女性朋友比較多？
Hard to say.	很難說。
It's about even.	幾乎一樣多。

**

meet〔mit〕*v.* 遇見；認識
kindergarten〔ˈkɪndəˌgɑrtn̩〕*n.* 幼稚園
old〔old〕*adj.* 老的；認識久的
guy〔gaɪ〕*n.*（男）人；傢伙
guy friend 男性朋友
girl friend 女性朋友
hard〔hɑrd〕*adj.* 困難的　　about〔əˈbaʊt〕*adv.* 大約；幾乎
even〔ˈivən〕*adj.* 相同的

guy friends and girl friends

【背景說明】

Oral Test 14

1. ***They're a lot of fun***.（他們非常有趣。）（= *They're fun to be with.*）可說成：They make me happy.（他們使我很快樂。）

3. ***We meet up every weekend***.（我們每個週末都會見面。）***meet up*** 是 meet 的加強語氣，都作「見面」解。這句話可說成：We get together every Saturday or Sunday.（我們每個禮拜六或禮拜天都會聚在一起。）

4. ***We like KTVs***.（我們喜歡 KTV。）（= *We like karaoke bars.*）可說成：We enjoy KTVs.（我們喜歡 KTV。）
【karaoke〔,kæri'oki〕*n.* 卡拉 OK　bar〔bɑr〕*n.* 酒吧】

6. ***Josh is hilarious***.（喬許很好笑。）（= *Josh is very humorous.*）可說成：Josh is a super funny guy.（喬許是個超級好笑的人。）
【funny〔'fʌnɪ〕*adj.* 好笑的　guy〔gaɪ〕*n.* 人；傢伙】

9. ***Do you have more guy friends or girl friends?***（你的男性朋友還是女性朋友比較多？）（= *Are most of your friends male or female?*）【male〔mel〕*adj.* 男性的　female〔'fimel〕*adj.* 女性的】
可說成：Do you have more male or female friendships?（你的男性朋友還是女性朋友比較多？）***Hard to say***.（很難說。）（= *It's hard to say. = It's difficult to say.*）That's a tough question.（那是個困難的問題。）【tough〔tʌf〕*adj.* 困難的】
It's about even.（幾乎一樣多。）（= *It's almost the same.*）
也可說成：It's pretty close.（相當接近。）

Elementary Oral Tests

※ 請掃瞄 QR 碼，聽完題目後，練習回答兩句。

Oral Test 1

☐ 1. What's your name?

☐ 2. How old are you?

☐ 3. How are you doing?

☐ 4. Where are you from?

☐ 5. Where do you live?

☐ 6. Are you a student?

☐ 7. What grade are you in?

☐ 8. Do you have a nickname?

☐ 9. Tell me a little about yourself.

Oral Test 2

☐ 1. Who do you live with?

☐ 2. How big is your family?

☐ 3. Do you have any siblings?

☐ 4. What's her name?

☐ 5. How old is she?

☐ 6. What grade is she in?

☐ 7. What's your sister like?

☐ 8. Are you guys close?

☐ 9. What do you like to do together?

Oral Test 3

☐ 1. Do you have any interests in common?

☐ 2. Do you ever argue or disagree?

☐ 3. What do you fight about?

☐ 4. What are your parents' names?

☐ 5. May I ask what your parents do?

☐ 6. How old are they?

☐ 7. Do you get along with your parents?

☐ 8. What's your dad like?

☐ 9. What's your mom like?

____

____

Oral Test 4

☐ 1. Who are you more like?

____

____

☐ 2. Do you have any aunts or uncles?

____

____

☐ 3. Do you have many cousins?

____

____

☐ 4. Do you see your grandparents often?

____

____

☐ 5. How old are your grandparents?

____

____

☐ 6. Where do they live?

____

____

☐ 7. How often does your entire family get together?

____

____

☐ 8. When do you have family reunions?

____

____

☐ 9. When you're all together, what do you do?

____

____

Oral Test 5

☐ 1. Where were you born?

____

____

☐ 2. When were you born?

____

____

☐ 3. What year were you born?

____

____

☐ 4. What's your sign?

____

____

☐ 5. What's your middle name?

____

____

☐ 6. Where did you grow up?

____

____

☐ 7. Did you like the neighborhood where you grew up?

____

____

☐ 8. What was your childhood like?

____

____

☐ 9. What do you miss most about being a kid?

____

____

Oral Test 6

☐ 1. When's your birthday?

____

____

☐ 2. How old will you be?

____

____

☐ 3. Any birthday plans?

____

____

☐ 4. Will you have a party?

____

____

☐ 5. Do you like birthday parties?

____

____

☐ 6. Describe a typical party.

____

____

☐ 7. What would you like for your birthday?

____

____

☐ 8. What's the sweetest gift you've ever received?

____

____

☐ 9. What are your wishes for the upcoming year?

____

____

Oral Test 7

☐ 1. What's your home like?

____

____

☐ 2. What type of home do you live in?

____

____

☐ 3. What's your neighborhood like?

____

____

☐ 4. Do you have any pets?

____

____

☐ 5. Why not?

____

____

☐ 6. Do you want a pet?

____

____

☐ 7. Do you do chores?

____

____

☐ 8. Do you have an allowance?

____

____

☐ 9. Do you have a curfew?

____

____

Oral Test 8

☐ 1. Do you get enough sleep?

____

____

☐ 2. How many hours do you get?

☐ 3. Do you sleep well?

☐ 4. What do you do when you have trouble sleeping?

☐ 5. What time do you usually go to bed?

☐ 6. What time do you usually get up?

☐ 7. Do you often dream?

☐ 8. Do you remember your dreams?

☐ 9. Did you sleep well?

Oral Test 9

☐ 1. What's your daily routine?

☐ 2. What's your weekly routine?

☐ 3. What do you usually do on weekends?

☐ 4. What are you doing this weekend?

☐ 5. How much free time do you have?

____

____

☐ 6. What do you do when you have free time?

____

____

☐ 7. When do you take a break?

____

____

☐ 8. If you had more free time, what would you do?

____

____

☐ 9. "Time is money." Do you agree or disagree? Why?

____

____

Oral Test 10

☐ 1. What's your favorite color?

____

____

☐ 2. What's your favorite animal?

____

____

☐ 3. What's your favorite hobby?

____

____

☐ 4. What's your favorite part of the day?

____

____

☐ 5. What's your favorite day of the week?

____

____

☐ 6. What's your favorite snack?

____

____

☐ 7. Who is your favorite superhero?

____

____

☐ 8. What's your favorite season?

____

____

☐ 9. What city do you like the most?

____

____

Oral Test 11

☐ 1. What languages do you speak?

____

____

☐ 2. When did you start learning English?

____

____

☐ 3. How long have you been learning English?

____

____

☐ 4. How's your English?

____

____

☐ 5. Can you read English well?

____

____

☐ 6. How do you practice speaking?

____

____

☐ 7. Do you take any English classes?

____

____

☐ 8. What's challenging about learning a language?

____

____

☐ 9. What's difficult about learning English?

____

____

Oral Test 12

☐ 1. Do you play any sports?

____

____

☐ 2. How long have you been playing?

____

____

☐ 3. What position do you play?

____

____

☐ 4. What's the objective of the game?

____

____

☐ 5. How many players are there?

____

____

☐ 6. Did your team play well this season?

____

____

☐ 7. Did you have a good coach?

____

____

☐ 8. What kind of league is it?

____

____

☐ 9. When's your next game?

____

____

Oral Test 13

☐ 1. How do you make new friends?

____

____

☐ 2. Do you make friends easily?

____

____

☐ 3. Did you have any childhood friends?

____

____

☐ 4. Do you have any long-distance friends?

____

____

☐ 5. How do you keep in touch?

____

____

☐ 6. Do you have a close group of friends?

☐ 7. Have you made any friends gaming?

☐ 8. Have you ever met them in person?

☐ 9. What makes a good friend?

Oral Test 14

☐ 1. Tell me about your closest friends. What are they like?

☐ 2. What do you and your friends like to do?

☐ 3. How often do you get together?

☐ 4. Where do you like to go?

☐ 5. Do you have a best friend?

☐ 6. What is he like?

☐ 7. Where did you meet him?

☐ 8. How long have you known each other?

☐ 9. Do you have more guy friends or girl friends?

英語口試 — 中級

Intermediate

What was your experience at school like?

I was a good student. My classmates and teachers liked me.

英語口試「中級」Oral Test 15~32

1. 「中級」的句子比較長或難，不容易背到變成直覺。
2. 要將「初級」背到滾瓜爛熟，再背「中級」。
3. 把這些問與答當成課本讀即可。
4. Intermediate Oral Tests的錄音QR碼只有唸問題，保留足夠的時間讓你練習回答。

Oral Test 15

【問與答一起背】

□ 1. ***What was your experience at school like?***	你在學校的經驗如何？
I was a good student.	我是個好學生。
My classmates and teachers liked me.	我的同學和老師都喜歡我。
□ 2. ***What's your happiest memory?***	你最快樂的回憶是什麼？
The day I passed my entrance exam.	我通過入學考試的那一天。
I felt so relieved.	我覺得大大地鬆了一口氣。
□ 3. ***What are your happiest childhood memories?***	你最快樂的童年回憶是什麼？
Getting money on Chinese New Year's Eve.	在除夕拿到壓歲錢。
Eating dinner with my family.	和家人吃年夜飯。

** ______________________

experience〔ɪk'spɪrɪəns〕*n.* 經驗

memory〔'mɛmərɪ〕*n.* 記憶；回憶　pass〔pæs〕*v.* 通過

entrance〔'ɛntrəns〕*n.* 進入；入學　***entrance exam*** 入學考試

so〔so〕*adv.* 非常　relieved〔rɪ'livd〕*adj.* 放心的；鬆了一口氣的

childhood〔'tʃaɪld,hʊd〕*n.* 童年　***Chinese New Year's Eve*** 除夕

□ 4. ***What is something most people don't know about you?***	大多數的人不知道關於你的什麼事？
I can speak English.	我會說英文。
They might not expect that.	他們可能沒想到我會。
□ 5. ***Where is your hometown?***	你的故鄉在哪裡？
It's in the countryside.	在鄉下。
It's just a few hours south.	只要往南幾個小時的路程。
□ 6. ***What is it like?***	它是什麼樣子？
It's peaceful and quiet.	非常寧靜。
It's a small town near the mountains.	它是個靠近山區的小鎮。

**

expect (ɪkˈspɛkt) *v.* 預期
hometown (ˈhomˈtaʊn) *n.* 故鄉
countryside (ˈkʌntrɪˌsaɪd) *n.* 鄉村地區
south (saʊθ) *adv.* 往南
like (laɪk) *prep.* 像　peaceful (ˈpisfəl) *adj.* 寧靜的
quiet (ˈkwaɪət) *adj.* 安靜的　town (taʊn) *n.* 城鎮
mountain (ˈmaʊntn̩) *n.* 山

countryside

□ **7.** ***What were your childhood fears?***	你童年時期會怕什麼？
I used to be afraid of the dark.	我以前會怕黑。
I hated spiders, too.	我也討厭蜘蛛。
□ **8.** ***Did you have many friends?***	你有很多朋友嗎？
Not too many.	不是太多。
I had two really close friends.	我有兩個眞的很親密的朋友。
□ **9.** ***What did you do in your childhood?***	你們童年時期會做什麼？
We rode bikes a lot.	我們常常騎腳踏車。
We swam at the pool.	我們會在游泳池裡游泳。

**

fear〔 fɪr 〕*n.* 恐懼　***used to*** 以前
be afraid of 害怕　dark〔 dɑrk 〕*n.* 黑暗
hate〔 het 〕*v.* 討厭　spider〔ˈspaɪdɚ〕*n.* 蜘蛛
close〔 klos 〕*adj.* 親密的　ride〔 raɪd 〕*v.* 騎
bike〔 baɪk 〕*n.* 腳踏車（= *bicycle*）
a lot 常常　swim〔 swɪm 〕*v.* 游泳
pool〔 pul 〕*n.* 游泳池（= *swimming pool*）

bike

Oral Test 16

Intermediate

【問與答一起背】

□ 1. ***Where do you go to school?***	你在哪裡上學？
Central High School.	中央高中。
It's not too far from here.	離這裡不會太遠。
□ 2. ***How's school going?***	學校的情況如何？
Great.	很棒。
I really like senior high.	我真的很喜歡高中。
□ 3. ***How's your school year so far?***	到目前為止，你在學校的這一年如何？
So far so good.	到目前為止還不錯。
I'm having a super year.	我今年過得很好。

**

go to school 上學　　central ('sɛntrəl) *adj.* 中央的
high school 高中　　school (skul) *n.* 學校；課業
go (go) *v.* 進展　　great (gret) *adj.* 很棒的
senior high 高中 (= *senior high school*)
school year 學年　　***so far*** 到目前為止
so far so good 到目前為止還好　　super ('supɚ) *adj.* 極好的

SENIOR HIGH SCHOOL

□ **4.** ***What's your favorite subject?***	你最喜愛的科目是什麼？
Definitely English.	當然是英文。
I have a lot of fun in that class.	上英文課我很愉快。
□ **5.** ***What's your least favorite subject?***	你最不喜歡的科目是什麼？
Physics.	物理。
There are too many formulas.	有太多公式了。
□ **6.** ***Who's your favorite teacher?***	你最喜愛的老師是誰？
Mr. Liu is my favorite.	我最喜愛的是劉老師。
I really like him.	我真的很喜歡他。

** ———————————

favorite (ˈfevərɪt) *adj.* 最喜愛的 *n.* 最喜愛的人或物

subject (ˈsʌbdʒɪkt) *n.* 科目

definitely (ˈdɛfənɪtlɪ) *adv.* 當然

have fun 玩得愉快　　least (list) *adv.* 最不

physics (ˈfɪzɪks) *n.* 物理學

formula (ˈfɔrmjələ) *n.* 公式

□ 7. ***Who's your least favorite teacher?***	你最不喜愛的老師是誰？
Mr. Brown, my PE teacher.	布朗先生，我的體育老師。
He yells a lot.	他常常大叫。
□ 8. ***Does your school have uniforms?***	你的學校有制服嗎？
Yes, it does.	是的，有。
They're blue and gray.	它們是藍色和灰色的。
□ 9. ***Do you like having uniforms?***	你喜歡有制服嗎？
I don't mind uniforms.	我不介意制服。
I'm used to it.	我習慣穿制服。

**

PE 體育（=*physical education*）
yell〔jɛl〕*v.* 大叫　***a lot*** 常常
uniform〔ˈjunəˌfɔrm〕*n.* 制服
gray〔gre〕*adj.* 灰色的
mind〔maɪnd〕*v.* 介意
be used to 習慣於

uniform

Oral Test 17

【問與答一起背】

☐ 1. ***Do you think school uniforms are a good idea?***	你認爲學校制服是個好主意嗎？
I think they're ok.	我認爲制服很好。
They save me time.	它們節省了我的時間。
☐ 2. ***What clubs does your school have?***	你們學校有什麼社團？
Debate, science, art, etc.	辯論、科學、藝術等。
We have a lot of clubs to choose from.	我們有很多社團可以選擇。
☐ 3. ***Are you in a club?***	你有參加社團嗎？
I'm in the drama club.	我是戲劇社的。
I love being onstage.	我喜歡上台。

**

uniform (ˈjunəˌfɔrm) *n.* 制服　ok (ˈoˈke) *adj.* 好的；可以的
save (sev) *v.* 使節省　club (klʌb) *n.* 社團
debate (dɪˈbet) *n.* 辯論　science (ˈsaɪəns) *n.* 科學
etc. (ɛtˈsɛtrə) 等等　choose (tʃuz) *v.* 選擇
drama (ˈdrɑmə) *n.* 戲劇
onstage (ˌɑnˈstedʒ) *adj., adv.* 在舞台上（的）

science

Intermediate

Intermediate

□ 4. ***What does your club do?***	你的社團都做些什麼？
We put on performances.	我們會表演。
Plays, musicals, talent shows, etc.	戲劇、音樂劇、才藝表演等。
□ 5. ***Why did you choose that club?***	你爲何會選擇那個社團？
I heard it was fun.	我聽說它很有趣。
I like acting, and I'm learning a lot.	我喜歡表演，而且我學到很多。
□ 6. ***What do you do after school?***	你放學後會做什麼？
I take evening lessons.	我會上課後輔導。
I go to a cram school for math and English.	我會去補習班補數學和英文。

** ______________________

put on 上演（戲劇）　performance〔pəˈfɔrməns〕*n.* 表演
play〔ple〕*n.* 戲劇　musical〔ˈmjuzɪkḷ〕*n.* 音樂劇
talent〔ˈtælənt〕*n.* 才能　show〔ʃo〕*n.* 表演
talent show 才藝表演　fun〔fʌn〕*adj.* 有趣的
act〔ækt〕*v.* 表演　***after school*** 放學後
take〔tek〕*v.* 上（課）　cram〔kræm〕*v.* 填塞；死記硬背
cram school 補習班　math〔mæθ〕*n.* 數學（= *mathematics*）

□ 7. ***What are you doing after this test?***	這場考試之後你會做什麼？
I'm going to meet my friend.	我會去和朋友見面。
We're going to a movie.	我們會去看電影。
□ 8. ***How are your grades?***	你的成績如何？
I have good grades.	我的成績很好。
All A's or B's.	全都是甲等或乙等。
□ 9. ***How's test preparation going?***	考試準備得如何？
It's going well.	很順利。
But I'm still a little nervous about it.	但我還是有一點緊張。

** ───────────

meet〔mit〕*v.* 和…會面　***go to a movie*** 去看電影

grade〔gred〕*n.* 成績

A〔e〕*n.*（五個等第中的）甲（等）

B〔bi〕*n.*（五個等第中的）乙（等）

preparation〔ˌprɛpəˈreʃən〕*n.* 準備

go〔go〕*v.* 進展　***go well*** 進展順利

nervous〔ˈnɝvəs〕*adj.* 緊張的

grade

【背景說明】

Oral Test 15

4. ***They might not expect that.*** (他們可能沒想到我會。) (= *They might not think I can.* = *They probably don't think I am able to.*)

5. ***It's just a few hours south.*** (只要往南幾個小時的路程。) (= *It's only a few hours south of here.*)

Oral Test 16

2. ***How's school going?*** (學校的情況如何？) (= *How is everything at school going?*)

3. ***How's your school year so far?*** (到目前爲止，你在學校的這一年如何？) (= *Up until now, how is school going?*) ***I'm having a super year.*** (我今年過得很好。) (= *This year is going great.*) 美國人很強調，今年我過得如何，明年我要怎樣，他們常說：So far, it's been a wonderful year. (到目前爲止，今年過得很好。) I'm having a terrific year. (我今年過得很好。)
【terrific (tə'rɪfɪk) *adj.* 很棒的】

7. ***He yells a lot.*** (他常常大叫。) (= *He yells often.*) 可說成：He yells at his students a lot. (他常常對他的學生大叫。) He often scolds. (他常常責罵。)【scold (skold) *v.* 責罵】He frequently shouts. (他經常吼叫。) He easily gets angry. (他很容易生氣。)

8. ***They're blue and gray.*** (它們是藍色和灰色的。) 美國私立學校的制服，通常上衣是藍色，下半身是灰色。They're blue on the top and gray on the bottom. (制服上面是藍色，下面是灰色。)【top (tap) *n.* 頂端　bottom ('batəm) *n.* 底部】Shirts are

blue; pants and skirts are gray.（襯衫是藍色的；褲子和裙子是灰色的。）【pants〔pænts〕*n.pl.* 褲子】

9. ***I'm used to it***.（我習慣穿制服。）（= *I'm used to wearing a uniform.*）可說成：I'm accustomed to it.（我習慣穿制服。）【***be accustomed to*** 習慣於（= *be used to*）】

【背景說明】

Oral Test 17

3. ***Are you in a club?***（你有參加社團嗎？）（= *Are you a member of a club?* = *Have you joined any clubs?*）***I love being onstage***.（我喜歡上台。）可說成：I enjoy performing.（我喜歡表演。）I really like being in public.（我很喜歡在眾人面前。）【***in public*** 在眾人面前】It's fun to be in front of many people.（在很多人面前很有趣。）【***in front of*** 在…面前】

4. ***We put on performances***.（我們會表演。）（= *We perform plays.* = *We present shows.*）【play〔ple〕*n.* 戲劇　present〔prɪ'zɛnt〕*v.* 呈現　show〔ʃo〕*n.* 表演；節目】可說成：We give presentations.（我們會表演。）【presentation〔,prɛzn̩'teʃən〕*n.* 演出】We entertain.（我們會娛樂大家。）【entertain〔,ɛntɚ'ten〕*v.* 娛樂；供人娛樂】

8. ***All A's or B's***.（全部是甲等或乙等。）（= *All my scores are either A's or B's.*）

9. ***How's test preparation going?***（考試準備得如何？）（= *How is your studying going?*）***It's going well***.（很順利。）（= *It's going good.* = *It's going fine.*）可說成：The results are good.（效果很好。）【result〔rɪ'zʌlt〕*n.* 結果；效果】I'm making progress.（我有在進步。）【progress〔'prɑgrɛs〕*n.* 進步　***make progress*** 進步】

Intermediate

Oral Test 18

【問與答一起背】

□ 1. ***Are you a good test-taker?***	你是考試高手嗎？
Yes, I am.	是的，我是。
I'm usually pretty calm.	我通常都很鎮定。
□ 2. ***How did your last test go?***	你上次考試考得如何？
It was terrible.	很糟。
I didn't pass.	我不及格。
□ 3. ***How did you do on your exams?***	你考試考得如何？
I did great.	我考得很好。
I passed them all.	我全都及格。

** ______________________

test-taker *n.* 參加考試的人

calm〔kɑm〕*adj.* 鎮定的；冷靜的

go〔go〕*v.* 進展　terrible〔ˈtɛrəbḷ〕*adj.* 很糟的

pass〔pæs〕*v.* 通過；(考試) 及格

do〔du〕*v.* 表現　***do great*** 考得很好

test-taker

□ 4. ***Do you have a school in mind?***	你心中有理想的學校嗎？
I have a few in mind.	我心中有一些學校。
Taiwan University is one.	台灣大學是其中之一。
□ 5. ***What university do you want to attend?***	你想唸什麼大學？
Taiwan University.	台灣大學。
That's my dream school.	那是我夢想中的學校。
□ 6. ***Have you applied anywhere yet?***	你已經申請任何學校了嗎？
I haven't started applying.	我還沒開始申請。
But I plan to do it soon.	但我打算很快就申請。

**

in mind 在心中　university (ˌjunəˈvɝsətɪ) *n.* 大學
attend (əˈtɛnd) *v.* 就讀
dream (drim) *adj.* 理想的；夢想的
apply (əˈplaɪ) *v.* 申請
anywhere (ˈɛnɪˌhwɛr) *adv.* 任何地方
yet (jɛt) *adv.* 已經
plan (plæn) *v.* 打算

university

□ 7. ***What do you want to major in?***	你想要主修什麼？
I'm not sure.	我不確定。
It's a big decision.	那是個重大的決定。
□ 8. ***What do you want to study?***	你想要讀什麼？
English.	英文。
That's my first choice.	那是我的第一志願。
□ 9. ***What do you want to be someday?***	未來你想做什麼？
Maybe a business owner.	也許當個老闆。
I might open a restaurant.	我可能會開一間餐廳。

** ___

major〔ˈmedʒɚ〕*v.* 主修 < *in* >

big〔bɪg〕*adj.* 大的；重要的　　decision〔dɪˈsɪʒən〕*n.* 決定

choice〔tʃɔɪs〕*n.* 選擇　　***first choice*** 第一志願

someday〔ˈsʌmˏde〕*adv.* 將來有一天

business〔ˈbɪznɪs〕*n.* 企業

owner〔ˈonɚ〕*n.* 擁有者

open〔ˈopən〕*v.* 使開張

restaurant〔ˈrɛstərənt〕*n.* 餐廳

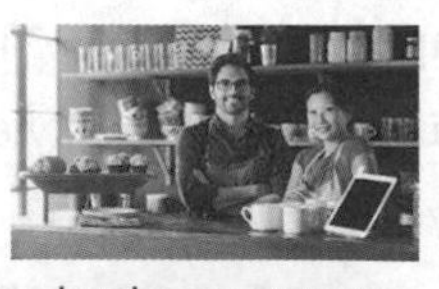

business owner

【背景說明】

Oral Test 18

1. ***Are you a good test-taker?***（你是考試高手嗎？）可說成：Are you good at taking tests?（你是不是很會考試？）【***be good at*** 擅長】Are you an experienced test-taker?（你不是對考試很有經驗？）【experienced〔ɪksˈpɪrɪənst〕*adj.* 有經驗的】Do you test well?（你很會考試嗎？）【***test well*** 考得好】

2. ***How did your last test go?***（你上次考試考得如何？）可說成：How did you do on your last test?（你上次考試考得如何？）What did you score on your last test?（上次考試你考幾分？）【score〔skor〕*v.* 得（分）】

3. ***I did great.***（我考得很好。）可說成：I did excellent. 或 I did very well. 意思相同。【excellent〔ˈɛksḷənt〕*adj.* 極佳的】

5. ***That's my dream school.***（那是我夢想中的學校。）（= *That's the school of my dreams.*）可說成：That's my top choice school.（那是我首選的學校。）（= *That's my number one school.* = *It's the school I most want to attend.*）

9. ***What do you want to be someday?***（未來你想做什麼？）（= *What's your future career choice?* = *What job do you want in the future?*）【career〔kəˈrɪr〕*n.* 職業】***Maybe a business owner.***（也許當個老闆。）（= *Maybe a boss.*）可說成：Possibly, I'll have my own business.（也許我會有自己的事業。）Perhaps I'll own a business.（也許我會擁有自己的事業。）

Oral Test 19

【問與答一起背】

□ 1. ***Are you a morning or a night person?***	你是個喜歡早起的人，還是個夜貓子？
I'm a night owl.	我是個夜貓子。
I hate getting up early.	我討厭早起。
□ 2. ***What time do you go to school?***	你幾點去上學？
I leave for school at 7 am.	我在早上七點去上學。
My first class is at 7:45.	我的第一堂課是在七點四十五分。
□ 3. ***What time do you get out of school?***	你幾點放學？
I get out at 5 pm.	我下午五點放學。
It's a long day.	眞是漫長的一天。

get up

** ________________________

morning person 喜歡早起的人

night person 夜貓子；喜歡白天睡覺，晚上活動的人

owl〔aʊl〕*n.* 貓頭鷹　***night owl*** 夜貓子　hate〔het〕*v.* 討厭

get up 起床　am〔ˈeˈɛm〕*adv.* 上午（= *a.m.*）

leave for 動身前往　***go out of*** 離開

get out 離開　pm〔ˈpiˈɛm〕*adv.* 下午（= *p.m.*）

Intermediate

□ 4. ***What time do your parents go to work?***	你的父母幾點去上班？
They go to work at 7:30.	他們在七點半去上班。
Both of them have a long commute.	他們兩人通勤的距離很長。
□ 5. ***What time do you start your homework?***	你幾點開始做功課？
I start my homework at around 6:30 pm.	我大約晚上六點半開始做功課。
I study for three hours.	我會讀三小時的書。
□ 6. ***How often do you take a break?***	你多久休息一次？
I take a break once every hour.	我每個小時休息一次。
I take a break for 15 minutes.	我會休息十五分鐘。

** ——————————

work〔wɜk〕*n.* 工作地點；工作場所

go to work 去上班　　long〔lɔŋ〕*adj.* 長的；長久的

commute〔kə'mjut〕*n.* 每天上下班的路程；通勤

homework〔'hom,wɜk〕*n.* 家庭作業；功課

around〔ə'raund〕*adv.* 大約　　***take a break*** 休息一下

once〔wʌns〕*adv.* 一次

Intermediate

□ 7. ***What's the best part of your week?***	一星期中你最喜歡什麼時候？
The weekend.	週末。
I live for the weekend!	我爲了週末而活！
□ 8. ***What are you looking forward to right now?***	你現在正在期待什麼？
Vacation.	假期。
I can't wait for summer vacation.	我等不及要過暑假。
□ 9. ***Do you keep a diary or journal?***	你會寫日記嗎？
Yes, I do.	是的，我會。
I have a diary.	我有日記。

** ___

weekend〔'wik'ɛnd〕*n.* 週末
look forward to + N./V-ing 期待…
right now 現在　vacation〔ve'keʃən〕*n.* 假期
diary〔'daɪərɪ〕*n.* 日記
journal〔'dʒɝnḷ〕*n.* 日記
keep a diary 寫日記（= *keep a journal*）

journal

【背景說明】

Oral Test 19

1. 「夜貓子」叫作 ***night owl*** (= *night person*)。你喜歡晚睡，你就可以說：***I'm a night person***.（我是個夜貓子。）(= *I'm a night owl.*) 你比較喜歡早起，你就可以說：I'm a morning person.（我喜歡早起。）(= *I'm an early riser.* = *I'm an early bird.*)【riser〔'raɪzɚ〕*n.* 起床的人　***early bird*** 早起的人】

3. ***What time do you get out of school?***（你幾點放學？）(= *When is your school over?* = *When do your classes end?*) ***It's a long day***.（眞是漫長的一天。）表示時間過得很慢。I do a lot.（我做了很多事。）It's a difficult day.（今天很辛苦。）

4. ***Both of them have a long commute***.（他們兩人通勤的距離很長。）(= *Both of them commute a long distance to work.* = *Both of them must travel a long distance to work.*)

7. ***What's the best part of your week?***（一星期中你最喜歡什麼時候？）(= *What's your favorite part of the week?* = *Which day of the week do you like best?*) ***I live for the weekend!***（我爲了週末而活！）可說成：My whole life is centered around the weekend!（我全部的生活都以週末爲中心！）【***be centered around*** 以…爲中心】I love the weekend!（我喜愛週末！）I endure weekdays to enjoy the weekend.（爲了享受週末，我忍受平日。）
【weekday〔'wik,de〕*n.* 平日　endure〔ɪn'djur〕*v.* 忍受】

9. ***Do you keep a diary or journal?***（你會寫日記嗎？）(= *Do you write in a diary?* = *Do you write daily in a diary or journal?*) 可說成：Do you have a journal?（你有沒有日記？）

Oral Test 20

【問與答一起背】

□ 1. ***What kind of music do you like?*** 你喜歡什麼種類的音樂？

Easy listening music. 輕鬆的音樂。

I like rock music, too. 我也喜歡搖滾樂。

□ 2. ***Why do you like it?*** 你爲什麼喜歡它？

It's relaxing. 它很令人放鬆。

It makes me feel happy. 它使我覺得很快樂。

□ 3. ***Do you have a favorite band or artist?*** 你有最喜愛的樂團或藝人嗎？

Yes, I have many favorites. 有，我有很多特別喜愛的。

I like BIGBANG, Jay Chou, and the Beatles. 我喜歡 BIGBANG、周杰倫，和披頭四合唱團。

** ______________________

easy listening 輕鬆的音樂

rock〔rɑk〕*n.* 搖滾樂　　relaxing〔rɪ'læksɪŋ〕*adj.* 令人放鬆的

favorite〔'fevərɪt〕*adj.* 最喜愛的　*n.* 最喜愛的人或物

band〔bænd〕*n.* 樂團　　artist〔'ɑrtɪst〕*n.* 藝術家；藝人

big bang 宇宙大爆炸　　Beatles〔'bitl̩z〕*n.* 披頭四合唱團

□ 4. ***What music is popular in your country right now?***	你的國家現在流行什麼音樂？
Pop music and hip hop.	流行音樂和嘻哈樂。
Everyone's listening to Ed Sheeran.	大家都在聽紅髮艾德的歌。
□ 5. ***Do you have a favorite song?***	你有最喜愛的歌嗎？
Oh, I have many.	喔，我有很多。
Too many to answer.	多到無法回答。
□ 6. ***Can you recommend any music or groups?***	你能推薦任何的音樂或團體嗎？
Sure, I could make you a list.	當然，我可以列一張清單給你。
But it depends on your taste.	但這要視你的喜好而定。

Intermediate

Ed Sheeran

**

popular〔ˈpɑpjələ˞〕*adj.* 受歡迎的；流行的
country〔ˈkʌntrɪ〕*n.* 國家　***right now*** 現在
pop〔pɑp〕*adj.* 流行的　hip hop〔ˈhɪp ˌhɑp〕*n.* 嘻哈樂
Ed Sheeran〔ˈɛd ˈʃɪrən〕*n.* 紅髮艾德　***too…to*** 太…以致於不
recommend〔ˌrɛkəˈmɛnd〕*v.* 推薦　group〔grup〕*n.* 團體
make a list 列一張清單　***depend on*** 視…而定
taste〔test〕*n.* 品味；愛好

□ 7. ***Have you ever played an instrument?***	你曾經彈過樂器嗎？
Yes, I take piano lessons.	是的，我上過鋼琴課。
I've also tried guitar.	我也試過吉他。
□ 8. ***How long have you played?***	你彈了多久？
Almost one year now.	到現在大約一年。
I'm still learning.	我還在學。
□ 9. ***Can you play for me sometime?***	你能找時間爲我彈奏嗎？
Sure, anytime.	當然，隨時都可以。
I can play one or two songs.	我可以彈一、兩首歌。

** ______

play〔ple〕*v.* 演奏；彈奏
instrument〔ˈɪnstrəmənt〕*n.* 樂器（= *musical instrument*）
take〔tek〕*v.* 上（課）
piano〔pɪˈæno〕*n.* 鋼琴
guitar〔gɪˈtɑr〕*n.* 吉他
sometime〔ˈsʌm,taɪm〕*adv.* 某時
sure〔ʃur〕*adv.* 當然　anytime〔ˈɛnɪ,taɪm〕*adv.* 在任何時候

piano

Oral Test 21

【問與答一起背】

□ 1. ***How does music make you feel?***	音樂給你什麼樣的感覺？
It makes me feel better.	它使我覺得更好。
It always cheers me up.	它總是能使我振作精神。
□ 2. ***Do you like to sing?***	你喜歡唱歌嗎？
Yes, I like to sing.	是的，我喜歡唱歌。
But I don't sing very well.	但是我唱得不是很好。
□ 3. ***Have you ever sung karaoke?***	你曾經唱過卡拉 OK 嗎？
Oh yeah, many times.	喔，唱過，很多次。
I'm going to go this weekend.	我這個週末要去。

**

cheer** sb. **up 使某人振作精神
ever〔'ɛvɚ〕*adv.* 曾經
karaoke〔,kæri'oki〕*n.* 卡拉 OK
yeah〔jɛ〕*adv.* 是的（= *yes*）
time〔taɪm〕*n.* 次　　weekend〔'wik'ɛnd〕*n.* 週末

karaoke

□ 4. ***What's your favorite karaoke song to sing?***	你最愛唱的卡拉 OK 歌曲是什麼？
I don't know.	我不知道。
I don't have one favorite.	我沒有最喜愛的。
□ 5. ***Do you like to dance?***	你喜歡跳舞嗎？
I seldom dance.	我很少跳舞。
I have two left feet.	我非常笨拙。
□ 6. ***How do you listen to music?***	你如何聽音樂？
I listen on my phone.	我用我的手機聽。
At home I use a bluetooth speaker.	在家我會用藍牙喇叭。

**

favorite〔ˈfevərɪt〕*adj.* 最喜愛的 *n.* 最喜愛的人或物
left〔lɛft〕*adj.* 左邊的 feet〔fit〕*n. pl.* 腳
have two left feet 非常笨拙
phone〔fon〕*n.* 電話【在此指 cell phone（手機）】
bluetooth〔ˈblu,tuθ〕*n.* 藍牙【一種無線通訊技術標準，用來讓固定與動行裝置，在短距離間交換資料，以形成個人區域網路】
speaker〔ˈspikɚ〕*n.* 擴音器；喇叭

have two left feet

□ **7.** ***Do you like classical music?***	你喜歡古典音樂嗎？
Sure, from time to time.	當然，有時候。
But it's not my favorite.	但它不是我最喜愛的。
□ **8.** ***Do you like country music?***	你喜歡鄉村音樂嗎？
I think it's ok.	我認爲還可以。
I don't know much about it.	我對它並不是很了解。
□ **9.** ***Have you ever been to a concert?***	你曾經去參加過演唱會嗎？
No, never.	不，從來沒有。
But I'll see a concert someday.	但將來有一天我一定會去看演唱會。

** ______________

classical〔ˈklæsɪkḷ〕*adj.* 古典的

from time to time 偶爾；有時候

country〔ˈkʌntrɪ〕*n.* 鄉村　***country music*** 鄉村音樂

ok〔ˈoˈke〕*adj.* 可以的

concert〔ˈkɑnsɜt〕*n.* 音樂會；演唱會

someday〔ˈsʌmˌde〕*adv.* 將來有一天

concert

【背景說明】

Oral Test 20

1. ***Easy listening music.***（輕鬆的音樂。）可說成：I like relaxing music.（我喜歡輕鬆的音樂。）

3. ***Do you have a favorite band or artist?***（你有最喜愛的樂團或藝人嗎？）可說成：Which music group or singer do you like best?（你最喜歡哪個樂團或歌手？）Who is your favorite music artist?（誰是你最喜愛的歌手？）

5. ***Too many to answer.***（多到無法回答。）可說成：I like so many—I can't answer.（我喜歡很多——我無法回答。）It's difficult to answer because I like so many.（很難回答，因爲我喜歡的很多。）

Oral Test 21

5. ***I have two left feet.*** 字面的意思是「我有兩隻左腳。」引申爲「我非常笨拙。」(= *I'm clumsy.*)【clumsy〔'klʌmzɪ〕*adj.* 笨拙的】在此可說成：I'm not a good dancer.（我不太會跳舞。）(= *I'm an awful dancer.*)【awful〔'ɔfl̩〕*adj.* 糟糕的】

6. ***I listen*** *on my phone.*（我用我的手機聽。）(= *I listen to music on my phone.*)

7. ***Sure, from time to time.***（當然，有時候。）(= *Yes, once in a while.* = *Of course, sometimes.*)【***once in a while*** 偶爾；有時候】

Oral Test 22

【問與答一起背】

□ 1. ***Do you like reading? Why or why not?***	你喜歡閱讀嗎？爲什麼喜歡，或爲什麼不？
Yes, I like to read.	是的，我喜歡閱讀。
A good book is an adventure, so I read a lot.	一本好書令人興奮，所以我讀很多書。
□ 2. ***What kind of books do you like?***	你喜歡什麼種類的書？
I like to read fantasy.	我喜歡看奇幻小說。
I also love mysteries.	我也喜愛推理小說。
□ 3. ***Do you have a favorite book?***	你有最喜愛的書嗎？
I don't.	我沒有。
I can't pick a favorite.	我無法挑一本最喜愛的書。

** ——————————

adventure〔əd'vɛntʃə〕*n.* 冒險
fantasy〔'fæntəsɪ〕*n.* 奇幻作品；奇幻小說
mystery〔'mɪstrɪ〕*n.* 推理小說
pick〔pɪk〕*v.* 挑選
favorite〔'fevərɪt〕*adj.* 最喜愛的 *n.* 最喜愛的人或物

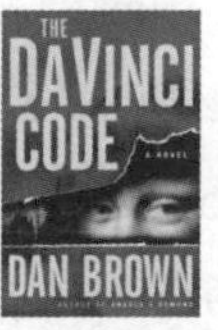

mystery

□ 4. ***What was the last book you read?***	你最近看的是什麼書？
One Word English.	《英文一字金》。
It was recommended by a friend.	那是一位朋友推薦的。
□ 5. ***How did you like it?***	你喜歡嗎？
I loved it.	我很愛。
It's helped me a lot.	它幫助我很多。
□ 6. ***Are you reading anything now?***	你現在有在閱讀任何書嗎？
Not right now.	現在沒有。
I have to look for a new book.	我必須尋找一本新書。

** ―――――――――――――

last〔 læst 〕*adj.* 最後的；上一次的

One Word English 英文一字金【書名】

recommend〔,rɛkə'mɛnd〕*v.* 推薦

right now 現在

look for 尋找

□ **7.** ***Do you have a favorite author?***	你有最喜愛的作家嗎？
Yes, Dan Brown.	有，丹•布朗。
I love his books.	我很喜愛他的書。
□ **8.** ***Can you recommend a good book?***	你能推薦一本好書嗎？
I recommend One Word English.	我推薦《英文一字金》。
It's how I learned English.	那是我學英文的方法。
□ **9.** ***Did you read much as a kid?***	你小時候有讀很多書嗎？
No, not too much.	不，沒有很多。
I did read comic books.	我的確會看漫畫書。

**

author〔'ɔθɚ〕*n.* 作者；作家

Dan Brown〔'dæn 'braʊn〕*n.* 丹•布朗

recommend〔,rɛkə'mɛnd〕*v.* 推薦

kid〔kɪd〕*n.* 小孩　***as a kid*** 小時候（= *as a child*）

「do + 原形動詞」可加強動詞的語氣，表「眞的…」。

comic〔'kɑmɪk〕*adj.* 漫畫的　***comic book*** 漫畫書

Intermediate

【背景說明】

Oral Test 22

1. ***adventure*** 主要的意思是「冒險」，對美國人來說，一點小事、一點小刺激、令人興奮的，都叫「冒險」。***A good book is an adventure***. 字面的意思是「一本好書是一場冒險。」引申為「一本好書令人興奮。」(= *A good book is exciting to read.* = *A good book is thrilling and fun to read.*)【thrilling〔'θrɪlɪŋ〕*adj.* 令人興奮的】

2. ***I like to read fantasy***. (我喜歡看奇幻小說。)(= *I like to read make-believe stories.* = *I enjoy reading fiction.* = *I like imaginary stories.*)【make-believe *adj.* 虛構的　imaginary〔ɪ'mædʒən,ɛrɪ〕*adj.* 虛構的】「虛構的小說」叫作 fiction 或 fantasy，如「哈利波特系列」(Harry Potter series)。***I also love mysteries***. (我也喜愛推理小說。) 如「偵探小說」(detective story)，最有名的是「福爾摩斯」(Sherlock Holmes)。

5. ***How did you like it?*** (你喜歡嗎？)(= *Did you like it?*) 可說成：Did you enjoy it? (你喜歡嗎？) How did you feel about it? (你覺得如何？) 美國人喜歡用 How do you like it? 來代替 Do you like it? 如在餐桌上，看到美國人在吃牛排，可問他：How do you like your steak? (你喜不喜歡你的牛排？) 通常他們會回答：It is delicious. I'm really enjoying it. (很好吃。我真的很喜歡。)【steat〔stek〕*n.* 牛排】

9. ***I did read comic books***. (我的確會看漫畫書。) did 用於加強語氣。可說成：I read cartoon books. (我會看漫畫書。)(= *I read funny picture books.*)
【***cartoon book*** 漫畫書　***picture book*** (兒童的) 圖畫書】

Oral Test 23

【問與答一起背】

□ 1. ***Do you like sports?***	你喜歡運動嗎？
Yes, I do.	是的，我喜歡。
I'm a big basketball fan.	我是個超級籃球迷。
□ 2. ***Why do you like sports?***	你爲什麼喜歡運動？
I like competing.	我喜歡競爭。
It's exciting.	那很刺激。
□ 3. ***Have you ever played a sport?***	你曾經從事任何運動嗎？
Yeah, I was on a baseball team.	是的，我參加過棒球隊。
Now I play basketball with my friends.	現在我會和朋友打籃球。

Intermediate

** ________________

sport〔sport〕*n.* 運動；競賽
basketball〔ˈbæskɪtˌbɔl〕*n.* 籃球
fan〔fæn〕*n.* 迷　compete〔kəmˈpit〕*v.* 競爭
exciting〔ɪkˈsaɪtɪŋ〕*adj.* 令人興奮的；刺激的
play〔ple〕*v.* 參加（競賽）　yeah〔jɛ〕*adv.* 是的（= *yes*）
baseball〔ˈbesˌbɔl〕*n.* 棒球　team〔tim〕*n.* 隊

□ 4. ***Did you play any sports as a child?***	你小時候參加過任何運動嗎？
Yes, I did.	是的，我有。
I played baseball in junior high.	我國中時會打棒球。
□ 5. ***Do you have a favorite sport?***	你有最喜愛的運動嗎？
I enjoy basketball.	我喜歡籃球。
It's easy to arrange a game.	要安排比賽很容易。
□ 6. ***What sports are popular in your country?***	在你的國家，受歡迎的運動是什麼？
Table tennis and badminton.	桌球和羽毛球。
But baseball is even more popular.	不過棒球更受歡迎。

baseball

** ——————————

as a child 小時候　***junior high*** 國中（= *junior high school*）
enjoy〔ɪnˈdʒɔɪ〕*v.* 喜歡　arrange〔əˈrendʒ〕*v.* 安排
game〔gem〕*n.* 比賽　popular〔ˈpɑpjələ˞〕*adj.* 受歡迎的
country〔ˈkʌntrɪ〕*n.* 國家　tennis〔ˈtɛnɪs〕*n.* 網球
table tennis 桌球　badminton〔ˈbædmɪntən〕*n.* 羽毛球
even〔ˈivən〕*adv.* 甚至；更加【強調比較級】

□ 7. ***Do you watch professional sports?***	你會看職業的運動嗎？
Once in a while.	偶爾。
I like to watch baseball.	我喜歡看棒球。
□ 8. ***Do you have a favorite team?***	你有最喜愛的球隊嗎？
Yes, the Yankees.	有，洋基隊。
My whole family loves them.	我們全家都很愛他們。
□ 9. ***What is your opinion of professional athletes?***	你對職業運動員有何看法？
I respect and admire most.	我尊敬和欽佩大部份的職業運動員。
The players work hard to succeed.	球員要很努力才能成功。

**

professional (prəˈfɛʃənḷ) *adj.* 職業的
once in a while 偶爾；有時候　team (tim) *n.* 隊
Yankees (ˈjæŋkɪz) *n.* (紐約) 洋基隊
whole (hol) *adj.* 全部的；整個的
opinion (əˈpɪnjən) *n.* 意見；看法　athlete (ˈæθlit) *n.* 運動員
respect (rɪˈspɛkt) *v.* 尊敬　admire (ədˈmaɪr) *v.* 欽佩
player (ˈpleɚ) *n.* 球員　***work hard*** 努力
succeed (səkˈsid) *v.* 成功

Oral Test 24

Intermediate

【問與答一起背】

□ 1. ***Do you like to watch TV?***	你喜歡看電視嗎？
Oh, sure!	喔，當然！
Watching TV is relaxing.	看電視能讓人放鬆。
□ 2. ***Do you have a favorite show or program?***	你有最喜愛的節目嗎？
I have a few.	我有一些。
But dramas are my favorite.	但戲劇是我的最愛。
□ 3. ***How often do you watch TV?***	你多久看一次電視？
Not so often.	不是很常。
Mostly on the weekends.	大多是在週末。

**

sure〔ʃur〕*adv.* 當然　relaxing〔rɪˈlæksɪŋ〕*adj.* 令人放鬆的
favorite〔ˈfevərɪt〕*adj.* 最喜愛的　*n.* 最喜愛的人或物
show〔ʃo〕*n.* 節目　program〔ˈprogræm〕*n.* 節目
a few 一些　drama〔ˈdrɑmə〕*n.* 戲劇
so〔so〕*adv.* 非常（= *very*）　mostly〔ˈmostlɪ〕*adv.* 大多
weekend〔ˈwikˈɛnd〕*n.* 週末

□ 4. ***What's your favorite way to watch TV: TV set, computer, iPad, or cell phone?***	你最喜愛用什麼方式看電視：電視機、電腦、iPad，或是手機？
TV set.	電視機。
I like seeing things on a big screen.	我喜歡用大螢幕看東西。
□ 5. ***What shows are popular in your country?***	在你的國家什麼節目受人歡迎？
Dramas are popular.	戲劇很受歡迎。
A lot of people like game shows, too.	很多人也喜歡遊戲節目。
□ 6. ***What are you watching these days?***	你最近在看什麼？
Nothing right now.	現在沒在看。
My favorite show just ended.	我最喜愛的節目剛結束。

** ______________________

TV set 電視機　computer〔kəm'pjutɚ〕*n.* 電腦
cell phone 手機　screen〔skrin〕*n.* 螢幕
popular〔'pɑpjəlɚ〕*adj.* 受歡迎的
drama〔'drɑmə〕*n.* 戲劇　***game show*** 遊戲節目
these days 最近（= *recently*）　***right now*** 現在
just〔dʒʌst〕*adv.* 剛剛　end〔ɛnd〕*v.* 結束

cell phone

□ 7. ***What was the last show you watched?***	你最近看的是什麼節目？
Last night I saw "American Idol."	昨晚我看了「美國偶像」。
It's a weekly talent show.	那是一週一次的達人秀。
□ 8. ***Can you recommend a good show?***	你可以推薦一個好的節目嗎？
Ok, let me think.	好的，讓我想想。
I suggest watching "Friends" or "Sex in the City".	我建議看「六人行」或「慾望城市」。
□ 9. ***Do you watch TV news?***	你會看電視新聞嗎？
No, not so much.	不會，不是很常看。
I prefer to read the news.	我比較喜歡閱讀新聞。

** ______

idol〔ˈaɪdḷ〕*n.* 偶像　***American Idol*** 美國偶像【節目名】
weekly〔ˈwiklɪ〕*adj.* 每週一次的　***talent show*** 才藝表演；達人秀
recommend〔ˌrɛkəˈmɛnd〕*v.* 推薦
suggest〔səgˈdʒɛst〕*v.* 建議　***Friends*** 六人行【影集名】
Sex and the City 慾望城市【影集名】
news〔njuz〕*n.* 新聞　much〔mʌtʃ〕*adv.* 常常
prefer〔prɪˈfɝ〕*v.* 比較喜歡

Oral Test 25

【問與答一起背】

☐ 1. ***Which TV news station does your family watch?***	你們家會看哪一個電視新聞台？
Sometimes TTV.	有時看台視。
Sometimes CNN.	有時看 CNN。
☐ 2. ***Do you have a favorite channel?***	你有最喜愛的頻道嗎？
Yes, the movie channels.	有，電影台。
Like HBO and Star Movies.	像是 HBO 和 Star Movies。
☐ 3. ***Do you like any foreign shows?***	你喜歡任何外國節目嗎？
Not too many.	不是很多。
I enjoy Chinese programs the most.	我最喜歡中文節目。

Intermediate

**

news station 新聞台　　TTV *n.* 台視（= *Taiwan TV*）
CNN *n.* 美國有線電視新聞網（= *Cable News Network*）
channel（ˈtʃænḷ）*n.* 頻道　　like（laɪk）*prep.* 像
foreign（ˈfɔrɪn）*adj.* 外國的　　enjoy（ɪnˈdʒɔɪ）*v.* 喜歡

□ 4. ***Do you ever watch reruns of old shows?***	你曾經看過舊的節目重播嗎？
Of course, I do.	當然，我看過。
I watch them with my parents.	我會和我的父母一起看。
□ 5. ***Do you like cartoons?***	你喜歡卡通嗎？
I used to.	我以前喜歡。
But now I prefer dramas.	但現在我比較喜歡戲劇。
□ 6. ***Did you watch cartoons as a kid?***	你小時候會看卡通嗎？
Yes, I did every day.	會，我每天都看。
I was crazy about cartoons.	我非常喜歡卡通。

** ________________

ever〔ˈɛvɚ〕*adv.* 曾經　rerun〔ˈriˌrʌn〕*n.* 重新上映

of course 當然　cartoon〔kɑrˈtun〕*n.* 卡通

used to 以前　prefer〔prɪˈfɝ〕*v.* 比較喜歡

drama〔ˈdrɑmə〕*n.* 戲劇

crazy〔ˈkrezɪ〕*adj.* 瘋狂的；喜歡的

be crazy about 很喜歡

cartoon

☐ **7.** ***Ever watch anime?***	曾經看過動畫片嗎？
Sometimes.	有時候。
Some are great.	有些很棒。
☐ **8.** ***Ever watch science channels like Discovery?***	曾經看過像是 Discovery 這樣的科學頻道嗎？
Yes, I do quite a bit.	是的，我常常看。
They have some interesting shows.	他們有一些有趣的節目。
☐ **9.** ***Does your family watch TV during meals?***	你的家人在用餐時會看電視嗎？
Yes, we often do.	是的，我們經常如此。
We enjoy watching TV while we eat.	我們喜歡邊吃飯邊看電視。

** ________________

anime〔ˈænəme〕*n.* 動漫；動畫片；卡通 great〔gret〕*adj.* 很棒的
science〔ˈsaɪəns〕*n.* 科學 discovery〔dɪsˈkʌvərɪ〕*n.* 發現
quite a bit 常常（= *a lot*）
interesting〔ˈɪntrɪstɪŋ〕*adj.* 有趣的
during〔ˈdjʊrɪŋ〕*prep.* 在…期間
meal〔mil〕*n.* 一餐；用餐時間

Intermediate

Oral Test 26

Intermediate

【問與答一起背】

☐ 1. ***What was the last movie you saw?*** 你最近看的是什麼電影？

I just watched *Avengers*. 我剛看過「復仇者聯盟」。

I really enjoyed it. 我真的很喜歡。

☐ 2. ***Do you have a favorite movie?*** 你有最喜愛的電影嗎？

Yes, I have a favorite. 有，我有一部最喜愛的電影。

The first *Harry Potter* was amazing. 「哈利波特」第一集很棒。

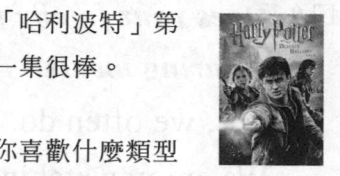

☐ 3. ***What sort of movies do you like?*** 你喜歡什麼類型的電影？

I like comedies. 我喜歡喜劇。

I like action movies, too. 我也喜歡動作片。

**

last〔 læst 〕*adj.* 最後的；上一次的
avenger〔 ə'vendʒɚ 〕*n.* 復仇者　***Avengers*** 復仇者聯盟【電影名】
Harry Potter〔'hærɪ 'pɑtɚ 〕*n.* 哈利波特
amazing〔 ə'mezɪŋ 〕*adj.* 驚人的；很棒的
sort〔 sɔrt 〕*n.* 種類　comedy〔'kɑmədɪ 〕*n.* 喜劇
action movie 動作片

☐ 4. ***How are the movies in your country?*** — 你們國家的電影如何？

They're not too bad. — 不會太差。

They're getting better. — 現在越來越好。

☐ 5. ***How often do you watch movies in English?*** — 你多久看一次英文電影？

All the time. — 一直都看。

I usually watch movies in English. — 我通常都看英文片。

☐ 6. ***Do you have a favorite actor or actress?*** — 你有最喜愛的男演員或女演員嗎？

I like Tom Cruise movies. — 我喜歡湯姆克魯斯的電影。

I really like Julia Roberts, too. — 我也很喜歡茱莉亞蘿勃茲。

**

all the time 一直　　actor (ˈæktɚ) *n.* 男演員

actress (ˈæktrɪs) *n.* 女演員

Tom Cruise (ˈtɑm ˈkruz) *n.* 湯姆克魯斯

Julia Roberts (ˈdʒuljə ˈrɑbɚz) *n.* 茱莉亞蘿勃茲

Julia Roberts

□ 7. ***Can you recommend a good movie?***	你能推薦一部好電影嗎？
I recommend *The Godfather*.	我推薦「教父」。
I suggest *Titanic*, too.	我也建議「鐵達尼號」。
□ 8. ***Do you like horror movies?***	你喜歡恐怖片嗎？
I love scary movies.	我很愛恐怖片。
I'm a big horror movie fan.	我是超級恐怖電影迷。
□ 9. ***If there were a movie about your life, what kind would it be?***	如果有一部關於你的人生的電影，它會是什麼類型的？
A drama or a comedy.	劇情片或喜劇。
I've experienced a lot so far.	到目前爲止我經歷了很多事。

**

recommend (ˌrɛkəˈmɛnd) *v.* 推薦

The Godfather 教父【電影名】

suggest (səgˈdʒɛst) *v.* 建議

Titanic (taɪˈtænɪk) *n.* 鐵達尼號

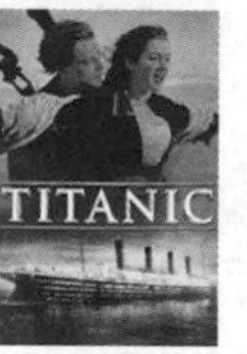

horror (ˈhɑrɚ) *n.* 恐怖　　scary (ˈskɛrɪ) *adj.* 可怕的

fan (fæn) *n.* (影) 迷　　kind (kaɪnd) *n.* 種類

drama (ˈdrɑmə) *n.* 戲劇；劇情片　　comedy (ˈkɑmədɪ) *n.* 喜劇

experience (ɪkˈspɪrɪəns) *v.* 經歷　　***so far*** 到目前爲止

【背景說明】

Oral Test 23

9. ***I respect and admire most.***（我尊敬和欽佩大部份的職業運動員。）（= *I respect and admire most of them.*）可說成：I think highly of them.（我認爲他們很了不起。）【***think highly of*** 對…評價很高；認爲…很了不起】I have a high opinion of many.（我對很多職業運動員有很高的評價。）【***have a high opinion of*** 對…有很高的評價】

Oral Test 24

5. ***A lot of people like game shows, too.***（很多人也喜歡遊戲節目。）可說成：People like shows where you can win money.（人們喜歡可以贏得獎金的節目。）Game shows with competition are popular.（競賽型的遊戲節目很受歡迎。）Programs where people compete against each other are popular.（有人互相競爭的節目很受歡迎。）【compete〔kəmˈpit〕*v.* 競爭】

Oral Test 25

4. ***Do you ever watch reruns of old shows?***（你曾經看過舊的節目重播嗎？）（= *Do you ever watch replays of shows from many years ago?*）【replay〔riˈple〕*n.* 重播】

6. ***I was crazy about cartoons.***（我非常喜歡卡通。）（= *I liked cartoons very much.*）可說成：I loved to watch cartoons whenever I could.（一有空我就愛看卡通。）

7. ***Ever watch anime?***（曾經看過動畫片嗎？）【anime〔ˈænəˌme〕*n.* 動漫；動畫片；卡通】源自 Do you ***ever watch anime***? 可說成：Have you ever watched a cartoon movie?（你曾經看過卡通片嗎？）

Intermediate

8. ***Yes, I do quite a bit.*** (是的，我常常看。) (= *Yes, I do a lot.* = *Yes, I often do.*) ***quite a bit*** 字面的意思是「相當多的一點」，引申爲「很多；常常」(= *a lot* = *much* = *often*)。同樣地，quite a few 則是「很多」(= *many*)。

9. ***Does your family watch TV during meals?*** (你的家人在用餐時會看電視嗎？) (= *Does your family watch TV while eating?*) 可說成：At home, does your family watch TV while eating? (你的家人在家吃飯時會看電視嗎？)

Oral Test 26

7. ***I suggest Titanic, too.*** (我也建議「鐵達尼號」。) 可說成：I propose you watch the Titanic movie. (我建議你看「鐵達尼號」這部電影。)【propose (prəˈpoz) *v.* 提議】You should see the movie "Titanic". (你應該看「鐵達尼號」這部電影。)

8. ***I'm a big horror movie fan.*** (我是超級恐怖電影迷。) (= *I like terrifying movies.* = *I love to watch frightening movies.*) 【terrifying (ˈtɛrəˌfaɪɪŋ) *adj.* 可怕的 frightening (ˈfraɪtṇɪŋ) *adj.* 可怕的】可說成：I really enjoy movies that scare me. (我很喜歡看會使我害怕的電影。)【scare (skɛr) *v.* 驚嚇】

9. ***I've experienced a lot so far.*** (到目前爲止我經歷了很多事。) (= *I have had many different experiences.*) 可說成：So much has happened to me already. (已經有很多事發生在我身上。) Many things have happened to me. (有很多事發生在我身上。)

Oral Test 27

【問與答一起背】

□ 1. ***What's your favorite game?***	你最喜愛的遊戲是什麼？
Pokémon for sure.	當然是寶可夢。
The Pokémon games are never boring.	寶可夢遊戲絕不會無聊。
□ 2. ***What games did you play as a kid?***	你小時候會玩什麼遊戲？
Tag and hide-and-seek.	捉人遊戲和捉迷藏。
We played outside a lot.	我們常常在外面玩。
□ 3. ***What games do you still play now? Why?***	你現在仍然會玩什麼遊戲？爲什麼？
I still play video games.	我仍然會玩電玩遊戲。
They are just as fun as when I was a child.	它們和我的小時候一樣有趣。

** ______________________

Pokémon〔ˈpokeˌmon〕*n.* 寶可夢　***for sure*** 當然
boring〔ˈborɪŋ〕*adj.* 無聊的　***as a kid*** 小時候
tag〔tæg〕*n.*（兒童的）捉人遊戲
hide-and-seek〔ˈhaɪdənˈsik〕*n.* 捉迷藏
outside〔ˈaʊtˈsaɪd〕*adv.* 在外面　***a lot*** 常常（= *often*）
video〔ˈvɪdɪˌo〕*adj.*（電視）影像的　***video game*** 電玩遊戲

Intermediate

□ 4. ***How competitive are you when it comes to games?*** 一提到遊戲，你有多喜歡競爭？

I'm super competitive. 我超級喜歡競爭的。

I play to win. 我玩遊戲是爲了要贏。

□ 5. ***Do you play video games?*** 你會玩電玩遊戲嗎？

Yes, I do. 是的，我會。

I'm a gamer. 我是個玩家。

□ 6. ***How often do you play video games?*** 你多久玩一次電玩遊戲？

Once or twice a week. 一星期一或兩次。

Whenever I have the time. 每當我有時間玩時。

**

competitive〔kəm'pɛtətɪv〕*adj.* 好競爭的

when it comes to 一提到

super〔'supɚ〕*adv.* 十分；非常

gamer〔'gemɚ〕*n.* 玩家　　once〔wʌns〕*adv.* 一次

twice〔twaɪs〕*adv.* 兩次

whenever〔hwɛn'ɛvɚ〕*conj.* 每當

video game

□ 7. ***What games are popular now?***	現在流行什麼遊戲？
I think Fortnite is popular now.	我認爲「要塞英雄」現在很流行。
Minecraft is well liked, too.	「當個創世神」也相當受喜愛。
□ 8. ***Do you prefer Xbox or PlayStation?***	你比較喜歡 Xbox 還是 PlayStation？
Neither.	兩個都不喜歡。
I like Nintendo better.	我比較喜歡任天堂。
□ 9. ***Do you play any games on your phone?***	你會用你的手機玩任何遊戲嗎？
Sure, I play a few.	當然，我會玩一些。
I play Pokémon Go.	我會玩「精靈寶可夢」。

** ————————————

popular〔ˈpɑpjələ˞〕*adj.* 受歡迎的
Fortnite〔ˈfɔrtˌnaɪt〕*n.* 要塞英雄【遊戲名】
Minecraft〔ˈmaɪnˌkræft〕*n.* 當個創世神【遊戲名】
well〔wɛl〕*adv.* 相當地　　prefer〔prɪˈfɝ〕*v.* 比較喜歡
X-box 是微軟創立的電子遊戲品牌。
PlayStation（官方簡稱 PS）是由索尼互動娛樂創立並開發，從第五代到第八代的一系列電子遊戲機。
neither〔ˈniðə˞〕*pron.* 兩者皆不　　Nintendo〔nɪnˈtɛndo〕*n.* 任天堂
phone〔fon〕*n.* 電話；手機【在此指 cell phone】
Pokémon Go 精靈寶可夢【遊戲名】

Oral Test 28

【問與答一起背】

□ 1. ***What motivates you?***	什麼能激勵你？
My parents motivate me.	我的父母會激勵我。
I want to make them proud.	我想要使他們感到驕傲。
□ 2. ***What is something you love a lot?***	你非常喜愛的事物是什麼？
I love learning English.	我很愛學英文。
It's fun for me.	我覺得很有趣。
□ 3. ***What are you working towards?***	你的目標是什麼？
I'm working towards graduation.	我正在努力要畢業。
I'm working towards college.	我的目標是上大學。

**

motivate〔ˈmotəˌvet〕*v.* 激勵
proud〔praʊd〕*adj.* 驕傲的；感到光榮的　***a lot*** 非常
fun〔fʌn〕*adj.* 有趣的　towards〔tordz〕*prep.* 朝向
work towards 努力達成；努力完成
graduation〔ˌgrædʒʊˈeʃən〕*n.* 畢業　college〔ˈkɑlɪdʒ〕*n.* 大學

Intermediate

□ **4.** ***What inspires you?*** 什麼能激勵你？

My best friend inspires me. 我最好的朋友能激勵我。

He's really talented. 他眞的很有才能。

□ **5.** ***Do you have a role model?*** 你有想要效法的榜樣嗎？

My favorite teacher is my hero! 我最喜愛的老師是我的英雄！

He is intelligent and tireless. 他很聰明又孜孜不倦。

□ **6.** ***How did he impact you?*** 他如何影響你？

He pushed me towards college. 他督促我上大學。

He challenged me to do my best. 他激發我盡全力。

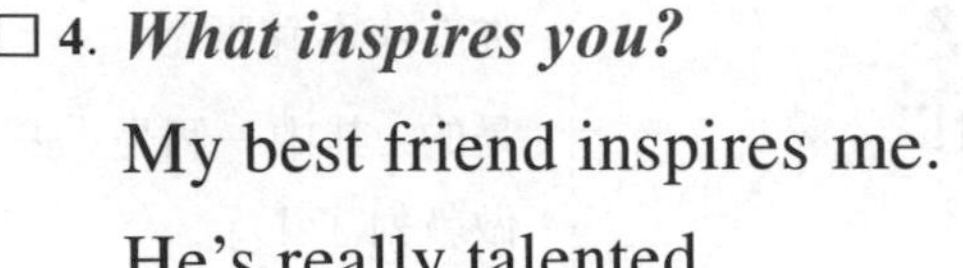

role model

**

inspire (ɪnˈspaɪr) *v.* 激勵

talented (ˈtæləntɪd) *adj.* 有才能的　role (rol) *n.* 角色

model (ˈmɑdḷ) *n.* 榜樣　***role model*** 行爲榜樣；模範

hero (ˈhɪro) *n.* 英雄　intelligent (ɪnˈtɛlədʒənt) *adj.* 聰明的

tireless (ˈtaɪrlɪs) *adj.* 孜孜不倦的

impact (ˈɪmpækt) *v.* 影響　push (pʊʃ) *v.* 催促；驅使

challenge (ˈtʃælɪndʒ) *v.* 要求；激發；督促　***do one's best*** 盡力

□ 7. ***Do you have a motto?***	你有座右銘嗎？
Yes, one is "Just do it!"	是的，其中一個是「去做就對了！」
The other is: study hard, work hard, play hard.	另一個是：用功讀書、努力工作、拼命玩樂。
□ 8. ***Do you have a philosophy of life?***	你有人生哲學嗎？
Never give up; don't quit!	絕不放棄；不要放棄！
Also, make it happen.	還有，去做吧。
□ 9. ***What's an issue you care about?***	你關心什麼議題？
I'm worried about conservation.	我很擔心自然資源的保護。
I care about protecting the environment.	我關心保護環境。

**

motto〔ˈmɑto〕*n.* 座右銘　***one…the other***　（兩者）一個…另一個
Just do it. 去做就對了；趕快做。
hard〔hɑrd〕*adv.* 拼命地；努力地　philosophy〔fəˈlɑsəfɪ〕*n.* 哲學
philosophy of life 人生哲學；人生觀　***give up*** 放棄
quit〔kwɪt〕*v.* 放棄　also〔ˈɔlso〕*adv.* 而且；此外
Make it happen. 去做吧。　issue〔ˈɪʃjʊ〕*n.* 議題；問題
care about 關心　***be worried about*** 擔心
conservation〔ˌkɑnsəˈveʃən〕*n.*（對自然資源的）保護
protect〔prəˈtɛkt〕*v.* 保護　environment〔ɪnˈvaɪrənmənt〕*n.* 環境

Oral Test 29

【問與答一起背】

□ **1.** ***Do you have a pet?***	你有養寵物嗎？
Yes, I do.	是的，我有。
I have a dog.	我有一隻狗。
□ **2.** ***Is it a he or a she?***	牠是公的還是母的？
He's male.	牠是公的。
He's a good boy.	牠是個好孩子。
□ **3.** ***What's his name?***	牠叫什麼名字？
His name is Lucky.	牠的名字是來福。
Maybe that's a common name.	也許那是個很普通的名字。

** ———————————

pet〔pɛt〕*n.* 寵物　***have a pet*** 養寵物
he〔hi〕*n.* 雄性動物　she〔ʃi〕*n.* 雌性動物
male〔mel〕*adj.* 雄性的；公的
boy〔bɔɪ〕*n.*【口語】兒子　lucky〔ˈlʌkɪ〕*adj.* 幸運的
common〔ˈkɑmən〕*adj.* 常見的；普通的

□ 4. ***How old is he?***	牠今年幾歲？
He's two years old.	牠今年兩歲。
He's not a puppy anymore.	牠已經不再是小狗了。
□ 5. ***What breed is he?***	牠是什麼品種？
He's a mix.	牠是隻雜種狗。
We're not sure what kind.	我們不確定是哪一種。
□ 6. ***Where did you get him?***	你在哪裡得到牠的？
Lucky was a stray.	來福是隻流浪狗。
I found him on the street.	我在街上發現牠的。

**

not…anymore 不再…

puppy〔ˈpʌpɪ〕*n.* 小狗

breed〔brid〕*n.* 品種

mix〔mɪks〕*n.* 混合物；雜種狗

sure〔ʃʊr〕*adj.* 確定的　　kind〔kaɪnd〕*n.* 種類

stray〔stre〕*n.* 野狗；流浪狗　*adj.* 迷失的

puppy

□ 7. ***How long have you had him?***	你養牠養多久了？
One year now.	到現在一年了。
He's become part of the family.	牠已經成爲家庭的一份子。
□ 8. ***Does he know any tricks?***	牠會任何把戲嗎？
Lucky can "shake."	來福會「握手」。
I'm teaching him to fetch.	我正在教牠去把東西拿回來。
□ 9. ***Where do you walk him?***	你會在哪裡遛狗？
I walk him in the park.	我會在公園遛狗。
He likes to sniff there.	牠喜歡在那裡嗅一嗅。

**

part〔pɑrt〕*n.* 部份　trick〔trɪk〕*n.* 把戲
shake〔ʃek〕*v.* 握手　fetch〔fɛtʃ〕*v.* 去把東西拿來
walk〔wɔk〕*v.* 遛（狗）
sniff〔snɪf〕*v.* 聞；嗅

walk a dog

【背景説明】

Oral Test 27

4. ***How competitive are you when it comes to games?***（一提到遊戲，你有多喜歡競爭？）這句話的意思是，「當你玩遊戲時，你認眞還是不認眞？」可説成：Do you play games just for fun?（你玩遊戲只是爲了好玩嗎？）Are you a serious game player?（你玩遊戲是很認眞的嗎？）Do you hate to lose?（你是不是不喜歡輸？）
I'm super competitive.（我超級喜歡競爭的。）(= *I'm serious. I always play to win. I hate to lose.*) ***I play to win***.（我玩遊戲是爲了要贏。）(= *I always try to win.*) I never just let people win to be nice.（我從不會爲了當好人讓別人贏。）

5. ***I'm a gamer***.（我是個玩家。）(= *I'm an experienced player.*)
【experienced（ɪk'spɪrɪənst）*adj.* 有經驗的】可説成：I play a lot.（我常常玩。）I'm a good player.（我很會玩遊戲。）

Oral Test 28

1. ***What motivates you?***（什麼能激勵你？）(= *What can motivate you?*) 可説成：***What*** or who ***motivates you***?（什麼東西或什麼人能激勵你？）

3. ***What are you working towards?*** 字面的意思是「你正在努力完成什麼？」引申爲「你的目標是什麼？」(= *What's your goal?*)
I'm working towards graduation.（我正在努力要畢業。）
(= *I'm working hard so I can graduate.*) ***I'm working towards college***.（我的目標是上大學。）(= *My goal is to attend college.*)

可說成：I'm working hard for college.（我正在努力要上大學。）I hope to enter a university.（我希望能上大學。）原則上，在美國，college 是「學院」，有兩年制，也有四年制，而社區學院（community college）則是不需要考試就可以進去。university 是「大學」，較難進入，但是，一般說來，college 是「大學」的通稱。

6. ***He challenged me to do my best.***（他激發我盡全力。）(= *He urged me to try my best.*) 在句中，challenge 不作「挑戰」解，是作「要求；激發；督促」解 (= *urge*)。

9. ***What's an issue*** *you care about?*（你關心什麼議題？）(= *What issue do you care about?*) 可說成：What is a subject you are concerned about?（你關心什麼問題？）【subject〔'sʌbdʒɪkt〕*n.* 主題；問題】

Oral Test 29

2. ***He's a good boy.***（牠是個好孩子。）(= *He's a good dog.*) 美國人常把狗擬人化，代名詞用 he 或 she。

5. ***He's a mix.***（牠是隻雜種狗。）(= *He's a cross breed.*)【cross〔krɔs〕*adj.* 雜種的　breed〔brid〕*n.* 品種】He's not a pure breed.（它不是純種狗。）【pure〔pjʊr〕*adj.* 純的】

6. ***Lucky was a stray.***（來福是隻流浪狗。）(= *Lucky had no home.*) 可說成：Lucky lived on the street.（來福住在街上。）

Oral Test 30

【問與答一起背】

□ 1. ***What brand of dog food do you buy?***	你會買什麼品牌的狗食？
Chicken-Chow dog food.	Chicken-Chow 狗食。
It's a safe and healthy brand.	它是個安全又健康的品牌。
□ 2. ***Is he house-trained?***	有訓練牠不在室內上廁所嗎？
Lucky's house-trained.	來福已經受過不會在室內上廁所的訓練。
He hasn't had an accident in months.	牠好幾個月都沒有在家裡上廁所。
□ 3. ***Hi, may I pet your dog?***	嗨，我可以摸一下你的狗嗎？
Of course.	當然。
Go ahead, he won't bite.	儘管摸，牠不會咬人。

**

brand〔brænd〕*n.* 品牌　***dog food*** 狗食

safe〔sef〕*adj.* 安全的　healthy〔ˈhɛlθɪ〕*v.* 健康的

house-trained〔ˈhaʊzˌtrend〕*adj.*（寵物）受過訓練不在室內便溺的

accident〔ˈæksədənt〕*n.* 意外

in months 已經好幾個月（= *for months*）　pet〔pɛt〕*v.* 撫摸

go ahead 儘管做吧　bite〔baɪt〕*v.* 咬；咬人

□ 4. ***Is he friendly?***	牠友善嗎？
He's super friendly.	牠超級友善的。
He loves people.	牠很喜歡人。
□ 5. ***Does he like to be petted?***	牠喜歡被撫摸嗎？
Yes, he loves to be petted.	是的，牠很喜歡被撫摸。
He especially loves belly rubs.	牠尤其喜愛被搓揉肚子。
□ 6. ***Is he good with kids?***	牠很會跟小孩相處嗎？
He's great with kids.	牠跟小孩處得很好。
He's very gentle.	牠非常溫和。

friendly

**

friendly〔ˈfrɛndlɪ〕*adj.* 友善的

super〔ˈsupɚ〕*adv.* 十分；非常；超

especially〔əˈspɛʃəlɪ〕*adv.* 尤其；特別是

belly〔ˈbɛlɪ〕*n.* 肚子　rub〔rʌb〕*n.* 摩擦；按摩

belly rub 搓揉肚子　***be good with*** 善於對待

gentle〔ˈdʒɛntl̩〕*adj.* 溫和的

□ 7. ***Will he bite?***	牠會咬人嗎？
No, he won't bite.	不，牠不會咬人。
He's very well-trained and friendly.	牠被訓練得很好，而且又友善。
□ 8. ***Does your dog chase birds?***	你的狗會追小鳥嗎？
He loves to chase birds!	牠很愛追小鳥！
Sometimes he chases his tail.	有時候牠會追自己的尾巴。
□ 9. ***Do you like cats or dogs more?***	你比較喜歡貓還是狗？
I like dogs more.	我比較喜歡狗。
They have a friendlier personality.	牠們的個性比較友善。

**

well-trained 〔,wɛl'trend〕*adj.* 訓練有素的

sometimes 〔'sʌm,taɪmz〕*adv.* 有時候

chase 〔tʃes〕*v.* 追

tail 〔tel〕*n.* 尾巴

personality 〔,pɝsn̩'ælətɪ〕*n.* 個性；性格

well-trained

【背景說明】

Oral Test 30

2. ***Is he house-trained?*** (有訓練牠不在室內上廁所嗎？) (= *Is he trained to go pee outside?*)【pee〔pi〕*v.* 尿尿；小便】***He hasn't had an accident in months.*** 字面的意思是「牠好幾個月都沒出過意外了。」在此表示「牠好幾個月都沒有在家裡上廁所。」(= *He hasn't peed in the house in months.*)

3. ***Go ahead, he won't bite.*** (儘管摸，牠不會咬人。) (= *You can—he's safe.*)

5. ***He especially loves belly rubs.*** (牠尤其喜愛被搓揉肚子。) (= *He really enjoys getting his belly scratched.* = *He likes belly massages.*)【scratch〔skrætʃ〕*v.* 抓；搔　massage〔mə'sɑʒ〕*n.* 按摩】

6. ***Is he good with kids?*** (牠很會跟小孩相處嗎？) (= *Does he get along with children?* = *Does he play well around kids?*)【***get along with*** 和…處得好　***play around*** 在…附近玩耍】

9. ***Do you like cats or dogs more?*** (你比較喜歡貓還是狗？) (= *Do you prefer cats or dogs?* = *Are you more of a cat person or a dog person?*)【prefer〔prɪ'fɝ〕*v.* 比較喜歡　***more of*** 更大程度上的…　***cat person*** 喜歡貓的人　***dog person*** 喜歡狗的人】

Oral Test 31

【問與答一起背】

□ 1. ***What do you find easy about English?***	你覺得學英文有什麼是容易的嗎？
I can practice anywhere.	我可以在任何地方練習。
English signs, movies, etc. are everywhere.	英文告示、英文電影等，到處都有。
□ 2. ***How are you learning English?***	你如何學英文？
I'm studying One Word English.	我正在研讀《英文一字金》。
I take practice quizzes.	我會做練習小考。
□ 3. ***Are you good at reciting?***	你擅長背誦嗎？
I'm about average.	我很普通。
I'm getting better.	我正在進步中。

**

practice ('præktɪs) *v. n.* 練習　sign (saɪn) *n.* 告示
etc. (ɛt'sɛtrə) 等等　take (tek) *v.* 參加（考試）
quiz (kwɪz) *n.* 小考　***be good at*** 擅長
recite (rɪ'saɪt) *v.* 背誦；朗誦　average ('ævərɪdʒ) *n.* 一般標準
about average 平凡的；普通的；中等的　get (gɛt) *v.* 變得

□ 4. ***How do you memorize vocabulary?***	你如何背單字？
I start by speaking out loud.	我一開始會唸出聲音來。
Then I repeat and repeat.	然後我會一直重複唸。
□ 5. ***Why do you want to learn English?***	你為什麼要學英文？
Knowing English is super helpful.	懂英文是非常有用的。
I might find more job opportunities.	我可以找到更多的工作機會。
□ 6. ***What are your language learning goals?***	你的語言學習目標是什麼？
To pass my English exam.	通過我的英文考試。
To improve my English skills.	增進我的英文技能。

** ______

memorize (ˈmɛməˌraɪz) *v.* 背誦；記憶
vocabulary (vəˈkæbjəˌlɛrɪ) *n.* 字彙　***out loud*** 出聲地
repeat (rɪˈpit) *v.* 重複地說　super (ˈsupɚ) *adv.* 十分；相當
helpful (ˈhɛlpfəl) *adj.* 有幫助的；有用的
opportunity (ˌɑpɚˈtjunətɪ) *n.* 機會
language (ˈlæŋgwɪdʒ) *n.* 語言　goal (gol) *n.* 目標
pass (pæs) *v.* 通過　improve (ɪmˈpruv) *v.* 改善
skill (skɪl) *n.* 技能

□ 7. ***Why choose One Word English?***	為什麼選擇《英文一字金》？
Because it works.	因為它很有效。
The method has helped me a lot.	這個方法對我幫助很大。
□ 8. ***Are you interested in taking the TOEIC test?***	你對參加多益測驗有興趣嗎？
I'm interested.	我有興趣。
I plan to take it at some point.	我打算在某個時刻考。
□ 9. ***Do you want to study abroad?***	你想要出國唸書嗎？
Sure, I want to.	當然，我想要。
That's my future plan.	那是我未來的計劃。

** ______________________

choose〔tʃuz〕*v.* 選擇
work〔wɝk〕*v.* 有效　method〔ˈmɛθəd〕*n.* 方法
interested〔ˈɪntrɪstɪd〕*adj.* 有興趣的 < *in* >
take〔tek〕*v.* 參加（考試）
TOEIC 多益測驗（= *Test of English for International Communication* 國際溝通英語測驗）【是國際職場英語溝通能力評量標準，為針對英語非母語人士所設計之英語能力測驗】
some〔sʌm〕*adj.* 某個　point〔pɔɪnt〕*n.* 時刻
abroad〔əˈbrɔd〕*adv.* 到國外　future〔ˈfjutʃɚ〕*adj.* 未來的

ETS TOEIC

Oral Test 32

【問與答一起背】

□ 1. ***How do you deal with your problems?***	你如何處理你的問題？
I think carefully.	我會仔細思考。
I talk with family or friends.	我會和家人或朋友談一談。
□ 2. ***What's one problem you are dealing with now?***	你現在正在處理什麼問題？
I'm too busy.	我太忙了。
I'm trying to balance study and fun.	我正努力要在讀書和娛樂之間取得平衡。
□ 3. ***What do you plan to do about it?***	你打算怎麼處理這件事？
I'll organize my time better.	我會更妥善安排我的時間。
I plan to set aside more time for study.	我打算撥出更多時間讀書。

study

Intermediate

**

deal with 應付；處理　balance (ˈbæləns) *v.* 使平衡
study (ˈstʌdɪ) *n.* 讀書；學業　fun (fʌn) *n.* 娛樂；樂趣
organize (ˈɔrgənˌaɪz) *v.* 組織；安排　plan (plæn) *v.* 打算
do about 對…採取措施　***set aside*** 留出；撥出

□ **4.** ***What other issues have you solved, and how?***	你解決過什麼其他的問題，而且是如何解決的？
I wasn't doing so well in math.	我的數學不是很好。
I got help from my teacher.	我向老師求助。
□ **5.** ***Have you ever turned a problem into an opportunity?***	你曾經把問題變成機會嗎？
Sure. My class once needed money for a trip.	當然。我們班曾經需要錢去旅行。
We started a small business selling snacks.	我們創立了一個小事業，賣點心。
□ **6.** "***Problems don't matter. Solutions do.***" ***Do you agree or disagree?***	「問題不重要。解決之道才重要。」你同不同意？
Yes, I totally agree.	是的，我完全同意。
I think success comes from solving problems.	我認為成功來自解決問題。

**

issue〔ˈɪʃju〕*n.* 問題　　solve〔sɑlv〕*v.* 解決
do well 表現好；考得好　　***turn A into B*** 使 A 變成 B
opportunity〔ˌɑpɚˈtjunətɪ〕*n.* 機會　　once〔wʌns〕*adv.* 曾經
start a business 創業　　snack〔snæk〕*n.* 點心
matter〔ˈmætɚ〕*v.* 重要　　solution〔səˈluʃən〕*n.* 解決之道
agree〔əˈgri〕*v.* 同意　　disagree〔ˌdɪsəˈgri〕*v.* 不同意
totally〔ˈtotl̩ɪ〕*adv.* 完全　　success〔səkˈsɛs〕*n.* 成功

□ 7. ***Do you ever get stressed out?***	你曾經壓力很大嗎？
Yes, I stress over exams.	是的，我會擔心考試。
Big exams make me nervous.	大考會使我緊張。
□ 8. ***How do you relieve stress?***	你如何減輕壓力？
I take a walk.	我會去散步。
I do something fun.	我會做些有趣的事。
□ 9. ***Is it ok to get nervous?***	可以感到緊張嗎？
Yes, it's a normal feeling.	是的，它是正常的感覺。
It's actually a healthy reaction.	它其實是一種健康的反應。

** ______________________

stress

stress〔strɛs〕*v.* 加壓力於；使緊張；緊張；焦慮；擔心 *n.* 壓力（= *worry*）
stressed out 有壓力的；緊張的（= *stressed*）
stress over 擔心 big〔bɪg〕*adj.* 重大的
nervous〔ˈnɝvəs〕*adj.* 緊張的 relieve〔rɪˈliv〕*v.* 減輕
take a walk 去散步 fun〔fʌn〕*adj.* 有趣的
ok〔ˈoˈke〕*adj.* 好的；可以的 normal〔ˈnɔrml̩〕*adj.* 正常的
actually〔ˈæktʃuəlɪ〕*adv.* 實際上 healthy〔ˈhɛlθɪ〕*adj.* 健康的
reaction〔rɪˈækʃən〕*n.* 反應

【背景說明】

Oral Test 31

1. ***What do you find easy about English?***（你覺得學英文有什麼是容易的嗎？）（= *To you what is easy about English?* = *What's an easy aspect of learning English?*）【aspect〔ˈæspɛkt〕*n.* 方面】可說成：What is convenient about English studying?（關於學英文，有什麼方便的方法？）

2. ***I take practice quizzes.***（我會做練習小考。）（= *I quiz myself a lot.* = *I practice by take quizzes.* = *I take practice tests a lot.*）【quiz〔kwɪz〕*n.* 小考 *v.* 查問 ***a lot*** 常常】

3. ***I'm about average.***（我很普通。）（= *I'm in the middle.* = *My level is in the middle.*）【middle〔ˈmɪdl̩〕*n.* 中間】可說成：I'm not the worst; I'm not the best. I'm at the intermediate level.（我不是最差的；我不是最好的。我的程度中等。）【intermediate〔ˌɪntəˈmidɪɪt〕*adj.* 中級的】

4. ***I start by speaking out loud.***（我一開始會唸出聲音來。）（= *I start by speaking aloud.*）【aloud〔əˈlaʊd〕*adv.* 出聲地】可說成：I begin by reciting.（我先從背誦開始。）【recite〔rɪˈsaɪt〕*v.* 背誦】

7. ***Why choose One Word English?***（爲什麼選擇《英文一字金》？）（= *Why do you choose One Word English?*）也可說成：Why do you choose this method?（你爲什麼選擇這個方法？）

8. ***I plan to take it at some point***.（我打算在某個時刻考。）（= *I plan to take it sometime in the future.*）可說成：Eventually I'll take it.（我終將參加考試。）【eventually〔ɪ'vɛntʃuəlɪ〕*adv.* 最後】I'm planning on taking it.（我打算參加考試。）【***plan on*** 打算】It's in my future plans.（這是我未來的計劃。）It's a test I plan to take.（這是我計劃要參加的考試。）

Oral Test 32

1. ***I think carefully***.（我會仔細思考。）（= *I consider the problem carefully.*）可說成：I think about the situation.（我會思考這個情況。）

2. ***I'm trying to balance study and fun***.（我正努力要在讀書和娛樂之間取得平衡。）可說成：I'm trying to use time wisely.（我正在努力聰明地運用時間。）I'm trying to manage my time better.（我正在努力更妥善管理我的時間。）【manage〔'mænɪdʒ〕*v.* 經營；管理】I'm attempting to be more time-efficient.（我試圖更有效率地運用時間。）【attempt〔ə'tɛmpt〕*v.* 企圖；嘗試
efficient〔ɪ'fɪʃənt〕*adj.* 有效率的　　time-efficient *adj.* 省時的】

5. ***We started a small business selling snacks***.（我們創立一個小事業賣點心。）可說成：We established our own business.（我們創立了自己的事業。）【establish〔ə'stæblɪʃ〕*v.* 建立】We set up a snack business.（我們創立了一個賣點心的事業。）（= *We opened a small snack business.*）【***set up*** 建立】

7. ***Do you ever get stressed out?***（你曾經壓力很大嗎？）（= *Do you ever get too nervous?*）***Yes, I stress over exams***.（是的，我會擔心考試。）（= *Sure, tests make me nervous.*）

Intermediate

Intermediate Oral Tests

※ 請掃瞄 QR 碼，聽完題目後，練習回答兩句。

Oral Test 15

☐ 1. What was your experience at school like?

____

____

☐ 2. What's your happiest memory?

____

____

☐ 3. What are your happiest childhood memories?

____

____

☐ 4. What is something most people don't know about you?

____

____

☐ 5. Where is your hometown?

____

____

☐ 6. What is it like?

____

____

☐ 7. What were your childhood fears?

____

____

☐ 8. Did you have many friends?

____

____

☐ 9. What did you do in your childhood?

____

____

Oral Test 16

☐ 1. Where do you go to school?

____

____

☐ 2. How's school going?

____

____

☐ 3. How's your school year so far?

____

____

☐ 4. What's your favorite subject?

____

____

☐ 5. What's your least favorite subject?

____

____

☐ 6. Who's your favorite teacher?

____

____

☐ 7. Who's your least favorite teacher?

____

____

☐ 8. Does your school have uniforms?

____

____

☐ 9. Do you like having uniforms?

____

____

Oral Test 17

☐ 1. Do you think school uniforms are a good idea?

____

____

☐ 2. What clubs does your school have?

____

____

☐ 3. Are you in a club?

____

____

☐ 4. What does your club do?

____

____

☐ 5. Why did you choose that club?

____

____

☐ 6. What do you do after school?

☐ 7. What are you doing after this test?

☐ 8. How are your grades?

☐ 9. How's test preparation going?

Oral Test 18

☐ 1. Are you a good test-taker?

☐ 2. How did your last test go?

☐ 3. How did you do on your exams?

☐ 4. Do you have a school in mind?

☐ 5. What university do you want to attend?

☐ 6. Have you applied anywhere yet?

☐ 7. What do you want to major in?

☐ 8. What do you want to study?

☐ 9. What do you want to be someday?

Oral Test 19

☐ 1. Are you a morning or a night person?

____

____

☐ 2. What time do you go to school?

____

____

☐ 3. What time do you get out of school?

____

____

☐ 4. What time do your parents go to work?

____

____

☐ 5. What time do you start your homework?

____

____

☐ 6. How often do you take a break?

____

____

☐ 7. What's the best part of your week?

____

____

☐ 8. What are you looking forward to right now?

____

____

☐ 9. Do you keep a diary or journal?

____

____

Oral Test 20

☐ 1. What kind of music do you like?

____

____

☐ 2. Why do you like it?

____

____

☐ 3. Do you have a favorite band or artist?

____

____

☐ 4. What music is popular in your country right now?

☐ 5. Do you have a favorite song?

☐ 6. Can you recommend any music or groups?

☐ 7. Have you ever played an instrument?

☐ 8. How long have you played?

☐ 9. Can you play for me sometime?

Oral Test 21

☐ 1. How does music make you feel?

☐ 2. Do you like to sing?

☐ 3. Have you ever sung karaoke?

☐ 4. What's your favorite karaoke song to sing?

☐ 5. Do you like to dance?

☐ 6. How do you listen to music?

☐ 7. Do you like classical music?

____

____

☐ 8. Do you like country music?

____

____

☐ 9. Have you ever been to a concert?

____

____

Oral Test 22

☐ 1. Do you like reading? Why or why not?

____

____

☐ 2. What kind of books do you like?

____

____

☐ 3. Do you have a favorite book?

____

____

☐ 4. What was the last book you read?

____

____

☐ 5. How did you like it?

____

____

☐ 6. Are you reading anything now?

____

____

☐ 7. Do you have a favorite author?

____

____

☐ 8. Can you recommend a good book?

____

____

☐ 9. Did you read much as a kid?

____

____

Oral Test 23

☐ 1. Do you like sports?

____

____

☐ 2. Why do you like sports?

☐ 3. Have you ever played a sport?

☐ 4. Did you play any sports as a child?

☐ 5. Do you have a favorite sport?

☐ 6. What sports are popular in your country?

☐ 7. Do you watch professional sports?

☐ 8. Do you have a favorite team?

☐ 9. What is your opinion of professional athletes?

Oral Test 24

☐ 1. Do you like to watch TV?

☐ 2. Do you have a favorite show or program?

☐ 3. How often do you watch TV?

☐ 4. What's your favorite way to watch TV: TV set, computer, iPad, or cell phone?

☐ 5. What shows are popular in your country?

____

____

☐ 6. What are you watching these days?

____

____

☐ 7. What was the last show you watched?

____

____

☐ 8. Can you recommend a good show?

____

____

☐ 9. Do you watch TV news?

____

____

Oral Test 25

☐ 1. Which TV news station does your family watch?

____

____

☐ 2. Do you have a favorite channel?

____

____

☐ 3. Do you like any foreign shows?

____

____

☐ 4. Do you ever watch reruns of old shows?

____

____

☐ 5. Do you like cartoons?

____

____

☐ 6. Did you watch cartoons as a kid?

____

____

☐ 7. Ever watch anime?

____

____

☐ 8. Ever watch science channels like Discovery?

____

____

☐ 9. Does your family watch TV during meals?

____

____

Oral Test 26

☐ 1. What was the last movie you saw?

____

____

☐ 2. Do you have a favorite movie?

____

____

☐ 3. What sort of movies do you like?

____

____

☐ 4. How are the movies in your country?

____

____

☐ 5. How often do you watch movies in English?

____

____

☐ 6. Do you have a favorite actor or actress?

____

____

☐ 7. Can you recommend a good movie?

____

____

☐ 8. Do you like horror movies?

____

____

☐ 9. If there were a movie about your life, what kind would it be?

____

____

Oral Test 27

☐ 1. What's your favorite game?

____

____

☐ 2. What games did you play as a kid?

____

____

☐ 3. What games do you still play now? Why?

☐ 4. How competitive are you when it comes to games?

☐ 5. Do you play video games?

☐ 6. How often do you play video games?

☐ 7. What games are popular now?

☐ 8. Do you prefer Xbox or PlayStation?

☐ 9. Do you play any games on your phone?

Oral Test 28

☐ 1. What motivates you?

☐ 2. What is something you love a lot?

☐ 3. What are you working towards?

☐ 4. What inspires you?

☐ 5. Do you have a role model?

☐ 6. How did he impact you?

☐ 7. Do you have a motto?

☐ 8. Do you have a philosophy of life?

☐ 9. What's an issue you care about?

Oral Test 29

☐ 1. Do you have a pet?

☐ 2. Is it a he or a she?

☐ 3. What's his name?

☐ 4. How old is he?

☐ 5. What breed is he?

☐ 6. Where did you get him?

☐ 7. How long have you had him?

☐ 8. Does he know any tricks?

☐ 9. Where do you walk him?

Oral Test 30

☐ 1. What brand of dog food do you buy?

☐ 2. Is he house-trained?

☐ 3. Hi, may I pet your dog?

☐ 4. Is he friendly?

☐ 5. Does he like to be petted?

☐ 6. Is he good with kids?

☐ 7. Will he bite?

☐ 8. Does your dog chase birds?

☐ 9. Do you like cats or dogs more?

Oral Test 31

☐ 1. What do you find easy about English?

☐ 2. How are you learning English?

☐ 3. Are you good at reciting?

☐ 4. How do you memorize vocabulary?

☐ 5. Why do you want to learn English?

☐ 6. What are your language learning goals?

☐ 7. Why choose One Word English?

____

____

☐ 8. Are you interested in taking the TOEIC test?

____

____

☐ 9. Do you want to study abroad?

____

____

Oral Test 32

☐ 1. How do you deal with your problems?

____

____

☐ 2. What's one problem you are dealing with now?

____

____

☐ 3. What do you plan to do about it?

____

____

☐ 4. What other issues have you solved, and how?

____

____

☐ 5. Have you ever turned a problem into an opportunity?

____

____

☐ 6. "Problems don't matter. Solutions do." Do you agree or disagree?

____

____

☐ 7. Do you ever get stressed out?

____

____

☐ 8. How do you relieve stress?

____

____

☐ 9. Is it ok to get nervous?

____

____

英語口試——中高級

High-Intermediate

How do you get around every day?
I usually take the metro. Occasionally I take a bus.

英語口試「中高級」Oral Test 33~54

1. 「中高級」的句子比較長或難，不容易背到變成直覺。
2. 要將「初級」和「中級」背到滾瓜爛熟，再背「中高級」。
3. 把這些問與答當成課本讀即可。
4. High-Intermediate Oral Tests的錄音QR碼只有唸問題，保留足夠的時間讓你練習回答。

Oral Test 33

【問與答一起背】

□ 1. ***How do you get around every day?***	你每天的交通方式是什麼？
I usually take the metro.	我通常搭地鐵。
Occasionally I take a bus.	我偶爾會搭公車。
□ 2. ***How do you get to school?***	你如何到學校？
By bike.	騎腳踏車。
If it's raining, I take a bus.	如果下雨，我會搭公車。
□ 3. ***How far is your home from school?***	你家距離學校多遠？
Just ten minutes away.	只有十分鐘的距離。
I have no excuse for being late.	我沒有遲到的藉口。

** ______________________

metro

get around 四處走動
take〔tek〕*v.* 搭乘
metro〔ˈmɛtro〕*n.* 地鐵　occasionally〔əˈkeʒənḷɪ〕*adv.* 偶爾
get to 到達　bike〔baɪk〕*n.* 腳踏車（= *bicycle*）
how far 多遠　away〔əˈwe〕*adv.* 離…有一定距離
excuse〔ɪkˈskjus〕*n.* 藉口　late〔let〕*adj.* 遲到的

High-Intermediate

□ 4. ***Can you drive?***	你會開車嗎？
Yes, I can.	是的，我會。
I learned last year.	我去年學的。
□ 5. ***Do you have your license?***	你有駕照嗎？
I do have my license.	我的確有駕照。
I passed the test on the first try.	我第一次就通過考試了。
□ 6. ***Are you a good driver?***	你開車技術好嗎？
I'm a decent driver.	我開車很守規矩。
I drive safe and slow.	我開車又安全又慢。

** ___

drive〔draɪv〕*v.* 開車

license〔ˈlaɪsn̩s〕*n.* 執照【在此指 driver's license（駕照）】

I do have… 我眞的有…

pass〔pæs〕*v.* 通過　　try〔traɪ〕*n.* 嘗試

driver〔ˈdraɪvɚ〕*n.* 駕駛人

decent〔ˈdisn̩t〕*adj.* 高尚的；相當好的

safe〔sef〕*adv.* 安全地

slow〔slo〕*adv.* 緩慢地

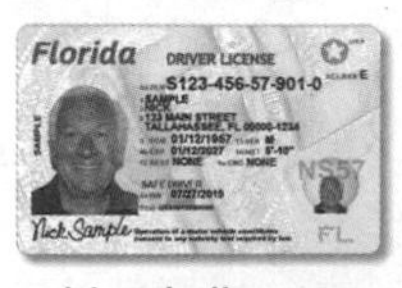

driver's license

☐ **7.** ***When did you get your license?***	你是何時拿到駕照的？
I got it three years ago.	我三年前拿到駕照。
It's made my life much easier.	它使我的生活輕鬆很多。
☐ **8.** ***Who taught you to drive?***	誰教你開車？
A driving instructor.	一位駕駛教練。
I went to a driving school.	我去上了駕訓班。
☐ **9.** ***How long did it take you to learn how to drive?***	你學開車學了多久？
A few months.	幾個月。
Almost half a year.	將近半年。

**

easy〔ˈizi〕*adj.* 容易的；輕鬆的

instructor〔ɪnˈstrʌktɚ〕*n.* 指導者；教練

driving instructor 駕駛教練

driving school 駕訓班　　take〔tek〕*v.* 花費

almost〔ˈɔlˌmost〕*adv.* 幾乎；將近

instructor

【背景說明】

Oral Test 33

1. ***How do you get around every day?*** 字面的意思是「你每天如何四處走動？」也就是「你每天的交通方式是什麼？」是坐計程車、公車，還是騎腳踏車？可說成：What's your daily mode of transportation?（你每天的交通方式是什麼？）【mode〔mod〕*n.* 模式；方式】How do you travel around?（你如何四處走動？）【travel〔ˈtrævḷ〕*v.* 行進；前進】

3. ***Just ten minutes away.***（只有十分鐘的距離。）（= *Just ten minutes from here.*）可說成：Only about ten minutes away.（只有大約十分鐘的距離。）It's not far, just ten minutes away.（不遠，只離這裡十分鐘。）

5. ***I passed the test on the first try.***（我第一次就通過考試了。）（= *I passed the test the first time.*）

6. ***I'm a decent driver.***（我開車很守規矩。）可說成：I'm a pretty good driver.（我開車技術相當不錯。）***I drive safe and slow.***（我開車又安全又慢。）不可說成：*I drive slow and safe.*（誤）可說成：I drive carefully.（我開車很小心。）（= *I drive cautiously.*）【cautiously〔ˈkɔʃəslɪ〕*adv.* 小心地；謹慎地】

7. ***It's made my life much easier.***（它使我的生活輕鬆很多。）（= *Life is easier for me now.* = *My life is more relaxed now.*）【relaxed〔rɪˈlækst〕*adj.* 輕鬆的】

Oral Test 34

【問與答一起背】

☐ 1. ***Are you in college?***
Yes, I'm in college.
I'm a sophomore.

你在唸大學嗎？
是的，我正在唸大學。
我是大二學生。

☐ 2. ***Where do you go to college?***
I go to National Taiwan University.
That's in Taipei.

你讀哪裡的大學？
我就讀台灣大學。
那是在台北。

☐ 3. ***What's your major?***
I'm majoring in English and Business.
I think that's a good combination.

你主修的科目是什麼？
我主修英文和商業。
我認爲那是個很好的組合。

**

college (ˈkɑlɪdʒ) *n.* 大學
sophomore (ˈsɑfm̩ˌor) *n.* 大二學生
go to 就讀　national (ˈnæʃənl̩) *adj.* 國立的
university (ˌjunəˈvɝsətɪ) *n.* 大學
major (ˈmedʒɚ) *n.* 主修科目　*v.* 主修 < *in* >
business (ˈbɪznɪs) *n.* 商業　combination (ˌkɑmbəˈneʃən) *n.* 組合

High-Intermediate

□ 4. ***Why did you choose it?***	你爲什麼選擇它？
I think both degrees will be useful.	我認爲雙學位會是有用的。
Especially the English degree.	特別是英文學位。
□ 5. ***What degree are you pursuing?***	你正在攻讀什麼學位？
I'm getting my bachelor's.	我快要拿到我的學士學位。
Maybe I'll go for a master's in a few years.	也許過幾年我會攻讀碩士學位。
□ 6. ***What year are you in?***	你現在幾年級？
I'm a freshman in college.	我是大學新鮮人。
My first year has been very exciting.	我在大學的第一年過得很刺激。

**

choose〔tʃuz〕*v.* 選擇
degree〔dɪ'gri〕*n.* 學位　useful〔'jusfəl〕*adj.* 有用的
especially〔ə'spɛʃəlɪ〕*adv.* 尤其；特別是
pursue〔pɚ'su〕*v.* 追求
bachelor〔'bætʃələ˞〕*n.* 學士
my bachelor's 在此指 my bachelor's degree（我的學士學位）。　master〔'mæstɚ〕*n.* 碩士
a master's 在此指 a master's degree（碩士學位）。
year〔jɪr〕*n.* 年；年級　freshman〔'frɛʃmən〕*n.* 大一新生；新鮮人
exciting〔ɪk'saɪtɪŋ〕*adj.* 刺激的；令人興奮的

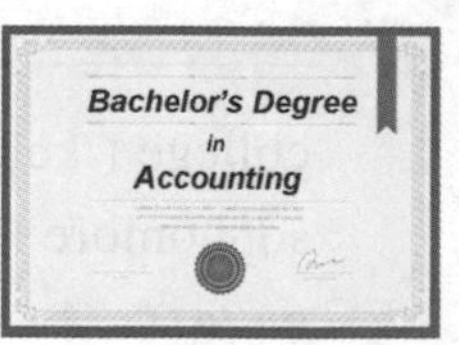

High-Intermediate

□ **7.** ***What classes are you taking?***	你正在上什麼課？
I'm taking a marketing class.	我正在上行銷課。
I'm also taking English Literature.	我也在上英國文學。

□ **8.** ***When will you graduate?***	你何時會畢業？
I plan to graduate on time.	我打算準時畢業。
I'll have my bachelor's in 3 years.	我再過三年會拿到學士學位。

□ **9.** ***What are your plans after graduation?***	你畢業後的計劃是什麼？
I plan to find a job.	我打算找工作。
I also plan to share an apartment.	我也打算和別人合住一間公寓。

**

take〔 tek 〕*v.* 上（課）　marketing〔ˈmɑrkɪtɪŋ 〕*n.* 行銷
literature〔ˈlɪtərətʃɚ 〕*n.* 文學
graduate〔ˈgrædʒuˌet 〕*v.* 畢業　plan〔 plæn 〕*v.* 打算　*n.* 計劃
on time 準時　in〔 ɪn 〕*prep.* 再過…
graduation〔ˌgrædʒuˈeʃən 〕*n.* 畢業　share〔 ʃɛr 〕*v.* 分享；共用
apartment〔 əˈpɑrtmənt 〕*n.* 公寓

Oral Test 35

【問與答一起背】

□ 1. ***How do you like college so far?***	到目前爲止，你喜不喜歡大學？
I love it so far.	到目前爲止，我很喜歡。
It's been exciting and eye-opening.	很令人興奮，而且讓人大開眼界。
□ 2. ***Have you made any friends?***	你有交到任何朋友嗎？
Sure, I've made friends.	當然，我交了朋友。
I've met a lot of cool people already.	我已經認識很多很酷的人。
□ 3. ***Do you live on campus or at home?***	你住在校園還是家裡？
I live on campus.	我住在校園。
I live in one of the campus dorms.	我住在校園的宿舍。

**

How do you like～? 你喜不喜歡～？　***so far*** 到目前爲止
exciting (ɪk'saɪtɪŋ) *adj.* 令人興奮的；刺激的
eye-opening *adj.* 令人大開眼界的　***make friends*** 交朋友
meet (mit) *v.* 認識　cool (kul) *adj.* 很酷的
campus ('kæmpəs) *n.* 校園　dorm (dɔrm) *n.* 宿舍

☐ **4.** ***What's your dormitory like?*** 你的宿舍是什麼樣子的？

It's super old. 它相當舊。

It's old but comfortable. 它很舊，但很舒適。

☐ **5.** ***Do you have a roommate?*** 你有室友嗎？

I have a roommate. 我有一個室友。

His name is Kyle. 他的名字是凱爾。

☐ **6.** ***Do you like your roommate?*** 你喜歡你的室友嗎？

I like Kyle. 我喜歡凱爾。

He shares his food. 他會分享他的食物。

** ______________________

dormitory〔ˈdɔrmə,torɪ〕*n.* 宿舍（= *dorm*）

super〔ˈsupɚ〕*adv.* 非常；超

comfortable〔ˈkʌmfɚtəbl̩〕*adj.* 舒適的

roommate〔ˈrum,met〕*n.* 室友

Kyle〔kaɪl〕*n.* 凱爾

share〔ʃɛr〕*v.* 分享

roommate

□ 7. ***Are you involved in any clubs?***	你有參加任何社團嗎？
Yes, I'm in an English book club.	有，我在英文書社。
I'm on the table tennis team, too.	我也參加桌球隊。
□ 8. ***Are you in a fraternity or sorority?***	你有加入兄弟會或姊妹會嗎？
No, I'm not.	不，我沒有。
I'm not interested in that.	我對那個沒興趣。
□ 9. ***Do you have a part-time job?***	你有兼職的工作嗎？
No, I'm not working now.	沒有，我現在沒有在工作。
I'm focusing on my studies.	我正專注於我的學業。

**

table tennis

involve (ɪn'vɑlv) *v.* 使牽涉在內
be involved in 參與　club (klʌb) *n.* 社團
table tennis 桌球　team (tim) *n.* 隊
fraternity (frə'tɝnətɪ) *n.* 兄弟會　sorority (sə'rɔrətɪ) *n.* 姊妹會
interested ('ɪntrɪstɪd) *adj.* 有興趣的
be interested in 對…有興趣　part-time ('pɑrt'taɪm) *adj.* 兼職的
focus on 專注於　studies ('stʌdɪz) *n. pl.* 學業

High-Intermediate

Oral Test 36

【問與答一起背】

□ 1. ***How are your classes going?***	你的課上得如何？
So far so good.	到目前爲止還好。
I'm doing well in every class.	我每一門課都表現得很好。
□ 2. ***How are your professors?***	你的教授如何？
Most are excellent.	大部分都很優秀。
A few are boring.	有一些很無聊。
□ 3. ***What's your favorite class?***	你最喜愛的課是什麼？
I like public speaking the most.	我最喜歡公開演說課。
It's fun and useful.	它很有趣而且有用。

**

go〔go〕*v.* 進展　***so far so good*** 到目前爲止還好

do〔du〕*v.* 表現　professor〔prəˈfɛsɚ〕*n.* 教授

excellent〔ˈɛksḷənt〕*adj.* 優秀的

boring〔ˈborɪŋ〕*adj.* 無聊的

like…the most 最喜歡…

public speaking 公開演說　fun〔fʌn〕*adj.* 有趣的

useful〔ˈjusfəl〕*adj.* 有用的

public speaking

□ 4. ***What's your easiest class?***	你最容易的課是什麼？
I'm really good at history.	我眞的很精通歷史。
I can relax in history class.	我上歷史課可以很放鬆。
□ 5. ***What's your hardest class?***	你最困難的課是什麼？
Business management is tough.	商業管理很困難。
It's a challenge for me.	它對我而言是個挑戰。
□ 6. ***How are your grades looking?***	你的成績看起來如何？
They're pretty good.	相當好。
I'm far from failing.	我絕對不會不及格。

** ______________________

be good at 精通　　history (ˈhɪstrɪ) *n.* 歷史

relax (rɪˈlæks) *v.* 放鬆　　hard (hɑrd) *adj.* 困難的

business (ˈbɪznɪs) *n.* 商業

management (ˈmænɪdʒmənt) *n.* 管理

tough (tʌf) *adj.* 困難的

challenge (ˈtʃælɪndʒ) *n.* 挑戰

grade (gred) *n.* 成績

pretty (ˈprɪtɪ) *adv.* 相當

far from 絕不；一點也不　　fail (fel) *v.* 失敗；不及格

challenge

□ 7. ***Are you studying hard?***	你很用功讀書嗎？
Yes, I study 4 to 5 hours a day.	是的，我一天讀書四至五小時。
I'm in two study groups.	我參加了兩個讀書會。
□ 8. ***Have you been to any college parties?***	你有參加過任何大學派對嗎？
I've been to a couple.	我去過幾個。
They were a lot of fun.	它們很有趣。
□ 9. ***Have you attended any college games?***	你去過任何大學的比賽嗎？
I saw a girls' volleyball game.	我看過女子排球比賽。
I'm also a fan of our basketball team.	我也是我們籃球隊的球迷。

** ________________________

study hard 用功讀書　　***study group*** 讀書會

college〔ˈkɑlɪdʒ〕*n.* 大學

a couple 幾個；兩三個　　***be a lot of fun*** 很有趣

attend〔əˈtɛnd〕*v.* 去；參加　　game〔gem〕*n.* 比賽

volleyball〔ˈvɑlɪˌbɔl〕*n.* 排球

fan〔fæn〕*n.*（球）迷　　team〔tim〕*n.* 隊

volleyball

【背景說明】

Oral Test 34

2. ***Where do you go to college?***（你讀哪裡的大學？）可說成：What school do you attend?（你讀什麼學校？）(= *What school are you in?*) What's the name of your school?（你的學校是什麼名字？）

5. ***What degree are you pursuing?***（你正在攻讀什麼學位？）（= *What degree are you going after?*）【***go after*** 追求（= *go for*）】

6. ***What year are you in?***（你現在幾年級？）(= *What grade are you in?*) 也可說成：Are you a freshman, sophomore, junior, or senior?（你是大一、大二、大三，或大四學生？）
【freshman〔'frɛʃmən〕*n.* 大一新生　sophomore〔'sɑfm̩,or〕*n.* 大二學生　junior〔'dʒunjɚ〕*n.* 大三學生　senior〔'sinjɚ〕*n.* 大四學生】

9. ***I also plan to share an apartment.***（我也打算和別人合住一間公寓。）(= *I'll also rent a place with a roommate.*)
【roommate〔'rum,met〕*n.* 室友】

Oral Test 35

1. ***How do you like college so far?***（到目前為止，你喜不喜歡大學？）(= *How's college so far?*) ***It's been exciting and eye-opening.***（很令人興奮，而且讓人大開眼界。）可說成：

It's fun and interesting.（非常有趣。）【fun〔fʌn〕*adj.* 有趣的】 It's never boring.（絕對不會無聊。）I'm learning new things.（我正在學新東西。）

7. ***Are you involved in any clubs?***（你有參加任何社團嗎？）（= *Do you belong to any clubs? = Have you joined any clubs? = Do you participate in any clubs?*）
【***belong to*** 屬於 participate〔pɑrˈtɪsə,pet〕*v.* 參與 <*in*>】可說成：Are you a member of any clubs?（你是任何社團的成員嗎？）

9. ***I'm focusing on my studies.***（我正專注於我的學業。）可說成：I totally concentrate on my classes.（我完全專心於我的課業。）
【concentrate〔ˈkɑnsn̩,tret〕*v.* 專心 <*on*>】I'm just paying attention to getting good grades.（我只是專注於得到好成績。）
【***pay attention to*** 注意】

Oral Test 36

1. ***How are your classes going?***（你的課上得如何？）可簡單地說：How's school?（課業如何？）Are you doing OK in school?（你在學校表現得好嗎？）【do〔du〕*v.* 表現】***So far so good.***（到目前爲止還好。）（= *Up till now, I'm doing good.*）【***up till now*** 到目前爲止】***I'm doing well in every class.***（我每一門課都表現得很好。）（= *I'm doing fine in every subject.*）

Oral Test 37

【問與答一起背】

□ 1. ***Do you like living in a city?***	你喜歡住在城市嗎？
I do like it.	我眞的很喜歡。
I like it more than the country.	我喜歡它甚於鄉村。
□ 2. ***What do you like about it?***	你喜歡它的什麼？
The convenience.	方便。
You can walk to almost anywhere.	你幾乎可以用走的去任何地方。
□ 3. ***Is there anything you dislike?***	你有任何不喜歡的嗎？
The air pollution.	空氣污染。
The air's not fresh.	空氣不新鮮。

** ──────────

「do + 原形 V.」表加強動詞的語氣，作「眞的…」解。

country〔ˈkʌntrɪ〕*n.* 國家；鄉下

convenience〔kənˈvinjəns〕*n.* 方便

dislike〔dɪsˈlaɪk〕*v.* 不喜歡　　air〔ɛr〕*n.* 空氣

pollution〔pəˈluʃən〕*n.* 污染

fresh〔frɛʃ〕*adj.* 新鮮的

pollution

□ 4. ***Would you rather live in the city or countryside?***	你寧願住在城市還是鄉下？
The city.	城市。
The country is too quiet.	鄉下太安靜了。
□ 5. ***Where is the best place to eat in your neighborhood?***	在你們那一區去哪裡吃東西最好？
The corner noodle shop.	轉角的麵店。
They're the best in town.	他們是城裡最好的。
□ 6. ***Where is the best place to shop in your neighborhood?***	你們那一區最佳的購物地點是哪裡？
The department store.	百貨公司。
It has everything you need.	它有你需要的一切。

** ______________________________

would rather 寧願
countryside (ˈkʌntrɪ,saɪd) *n.* 鄉間；鄉村地區
quiet (ˈkwaɪət) *adj.* 安靜的
neighborhood (ˈnebɚ,hʊd) *n.* 鄰近地區
corner (ˈkɔrnɚ) *n.* 角落；轉角
noodle (ˈnudḷ) *n.* 麵 ***in town*** 在城裡
shop (ʃɑp) *v.* 購物 ***department store*** 百貨公司

department store

□ **7.** ***What do you think of your neighbors?***	你認為你的鄰居如何？
Most neighbors are friendly.	大部份的鄰居都很友善。
Some with small kids are noisy.	有些有小孩的會很吵。
□ **8.** ***Do you know your neighbors?***	你認識你的鄰居嗎？
I know most of them.	我認識大部份的鄰居。
Most people have lived in the building for years.	大部份的人住在這棟大樓已經很多年了。
□ **9.** ***Is there anything your neighbors do that annoys you?***	鄰居會做什麼使你心煩的事嗎？
One neighbor's dog barks a lot.	有個鄰居的狗常常吠叫。
It's annoying at night.	那在晚上很令人心煩。

** ————————————

think of 認為　　neighbor (ˈnebɚ) *n.* 鄰居

friendly (ˈfrɛndlɪ) *adj.* 友善的

noisy (ˈnɔɪzɪ) *adj.* 吵鬧的

building (ˈbɪldɪŋ) *n.* 建築物；大樓

annoy (əˈnɔɪ) *v.* 使心煩

bark (bɑrk) *v.* 吠叫　　***a lot*** 常常

annoying (əˈnɔɪɪŋ) *adj.* 令人心煩的

High-Intermediate

Oral Test 38

【問與答一起背】

□ 1. ***What's your favorite kind of food?***	你最喜愛什麼種類的食物？
Italian food.	義大利菜。
I could eat it every day.	我可以每天吃。
□ 2. ***What's your favorite pizza?***	你最喜愛的披薩是什麼？
Hawaiian.	夏威夷披薩。
I love the combination of flavors.	我喜愛不同口味的組合。
□ 3. ***What's your favorite ice cream flavor?***	你最喜愛的冰淇淋口味是什麼？
Strawberry.	草莓。
But I like just about every flavor.	但我幾乎每一種口味都喜歡。

pizza

** ──────────

Italian〔ɪ'tæljən〕*adj.* 義大利的　　pizza〔'pitsə〕*n.* 披薩
Hawaiian〔hə'waɪɪjən〕*adj.* 夏威夷的
combination〔,kɑmbə'neʃən〕*n.* 結合；組合
flavor〔'flevɚ〕*n.* 口味　***ice cream*** 冰淇淋
strawberry〔'strɔ,bɛrɪ〕*n.* 草莓　***just about*** 幾乎

Hawaiian

High-Intermediate

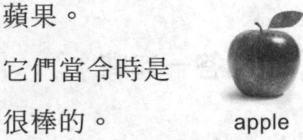

□ 4. ***What's your favorite fruit?***	你最喜愛的水果是什麼？
Apples.	蘋果。
They're great when they're in season.	它們當令時是很棒的。
□ 5. ***What's your favorite drink?***	你最喜愛的飲料是什麼？
Coffee.	咖啡。
I love bubble milk tea, too.	我也愛泡沫奶茶。
□ 6. ***What food is your country known for?***	你的國家有名的食物是什麼？
Beef noodle soup.	牛肉麵。
It's a delicious dish.	它是一道美味的菜餚。

apple

**

favorite〔ˈfevərɪt〕*adj.* 最喜愛的 *n.* 最喜愛的人或物
season〔ˈsizn̩〕*n.* 季節
in season （水果、蔬菜等）當令的；應時的
drink〔drɪŋk〕*n.* 飲料 coffee〔ˈkɔfɪ〕*n.* 咖啡
bubble〔ˈbʌbl̩〕*n.* 泡泡 ***bubble tea*** 泡沫紅茶
milk tea 奶茶 ***be known for*** 以…聞名
beef〔bif〕*n.* 牛肉 noodle〔ˈnudl̩〕*n.* 麵
soup〔sup〕*n.* 湯 ***beef noodle soup*** 牛肉麵
delicious〔dɪˈlɪʃəs〕*adj.* 美味的 dish〔dɪʃ〕*n.* 菜餚

beef noodle soup

High-Intermediate

□ 7. ***What foods do you dislike?***	你不喜歡什麼食物？
I don't like bitter foods.	我不喜歡苦的食物。
And I can't eat food that's too spicy.	而且我無法吃太辣的食物。
□ 8. ***Is there anything you don't eat?***	有什麼東西是你不吃的嗎？
No, not really.	不，其實沒有。
I eat pretty much everything.	我幾乎什麼都吃。
□ 9. ***Do you have any food allergies?***	你有沒有對任何食物過敏？
No, I don't.	不，我沒有。
I'm lucky that way.	我能那樣眞的很幸運。

**

dislike (dɪsˈlaɪk) *v.* 不喜歡
bitter (ˈbɪtɚ) *adj.* 苦的
spicy (ˈspaɪsɪ) *adj.* 辣的
pretty much 幾乎 (= *just about* = *almost*)
allergy (ˈælədʒɪ) *n.* 過敏症
lucky (ˈlʌkɪ) *adj.* 幸運的 ***that way*** 那樣

allergy

【背景說明】

Oral Test 37

1. ***I do like it***.（我眞的很喜歡。）是 I like it. 的加強語氣。可說成：I really enjoy it.（我眞的很喜歡。）It's really nice.（它眞的很好。）(= *It's great*.)【enjoy〔ɪn'dʒɔɪ〕*v.* 喜歡】

5. ***They're the best in town***. 字面的意思是「它們是城裡最好的。」也就是「它們是這個區域中最好的。」(= *They're the best in this area.*) ***in town*** 字面的意思是「在小鎮裡」，但在大城市、小鄉鎮，都可用 ***in town***，這是美國人的習慣說法。如：This is the best food ***in town***.（這是這裡最好的食物。）This is the best park ***in town***.（這是這個城市最好的公園。）***in town*** 要依前後句意來翻譯。

Oral Test 38

1. ***I could eat it every day***. 字面的意思是「我可以每天吃。」用假設法助動詞 could，表示事實上不可能每天吃，引申爲「我非常喜歡吃。」(= *I like it so much. = It's so good.*) 美國人也常說：I can't get enough.（我怎麼吃都不夠。）I'm never tired of it.（我絕不會厭倦。）(= *I'm never tired of eating it.*)
【***be tired of*** 厭倦】

2. ***I love the combination of flavors***.（我喜愛不同口味的組合。）(= *I like the taste of the flavors together. = The combined flavors are delicious.*) 可說成：I love the cheese, tomato, and

pineapple all together.（我喜歡起司、蕃茄，和鳳梨全部加在一起。）【cheese〔tʃiz〕*n.* 起司　tomato〔tə'meto〕*n.* 蕃茄　pineapple〔'paɪn,æpl̩〕*n.* 鳳梨】

3. ***I like just about every flavor.***（我幾乎每一種口味都喜歡。）（= *I like almost all flavors.*）可說成：Almost every flavor tastes good to me.（幾乎每一種口味對我來說都很好吃。）

6. 中國人說「牛肉麵」，美國人說「牛肉麵湯」(***beef noodle soup***)。中國人說「稀飯」，美國人說 rice soup，在美國人眼裡是「湯」。如果只說 beef noodles，美國人會認為是「牛肉乾麵」(beef with noodles)。

8. ***I eat pretty much everything.***（我幾乎什麼都吃。）(= *I eat almost any type of food.*) 可說成：I seldom refuse any type of food.（我很少拒絕任何類型的食物。）【refuse〔rɪfjuz〕*v.* 拒絕】I'll eat just about anything.（我幾乎什麼都吃。）【***just about*** 幾乎（= *almost*）】

9. ***Do you have any food allergies?***（你有沒有對任何食物過敏？）（= *Are you allergic to any foods?*）【allergic〔ə'lɝdʒɪk〕*adj.* 過敏的】可說成：Any foods you can't eat?（有沒有你不能吃的食物？）(= *Are there any foods you can't eat?*) ***I'm lucky that way.***（我能那樣真的很幸運。）(= *I'm lucky concerning that.*)【concerning〔kən'sɝnɪŋ〕*prep.* 關於】可說成：I'm blessed with no allergies.（我真幸福，沒有過敏。）【blessed〔'blɛsɪd〕*adj.* 幸福的】I'm fortunate with my health.（我很幸運，身體很健康。）

Oral Test 39

【問與答一起背】

□ 1. ***Do you like spicy food?***	你喜歡辣的食物嗎？
I don't like it.	我不喜歡。
I avoid it.	我會避開它。
□ 2. ***Do you like sweets?***	你喜歡甜食嗎？
I love sweets.	我很愛甜食。
I have a sweet tooth.	我喜歡吃甜食。
□ 3. ***Do you drink coffee?***	你喝咖啡嗎？
Yes, I love coffee.	是的，我很愛咖啡。
I drink it every day.	我每天喝咖啡。

**

spicy (ˈspaɪsɪ) *adj.* 辣的

avoid (əˈvɔɪd) *v.* 避免；避開

sweets (swits) *n. pl.* 甜食　　tooth (tuθ) *n.* 牙齒

have a sweet tooth 喜歡吃甜食

coffee (ˈkɔfɪ) *n.* 咖啡

□ 4. ***How do you like your coffee?***	你喜歡什麼樣的咖啡？
I like my coffee black.	我喜歡黑咖啡。
I like it dark and bitter.	我喜歡又黑又苦的咖啡。
□ 5. ***Do you like it hot or iced?***	你喜歡熱的還是冰的咖啡？
I prefer hot coffee.	我比較喜歡熱咖啡。
But I'll have an iced coffee on a hot day.	但在大熱天我會喝冰咖啡。
□ 6. ***How much coffee do you drink?***	你會喝多少咖啡？
Just a cup a day.	每天只喝一杯。
Any more than that and I can't sleep.	如果比那個多，我就會睡不著。

**

black〔blæk〕*adj.*（咖啡）不加牛奶的
dark〔dɑrk〕*adj.* 黑暗的
bitter〔ˈbɪtɚ〕*adj.* 苦的
iced〔aɪst〕*adj.* 冰的
prefer〔prɪˈfɝ〕*v.* 比較喜歡
have〔hæv〕*v.* 喝

black coffee

□ 7. ***Do you drink tea?***	你喝茶嗎？
Yes, I drink tea.	是的，我喝茶。
I like oolong tea.	我喜歡烏龍茶。
□ 8. ***Are you a vegetarian?***	你吃素嗎？
No, I'm not.	不，我不是。
I like eating meat.	我喜歡吃肉。
□ 9. ***Are you a vegan?***	你是嚴守素食主義的人嗎？
No, I'm not.	不，我不是。
It's too restrictive.	那樣限制太多了。

** ──────────

oolong (ˈulɔŋ) *n.* 烏龍茶

vegetarian (ˌvɛdʒəˈtɛrɪən) *n.* 素食者

meat (mit) *n.* 肉

vegan (ˈvɛgən) *n.* 嚴守素食主義的人

restrictive (rɪˈstrɪktɪv) *adj.* 限制的；拘束的

oolong tea

Oral Test 40

【問與答一起背】

□ 1. ***What's your favorite restaurant?***	你最喜愛的餐廳是什麼餐廳？
My favorite restaurant is Red Lobster.	我最喜愛的餐廳是紅龍蝦。
I also like Pizza Hut.	我也喜歡必勝客。
□ 2. ***How often do you eat out?***	你多久會出去吃一次？
Two or three times a week.	一星期兩次或三次。
I'm not much of a cook.	我不太會做菜。
□ 3. ***Do you prefer eating in or out?***	你比較喜歡在家裡吃還是出去吃？
I prefer eating out.	我比較喜歡出去吃。
It's fun and relaxing.	那樣很有趣而且輕鬆。

＊＊

favorite (ˈfevərɪt) *adj.* 最喜愛的　restaurant (ˈrɛstərənt) *n.* 餐廳
lobster (ˈlɑbstɚ) *n.* 龍蝦　Pizza Hut (ˈpitsə ˈhʌt) *n.* 必勝客
eat out 出去吃　time (taɪm) *n.* 次
not much of a 算不上好的　cook (kuk) *n.* 廚師
prefer (prɪˈfɝ) *v.* 比較喜歡　***eat in*** 在家裡吃
fun (fʌn) *adj.* 有趣的　relaxing (rɪˈlæksɪŋ) *adj.* 使人放鬆的

High-Intermediate

□ 4. ***Have you ever worked in a restaurant?***	你曾經在餐廳工作過嗎？
Yes, I have.	是的，我在餐廳工作過。
I used to work at McDonald's.	我以前在麥當勞工作。
□ 5. ***How often do you eat takeout?***	你多久吃一次外賣的食物？
A few times a week.	一星期好幾次。
It's really convenient.	眞的很方便。
□ 6. ***Do you want to order pizza?***	你想要訂披薩嗎？
Yes, please!	是的，麻煩你！
Let's get half cheese half vegetable.	我們買一半起司一半蔬菜的吧。

**

ever〔ˈɛvɚ〕*adv.* 曾經　***used to*** 以前

McDonald's〔məkˈdɑnl̩dz〕*n.* 麥當勞

takeout〔ˈtekˌaʊt〕*n.* 外賣的食物　time〔taɪm〕*n.* 次

convenient〔kənˈvinjənt〕*adj.* 方便的

order〔ˈɔrdɚ〕*v.* 點（餐）；訂購　get〔gɛt〕*v.* 買

cheese〔tʃiz〕*n.* 起司　vegetable〔ˈvɛdʒɪtəbl̩〕*n.* 蔬菜

□ 7. ***Are tips at restaurants common where you live?***	在你住的地方，去餐廳通常會給小費嗎？
Tips are not common.	小費並不常見。
Usually it's added to your check.	通常是加在帳單裡。
□ 8. ***How much is a reasonable tip?***	小費要給多少才合理？
10-15%.	百分之十至十五。
A 20% tip is better.	百分之二十的小費更好。
□ 9. ***How much should I tip?***	我應該給多少小費？
For waiters tip 10-15%.	給服務生百分之十至十五的小費。
You should tip $5 per night for housekeeping.	打掃房間每晚應該給 5 美元的小費。

**

tip〔tɪp〕*n.* 小費　*v.* 給小費；給…小費
common〔ˈkɑmən〕*adj.* 常見的
add〔æd〕*v.* 添加；增加
be added to 被加到…　　check〔tʃɛk〕*n.* 帳單
reasonable〔ˈriznəbl̩〕*adj.* 合理的
waiter〔ˈwetɚ〕*n.* 服務生　　per〔pɚ〕*prep.* 每一
housekeeping〔ˈhaʊsˌkipɪŋ〕*n.*（旅館的）清潔部門；打掃房間

waiter

【背景說明】

Oral Test 39

2. ***I have a sweet tooth***.（我喜歡吃甜食。）(= *I like to eat sweets.*)

4. ***How do you like your coffee?***（你喜歡什麼樣的咖啡？）(= *What do you want in your coffee?*) 通常店員都會問你這句話。你喜歡黑咖啡的話，就說：***I like my coffee black***.（我喜歡黑咖啡。）(= *I like my coffee straight.*)【straight〔stret〕*adj.* 純粹的；不摻雜的】如果想加奶精和糖時，可說：I like my coffee with cream and sugar.（我喜歡有奶精和糖的咖啡。）【cream〔krim〕*n.* 奶精 sugar〔'ʃʊgɚ〕*n.* 糖】

5. ***Do you like it hot or iced?***（你喜歡熱的還是冰的咖啡？）(= *Do you prefer coffee hot or cold?*)

6. ***Any more than that and I can't sleep***.（如果比那個多，我就會睡不著。）(= *Too much and I'm unable to sleep.*)

9. ***Are you a vegan?***（你是嚴守素食主義的人嗎？）***vegan*** 是連乳製品和雞蛋都不吃的素食主義者。

Oral Test 40

2. ***I'm not much of a cook***.（我不太會做菜。）(= *I'm not a good cook.* = *I'm mediocre at cooking.*)【mediocre〔,midɪ'okɚ〕*adj.* 平凡的；普通的】

3. ***Do you prefer eating in or out?***（你比較喜歡在家裡吃還是出去吃？）(= *Do you prefer eating at home or going out to eat?*)

5. ***How often do you eat takeout?***（你多久吃一次外賣的食物？）(= *How often do you order takeout?* = *How often do you order food to go?*)【order〔'ɔrdɚ〕*v.* 點（餐）；訂購　***to go*** 外帶】也可說成：How often do you bring already cooked food home?（你多久會帶一次已經煮好的食物回家？）

6. ***Let's get half cheese half vegetable.***（我們買一半起司一半蔬菜的吧。）可說成：Let's order a pizza that is half cheese and half vegetable.（我們訂一個一半起司一半蔬菜的披薩吧。）

7. 在美國餐廳吃飯要付小費，通常是 10%～15%，如果六個人以上，怕你不付小費，會自動加 15% 在你的帳單上。在美國餐廳吃飯，又加稅、又加小費，往往會超過你的預算。

Are tips at restaurants common where you live?（在你住的地方，去餐廳通常會給小費嗎？）(= *Is is customary to tip at restaurants where you live?*)【customary〔'kʌstəm,ɛrɪ〕*adj.* 習慣性的；慣例的】

Oral Test 41

【問與答一起背】

□ 1. ***Are you on social media?***	你會使用社群媒體嗎？
Oh, definitely!	喔，當然！
I post something every day.	我每天都會發佈一些東西。
□ 2. ***Do you have a Facebook page?***	你有臉書嗎？
Yes, I do.	是的，我有。
It's a great way to keep in touch.	它是一個保持聯絡的好方法。
□ 3. ***What kind of information do you put on there?***	你會在那裡放什麼種類的資料？
Only basic information.	只有基本資料。
I never give my age or address.	我從不提供我的年齡或地址。

Facebook

**

social〔ˈsoʃəl〕*adj.* 社交的　media〔ˈmidɪə〕*n. pl.* 媒體
definitely〔ˈdɛfənɪtlɪ〕*adv.* 當然　post〔post〕*v.* 張貼；發佈
Facebook〔ˈfes,bʊk〕*n.* 臉書　page〔pedʒ〕*n.* 頁；頁面；網頁
keep in touch 保持聯絡　information〔,ɪnfəˈmeʃən〕*n.* 資訊；資料
basic〔ˈbesɪk〕*adj.* 基本的　give〔gɪv〕*v.* 給予（訊息）
address〔əˈdrɛs, ˈædrɛs〕*n.* 地址

□ 4. ***What info are you ok with people seeing?***	你可以讓人看到什麼資訊？
My pictures.	我的照片。
And I post my opinion on different things.	而且我會發佈我對不同事物的看法。
□ 5. ***How do you protect your privacy?***	你如何保護你的隱私？
I keep my passwords private.	我的密碼會保密。
I also never give out my phone number.	我也從不公佈我的電話號碼。
□ 6. ***Do you use Twitter?***	你有在用推特嗎？
I don't use Twitter.	我沒有在用推特。
Maybe I should check it out.	也許我該看看。

Twitter

**

info (ˈɪnfo) *n.* 資訊；情報（= *information*）
ok (ˈoˈke) *adj.* 可以的　opinion (əˈpɪnjən) *n.* 意見；看法
on (ɑn) *prep.* 關於　protect (prəˈtɛkt) *v.* 保護
privacy (ˈpraɪvəsɪ) *n.* 隱私　password (ˈpæs,wɝd) *n.* 密碼
private (ˈpraɪvɪt) *adj.* 機密的　***give out*** 公佈
Twitter (ˈtwɪtɚ) *n.* 推特　***check out*** 查看

□ 7. ***Do you have an Instagram account?*** 你有 Instagram 帳號嗎？

No, not yet. 不，還沒。

But I plan to make one soon. 但我打算很快就去申請。

□ 8. ***What do you watch on YouTube?*** 你會在 YouTube 上看什麼？

I like movie trailers. 我喜歡電影的預告片。

And I love animal videos. 而且我很喜愛動物影片。

□ 9. ***Do you use WeChat?*** 你會使用微信嗎？

I use WeChat for everything. 我用微信做每件事。

It's so convenient. 它非常方便。

** ______________________

Instagram〔ˈɪnstəˌgræm〕簡稱 IG，是 Facebook 公司旗下一款免費提供在線圖片及視頻分享的社交應用軟體，於 2010 年 10 月發布。

account〔əˈkaʊnt〕*n.* 帳戶；帳號　***not yet*** 尚未；還沒

YouTube〔ˈjuˈtjub〕是源自美國的影片分享網站，讓使用者上傳、觀看、分享，及評論影片。　trailer〔ˈtrelɚ〕*n.* 預告片

video〔ˈvɪdɪˌo〕*n.* 影片　WeChat〔ˈwiˈtʃæt〕*n.* 微信

convenient〔kənˈvinjənt〕*adj.* 方便的

【背景說明】

Oral Test 41

1. ***Are you on social media?***（你會使用社群媒體嗎？）可說成：Are you online?（你會上網嗎？）【online〔ˈɑnˌlaɪn〕*adj.* 線上的；在網路上的】Are you on the Internet?（你會上網嗎？）【Internet〔ˈɪntɚˌnɛt〕*n.* 網際網路】Do you have a website?（你有網站嗎？）【website〔ˈwɛbˌsaɪt〕*n.* 網站】Are you on Facebook?（你會上臉書嗎？）

3. ***I never give my age or address.***（我從不提供我的年齡或地址。）可說成：I don't release personal information.（我不會透露個人資料。）【release〔rɪˈlis〕*v.* 透露】I would never share private information about myself.（我絕不會分享關於自己的私人資料。）

4. ***What info are you ok with people seeing?***（你可以讓人看到什麼資訊？）可說成：What kind of information are you comfortable sharing?（你樂意和人分享什麼種類的資訊？）

8. ***I like movie trailers.***（我喜歡電影的預告片。）(= *I enjoy movie introductions.*) 可說成：I really like watching previews to upcoming movies.（我眞的很喜歡看即將上映的電影的預告片。）【preview〔ˈprivju〕*n.* 預告片　upcoming〔ˈʌpˌkʌmɪŋ〕*adj.* 即將來臨的】

9. ***I use WeChat for everything.***（我用微信做每件事。）可說成：I use WeChat for all my communications.（我會用微信來和人通訊。）【communications〔kəˌmjunəˈkeʃənz〕*n. pl.* 聯繫；通訊連絡】

High-Intermediate

Oral Test 42

【問與答一起背】

□ 1. ***What do you do on WeChat?***	你會在微信上做什麼？
I mostly message friends.	我大多是傳訊息給朋友。
I use it to share updates or photos.	我用它來分享最新資訊或照片。
□ 2. ***How many followers do you have?***	有多少人追蹤你？
Around 100.	大約一百人。
I know most of them in real life.	大部份都是我真的認識的人。
□ 3. ***What do you usually post?***	你通常會發佈什麼？
I'll post pictures of my dog.	我會發佈我的狗的照片。
Lots of food pictures, too.	也有很多食物的照片。

**

mostly〔'mɔstlɪ〕*adv.* 大多　message〔'mɛsɪdʒ〕*v.* 傳訊息給…
share〔ʃɛr〕*v.* 分享　update〔'ʌp'det〕*n.* 最新資訊
photo〔'foto〕*n.* 照片（= *photograph*）
follower〔'fɑloə〕*n.* 追隨者；追蹤者
around〔ə'raʊnd〕*adv.* 大約　***real life*** 實際生活；現實生活
post〔post〕*v.* 張貼；公告；發佈　***lots of*** 很多的

□ 4. ***What do you like about social media?***	你喜歡社群媒體的什麼？
It's good for communicating.	它很適合用來通訊。
I use it to keep up with friends.	我用它來和朋友保持聯絡。
□ 5. ***What don't you like about social media?***	你不喜歡社群媒體的什麼？
It's a bit addictive.	它會使人有點上癮。
I check it too often.	我太常去看了。
□ 6. ***How many times a day do you check social media?***	你一天會查看社群媒體幾次？
About five times a day.	一天大約五次。
I think that's too much.	我認爲太多了。

** ______

social〔ˈsoʃəl〕*adj.* 社會的；社交的

media〔ˈmidɪə〕*n. pl.* 媒體　***social media*** 社群媒體

communicate〔kəˈmjunəˌket〕*v.* 溝通；通訊

good〔gʊd〕*adj.* 好的；適合的　***keep up with*** 和…保持聯絡

a bit 有一點　addictive〔əˈdɪktɪv〕*adj.* 使人上癮的

check〔tʃɛk〕*v.* 查看　time〔taɪm〕*n.* 次

☐ **7.** ***Who are you following?*** 你有在追蹤誰？

I'm following my friends. 我追蹤我的朋友。

I follow some celebrities. 我追蹤一些名人。

☐ **8.** ***What's your favorite app?*** 你最喜愛的應用程式是什麼？

My favorite app is FaceTime. 我最喜愛的應用程式是 FaceTime。

I like to see the person I'm talking to. 我喜歡看到正在跟我談話的人。

☐ **9.** ***What's your favorite website?*** 你最喜愛的網站是什麼？

I'd say YouTube. 當然是 YouTube。

It's an ocean of entertainment. 它提供大量的娛樂。

YouTube

**

follow〔ˈfɑlo〕*v.* 跟隨；追蹤

celebrity〔səˈlɛbrətɪ〕*n.* 名人

app〔æp〕*n.* 應用程式（= *application*）

FaceTime 是一種視訊電話，由蘋果公司 CEO 賈伯斯於 2014 年發表，首先支援的是 iPhone 4。

website〔ˈwɛb,saɪt〕*n.* 網站　***I'd say*** 當然；的確

ocean〔ˈoʃən〕*n.* 大量；許多

entertainment〔,ɛntəˈtenmənt〕*n.* 娛樂

【背景說明】

Oral Test 42

1. ***What do you do on WeChat?***（你會在微信上做什麼？）(= *What activities are you doing on WeChat?*) ***I mostly message friends.***（我大多是傳訊息給朋友。）(= *Most of the time I'm communicating with friends.*) 可說成：Mainly, I contact friends.（我主要是和朋友連絡。）【mainly〔ˈmenlɪ〕*adv.* 主要地 contact〔ˈkɑntækt〕*v.* 連絡】***I use it to share updates or photos.***（我用它來分享最新資訊或照片。）可說成：I share news, events, and pictures.（我會分享消息、活動，和照片。）【event〔ɪˈvɛnt〕*n.* 事件；大型活動】I exchange information on it.（我會用它和人交換資訊。）(= *I exchange information by using it.*)【exchange〔ɪksˈtʃendʒ〕*v.* 交換】

4. ***I use it to keep up with friends.***（我用它來和朋友保持連絡。）(= *It helps me to stay in touch with friends.*)

5. ***It's a bit addictive.***（它會使人有點上癮。）(= *It's hard to stop doing it.*) ***I check it too often.***（我太常去看了。）(= *I go on it too much every day.*)

9. ***I'd say YouTube.***（當然是 YouTube。）(= *YouTube for sure.* = *It has to be YouTube.*) ***It's an ocean of entertainment.***（它提供大量的娛樂。）可說成：It has so many videos.（它有很多影片。）(= *It has a vast number of videos.*)
【video〔ˈvɪdɪˌo〕*n.* 影片　vast〔væst〕*adj.* 巨大的】

High-Intermediate

Oral Test 43

【問與答一起背】

□ 1. ***What do you like about texting?***	你喜歡傳簡訊的哪一點？
It's so convenient.	它很方便。
I can text anywhere.	我可以在任何地方傳簡訊。
□ 2. ***What don't you like about texting?***	你不喜歡傳簡訊的哪一點？
Some people don't answer.	有些人不會回覆。
I don't know if they read the text or not.	我不知道他們是否看了簡訊。
□ 3. ***Who do you text the most?***	你最常傳簡訊給誰？
My mom.	我媽媽。
She always wants to know what I'm doing.	她總是想知道我正在做什麼。

** ——————

text〔tɛkst〕*v.* 傳簡訊 *n.* 內文；簡訊　so〔so〕*adv.* 非常
convenient〔kən'vinjənt〕*adj.* 方便的
anywhere〔'ɛnɪˌhwɛr〕*adv.* 在任何地方　***if…or not*** 是否…

☐ **4.** ***Do you ever talk to strangers?***	你曾經和陌生人談話嗎？
No, never.	不，從沒有過。
It could be dangerous.	那可能很危險。
☐ **5.** ***Does speaking to foreigners make you nervous?***	和外國人說話會使你緊張嗎？
At first, definitely.	起初當然會。
Then I relax more.	然後我就會比較放鬆。
☐ **6.** ***Does public speaking make you nervous?***	公開演說會使你緊張嗎？
A little bit.	有一點。
But it gets easier with practice.	但是練習後就變得比較容易。

**

ever (ˈɛvɚ) *adv.* 曾經　stranger (ˈstrendʒɚ) *n.* 陌生人
dangerous (ˈdendʒərəs) *adj.* 危險的
foreigner (ˈfɔrɪnɚ) *n.* 外國人　nervous (ˈnɝvəs) *adj.* 緊張的
at first 起初　definitely (ˈdɛfənɪtlɪ) *adv.* 當然
then (ðɛn) *adv.* 然後　relax (rɪˈlæks) *v.* 放鬆
public speaking 公開演說　***a little bit*** 一點點
practice (ˈpræktɪs) *n.* 練習

□ 7. ***Do you like to argue?***	你喜歡爭論嗎？
Not at all.	一點也不。
I want everyone to get along.	我想要每個人都和睦相處。
□ 8. ***What kind of phone do you have?***	你有什麼種類的手機？
I have a smartphone.	我有一台智慧型手機。
I have an iPhone.	我有一台 iPhone。
□ 9. ***Which do you like better: Apple or Samsung?***	你比較喜歡哪一個：蘋果或三星？
Actually, I like them both.	事實上，我兩個都喜歡。
I think they're both good quality.	我認爲它們兩個品質都很好。

**

argue〔ˈɑrgjʊ〕*v.* 爭論　***not at all*** 一點也不
get along 和睦相處　kind〔kaɪnd〕*n.* 種類
phone〔fon〕*n.* 電話【在此指 cell phone（手機）】
smartphone〔ˈsmɑrt͵fon〕*n.* 智慧型手機
like better 比較喜歡　Samsung〔ˈsæm͵sʌŋ〕*n.* 三星【品牌名】
actually〔ˈæktʃʊəlɪ〕*adv.* 事實上　***good quality*** 品質好的

smartphone

【背景說明】

Oral Test 43

1. ***text*** 的主要意思是「內文」,「教科書」是 textbook。***text*** 也可當動詞,作「傳簡訊」解。***What do you like about texting?***(你喜歡傳簡訊的哪一點?)(= *What's an aspect of texting you like?*)【aspect〔ˈæspɛkt〕*n.* 方面】Why do you like texting?(你爲什麼喜歡傳簡訊?)***I can text anywhere.***(我可以在任何地方傳簡訊。)I can text people in most locations.(我可以在大部份的地點傳簡訊給別人。)I'm able to text wherever there is wi-fi.(只要有 wi-fi 的地方,我就可以傳簡訊。)

2. ***Some people don't answer.***(有些人不會回覆。)(= *Some people don't reply.* = *Some people don't respond.*)
【reply〔rɪˈplaɪ〕*v.* 回答;答覆　respond〔rɪˈspɑnd〕*v.* 回答;反應】

5. ***Then I relax more.***(然後我就會比較放鬆。)(= *Later, I become more relaxed.*) ***relax***「放鬆」(= *be relaxed*)。After a while, I'm not nervous.(過了一會兒,我就不緊張了。)
【***after a while*** 過了一會兒】

7. ***I want everyone to get along.***(我想要每個人都和睦相處。)
I just wish all people were friends.(我只希望所有的人都是朋友。)wish 後面用 were 表假設法的現在式。

9. ***I think they're both good quality.***(我認爲它們兩個品質都很好。)I feel both brands are fine.(我覺得這兩個品牌都很好。)
【brand〔brænd〕*n.* 品牌】

High-Intermediate

Oral Test 44

【問與答一起背】

□ 1. ***Are you dating anyone?***	你正在跟任何人約會嗎？
Yes, I am.	是的，我是。
I'm dating a classmate of mine.	我正在和一個同學約會。
□ 2. ***Are you seeing anyone?***	你正在和任何人談戀愛嗎？
Yes, I'm seeing someone.	是的，我正在談戀愛。
We have a good relationship.	我們的關係很好。
□ 3. ***How long have you been dating?***	你們約會多久了？
We've been dating for a month.	我們約會一個月了。
We met at a festival.	我們是在慶典上認識的。

** ─────────────

date (det) *v.* 和…約會

classmate (′klæs,met) *n.* 同班同學

***be seeing** sb.* 與某人談戀愛

relationship (rɪ′leʃən,ʃɪp) *n.* 關係

meet (mit) *v.* 認識　　festival (′fɛstəvḷ) *n.* 節日；慶典

classmates

High-Intermediate

□ **4.** ***How many dates have you been on lately?***	你最近約會幾次？
I've been on a couple.	我約會好幾次。
I'm not serious about anyone.	我沒有對任何人認眞。
□ **5.** ***How do you feel about dating?***	你覺得約會如何？
I feel it's a good way to meet people.	我覺得這是個認識人的好方法。
Sometimes a date goes well; sometimes it doesn't.	有時候約會進行得很順利；有時候不順利。
□ **6.** ***What are the best and worst first dates you've been on?***	你曾經擁有過最好或最差的初次約會是什麼？
The best date was to a movie.	最好的約會是去看電影。
The worst was to a crummy restaurant.	最差的是去一家很糟糕的餐廳。

** ______________

date〔 det 〕*v. n.* 約會　***be on a date*** 約會
lately〔ˈletlɪ〕*adv.* 最近　***a couple*** 幾個
serious〔ˈsɪrɪəs〕*adj.* 認眞的
go〔 go 〕*v.* 進展
crummy〔ˈkrʌmɪ〕*adj.* 劣質的；糟糕的

date

High-Intermediate

□ 7. ***What makes a good first date to you?***	對你來說，什麼會讓初次約會順利？
Having a nice conversation.	有好的對話。
Just chatting and laughing is good.	只要能聊天和笑就很好了。
□ 8. ***Do you prefer being single or in a relationship?***	你比較喜歡單身，還是有交往對象？
I prefer to be single.	我比較喜歡單身。
I enjoy the freedom of single life.	我喜歡單身生活的自由。
□ 9. ***What do you look for in a boyfriend?***	你要找什麼樣的男朋友？
I look for a sense of humor.	我會找有幽默感的。
A kind personality is a must.	親切的個性是必備條件。

** ___

make (mek) *v.* 構成；造就　nice (naɪs) *adj.* 好的
conversation (ˌkɑnvəˈseʃən) *n.* 對話　chat (tʃæt) *v.* 聊天
prefer (prɪˈfɝ) *v.* 比較喜歡　single (ˈsɪŋgḷ) *adj.* 單身的
relationship (rɪˈleʃənˌʃɪp) *n.* 關係；戀愛關係
in a relationship 穩定交往中　enjoy (ɪnˈdʒɔɪ) *v.* 享受；喜歡
freedom (ˈfridəm) *n.* 自由　***look for*** 尋找
boyfriend (ˈbɔɪˌfrɛnd) *n.* 男朋友　sense (sɛns) *n.* 感覺
humor (ˈhjumə) *n.* 幽默　kind (kaɪnd) *adj.* 親切的；好心的
personality (ˌpɝsṇˈælətɪ) *n.* 個性　must (mʌst) *n.* 必備之物

Oral Test 45

【問與答一起背】

□ 1. ***What are your plans for this weekend?***	你這個週末有什麼計劃？
I'm sleeping in.	我會睡到很晚。
After that, I'm not sure.	在那之後，我不太確定。
□ 2. ***What are your plans for this Saturday?***	你這個週六有什麼計劃？
I'll be studying.	我會讀書。
I have a big test next week.	我下星期有重要的考試。
□ 3. ***What are your plans for this summer?***	你這個夏天有什麼計劃？
I might go on vacation.	我可能會去度假。
I hope to travel abroad.	我希望能出國旅遊。

go on vacation

** ―――――――――――――

plan〔plæn〕*n.* 計劃　*v.* 打算；計劃
weekend〔ˈwikˈɛnd〕*n.* 週末
sleep in 早上起得晚；睡過頭　　sure〔ʃur〕*adj.* 確定的
big〔bɪg〕*adj.* 重要的　　***go on vacation*** 去度假
travel〔ˈtrævḷ〕*v.* 旅行　　abroad〔əˈbrɔd〕*adv.* 到國外

High-Intermediate

□ 4. ***What are your plans for the holidays?***	你假日有什麼計劃？
I'm going to visit my family.	我要去探望我的家人。
We always get together for the holidays.	我們在假日總是會聚在一起。
□ 5. ***What are your plans for Chinese New Year?***	你農曆新年有什麼計劃？
I'll visit my grandparents.	我會去探望我的祖父母。
We'll have a big meal together.	我們會一起吃頓大餐。
□ 6. ***What are your plans for learning English?***	你對於學英文有什麼計劃？
I'm taking a conversation class.	我正在上會話課。
I want to take a writing course, too.	我也想要上寫作課。

**

holiday〔ˈhɑləˌde〕*n.* 假日；節日
visit〔ˈvɪzɪt〕*v.* 拜訪；探望　***get together*** 團聚
Chinese New Year 農曆新年
grandparents〔ˈgrændˌpærənts〕*n. pl.* 祖父母
big〔bɪg〕*adj.* 豐盛的　meal〔mil〕*n.* 一餐
take〔tek〕*v.* 上（課）　conversation〔ˌkɑnvəˈseʃən〕*n.* 對話
writing〔ˈraɪtɪŋ〕*n.* 寫作　course〔kros〕*n.* 課程

meal

□ 7. ***What are your plans for this project?***	對於這個企劃你有什麼計劃？
I plan to split the workload.	我打算分配工作量。
I plan to finish by the deadline.	我計劃在截止日期前完成。
□ 8. ***Do you have a back-up plan?***	你有替代方案嗎？
I have a plan B.	我有替代方案。
But I don't think I'll need it.	但我不認為我會需要它。
□ 9. ***Want to make plans for this weekend?***	想要擬定這個週末的計劃嗎？
Definitely!	當然！
Let's get together.	我們聚一下吧。

**

project (ˈprɑdʒɛkt) *n.* 計劃；企劃
split (splɪt) *v.* 分配；分派
workload (ˈwɝkˌlod) *n.* 工作量
finish (ˈfɪnɪʃ) *v.* 完成
by (baɪ) *prep.* 在…之前　deadline (ˈdɛdˌlaɪn) *n.* 截止日期
back-up (ˈbækˌʌp) *adj.* 支援的；備用的
plan B 替代方案　***make a plan*** 擬定計劃
definitely (ˈdɛfənɪtlɪ) *adv.* 當然　***get together*** 聚集；聚會

project

【背景説明】

Oral Test 44

2. ***Are you seeing anyone?*** 字面的意思是「你正在看任何人嗎？」引申爲「你正在和任何人談戀愛嗎？」(= *Are you in love with anyone?*) 可説成：Are you seriously dating anyone? (你正在和任何人認眞地約會嗎？) Are you going steady with anyone? (你正在和任何人固定交往嗎？)

【steady (ˈstɛdɪ) *adj.* 穩定的　***go steady*** 與固定的異性交往】

4. ***How many dates have you been on lately?*** (你最近約會幾次？) (= *How often have you dated lately?*) ***I'm not serious about anyone.*** (我沒有對任何人認眞。) (= *I have no one to date seriously.*) 可説成：I'm just dating friends, no one seriously. (我只是和朋友約會，沒有一個認眞的。)

5. ***Sometimes a date goes well; sometimes it doesn't.*** (有時候約會進行得很順利；有時候不順利。) (= *Some dates are good, and some aren't.*) 可説成：Sometimes a date is fun, and sometimes it's not. (有時候約會很有趣，有時候無趣。)【fun (fʌn) *adj.* 有趣的】

7. ***What makes a good first date to you?*** (對你來說，什麼會讓初次約會順利？) (= *What makes a first date good?*) 可説成：What makes a first date successful? (什麼會讓初次約會順利成功？)

8. ***Do you prefer being single or in a relationship?*** (你比較喜歡單身，還是有交往對象？) (= *Would you rather be single or in a relationship?*) Would you rather be single or have a boyfriend? (你寧願單身，還是有男朋友？)【***would rather*** 寧願】

9. ***What do you look for in a boyfriend?***（你要找什麼樣的男朋友？）
可說成：What quality of a boyfriend is important to you?
（男朋友的什麼特質對你很重要？）【quality〔ˈkwɑlətɪ〕*n.* 特質】
A kind personality is a must.（個性好是必備條件。）He must be kind, gentle, and nice.（他必須親切、溫和，而且討人喜歡。）
【gentle〔ˈdʒɛntḷ〕*adj.* 溫和的　nice〔naɪs〕*adj.* 好的；親切的；討人喜歡的】

Oral Test 45

sleep in

1. ***I'm sleeping in.***（我會睡到很晚。）
= I'm sleeping late.
= I'll get up late.
= I'll be waking up late.

7. ***I plan to split the workload.***（我打算分配工作量。）
= I'm going to divide up my work.
= I'll separate it into parts.
I plan to finish by the deadline.（我計劃在截止日期前完成。）
= I'll get it done on time.【***on time*** 準時】

8. ***Do you have a back-up plan?***（你有替代方案嗎？）
= Do you have another plan if something goes wrong?
= If something happens, do you have another plan?
【***go wrong*** 出錯】
I have a plan B.（我有替代方案。）
= I have an alternative plan.【alternative〔ɔlˈtɝnətɪv〕*adj.* 替代的】

9. ***Let's get together.***（我們聚一下吧。）
= Let's meet.
= Let's spend time together.
= I hope we can meet.【spend〔spɛnd〕*v.* 度過】

Oral Test 46

【問與答一起背】

□ 1. ***How's your vision?***	你的視力如何？
Not so good.	不是很好。
I have to wear glasses.	我必須戴眼鏡。
□ 2. ***Are you nearsighted or farsighted?***	你是近視還是遠視？
I'm nearsighted.	我近視。
I can't see far away.	我不能看得很遠。
□ 3. ***Do you wear glasses?***	你有戴眼鏡嗎？
Yes, I do.	是的，我有。
I've worn glasses since sixth grade.	我從六年級就開始戴眼鏡了。

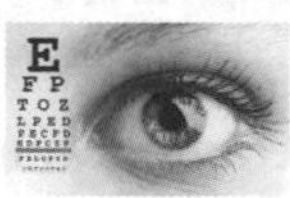

vision

** ______________________

vision〔ˈvɪʒən〕*n.* 視力
so〔so〕*adv.* 非常（= *very*）
glasses〔ˈglæsɪz〕*n. pl.* 眼鏡　nearsighted〔ˈnɪrˈsaɪtɪd〕*adj.* 近視的
farsighted〔ˈfɑrˈsaɪtɪd〕*adj.* 遠視的　***far away*** 很遠
grade〔gred〕*n.* 年級

□ 4. ***Do you prefer glasses or contacts?***	你比較喜歡眼鏡還是隱形眼鏡？
I prefer contact lenses.	我比較喜歡隱形眼鏡。
Glasses can get in my way.	眼鏡可能會妨礙我。
□ 5. ***Have you ever had braces?***	你曾經戴過牙套嗎？
Yeah, I used to have braces.	是的，我以前戴牙套。
I had braces in middle school.	我中學時戴過牙套。
□ 6. ***Do you catch colds a lot?***	你常感冒嗎？
No, not a lot.	不，不是很常。
I usually get one a year.	我通常一年感冒一次。

** ______________________

prefer〔prɪˈfɝ〕*v.* 比較喜歡
contact〔ˈkɑntækt〕*n.* 接觸；(*pl.*) 隱形眼鏡
lens〔lɛns〕*n.* 鏡片
contact lenses 隱形眼鏡（= *contacts*）
get in one's way 妨礙某人　　ever〔ˈɛvɚ〕*adv.* 曾經
braces〔ˈbresɪz〕*n.pl.* 牙套
have braces 戴牙套（= *wear braces*）　　***middle school*** 中學
cold〔kold〕*n.* 感冒　　***catch a cold*** 感冒（= *get a cold*）
a lot 常常　　usually〔ˈjuʒuəlɪ〕*adv.* 通常

contact lenses

High-Intermediate

□ 7. ***How would you treat a cold?***	你會如何治療感冒？
I'd take medicine.	我會吃藥。
I'd drink more water.	我會喝更多的水。
□ 8. ***When sick, do you prefer Western or Chinese medicine?***	生病時，你比較喜歡西醫還是中醫？
Chinese medicine.	中醫。
It works better for me.	它對我比較有效。
□ 9. ***Do you think diets are useful?***	你認爲節食有用嗎？
I think diets can work.	我認爲節食可能有用。
But I think extreme diets are unhealthy.	但我認爲極端的節食是不健康的。

** ___

treat〔trit〕*v.* 治療　　take〔tek〕*v.* 服用
When sick, ... 是 When *you are* sick, ... 的省略。
Western〔ˈwɛstən〕*adj.* 西方的；歐美的
medicine〔ˈmɛdəsn̩〕*n.* 醫學；醫療
Western medicine 西醫
Chinese medicine 中醫
work〔wɝk〕*v.* 有效
diet〔ˈdaɪət〕*n.* 飲食；節食
useful〔ˈjusfəl〕*adj.* 有用的　　extreme〔ɪkˈstrim〕*adj.* 極端的
unhealthy〔ʌnˈhɛlθɪ〕*adj.* 不健康的

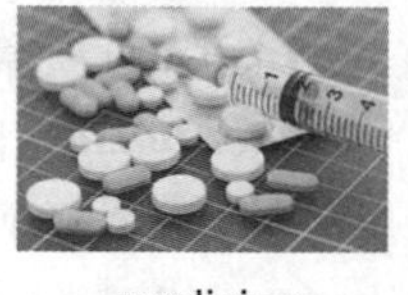
medicine

【背景説明】

Oral Test 46

2. ***I can't see far away***.（我不能看得很遠。）
   = I can't see far away very well.
   = I can't see objects far away very well.
   = I can't see long distances.
   = My long distance eyesight is poor.
   【object〔ˈɑbdʒɪkt〕*n.* 物體　distance〔ˈdɪstəns〕*n.* 距離
   eyesight〔ˈaɪˌsaɪt〕*n.* 視力】

4. ***Glasses can get in my way***.（眼鏡可能會妨礙我。）可說成：Glasses bothers me.（眼鏡會妨礙我。）Glasses feel awkward.（眼鏡使人覺得不方便。）【awkward〔ˈɔkwəd〕*adj.* 笨拙的；不自在的；不方便的】Glasses are not convenient.（眼鏡不方便。）

5. ***Have you ever had braces?***（你曾經戴過牙套嗎？）(= *Have you ever worn dental braces?*) Ever worn wires to straighten your teeth?（曾經戴過牙套矯正你的牙齒嗎？）
   (= *Have you ever worn…?*)
   【dental〔ˈdɛntḷ〕*adj.* 牙齒的；牙科的　wires〔waɪrz〕*n.pl.* 鐵絲；牙套
   straighten〔ˈstretṇ〕*v.* 把…弄直】

braces

8. ***It works better for me***.（它對我比較有效。）
   = It helps me more.
   = For me, it's more effective.
   【effective〔əˈfɛktɪv〕*adj.* 有效的】

Oral Test 47

【問與答一起背】

□ 1. ***What do you like to do?***	你喜歡做什麼？
I like to hang out with friends.	我喜歡和朋友出去玩。
We go to a café or a park.	我們會去咖啡廳或公園。
□ 2. ***What do you do for fun?***	你會做什麼好玩的事？
I read for fun.	我會爲了好玩而閱讀。
I like to read all kinds of books.	我喜歡讀各式各樣的書。
□ 3. ***What are your hobbies?***	你的嗜好是什麼？
I love to hike.	我喜愛健行。
I also like painting.	我也喜歡畫畫。

**

hang out with 和…出去玩
café (kəˈfe) *n.* 咖啡廳　fun (fʌn) *n.* 樂趣
for fun 爲了好玩　kind (kaɪnd) *n.* 種類
hobby (ˈhɑbɪ) *n.* 嗜好
hike (haɪk) *v.* 健行　paint (pent) *v.* 畫畫

hike

High-Intermediate

□ 4. ***Why do you like to hike?***	你爲什麼喜歡健行？
Hiking is so much fun.	健行很有趣。
And the exercise is good for me.	而且這個運動對我很好。
□ 5. ***How often do you go hiking?***	你多久去健行一次？
I go hiking at least once a week.	我一星期至少去健行一次。
I try to go whenever I can.	我儘量能去就去。
□ 6. ***How long have you been hiking?***	你已經健行多久了？
Two years now.	到現在兩年了。
I've been to many great places.	我去過很多很棒的地方。

**

fun〔fʌn〕*adj.* 有趣的

exercise〔ˈɛksɚˌsaɪz〕*n.* 運動

how often 多久一次

at least 至少　once〔wʌns〕*adv.* 一次

whenever〔hwɛnˈɛvɚ〕*conj.* 不論什麼時候（只要）；每當

how long 多久　***have been to*** 去過　great〔gret〕*adj.* 很棒的

exercise

□ 7. ***What made you start hiking?***	什麼使你開始健行？
I was bored.	我當時很無聊。
I wanted to see some nature.	我想要看一些大自然。
□ 8. ***How did you get into hiking?***	你是如何開始健行的？
My friend was in a hiking club.	我的朋友在健行社。
She invited me to join them.	她邀請我加入他們。
□ 9. ***What are your other interests?***	你其他的興趣是什麼？
Learning English is one.	學英文是其中之一。
I also like to take photos.	我也喜歡拍照。

**

nature

make〔mek〕*v.* 使
bored〔bord〕*adj.* 感到無聊的
nature〔ˈnetʃɚ〕*n.* 大自然
get into 開始從事
club〔klʌb〕*n.* 社團　invite〔ɪnˈvaɪt〕*v.* 邀請
join〔dʒɔɪn〕*v.* 加入
other〔ˈʌðɚ〕*adj.* 其他的　interest〔ˈɪntrɪst〕*n.* 興趣
photo〔ˈfoto〕*n.* 照片（= *photograph*）　***take photos*** 拍照

Oral Test 48

【問與答一起背】

□ 1. ***How about this weather?***	這個天氣如何？
It's pretty nice.	很好。
I can't complain.	我沒什麼好抱怨的。
□ 2. ***What will the weather be like tomorrow?***	明天的天氣會如何？
I'm not sure.	我不確定。
I haven't checked yet.	我還沒看。
□ 3. ***What's the forecast for next week?***	下星期的預報如何？
Rainy, which isn't too surprising.	會下雨，這不太令人驚訝。
This is the rainy season.	現在是雨季。

** ————————————

how about …如何　　weather〔ˈwɛðɚ〕*n.* 天氣
pretty〔ˈprɪtɪ〕*adv.* 相當　　complain〔kəmˈplen〕*v.* 抱怨
like〔laɪk〕*prep.* 像　　***not…yet*** 尚未；還沒
check〔tʃɛk〕*v.* 查看　　forecast〔ˈfor͵kæst〕*n.* 預報
rainy〔ˈrenɪ〕*adj.* 下雨的
surprising〔səˈpraɪzɪŋ〕*adj.* 令人驚訝的
season〔ˈsizn̩〕*n.* 季節；時期

□ 4. ***What's your favorite weather?***	你最喜愛什麼天氣？
Rain.	下雨。
I enjoy the soft sound of falling rain.	我喜歡雨落下時輕柔的聲音。
□ 5. ***What's your least favorite weather?***	你最不喜歡什麼天氣？
Hot and humid.	又熱又潮濕。
Summer is a terrible season for me.	夏天對我而言是個可怕的季節。
□ 6. ***Have you ever seen snow?***	你曾經看過雪嗎？
Yes, in China.	是的，在中國。
It's so fun to touch!	摸起來很有趣！

** ______________________

enjoy〔ɪn'dʒɔɪ〕*v.* 喜歡
soft〔sɔft〕*adj.* 柔和的　　falling〔'fɔlɪŋ〕*adj.* 落下的
least〔list〕*adv.* 最不　　humid〔'hjumɪd〕*adj.* 潮濕的
terrible〔'tɛrəbḷ〕*adj.* 可怕的
season〔'sizṇ〕*n.* 季節
ever〔'ɛvɚ〕*adv.* 曾經　　snow〔sno〕*n.* 雪
so〔so〕*adv.* 非常（= *very*）　　fun〔fʌn〕*adj.* 有趣的
touch〔tʌtʃ〕*v.* 觸碰

snow

□ **7.** ***What's the temperature outside?***	外面的溫度是幾度？
It's seven degrees Celsius.	攝氏七度。
It's pretty cold!	相當寒冷！
□ **8.** ***Is it going to rain this weekend?***	這個週末會下雨嗎？
It probably will.	可能會。
There's a sixty percent chance of rain.	降雨機率是百分之六十。
□ **9.** ***How cold does it get here in the winter?***	這裡冬天會變得多冷？
It never goes below zero.	從未到零下。
We never get snow or ice.	從未下雪或結冰。

＊＊ ________________

temperature (ˈtɛmpərətʃɚ) *n.* 溫度
outside (ˈaʊtˈsaɪd) *adv.* 在外面
degree (dɪˈgri) *n.* 度　Celsius (ˈsɛlsɪəs) *adj.* 攝氏的
weekend (ˈwikˈɛnd) *n.* 週末
probably (ˈprɑbəblɪ) *adv.* 可能
percent (pɚˈsɛnt) *adj.* 百分之…的
chance (tʃæns) *n.* 機會；可能性
get (gɛt) *v.* 變得；得到；有　go (go) *v.* 變成
below (bɪˈlo) *prep.* 在…之下　zero (ˈzɪro) *n.* 零度

temperature

【背景説明】

Oral Test 47

2. ***What do you do for fun?***（你會做什麼好玩的事？）

   = What do you do for enjoyment?

   = What are fun things you like to do?

   【enjoyment〔ɪnˈdʒɔɪmənt〕*n.* 樂趣；歡樂】

7. ***I wanted to see some nature.***（我想要看一些大自然。）

   = I wanted to be outside in nature.

   = I wanted to observe more natural environments.

   【observe〔əbˈzɝv〕*v.* 觀察；看　***natural environnment*** 自然環境】

8. ***How did you get into hiking?***（你是如何開始健行的？）

   = How did you become interested in hiking?

   = How did you get so involved in hiking?

   【interested〔ˈɪntrɪstɪd〕*adj.* 有興趣的　involved〔ɪnˈvɑlvd〕*adj.* 熱中於…的 <*in*>】

Oral Test 48

1. 美國人喜歡說：***I can't complain.***（我沒什麼好抱怨的。）這是他們的口頭禪，因爲美國小孩受教育時，老師常教導他們：Don't complain.（不要抱怨。）也可説成：It's very fine.（很好。）I'm satisfied.（我很滿意。）（= *I'm happy about it.*）

3. ***This is the rainy season***.（現在是雨季。）

rainy season

= It's the wet season.

= It's the time of year when it rains a lot.

【wet〔 wɛt 〕*adj.* 潮濕的；下雨的　***a lot*** 常常】

4. ***Rain***.（下雨。）

= Rainy weather.

= Wet weather.

6. ***It's so fun to touch!***（摸起來很有趣！）

= I enjoy touching it!

= I like to feel it!

= It's fun to feel it!

【feel〔 fil 〕*v.* 感覺；摸摸看；觸摸】

8. ***There's a sixty percent of chance of rain***.（降雨機率是百分之六十。）這句是氣象預報員會說的話。也可說成：It will most likely rain.（很可能會下雨。）（= *It will probably rain.*）

9. ***It never goes below zero***.（從未到零下。）

= It won't go below the freezing point.

= It never falls under the freezing point.

0–

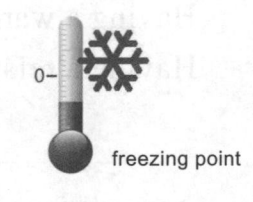

freezing point

【freeze〔 friz 〕*v.* 結冰　***freezing point*** 冰點】

We never get snow or ice.（從未下雪或結冰。）

中文裡不會說「我們」，而英文中卻用 we。

= We've never had snow or ice before.

= It's never gone below zero.

High-Intermediate

Oral Test 49

【問與答一起背】

□ 1. ***How do you start a conversation?***	你會如何開始一段對話？
First, I introduce myself.	首先，我會自我介紹。
Then, I start asking questions.	然後，我會開始問問題。
□ 2. ***What kind of questions do you ask?***	你會問什麼種類的問題？
I ask about the weather.	我會問關於天氣。
I ask about that person's day.	我會問那人當天過得如何。
□ 3. ***What makes it easy to talk to someone?***	什麼能使和別人說話較容易？
Having a warm smile.	有親切的笑容。
Having a relaxed manner.	有輕鬆的態度。

** ──────────

conversation (ˌkɑnvəˈseʃən) *n.* 對話
introduce (ˌɪntrəˈdjus) *v.* 介紹　　kind (kaɪnd) *n.* 種類
weather (ˈwɛðə) *n.* 天氣
warm (wɔrm) *adj.* 溫暖的；親切的　　smile (smaɪl) *n.* 微笑
relaxed (rɪˈlækst) *adj.* 放鬆的　　manner (ˈmænə) *n.* 態度

□ 4. ***What do you like to talk about?***	你喜歡談論什麼？
Recent news.	最近的新聞。
I like to talk about movies, too.	我也喜歡談論電影。
□ 5. ***What do you want to talk about?***	你想要談論什麼？
Anything.	任何事。
How about sports?	運動如何？
□ 6. ***What can you talk about for an hour?***	你談論什麼可以談一個小時？
Movies.	電影。
I'm a huge movie fan.	我是個超級電影迷。

**

talk about 談論
recent ('risn̩t) *adj.* 最近的
news (njuz) *n.* 新聞
How about~? ~如何？　sport (sport) *n.* 運動
huge (hjudʒ) *adj.* 巨大的　fan (fæn) *n.* 迷

NBC news

□ **7.** ***Do you like small talk?***	你喜歡閒聊嗎？
I don't mind small talk.	我不介意閒聊。
It's good for breaking the ice.	它很適合用來打破僵局。
□ **8.** ***Do you text or call more?***	你較常傳簡訊還是打電話？
I text more.	我比較常傳簡訊。
It's less likely to disturb someone.	這樣可能比較不會打擾別人。
□ **9.** ***Do you prefer to talk over the phone or in person?***	你比較喜歡講電話還是和本人談話？
I prefer to talk in person.	我比較喜歡面對面說話。
There are fewer misunderstandings.	那樣比較不會有誤會。

** ______________________

small talk 閒聊　　mind〔maɪnd〕*v.* 介意
good〔gʊd〕*adj.* 好的；適合的　　***break the ice*** 打破僵局
text〔tɛkst〕*v.* 傳簡訊　　likely〔ˈlaɪklɪ〕*adv.* 可能
disturb〔dɪˈstɝb〕*v.* 打擾　　prefer〔prɪˈfɝ〕*v.* 比較喜歡
talk over the phone 講電話　　***in person*** 親自；本身
misunderstanding〔ˌmɪsʌndəˈstændɪŋ〕*n.* 誤會

Oral Test 50

【問與答一起背】

□ 1. ***What's your idea of a healthy lifestyle?***	你認為什麼是健康的生活方式？
One involving exercise.	跟運動有關的生活方式。
Taking care of yourself is key.	照顧自己是關鍵。
□ 2. ***How do you stay fit?***	你如何保持健康？
I eat healthy foods.	我吃健康的食物。
I don't eat fried food.	我不吃油炸的食物。
□ 3. ***Do you like to exercise?***	你喜歡運動嗎？
I do.	我喜歡。
I go running every morning.	我每天早上去跑步。

**

idea〔aɪ'diə〕*n.* 想法
healthy〔'hɛlθɪ〕*adj.* 健康的　lifestyle〔'laɪf,staɪl〕*n.* 生活方式
involve〔ɪn'vɑlv〕*v.* 牽涉；包含；與…有關
exercise〔'ɛksə,saɪz〕*n. v.* 運動　***take care of*** 照顧
key〔ki〕*adj.* 極重要的；關鍵性的　stay〔ste〕*v.* 保持
fit〔fɪt〕*adj.* 健康的　fried〔fraɪd〕*adj.* 油炸的

□ 4. ***How often do you exercise?***	你多久運動一次？
Almost every day.	幾乎每天。
I try to exercise every day.	我試著每天運動。
□ 5. ***Do you work out?***	你會運動嗎？
Yes, I run.	是的，我會跑步。
I go to the gym.	我會上健身房。
□ 6. ***Why do you work out?***	你為什麼要運動？
To stay in shape.	要保持健康。
To improve my health.	要增進我的健康。

** ———

work out 運動　gym〔dʒɪm〕*n.* 健身房
in shape 健康的　***stay in shape*** 保持健康
improve〔ɪm'pruv〕*v.* 改善；增進
health〔hɛlθ〕*n.* 健康

work out

□ 7. ***Do you get yearly checkups?***	你會做年度的健康檢查嗎？
Always.	一直都會。
I believe in prevention.	我相信預防的重要。
□ 8. ***How often do you go to the doctor?***	你多久看一次醫生？
Only when I'm sick.	只有當我生病時。
I don't like doctors.	我不喜歡醫生。
□ 9. ***How often do you see a dentist?***	你多久看一次牙醫？
I get my teeth checked twice a year.	我一年檢查兩次牙齒。
I have an appointment next month.	我下個月有約。

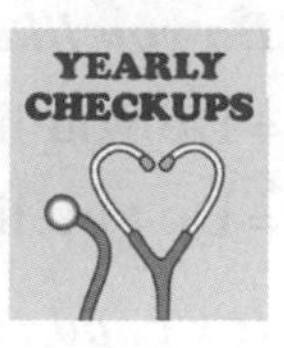

YEARLY CHECKUPS

** ______________________

yearly〔ˈjɪrlɪ〕*adj.* 每年的；一年一度的
checkup〔ˈtʃɛkˌʌp〕*n.* 健康檢查
believe in 相信…是好的
prevention〔prɪˈvɛnʃən〕*n.* 預防　***go to the doctor*** 去看醫生
dentist〔ˈdɛntɪst〕*n.* 牙醫　get〔gɛt〕*v.* 使
teeth〔tiθ〕*n. pl.* 牙齒　check〔tʃɛk〕*v.* 檢查
twice〔twaɪs〕*adv.* 兩次
appointment〔əˈpɔɪntmənt〕*n.* 約會；約診

【背景說明】

Oral Test 49

2. ***I ask about that person's day.***（我會問那人當天過得如何。）
   （= *I ask about how his day is going.*）

3. ***Having a relaxed manner.***（有輕鬆的態度。）
   = Having an easy-going attitude.
   = Having a comfortable style.
   = Making others feel at ease.
   【easy-going〔ˈizɪˌgoɪŋ〕*adj.* 悠哉的　style〔staɪl〕*n.* 風格；說話的態度　***at ease*** 自在的】

6. ***I'm a huge movie fan.***（我是個超級電影迷。）
   = I'm really into movies.
   = I love watching movies.
   = I'm crazy about watching movies.
   【***be into*** 熱中於　***be crazy about*** 熱中於；很喜歡】

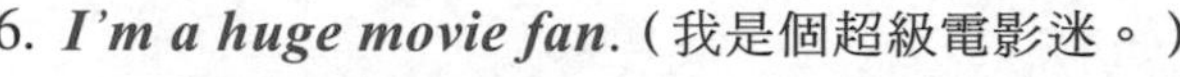

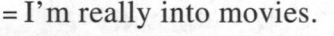

watch movies

7. ***Do you like small talk?***（你喜歡閒聊嗎？）
   = Do you like chatting?
   = Do you like to chat?【chat〔tʃæt〕*v.* 聊天】
   It's good for breaking the ice.（這對打破僵局有好處的。）
   = It's good for meeting people.
   = It helps in making friends.
   = It's useful for getting to know people.
   【meet〔mit〕*v.* 認識　***make friends*** 交朋友　***get to V.*** 得以…】

High-Intermediate

9. ***I prefer to talk in person.*** (我比較喜歡面對面說話。)
= I prefer to talk face to face.
= I prefer talking face to face.
= I like talking to people face to face.【***face to face*** 面對面】

Oral Test 50

1. ***What's your idea of a healthy lifestyle?***
(你認爲什麼是健康的生活方式？)
= What do you think a healthy lifestyle is?
= What do you think a healthy way to live is?

One involving exercise. (跟運動有關的生活方式。) 源自 One involving exercise is my idea of a healthy lifestyle.

Taking care of yourself is key. (照顧自己是關鍵。)
= Taking care of yourself is the key.
= It's important to treat yourself right.【treat (trit) *v.* 對待】

2. ***How do you stay fit?*** (你如何保持健康？)
= How do you stay in shape?
= How do you keep fit?
= How do you remain healthy?
= How do you remain in good health?

stay in shape

【***in shape*** 健康的　remain (rɪ'men) *v.* 保持】

7. ***I believe in prevention.*** (我相信預防的重要。) 任何及物動詞加介系詞，就形成另一個意思。believe 是「相信某人的話」，***believe in*** 是「相信…是好的」。諺語說：Prevention is better than cure. (預防勝於治療。)

High-Intermediate

Oral Test 51

【問與答一起背】

□ 1. ***What's your favorite holiday?***	你最喜愛的節日是什麼？
It's Chinese New Year.	農曆新年。
It's a lot of fun.	它很有趣。
□ 2. ***When is the holiday celebrated?***	何時會慶祝這個節日？
It's on Lunar New Year.	在農曆新年。
It's always in January or February.	它總是在一月或二月。
□ 3. ***What does the holiday stand for?***	這個節日代表什麼？
We celebrate family togetherness.	我們慶祝家人的團結。
It stands for family reunion.	它代表家人的團圓。

**

holiday (ˈhɑləˌde) *n.* 節日　***Chinese New Year*** 農曆新年
fun (fʌn) *n.* 樂趣　celebrate (ˈsɛləˌbret) *v.* 慶祝
lunar (ˈlunɚ) *adj.* 農曆的
Lunar New Year 農曆新年　***stand for*** 代表
togetherness (təˈgɛðɚnɪs) *n.* 團結友愛；和睦相處；親密無間
reunion (riˈjunjən) *n.* 團圓

High-Intermediate

☐ **4.** ***How do people celebrate this holiday?*** 人們如何慶祝這個節日？

They return home. 他們會回家。

They eat with their families. 他們會和家人一起吃飯。

☐ **5.** ***Are there any traditions you follow?*** 你們會遵循任何的傳統嗎？

Kids get money envelopes. 小孩子會拿到壓歲錢。

At night, we light fireworks. 晚上我們會放煙火。

☐ **6.** ***Are there any special foods you eat?*** 你們會吃什麼特別的食物？

We always eat dumplings. 我們一定會吃水餃。

The dumplings symbolize wealth. 水餃象徵財富。

** ___

return (rɪ'tɝn) *v.* 返回　tradition (trə'dɪʃən) *n.* 傳統
follow ('fɑlo) *v.* 遵循　envelope ('ɛnvə,lop) *n.* 信封
money envelope 壓歲錢　light (laɪt) *v.* 點燃
firework ('faɪr,wɝk) *n.* 煙火　***light fireworks*** 放煙火
special ('spɛʃəl) *adj.* 特別的
dumpling ('dʌmplɪŋ) *n.* 水餃
symbolize ('sɪmbl̩,aɪz) *v.* 象徵
wealth (wɛlθ) *n.* 財富

dumplings

□ 7. ***Why's this holiday your favorite?***	爲什麼這個節日是你最喜愛的？
Friends and relatives visit.	朋友和親戚會來拜訪。
We all enjoy being together.	我們全都喜歡聚在一起。
□ 8. ***What other holidays do you celebrate?***	你們會慶祝什麼其他的節日？
We have the Mid-Autumn Festival.	我們有中秋節。
It's also called the "Moon Festival."	它也被稱爲「月亮節」。
□ 9. ***What is the biggest, most important holiday?***	最重大的節日是什麼？
It's also Chinese New Year.	也是農曆新年。
I think it's everyone's favorite.	我認爲它是每個人的最愛。

**

favorite (ˈfevərɪt) *n.* 最喜愛的人或物　relative (ˈrɛlətɪv) *n.* 親戚
enjoy (ɪnˈdʒɔɪ) *v.* 喜歡
festival (ˈfɛstəvḷ) *n.* 節日；慶典
Mid-Autumn Festival 中秋節
moon (mun) *n.* 月亮
big (bɪg) *adj.* 重要的

Mid-Autumn Festival

Oral Test 52

【問與答一起背】

□ 1. ***What's your best holiday memory?***	你最美好的節日回憶是什麼？
Getting to shoot off fireworks.	能夠放煙火。
Also, lighting noisy firecrackers.	還有放很吵的鞭炮。
□ 2. ***Are there any holidays you really don't like?***	有任何你非常不喜歡的節日嗎？
Not really.	其實沒有。
Every holiday has a purpose.	每個節日都有它的目的。
□ 3. ***Any strange holidays or festivals?***	有任何奇怪的節日或節慶嗎？
We have a Tomb Sweeping Day.	我們有清明節。
It takes place in April.	是在四月。

**

firework

memory (ˈmɛmərɪ) *n.* 回憶　***get to V.*** 得以…
shoot off 發射　firework (ˈfaɪr,wɝk) *n.* 煙火
also (ˈɔlso) *adv.* 而且　light (laɪt) *v.* 點燃
noisy (ˈnɔɪzɪ) *adj.* 吵鬧的　firecrackers (ˈfaɪr,krækɚz) *n. pl.* 鞭炮
purpose (ˈpɝpəs) *n.* 目的；用途　tomb (tum) *n.* 墳墓
sweep (swip) *v.* 掃　***take place*** 發生；舉行

□ 4. ***Does your country celebrate Christmas?***	你的國家會慶祝聖誕節嗎？
Stores and churches do.	商店跟教堂會。
But not schools or companies.	但學校或公司不會。
□ 5. ***Does your country have a Veteran's Day?***	你的國家有退伍軍人嗎？
We have Armed Forces Day.	我們有軍人節。
But it's not a national holiday.	但它不是國定假日。
□ 6. ***Does your country have a Valentine's Day?***	你的國家有情人節嗎？
Yes, we have our own.	是的，我們有自己的。
It's in August.	是在八月。

church

**

celebrate〔ˈsɛləˌbret〕*v.* 慶祝
Christmas〔ˈkrɪsməs〕*n.* 聖誕節
church〔tʃɝtʃ〕*n.* 教堂　company〔ˈkʌmpənɪ〕*n.* 公司
veteran〔ˈvɛtərən〕*n.* 老兵；退伍軍人　armed〔ɑrmd〕*adj.* 武裝的
forces〔ˈforsɪz〕*n. pl.* 武裝力量　***armed forces*** 武裝部隊
Armed Forces Day 軍人節　national〔ˈnæʃənl̩〕*adj.* 國家的；國定的
national holiday 國定假日
Valentine's Day〔ˈvælənˌtaɪz ˌde〕*n.* 情人節

☐ **7.** ***Have you made a New Year's resolution?***	你有許下新年新希望嗎？
I have made them before.	我以前會。
But I didn't make any last year.	但我去年沒有許任何新年新希望。
☐ **8.** ***When is Mother's Day in your country?***	在你的國家母親節是什麼時候？
It's in May.	是在五月。
It's the second Sunday in May.	是五月的第二個星期天。
☐ **9.** ***When is Father's Day in your country?***	在你的國家父親節是什麼時候？
In my country, it's August 8th.	在我的國家是八月八日。
In Chinese, eight-eight sounds like "father."	中文裡的八八，聽起來像「爸爸」。

＊＊

resolution (ˌrɛzəˈluʃən) *n.* 決心；決心要做的事

New Year's resolution 新年新希望

Mother's Day 母親節

May (me) *n.* 五月 ***Father's Day*** 父親節

Chinese (tʃaɪˈniz) *n.* 中文 sound (saʊnd) *v.* 聽起來

Mother's Day

Oral Test 53

【問與答一起背】

□ 1. ***Can you cook?***	你會做菜嗎？
Yes, I can.	是的，我會。
I can cook a little.	我會做一點。
□ 2. ***What can you make?***	你會做什麼菜？
Grilled cheese.	烤起司。
I can also fry eggs.	我也會炒蛋。
□ 3. ***Do you have a specialty?***	你有拿手菜嗎？
Yes, tomato soup.	有，蕃茄湯。
I have a great recipe.	我有很棒的食譜。

** ___

fry

cook〔kuk〕*v.* 煮；做菜
grilled〔grɪld〕*adj.* 烤的
cheese〔tʃiz〕*n.* 起司　　fry〔fraɪ〕*v.* 油煎；油炒；油炸
specialty〔ˈspɛʃəltɪ〕*n.* 招牌菜；專長
tomato〔təˈmæto〕*n.* 蕃茄　　soup〔sup〕*n.* 湯
great〔gret〕*adj.* 很棒的　　recipe〔ˈrɛsəpɪ〕*n.* 食譜；烹飪法

□ **4.** ***Do you enjoy cooking?***	你喜歡做菜嗎？
Not really.	不是很喜歡。
I'd rather eat out.	我寧願出去吃。
□ **5.** ***How did you learn?***	你如何學習？
My mother taught me.	我媽媽教我的。
She's a great cook.	她很會做菜。
□ **6.** ***In your home, who usually cooks?***	你們家通常是誰做菜？
My mother.	我媽媽。
She rules the kitchen.	她掌管廚房。

** ______

enjoy〔ɪn'dʒɔɪ〕*v.* 喜歡
cook〔kuk〕*v.* 煮；做菜　*n.* 廚師
would rather 寧願　***eat out*** 出去吃飯
usually〔'juʒuəlɪ〕*adv.* 通常
rule〔rul〕*v.* 統治；支配
kitchen〔'kɪtʃɪn〕*n.* 廚房

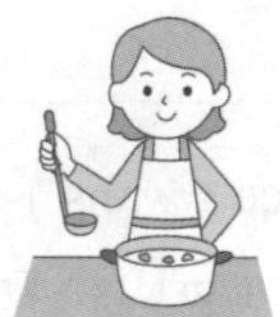
cook

□ 7. ***How often do you cook?***	你多久做一次菜？
Once or twice a week.	一星期一或兩次。
I get takeout most days.	我大部份的日子都是買外賣的食物。
□ 8. ***What are the advantages of cooking?***	做菜的優點是什麼？
It's cheaper.	比較便宜。
It can also be healthier.	也可能比較健康。
□ 9. ***What are the disadvantages of cooking?***	做菜的缺點是什麼？
It's time-consuming.	它很花時間。
And it takes some skill.	而且也需要一些技巧。

**

once〔wʌns〕*adv.* 一次　twice〔twaɪs〕*adv.* 兩次
get〔gɛt〕*v.* 買　takeout〔ˈtekˌaʊt〕*n.* 外賣的食物
advantage〔ədˈvæntɪdʒ〕*n.* 優點
cheap〔tʃip〕*adj.* 便宜的　healthy〔ˈhɛlθɪ〕*adj.* 健康的
disadvantage〔ˌdɪsədˈvæntɪdʒ〕*n.* 缺點
time-consuming〔ˈtaɪmkənˌsumɪŋ〕*adj.* 耗時的
take〔tek〕*v.* 需要　skill〔skɪl〕*n.* 技巧

takeout

Oral Test 54

【問與答一起背】

□ 1. ***Do you have any pet peeves?***	你有任何最討厭的事嗎？
I have one pet peeve.	我有一件最討厭的事。
It's when people cut in line.	那就是有人插隊的時候。
□ 2. ***Where do you like to go for fun?***	想要玩樂時，你會去哪裡？
I go to the night market.	我會去夜市。
I love to eat and shop.	我喜歡吃東西和購物。
□ 3. ***Do you have any bad habits?***	你有任何壞習慣嗎？
Yes, my room is often messy.	有，我的房間常常很雜亂。
I just can't seem to keep it neat.	我似乎就是無法使它保持整潔。

**

peeve〔 piv 〕*n.* 令人氣惱的東西；討厭的東西
pet peeve 最討厭的事　line〔 laɪn 〕*n.*（等待順序的）行列
cut in line 插隊　market〔ˈmɑrkɪt 〕*n.* 市場
night market 夜市　shop〔 ʃɑp 〕*v.* 購物
habit〔ˈhæbɪt 〕*n.* 習慣
messy〔ˈmɛsɪ 〕*adj.* 雜亂的
seem〔 sim 〕*v.* 似乎　neat〔 nit 〕*adj.* 整潔的

messy

□ 4. ***What are your good habits?***	你的好習慣是什麼？
I'm a serious student.	我是個認真的學生。
I prepare and study well.	我會好好準備並且把書唸好。
□ 5. ***Would you ever move to another country?***	你會搬到另一個國家嗎？
Sure, I would.	當然，我會。
But only an English speaking one.	但是只會搬到說英語的國家。
□ 6. ***Are there any natural disasters where you live?***	在你住的地方有任何的天災嗎？
Yes, earthquakes.	是的，地震。
There are also typhoons.	也會有颱風。

** ——————————

serious (ˈsɪrɪəs) *adj.* 認眞的　　prepare (prɪˈpɛr) *v.* 準備
would ever 會　　move (muv) *v.* 搬家
English speaking 說英文的　　natural (ˈnætʃərəl) *adj.* 天然的
disaster (dɪˈzæstɚ) *n.* 災害
natural disaster 天災
earthquake (ˈɝθˌkwek) *n.* 地震
typhoon (taɪˈfun) *n.* 颱風

typhoon

☐ 7. ***Is laughter the best medicine?***	笑是最好的藥嗎？
Yes, humor is healthy.	是的，幽默是健康的。
It affects your mind and body.	它會影響你的身心。
☐ 8. ***Do you like to watch comedy?***	你喜歡看喜劇嗎？
I love to watch comedies.	我喜歡看喜劇。
I like stand-up comedy, too.	我也喜歡單人表演的喜劇。
☐ 9. ***Are you afraid of anything?***	你有任何害怕的東西嗎？
I'm afraid of spiders.	我怕蜘蛛。
I don't like snakes, either.	我也不喜歡蛇。

** ____________________

laughter〔ˈlæftɚ〕*n.* 笑　medicine〔ˈmɛdəsn̩〕*n.* 藥
Laughter is the best medicine. 【諺】笑是最好的藥。
humor〔ˈhjumɚ〕*n.* 幽默　healthy〔ˈhɛlθɪ〕*adj.* 健康的
affect〔əˈfɛkt〕*v.* 影響　***mind and body*** 身心
comedy〔ˈkɑmədɪ〕*n.* 喜劇
stand-up〔ˈstændˌʌp〕*adj.*（笑話）單人表演的　*n.* 西式單口相聲
afraid〔əˈfred〕*adj.* 害怕的　***be afraid of*** 害怕
spider〔ˈspaɪdɚ〕*n.* 蜘蛛　snake〔snek〕*n.* 蛇
either〔ˈiðɚ, ˈaɪðɚ〕*adv.* 也（不）

spider

【背景說明】

Oral Test 51

3. ***We celebrate family togetherness.***（我們慶祝家人的團結。）
= We rejoice in our strong family unity.
= We commemorate our close family ties.
【rejoice（rɪ'dʒɔɪs）*v.* 高興　unity（'junətɪ）*n.* 團結
commemorate（kə'mɛmə,ret）*v.* 慶祝　close（klos）*adj.* 親密的
ties（taɪz）*n. pl.* 關係】

7. ***Friends and relatives visit.***（朋友和親戚會來拜訪。）
= Family and friends come visit us.
= People we care about come see us.
【***come visit*** 來拜訪（= *come and visit*）　***care about*** 關心；在乎】

Oral Test 52

1. ***Getting to shoot off fireworks.*** 這句話是名詞片語，完整句是 ***Getting to shoot off fireworks*** is my best holiday memory.（能夠放煙火是我最棒的節日回憶。）動名詞片語當主詞。可說成：Being allowed to launch rockets.（被允許放沖天炮。）
【launch（lɔntʃ）*v.* 發射　rocket（'rɑkɪt）*n.* 沖天炮】Being allowed by my parents to set off fireworks.（被我的父母允許放煙火。）【***set off*** 使爆炸】***Also, lighting noisy firecrackers.***（還有燃放很吵的鞭炮。）（= *Also, igniting loud firecrackers.*）
【ignite（ɪg'naɪt）*v.* 點燃】

2. ***Every holiday has a purpose.***（每個節日都有它的目的。）（= *There is a reason for every holiday.*）We celebrate or have holidays for a reason.（我們慶祝節日或放假都是有理由的。）

3. ***It takes place in April.***（是在四月。）可說成：It falls in April.（是在四月。）（= *It happens in April.* = *It occurs in April.*）【fall〔fɔl〕*v.* 來臨】

4. ***But not schools and companies.***（但學校或公司不會。）可說成：Public schools and private businesses do not.（公立學校和私人企業不會。）

7. ***Have you made a New Year's resolution?***（你有許下新年新希望嗎？）美國人習慣，到了新年，都會有一個新希望，決心在這一年當中，要做什麼事。可說成：Any New Year's plan to improve?（新的一年有沒有任何想要改進的計劃？）Did you make a New Year's promise?（你有沒有許下新年的承諾？）

Oral Test 53

3. ***Do you have a specialty?***（你有拿手菜嗎？）（= *What's the best dish you can cook?*）***I have a great recipe.***（我有很棒的食譜。）在此指 I know a special way to cook tomato soup.（我知道一個特別的方法煮蕃茄湯。）

4. ***Not really.***（不是很喜歡。）是委婉的否定（*used for saying "No" without being definite*）。例如：

   A: Do you like fast food?（你喜歡速食嗎？）
   B: ***Not really.***（不是很喜歡。）
   （= *Not too much.* = *Not in particular.*）

5. ***She's a great cook***. 字面的意思是「她是很棒的廚師。」也就是「她很會做菜。」(= *She makes delicious meals.*) cook (廚師) 不要和 cooker (鍋子) 搞混。

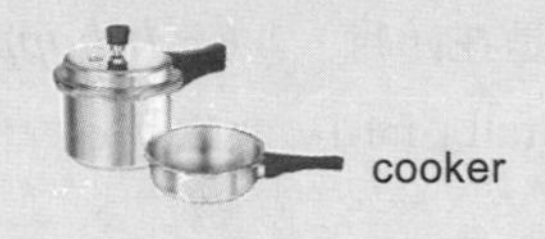

6. ***She rules the kitchen***. (她掌管廚房。) (= *She's the kitchen boss.* = *She is in charge of the kitchen.*)【***in charge of*** 負責；掌管】

7. ***I get takeout most days***. (我大部份的日子都是買外賣的食物。)
(= *I usually buy takeout.* = *I get takeout almost every day.*)

9. ***It's time-consuming***. (它很花時間。)
= It uses up too much time.
= It takes a lot of time to do it.
【***use up*** 用完；耗盡　take (tek) *v.* 需要；花費】

Oral Test 54

1. ***Do you have any pet peeves?*** (你有任何最討厭的事嗎？)
= What bothers you?
= Is there anything that really annoys you?
= Is there anything that bugs you?
【bother (ˈbɑðɚ) *v.* 困擾　annoy (əˈnɔɪ) *v.* 使心煩　bug (bʌg) *v.* 使煩惱】
peeve 是「討厭的東西」，***pet peeve*** 是「最討厭的東西」(= *pet hate*)。***pet*** 的主要意思是「寵物」，在 ***pet peeve*** 中，***pet*** 作「非常的；特別的」解。

High-Intermediate

It's when people cut in line.（那就是有人插隊的時候。）
= It's when people don't wait in line.
= I get upset when people fail to wait their turn.
【***wait in line*** 排隊等候　upset〔ʌp'sɛt〕*adj.* 不高興的
fail to V. 未能…　***wait*** *one's* ***turn*** 等輪到自己】

3. ***My room is often messy.***（我的房間常常很雜亂。）
= My room is untidy. = My room is not organized.
= I'm messy at home.
【untidy〔ʌn'taɪdɪ〕*adj.* 不整潔的　organized〔'ɔrgən,aɪzd〕*adj.* 有條理的】

4. ***I'm a serious student.***（我個是認真的學生。）（= *I'm an earnest student.*）可接著說：I don't waste time.（我不會浪費時間。）I care about schoolwork.（我很在乎學業。）I'm determined in school.（我在學校很認真。）【determined〔dɪ'tɝmɪnd〕*adj.* 堅決的】

5. ***Would you ever move to another country?***（你會搬到另一個國家嗎？）
= Would you be willing to live overseas?
= Would you ever live abroad?
【willing〔'wɪlɪŋ〕*adj.* 願意的　overseas〔'ovə'siz〕*adv.* 在海外
abroad〔ə'brɔd〕*adv.* 在國外】

8. ***I like stand-up comedy.***（我喜歡單人表演的喜劇。）
= I like live-performance comedy monologues.
= I like going to comedy clubs and watching comedians perfom.
= I enjoy watching people perform by telling jokes and humorous stories.
【live〔laɪv〕*adj.* 現場的　monologue〔'monḷ,ɔg〕*n.* 獨白；獨腳戲
comedian〔kə'midɪən〕*n.* 喜劇演員】

High-Intermediate Oral Tests

※ 請掃瞄 QR 碼，聽完題目後，練習回答兩句。

Oral Test 33

□ 1. How do you get around every day?

□ 2. How do you get to school?

□ 3. How far is your home from school?

□ 4. Can you drive?

□ 5. Do you have your license?

□ 6. Are you a good driver?

□ 7. When did you get your license?

□ 8. Who taught you to drive?

□ 9. How long did it take you to learn how to drive?

Oral Test 34

□ 1. Are you in college?

□ 2. Where do you go to college?

□ 3. What's your major?

☐ 4. Why did you choose it?

____

____

☐ 5. What degree are you pursuing?

____

____

☐ 6. What year are you in?

____

____

☐ 7. What classes are you taking?

____

____

☐ 8. When will you graduate?

____

____

☐ 9. What are your plans after graduation?

____

____

Oral Test 35

☐ 1. How do you like college so far?

____

____

☐ 2. Have you made any friends?

____

____

☐ 3. Do you live on campus or at home?

____

____

☐ 4. What's your dormitory like?

____

____

☐ 5. Do you have a roommate?

____

____

☐ 6. Do you like your roommate?

____

____

□ 7. Are you involved in any clubs?

____

____

□ 8. Are you in a fraternity or sorority?

____

____

□ 9. Do you have a part-time job?

____

____

Oral Test 36

□ 1. How are your classes going?

____

____

□ 2. How are your professors?

____

____

□ 3. What's your favorite class?

____

____

□ 4. What's your easiest class?

____

____

□ 5. What's your hardest class?

____

____

□ 6. How are your grades looking?

____

____

□ 7. Are you studying hard?

____

____

□ 8. Have you been to any college parties?

____

____

□ 9. Have you attended any college games?

____

____

Oral Test 37

☐ 1. Do you like living in a city?

____

____

☐ 2. What do you like about it?

____

____

☐ 3. Is there anything you dislike?

____

____

☐ 4. Would you rather live in the city or countryside?

____

____

☐ 5. Where is the best place to eat in your neighborhood?

____

____

☐ 6. Where is the best place to shop in your neighborhood?

____

____

☐ 7. What do you think of your neighbors?

____

____

☐ 8. Do you know your neighbors?

____

____

☐ 9. Is there anything your neighbors do that annoys you?

____

____

Oral Test 38

☐ 1. What's your favorite kind of food?

____

____

☐ 2. What's your favorite pizza?

____

____

☐ 3. What's your favorite ice cream flavor?

____

____

☐ 4. What's your favorite fruit?

____

____

☐ 5. What's your favorite drink?

____

____

☐ 6. What food is your country known for?

____

____

☐ 7. What foods do you dislike?

____

____

☐ 8. Is there anything you don't eat?

____

____

☐ 9. Do you have any food allergies?

____

____

Oral Test 39

☐ 1. Do you like spicy food?

____

____

☐ 2. Do you like sweets?

____

____

☐ 3. Do you drink coffee?

____

____

☐ 4. How do you like your coffee?

____

____

☐ 5. Do you like it hot or iced?

____

____

☐ 6. How much coffee do you drink?

____

____

☐ 7. Do you drink tea?

____

____

☐ 8. Are you a vegetarian?

____

____

☐ 9. Are you a vegan?

____

____

Oral Test 40

☐ 1. What's your favorite restaurant?

____

____

☐ 2. How often do you eat out?

____

____

☐ 3. Do you prefer eating in or out?

____

____

☐ 4. Have you ever worked in a restaurant?

____

____

☐ 5. How often do you eat takeout?

____

____

☐ 6. Do you want to order pizza?

____

____

☐ 7. Are tips at restaurants common where you live?

____

____

☐ 8. How much is a reasonable tip?

____

____

☐ 9. How much should I tip?

____

____

Oral Test 41

☐ 1. Are you on social media?

____

____

☐ 2. Do you have a Facebook page?

____

____

☐ 3. What kind of information do you put on there?

____

____

☐ 4. What info are you ok with people seeing?

____

____

☐ 5. How do you protect your privacy?

____

____

☐ 6. Do you use Twitter?

____

____

☐ 7. Do you have an Instagram account?

____

____

☐ 8. What do you watch on YouTube?

____

____

☐ 9. Do you use WeChat?

____

____

Oral Test 42

☐ 1. What do you do on WeChat?

____

____

☐ 2. How many followers do you have?

____

____

☐ 3. What do you usually post?

____

____

☐ 4. What do you like about social media?

☐ 5. What don't you like about social media?

☐ 6. How many times a day do you check social media?

☐ 7. Who are you following?

☐ 8. What's your favorite app?

☐ 9. What's your favorite website?

Oral Test 43

☐ 1. What do you like about texting?

☐ 2. What don't you like about texting?

☐ 3. Who do you text the most?

☐ 4. Do you ever talk to strangers?

☐ 5. Does speaking to foreigners make you nervous?

☐ 6. Does public speaking make you nervous?

☐ 7. Do you like to argue?

____

____

☐ 8. What kind of phone do you have?

____

____

☐ 9. Which do you like better: Apple or Samsung?

____

____

Oral Test 44

☐ 1. Are you dating anyone?

____

____

☐ 2. Are you seeing anyone?

____

____

☐ 3. How long have you been dating?

____

____

☐ 4. How many dates have you been on lately?

____

____

☐ 5. How do you feel about dating?

____

____

☐ 6. What are the best and worst first dates you've been on?

____

____

☐ 7. What makes a good first date to you?

____

____

☐ 8. Do you prefer being single or in a relationship?

____

____

☐ 9. What do you look for in a boyfriend?

____

____

Oral Test 45

☐ 1. What are your plans for this weekend?

____

____

☐ 2. What are your plans for this Saturday?

____

____

☐ 3. What are your plans for this summer?

____

____

☐ 4. What are your plans for the holidays?

____

____

☐ 5. What are your plans for Chinese New Year?

____

____

☐ 6. What are your plans for learning English?

____

____

☐ 7. What are your plans for this project?

____

____

☐ 8. Do you have a back-up plan?

____

____

☐ 9. Want to make plans for this weekend?

____

____

Oral Test 46

☐ 1. How's your vision?

____

____

☐ 2. Are you nearsighted or farsighted?

____

____

☐ 3. Do you wear glasses?

____

____

☐ 4. Do you prefer glasses or contacts?

____

____

☐ 5. Have you ever had braces?

____

____

☐ 6. Do you catch colds a lot?

____

____

☐ 7. How would you treat a cold?

____

____

☐ 8. When sick, do you prefer Western or Chinese medicine?

____

____

☐ 9. Do you think diets are useful?

____

____

Oral Test 47

☐ 1. What do you like to do?

____

____

☐ 2. What do you do for fun?

____

____

☐ 3. What are your hobbies?

____

____

☐ 4. Why do you like to hike?

____

____

☐ 5. How often do you go hiking?

____

____

☐ 6. How long have you been hiking?

____

____

☐ 7. What made you start hiking?

____

____

☐ 8. How did you get into hiking?

____

____

☐ 9. What are your other interests?

____

____

Oral Test 48

☐ 1. How about this weather?

____

____

☐ 2. What will the weather be like tomorrow?

____

____

☐ 3. What's the forecast for next week?

____

____

☐ 4. What's your favorite weather?

____

____

☐ 5. What's your least favorite weather?

____

____

☐ 6. Have you ever seen snow?

____

____

☐ 7. What's the temperature outside?

____

____

☐ 8. Is it going to rain this weekend?

____

____

☐ 9. How cold does it get here in the winter?

____

____

Oral Test 49

☐ 1. How do you start a conversation?

____

____

☐ 2. What kind of questions do you ask?

____

____

☐ 3. What makes it easy to talk to someone?

____

____

☐ 4. What do you like to talk about?

____

____

☐ 5. What do you want to talk about?

____

____

☐ 6. What can you talk about for an hour?

____

____

☐ 7. Do you like small talk?

____

____

☐ 8. Do you text or call more?

____

____

☐ 9. Do you prefer to talk over the phone or in person?

____

____

Oral Test 50

☐ 1. What's your idea of a healthy lifestyle?

____

____

☐ 2. How do you stay fit?

____

____

☐ 3. Do you like to exercise?

____

____

☐ 4. How often do you exercise?

____

____

☐ 5. Do you work out?

____

____

☐ 6. Why do you work out?

____

____

☐ 7. Do you get yearly checkups?

____

____

☐ 8. How often do you go to the doctor?

____

____

☐ 9. How often do you see a dentist?

____

____

Oral Test 51

☐ 1. What's your favorite holiday?

____

____

☐ 2. When is the holiday celebrated?

____

____

☐ 3. What does the holiday stand for?

____

____

□ 4. How do people celebrate this holiday?

____

____

□ 5. Are there any traditions you follow?

____

____

□ 6. Are there any special foods you eat?

____

____

□ 7. Why's this holiday your favorite?

____

____

□ 8. What other holidays do you celebrate?

____

____

□ 9. What is the biggest, most important holiday?

____

____

Oral Test 52

□ 1. What's your best holiday memory?

____

____

□ 2. Are there any holidays you really don't like?

____

____

□ 3. Any strange holidays or festivals?

____

____

□ 4. Does your country celebrate Christmas?

____

____

□ 5. Does your country have a Veteran's Day?

____

____

□ 6. Does your country have a Valentine's Day?

____

____

□ 7. Have you made a New Year's resolution?

____

____

□ 8. When is Mother's Day in your country?

____

____

□ 9. When is Father's Day in your country?

____

____

Oral Test 53

□ 1. Can you cook?

____

____

□ 2. What can you make?

____

____

□ 3. Do you have a specialty?

____

____

□ 4. Do you enjoy cooking?

____

____

□ 5. How did you learn?

____

____

□ 6. In your home, who usually cooks?

____

____

□ 7. How often do you cook?

____

____

□ 8. What are the advantages of cooking?

____

____

□ 9. What are the disadvantages of cooking?

____

____

Oral Test 54

☐ 1. Do you have any pet peeves?

____

____

☐ 2. Where do you like to go for fun?

____

____

☐ 3. Do you have any bad habits?

____

____

☐ 4. What are your good habits?

____

____

☐ 5. Would you ever move to another country?

____

____

☐ 6. Are there any natural disasters where you live?

____

____

☐ 7. Is laughter the best medicine?

____

____

☐ 8. Do you like to watch comedy?

____

____

☐ 9. Are you afraid of anything?

____

____

英語口試 — 高級

Advanced

英語口試「高級」Oral Test 55~80

1. 「高級」的句子更長也更難，不容易背到變成直覺。
2. 「初級」、「中級」，和「中高級」要背到滾瓜爛熟，再背「高級」。
3. 把這些問與答當成課本讀即可。
4. Advanced Oral Tests的錄音QR碼只有唸問題，保留足夠的時間讓你練習回答。

Advanced

Oral Test 55

【問與答一起背】

□ 1. ***Do you enjoy shopping?*** 你喜歡購物嗎？

I like to shop; it's fun. 我喜歡購物；很有趣。

I enjoy buying things I like. 我喜歡買自己喜歡的東西。

□ 2. ***Where do you like to shop for clothes?*** 你喜歡在哪裡買衣服？

I like department stores. 我喜歡百貨公司。

They have everything in one place. 那裡所有的東西都在同一個地方。

□ 3. ***Do you like outlet stores or the mall?*** 你喜歡名牌折扣店還是購物中心？

I like to shop at both. 我喜歡在這兩個地方購物。

I like discounted brand-name items. 我喜歡打折的名牌商品。

** ______________________

shop〔ʃɑp〕*v.* 購物　　fun〔fʌn〕*adj.* 有趣的

shop for 購買　　clothes〔kloz〕*n.pl.* 衣服

department store 百貨公司　　***outlet store*** 名牌折扣店

mall〔mɔl〕*n.* 購物中心；商場

discounted〔dɪsˈkaʊntɪd〕*adj.* 打折的

brand-name〔ˈbrændˌnem〕*adj.* 名牌的　　item〔ˈaɪtəm〕*n.* 物品

□ 4. ***In your city, where is a good place to go shopping?*** 在你的城市裡，哪裡是購物的好地方？

Street markets are good. 街上的市集很不錯。

The goods are cheap! 那裡的商品很便宜！

□ 5. ***How do you feel about online shopping?*** 你覺得網路購物如何？

It's very convenient. 非常方便。

I love online shopping. 我很愛網路購物。

□ 6. ***Do you prefer to shop online or in person?*** 你比較喜歡網購還是親自去買東西？

I like shopping in person. 我喜歡親自去買。

I can touch and try the product. 我可以觸摸並試用商品。

** ——————————

market〔'mɑrkɪt〕*n.* 市場

goods〔gʊdz〕*n. pl.* 商品　cheap〔tʃip〕*adj.* 便宜的

online〔'ɑn,laɪn〕*adj.* 線上的　*adv.* 在線上；在網路上

convenient〔kən'vinjənt〕*adj.* 方便的

prefer〔prɪ'fɝ〕*v.* 比較喜歡　***in person*** 親自

touch〔tʌtʃ〕*v.* 碰觸；觸摸　try〔traɪ〕*v.* 試用

product〔'prɑdəkt〕*n.* 產品

□ 7. ***What products do you prefer to shop online for?***	你比較喜歡在網路上購買什麼產品？
I shop online for devices.	我會上網買一些器具。
I bought my laptop online.	我在網路上買我的筆電。
□ 8. ***What products do you prefer to shop in stores for?***	你比較喜歡在商店購買什麼產品？
I buy clothing in stores.	我會在商店買衣服。
I buy shoes in stores, too.	我也會在商店買鞋子。
□ 9. ***What is your favorite e-commerce site?***	你最喜愛的電子商務網站是什麼？
Amazon is my favorite.	亞馬遜是我最喜愛的。
It sells just about everything.	它幾乎什麼都賣。

** ————————

shop for 購買　　device (dɪˈvaɪs) *n.* 裝置；器具
laptop (ˈlæpˌtɑp) *n.* 膝上型電腦；筆電
clothing (ˈkloðɪŋ) *n.* 衣服
e-commerce (ˈiˈkɑmɝs) *n.* 電子商務
favorite (ˈfevərɪt) *adj.* 最喜愛的
n. 最喜愛的人或物　　site (saɪt) *n.* 網站 (= *website*)
Amazon (ˈæməˌzɑn) *n.* 亞馬遜河；亞馬遜網路商店
just about 幾乎 (= *almost*)

laptop

【背景說明】

Oral Test 55

6. ***Do you prefer to shop online or in person?***（你比較喜歡網購還是親自去買東西？）

   = Do you like online shopping or traditional shopping better?

   【traditional〔trəˈdɪʃənl̩〕*adj.* 傳統的】

   I like shopping in person.（我喜歡親自去買。）

   = I like visiting the shop and looking at stuff.

   【visit〔ˈvɪzɪt〕*v.* 拜訪；去　stuff〔stʌf〕*n.* 東西】

7. ***I shop online for devices***.（我會上網買一些器具。）可說成：

   I buy computer stuff online.（我會上網買一些電腦的東西。）

9. ***What is your favorite e-commerce site?***（你最喜愛的電子商務網站是什麼？）

   = Which e-commerce website do you like best?

   It sells just about everything.（它幾乎什麼都賣。）

   = They offer a huge selection.

   = They sell everything from A to Z.

   = They sell everything you can imagine.

   【huge〔hjudʒ〕*adj.* 巨大的　selection〔səˈlɛkʃən〕*n.* 供挑選的東西
   from A to Z 從頭到尾；完全地　imagine〔ɪˈmædʒɪn〕*v.* 想像】

Advanced

Oral Test 56

【問與答一起背】

☐ 1. ***Do you have any favorite brands?***

你有任何最喜愛的品牌嗎？

I have no real favorites.

我沒有眞正的最愛。

I like many different brands.

我喜歡許多不同的品牌。

☐ 2. ***What style of clothes do you like?***

你喜歡什麼風格的衣服？

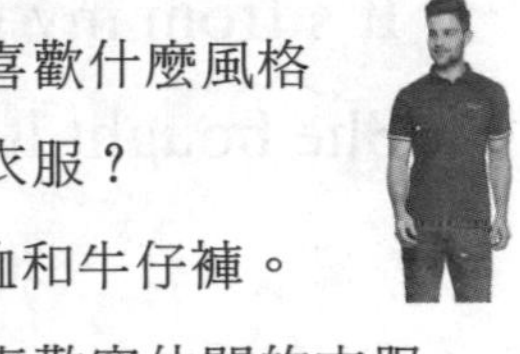

T-shirts and jeans.

T 恤和牛仔褲。

I like to dress casually.

我喜歡穿休閒的衣服。

☐ 3. ***Do you dress for style or comfort?***

你穿衣服是爲了流行還是舒適？

I dress for both.

我穿衣服兩種目的都有。

Being comfortable is important.

舒適是很重要的。

** ————————————

brand〔brænd〕*n.* 品牌　style〔staɪl〕*n.* 風格；流行
clothes〔kloðz, kloz〕*n. pl.* 衣服　T-shirt〔ˈti,ʃɝt〕*n.* T 恤
jeans〔dʒinz〕*n. pl.* 牛仔褲　dress〔drɛs〕*v.* 穿衣服
casually〔ˈkæʒuəlɪ〕*adv.* 休閒地　comfort〔ˈkʌmfɚt〕*n.* 舒適
comfortable〔ˈkʌmfɚtəbl̩〕*adj.* 舒服的

□ 4. ***Do you follow fashion trends?***	你會跟隨流行趨勢嗎？
Yes, I like new styles.	是的，我喜歡新的流行。
I want to look good.	我想要看起來好看。
□ 5. ***I like your jacket. Where did you get it?***	我喜歡你的夾克。你在哪裡買的？
It's from my mom.	是我媽媽給我的。
She bought it for me.	她買給我的。
□ 6. ***I like your shoes. How much were they?***	我喜歡你的鞋子。要多少錢？
About one hundred dollars.	大約一百美元。
I think they were worth it.	我認爲很值得。

** ――――――――――――

follow〔ˈfɑlo〕*v.* 跟隨；遵循
fashion〔ˈfæʃən〕*n.* 流行；時尚
trend〔trɛnd〕*n.* 趨勢
look〔lʊk〕*v.* 看起來
jacket〔ˈdʒækɪt〕*n.* 夾克　　get〔gɛt〕*v.* 得到；買
about〔əˈbaʊt〕*adv.* 大約　　worth〔wɜθ〕*adj.* 值得…的

jacket

□ 7. ***Nice watch. Is it waterproof?***	很棒的手錶。它防水嗎？
Thanks, it is.	謝謝，是的。
It's accurate, too.	它也很準確。
□ 8. ***How often do you shop at street markets?***	你多久會在街頭市集購物一次？
A few times a month.	一個月好幾次。
I can always find something I like.	我總是能找到喜歡的東西。
□ 9. ***Do you like to haggle for a lower price?***	你喜歡討價還價嗎？
I sure do.	我當然喜歡。
It's really fun to haggle.	討價還價非常有趣。

** ________________________

waterproof

waterproof〔'wɔtə,pruf〕*adj.* 防水的
accurate〔'ækjərɪt〕*adj.* 準確的
time〔taɪm〕*n.* 次　　once〔wʌns〕*adv.* 一次
haggle〔'hægḷ〕*v.* 討價還價；殺價
lower〔'loə〕*adj.* 較低的　　price〔praɪs〕*n.* 價格
sure〔ʃur〕*adv.* 確實地；當然　　fun〔fʌn〕*adj.* 有趣的

Advanced

Oral Test 57

【問與答一起背】

□ 1. ***Do you enjoy flying?***	你喜歡搭飛機嗎？
It depends.	看情形。
I like flights under five hours.	我喜歡五小時以內的飛行。
□ 2. ***Do you fly often?***	你常搭飛機嗎？
Yes, I fly a lot.	是的，我常搭飛機。
I often travel for business.	我常出差旅行。
□ 3. ***Which airline do you fly with most?***	你最常搭哪一家航空公司？
I fly them all.	他們我全部都會搭。
I look for the best schedule.	我會找最好的時間。

** ________________

enjoy〔ɪnˈdʒɔɪ〕*v.* 喜歡

fly〔flaɪ〕*v.* 搭飛機；搭（航空公司）飛機

depend〔dɪˈpɛnd〕*v.* 視…而定　***It depends.*** 看情形。

flight〔flaɪt〕*n.* 飛行；搭飛機旅行；班機　***a lot*** 常常

travel for business 出差旅行　airline〔ˈɛrˌlaɪn〕*n.* 航空公司

look for 尋找　schedule〔ˈskɛdʒul〕*n.* 時間表；時刻表

□ 4. ***Why do you prefer them?*** 你爲什麼比較喜歡他們？
I'm a bargain hunter. 我很會找便宜的東西。
I look for the best deal. 我會找最划算的交易。

□ 5. ***Ever fly business class?*** 曾經搭過商務艙嗎？
I rarely fly business class. 我很少搭商務艙。
It's a bit expensive for me. 它對我而言有點貴。

□ 6. ***Ever fly first class?*** 曾經搭過頭等艙嗎？
I've never tried it. 我從未嘗試過。
I can't afford it. 我負擔不起。

** ___

prefer (prɪ'fɝ) *v.* 比較喜歡　bargain ('bɑrgɪn) *n.* 便宜貨
hunter ('hʌntɚ) *n.* 獵人；搜索的人　***look for*** 尋找
deal (dil) *n.* 交易　ever ('ɛvɚ) *adv.* 曾經
fly (flaɪ) *v.* 飛；搭飛機
business class 乘坐商務艙
rarely ('rɛrlɪ) *adv.* 很少
a bit 有點　***first class*** 乘坐頭等艙
afford (ə'fɔrd) *v.* 負擔得起

business class

□ 7. ***How do you normally check in?***	你通常如何辦理登機手續？
I always check in online.	我總是在網路上辦理登機手續。
I do it at home the day before.	我會前一天在家裡做這件事。
□ 8. ***How much luggage do you bring?***	你會帶多少行李？
I travel light with one bag.	我會輕裝旅行，帶一個行李。
I also keep a carry-on.	我也會拿一個手提行李。
□ 9. ***Have you ever missed your flight?***	你曾經錯過班機嗎？
I've never missed my flight.	我從未錯過我的班機。
I go to the airport early.	我會早點到機場。

**

normally〔ˈnɔrmḷɪ〕*adv.* 通常　***check in*** 辦理登機手續
online〔ˈɑnˌlaɪn〕*adv.* 在線上；在網路上　***the day before*** 前一天
luggage〔ˈlʌgɪdʒ〕*n.* 行李　light〔laɪt〕*adv.* 不帶東西地；輕裝地
travel light 輕裝旅行　bag〔bæg〕*n.* 袋子；行李
carry-on〔ˈkærɪˌɑn〕*n.* 手提行李；隨身行李
miss〔mɪs〕*v.* 錯過
airport〔ˈɛrˈport〕*n.* 機場

airport

【背景說明】

Oral Test 56

3. ***Do you dress for style or comfort?***（你穿衣服是爲了流行還是舒適？）
   = Do you wear your clothing more for style or comfort?
   = Do you care more for fashion or comfort?【***care for*** 喜歡；想要】
   也可說成：Do you shop more for fashion or comfort?（你比較常爲了流行或是舒適而買東西？）

4. ***Do you follow fashion trends?***（你會跟隨流行趨勢嗎？）
   = Do you wear the latest styles?
   = Do you pay attention to the latest fashions?
   【latest〔ˈletɪst〕*adj.* 最新的　style〔staɪl〕*n.* 風格；樣式；(流行) 款式　***pay attention to*** 注意】

9. ***Do you like to haggle for a lower price?***（你喜歡討價還價嗎？）
   = Do you enjoy bargaining to lower the price?
   = Do you like to bargain?
   = Do you mind trying to negotiate for a lower price?
   【bargain〔ˈbɑrgɪn〕*v.* 討價還價　negotiate〔nɪˈgoʃɪˌet〕*v.* 協商；談判】

Oral Test 57

1. ***I like flights under five hours.***（我喜歡五小時以內的飛行。）
   = I like flights of less than five hours.
   = I like short flights.
   = I enjoy flying on short flights.
   = I don't like flying too long.

3. ***Which airline do you fly with most?***（你最常搭哪一家航空公司？）
   = What ailrline do you take most often?

I fly them all.（他們我全部都會搭。）

= I take them all. = I fly on every airline.

I look for the best schedule.（我會找最好的時間。）

= I try to find the best times.

= I search for the best times.

4. ***I'm a bargain hunter.***（我很會找便宜的東西。）

= I look for good bargains.

= I try hard to find cheaper prices.

I look for the best deal.（我會找最划算的交易。）

= I try for the best rates.

= I seach for low prices.【***try for*** 爭取　rate〔ret〕*n.* 價格】

5. ***Ever fly business class?***（曾經搭過商務艙嗎？）

= Do you ever fly business class?

= Have you ever flown business class before?

= Have you ever tried business class?

6. ***Ever fly first class?***（曾經搭過頭等艙嗎？）

= Do you ever fly first class?

= Have you ever flown first class?

= Have you ever tried first class travel?

first class

7. ***I do it at home the day before.***（我會前一天在家裡做這件事。）

（= *I check in at home 24 hours before.*）可說成：I check in on a computer 24 hours before my flight.（我會在班機時間二十四小時前，在電腦上辦理登機手續。）

8. ***I travel light with one bag.***（我會輕裝旅行，帶一個行李。）

= I'm a light traveler.

= I don't like to travel with more than one bag.

I also keep a carry-on.（我也會拿一個手提行李。）

= I also take a carry-on bag.

Advanced

Oral Test 58

【問與答一起背】

□ 1. ***Do you prefer the aisle or window seat?***	你比較喜歡靠走道還是靠窗的座位？
I prefer the aisle seat.	我比較喜歡靠走道的座位。
I like to stretch my legs.	我喜歡伸展我的腿。
□ 2. ***Do you have any plane tips?***	你有任何搭飛機的祕訣嗎？
I chew gum before take-off.	我在起飛前會嚼口香糖。
I always bring my own earbuds.	我一定會帶自己的耳機。
□ 3. ***How do you pass the time?***	你如何度過這段時間？
I watch movies.	我會看電影。
Sometimes I read.	有時候我會閱讀。

** ———————————

prefer (prɪ'fɝ) *v.* 比較喜歡
aisle (aɪl) *n.* 走道
aisle seat 靠走道的座位　　***window seat*** 靠窗的座位
stretch (strɛtʃ) *v.* 伸展（四肢）　　plane (plen) *n.* 飛機
tip (tɪp) *n.* 祕訣　　chew (tʃu) *v.* 嚼
gum (gʌm) *n.* 口香糖　　take-off ('tek,ɔf) *n.* 起飛
earbuds ('ɪr,bʌdz) *n. pl.* 耳機　　pass (pæs) *v.* 度過

□ 4. ***Do you ever chat with strangers on the plane?***	你曾經在飛機上和陌生人聊天嗎？
I do, sometimes.	我有時候會。
I might chitchat a bit.	我可能會閒聊一會兒。
□ 5. ***Do you like airline food?***	你喜歡飛機餐嗎？
No, I do not.	不，我不喜歡。
I think it's tasteless.	我認為飛機餐不好吃。
□ 6. ***Are you afraid of flying?***	你害怕搭飛機嗎？
No, I'm not scared.	不，我不會怕。
Flying doesn't bother me.	搭飛機不會困擾我。

**

ever ('ɛvɚ) *adv.* 曾經　chat (tʃæt) *v.* 聊天
stranger ('strendʒɚ) *n.* 陌生人
sometimes ('sʌm,taɪmz) *adv.* 有時候
chitchat ('tʃɪt,tʃæt) *v.* 閒談；聊天　***a bit*** 一會兒；一下子
airline food 飛機餐（= *airline meal*）
tasteless ('testlɪs) *adj.* 沒有味道的；不好吃的
be afraid of 害怕　fly (flaɪ) *v.* 搭飛機
scared (skɛrd) *adj.* 害怕的　bother ('bɑðɚ) *v.* 困擾

□ 7. ***Any funny stories about flying?***	有任何關於搭飛機的好笑的故事嗎？
Once, someone brought a dog.	有一次，有人帶了一隻狗。
That dog snored like a human.	那隻狗會像人一樣打呼。
□ 8. ***What's the longest flight you've ever taken?***	你搭過最久的班機是什麼航班？
The longest flight was 15 hours.	最久的航班是十五小時。
I thought it would never end.	我以爲永遠不會結束。
□ 9. ***Ever had a scary, bumpy flight?***	曾經有過可怕又顚簸的飛行經驗嗎？
Yes, I have flown through a storm.	有，我曾經搭飛機穿越暴風雨。
I hate flying in bad weather.	我討厭在壞天氣搭飛機。

** ————————

funny (ˈfʌnɪ) *adj.* 好笑的　snore (snor) *v.* 打呼
human (ˈhjumən) *n.* 人　long (lɔŋ) *adj.* 長久的
flight (flaɪt) *n.* 飛行；班機　take (tek) *v.* 搭乘
end (ɛnd) *v.* 結束　scary (ˈskɛrɪ) *adj.* 可怕的
bumpy (ˈbʌmpɪ) *adj.* 顚簸的
through (θru) *prep.* 穿越　storm (stɔrm) *n.* 暴風雨
hate (het) *v.* 討厭　weather (ˈwɛðɚ) *n.* 天氣

bumpy

Oral Test 58

2. ***Do you have any plane tips?***（你有任何搭飛機的祕訣嗎？）

= Do you have any air travel advice?

= Do you have any good suggestions for better air travel?

I chew gum before take-off.（我在起飛前會嚼口香糖。）

在飛機起飛或降落前，嚼口香糖能減輕耳朵壓力。

I always bring my own earbuds.（我一定會帶自己的耳機。）

= I always bring my own earphones.

= I always use my own earphones.

= I like to use my own earphones.

【earphones〔ˈɪr,fonz〕*n. pl.* 耳機】

earphones

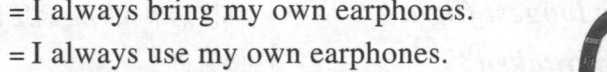

4. ***I might chitchat a bit.***（我可能會閒聊一會兒。）

= I might chat a little.

= Sometimes I'll engage in small talk.

= I occasionally have a light conversation.

【***engage in*** 參與　***small talk*** 聊天
occasionally〔əˈkeʒənḷɪ〕*adv.* 偶爾　***light conversation*** 隨便閒聊】

8. ***I thought it would never end.***（我以爲永遠不會結束。）

= I felt like it was forever.

= It seemed like we were flying forever.

9. ***Ever had a scary, bumpy flight?***（曾經有過可怕又顛簸的飛行經驗嗎？）

= Ever had a turbulent flight?

= Ever had a rough flight?

【turbulent〔ˈtɝbjələnt〕*adj.* 動盪的；亂流的　rough〔rʌf〕*adj.* 顛簸的】

這句話源自：Have you ever had...? 美國人在口語中常省略 Have you。

Oral Test 59

【問與答一起背】

□ 1. ***Do you like to travel?***	你喜歡旅行嗎？
I love it.	我很喜愛。
There are many places I want to see.	有很多我想看的地方。
□ 2. ***Why do you like to travel?***	你為什麼喜歡旅行？
I learn a lot.	我可以學到很多。
And it's always a lot of fun.	而且總是很有趣。
□ 3. ***How often do you travel?***	你多久旅行一次？
Not as much as I'd like.	不像我想要的那麼常去。
Maybe once or twice a year.	可能一年一次或兩次。

**

fun〔fʌn〕*n.* 樂趣；有趣的人或事物

It's a lot of fun. 很有趣。（= *It's great fun.*）

as much as I'd like 和我想要的一樣多

once〔wʌns〕*adv.* 一次　twice〔twaɪs〕*adv.* 兩次

□ 4. ***Have you ever been abroad?***	你曾經出過國嗎？
Yes, a few times.	是的，好幾次。
I've traveled overseas before.	我以前出國旅行過。
□ 5. ***What country do you most want to visit?***	你最想去什麼國家遊覽？
I want to go to China.	我想去中國。
To travel around China is my dream.	到中國各地旅遊是我的夢想。
□ 6. ***What is your dream vacation?***	你夢想中的假期是什麼？
To go to Hawaii.	去夏威夷。
It seems so beautiful.	那裡似乎很美。

**

ever〔ˈɛvɚ〕*adv.* 曾經
abroad〔əˈbrɔd〕*adv.* 到國外
overseas〔ˈovɚˈsiz〕*adv.* 到海外
dream〔drim〕*n.* 夢想 *adj.* 夢想中的
vacation〔veˈkeʃən〕*n.* 假期　Hawaii〔həˈwaɪjə〕*n.* 夏威夷
seen〔sim〕*v.* 似乎　so〔so〕*adv.* 非常（= *very*）

Hawaii

□ 7. ***What do you want to do there?***	你想在那裡做什麼？
I want to see the scenery.	我想要看風景。
I want to enjoy the beautiful beach.	我想要欣賞美麗的海灘。
□ 8. ***Why do you usually travel?***	你通常爲了什麼去旅行？
Usually it's to relax.	通常是爲了放鬆。
To get away and rejuvenate.	爲了離開一下，恢復精神。
□ 9. ***Where do you like to go on vacation?***	你喜歡去哪裡度假？
To mountains or beaches.	去山上或海邊。
I like to go somewhere new.	我喜歡去沒去過的地方。

** ──────────────

scenery〔ˈsinərɪ〕*n.* 風景　　beach〔bitʃ〕*n.* 海灘

usually〔ˈjuʒuəlɪ〕*adv.* 通常

relax〔rɪˈlæks〕*v.* 放鬆

get away 離開；外出

rejuvenate〔rɪˈdʒuvənˌet〕*v.* 恢復精神

go on vacation 去度假

somewhere〔ˈsʌmˌhwɛr〕*adv.* 在某處；到某處

new〔nju〕*adj.* 陌生的

go on vacation

Advanced

Oral Test 60

【問與答一起背】

□ 1. ***What kind of places would you like to go?***	你想要去什麼樣的地方？
Anywhere.	任何地方。
I'm not picky.	我不挑剔。
□ 2. ***Have you ever been camping?***	你曾經去露營過嗎？
No, I've never been.	不，我從來沒有過。
But I want to try.	不過我想試試看。
□ 3. ***Have you ever taken a cruise?***	你曾經乘船遊覽過嗎？
Not yet.	還沒有過。
They're a little expensive.	乘船遊覽有點貴。

** ─────────────

anywhere ('ɛnɪ,hwɛr) *adv.* 任何地方
picky ('pɪkɪ) *adj.* 挑剔的
ever ('ɛvɚ) *adv.* 曾經
camp (kæmp) *v.* 露營　cruise (kruz) *n.* 乘船遊覽
not yet 尚未；還沒　expensive (ɪk'spɛnsɪv) *adj.* 昂貴的

☐ 4. ***Ever been to Europe?***	曾經去過歐洲嗎？
Once.	一次。
I've been to France.	我去過法國。
☐ 5. ***Do you ever use English while traveling?***	你旅行時曾經使用過英文嗎？
Yes, all the time.	是的，一直都會使用。
It's a good language for travel.	對旅行而言，英文是很適合的語言。
☐ 6. ***Do you have any good travel stories?***	你有任何好的旅行故事嗎？
Yes, I have many.	是的，我有很多。
I always see cool things.	我總是看到很酷的事物。

＊＊ ——————

ever〔ˈɛvɚ〕*adv.* 曾經
Europe〔ˈjurəp〕*n.* 歐洲
travel〔ˈtrævl̩〕*v. n.* 旅行
all the time 一直；總是　　good〔gʊd〕*adj.* 好的；適合的
language〔ˈlæŋgwɪdʒ〕*n.* 語言
cool〔kul〕*adj.* 很酷的；很棒的

□ 7. ***Where did you spend your last vacation?*** 你上一次的假期去了什麼地方？

New York City. 紐約市。

I went there last summer. 我去年夏天去了那裡。

□ 8. ***What did you do?*** 你做了什麼？

I had a great time! 我玩得很愉快！

I saw some Broadway shows. 我看了一些百老匯的秀。

□ 9. ***Do you prefer traveling alone or with a group?*** 你比較喜歡獨自旅行還是跟團？

I like to travel alone. 我喜歡獨自旅行。

Groups are too inflexible. 跟團太沒有彈性了。

**

spend〔spɛnd〕*v.* 度過　***have a great time*** 玩得很愉快

Broadway〔ˈbrɔd͵we〕*n.* 百老匯【美國戲劇和音樂劇的重要地點】

show〔ʃo〕*n.* 節目；秀

prefer〔prɪˈfɝ〕*v.* 比較喜歡

alone〔əˈlon〕*adv.* 獨自地

group〔grup〕*n.* 團體

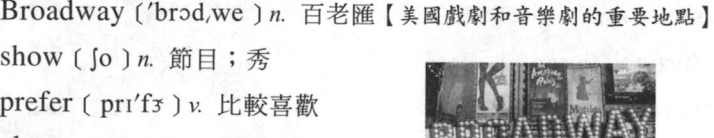

inflexible〔ɪnˈflɛksəbḷ〕*adj.* 缺乏彈性的；不可改變的

Advanced

【背景說明】

Oral Test 59

8. ***To get away and rejuvenate.***（爲了離開一下，恢復精神。）
   = To clear my mind and recharge my batteries.
   = To leave my troubles behind and to feel young again.
   這句話源自：I have to get away and rejuvenate.
   【***clear** one's **mind*** 使某人的頭腦清晰　recharge (ri'tʃardʒ) *v.* 給…再充電　battery ('bætərɪ) *n.* 電池　***leave…behind*** 留下；忘記】

9. ***Where do you like to go on vacation?***（你喜歡去哪裡度假？）
   句中的 on 表目的，含有「從事於」的意思，後面常接 business，errand，journey，trip 之類的字。【詳見「文法寶典」p.595】
   I'm going on vacation.（我要去度假。）
   = I'm going on holiday.

Oral Test 60

1. ***I'm not picky.***（我不挑剔。）
   = I'm not selective. = I'm easy to satisfy.
   = I'm open to trying. = I'm not hard to please.
   = I'm game for anything.
   【selective (sə'lɛktɪv) *adj.* 精挑細選的　***be open to*** 願意接受　please (pliz) *v.* 取悅　***be game for*** 對…有興趣】

9. ***Groups are too inflexible.***（跟團太沒有彈性了。）
   = Tour groups are too restrictive.
   = Groups have too many guidelines and rules.
   = Groups control your activities too much.
   【restrictive (rɪ'strɪktɪv) *adj.* 限制的
   guideline ('gaɪd,laɪn) *n.* 指導方針】

Oral Test 61

【問與答一起背】

□ 1. ***What's the most amazing place you have been to?***	你去過最棒的地方是哪裡？
Good question.	好問題。
Definitely Mt. Fuji in Japan.	當然是日本的富士山。
□ 2. ***What do you like to do when traveling?***	你旅行的時候喜歡做什麼？
I love to sightsee.	我喜愛觀光。
I also want to shop.	我也想要去購物。
□ 3. ***Do you know any travel tips?***	你知道任何旅行祕訣嗎？
Always travel light.	一定要輕裝旅行。
That way you have room for souvenirs.	那樣你就有空間可以放紀念品。

**

amazing (ə'mezɪŋ) *adj.* 令人驚奇的；很棒的
definitely ('dɛfənɪtlɪ) *adv.* 當然
Mt. (maʊnt) *n.* 山【源自 mount，用於山名】
sightsee ('saɪt,si) *v.* 觀光　tip (tɪp) *n.* 祕訣
light (laɪt) *adv.* 輕便地　***travel light*** 輕裝旅行
that way 那樣　room (rum) *n.* 空間
souvenir (,suvə'nɪr) *n.* 紀念品

travel light

□ 4. ***Where are you going for your next trip?***	你下一趟旅行要去哪裡？
I have no clue.	我不知道。
There are a lot of good choices.	有很多好的選擇。
□ 5. ***How much vacation time do you get a year?***	你一年有多少時間可以休假？
About 14 days.	大約十四天。
I usually take it in the summer.	我通常在夏天休假。
□ 6. ***Where are the best places to visit in your country?***	在你們國家最適合遊覽的地方是哪裡？
Taroko Gorge is stunning.	太魯閣非常美。
Taipei 101 is a must-see.	台北 101 是必看的景點。

**

clue (klu) *n.* 線索　***have no clue*** 不知道
choice (tʃɔɪs) *n.* 選擇
vacation (veˈkeʃən) *n.* 休假；假期
visit (ˈvɪzɪt) *v.* 參觀；遊覽
gorge (gɔrdʒ) *n.* 峽谷　***Taroko Gorge*** 太魯閣
stunning (ˈstʌnɪŋ) *adj.* 令人目眩的；極美的
must-see (ˈmʌstˈsi) *n.* 必須去看的東西

Taroko Gorge

□ 7. ***What are the best months to visit your country?***	哪幾個月最適合遊覽你的國家？
I'd say September to November.	我會說九月到十一月。
That's when the weather is best.	那是天氣最好的時候。
□ 8. ***What foods do you recommend tourists try?***	你會推薦觀光客嘗試什麼食物？
Our beef noodle soup.	我們的牛肉麵。
Maybe even stinky tofu.	或許甚至是臭豆腐。
□ 9. ***If you could go anywhere, where would you go?***	如果你可以去任何地方，你會去哪裡？
I'd go to Venice.	我會去威尼斯。
I think it's a beautiful city.	我認爲它是一個美麗的城市。

** ___

month〔 mʌnθ 〕*n.* 月
weather〔ˈwɛðɚ 〕*n.* 天氣
recommend〔ˌrɛkəˈmɛnd 〕*v.* 推薦　　tourist〔ˈturɪst 〕*n.* 觀光客
beef〔 bif 〕*n.* 牛肉　　noodle〔ˈnudl̩ 〕*n.* 麵
soup〔 sup 〕*n.* 湯　　***beef noodle soup*** 牛肉麵
stinky〔ˈstɪŋkɪ 〕*adj.* 臭的　　***stinky tofu*** 臭豆腐
Venice〔ˈvɛnɪs 〕*n.* 威尼斯【義大利都市】

stinky tofu

Oral Test 62

【問與答一起背】

□ 1. ***Do you have a passport?***	你有護照嗎？
Yes, I do.	是的，我有。
I've had one since I was in high school.	我從高中時就有護照了。
□ 2. ***What do you think of public transportation?***	你認爲大衆運輸如何？
I think it's great.	我認爲它很棒。
It's good for the environment.	它對環境有益。
□ 3. ***Do you use public transit often?***	你會常使用大衆運輸嗎？
Oh, yes.	喔，是的。
I take it to work every day.	我每天都搭大衆運輸去上班。

** ______________________________

passport〔ˈpæs,port〕*n.* 護照　***high school*** 高中
think of 認爲　public〔ˈpʌblɪk〕*adj.* 公共的；大衆的
transportation〔,trænspəˈteʃən〕*n.* 運輸；交通工具
public transportation 大衆運輸　great〔gret〕*adj.* 很棒的
environment〔ɪnˈvaɪrənmənt〕*n.* 環境
transit〔ˈtrænzɪt〕*n.* 運輸；運輸系統　take〔tek〕*v.* 搭乘

passport

□ 4. ***Do you have good public transportation where you live?***	在你住的地方有好的大眾運輸系統嗎？
The metro where I live is great.	在我住的地方地鐵很棒。
It's always clean and on time.	它總是乾淨又準時。
□ 5. ***Have you ever used Uber?***	你曾經叫過優步嗎？
Yes, I have.	是的，我曾經叫過。
Uber is pretty popular where I live.	優步在我住的地方相當受歡迎。
□ 6. ***Do you prefer Uber or taxis?***	你比較喜歡優步還是計程車？
I prefer Uber.	我比較喜歡優步。
I prefer it because it's cheaper.	我比較喜歡它，因爲它比較便宜。

** ______________________

metro (ˈmɛtro) *n.* 地鐵　　***on time*** 準時

ever (ˈɛvɚ) *adv.* 曾經

Uber (ˈubɚ) *n.* 優步【是一間交通網路公司，總部位於美國舊金山，以開發行動應用程式，連結乘客和司機，提供載客車輛租賃及實時共乘的分享型經濟服務】

Uber

pretty (ˈprɪtɪ) *adv.* 相當

popular (ˈpɑpjəlɚ) *adj.* 受歡迎的　　prefer (prɪˈfɝ) *v.* 比較喜歡

□ 7. ***Have you ever carpooled?***	你曾經汽車共乘嗎？
No, I haven't.	不，我不曾。
I don't know many people with a car.	我沒有認識很多有車的人。
□ 8. ***Have you ever seen an accident?***	你曾經看過車禍嗎？
Yes, I have.	是的，我看過。
I saw two cars collide.	我看過兩輛汽車相撞。
□ 9. ***Can you ride a motorcycle?***	你會騎摩托車嗎？
Yes, I can.	是的，我會。
I have my own bike.	我有我自己的摩托車。

**

carpool〔ˈkɑr,pul〕*v.* 汽車共乘
accident〔ˈæksədənt〕*n.* 意外；車禍
collide〔kəˈlaɪd〕*v.* 相撞
motorcycle〔ˈmotɚ,saɪkl̩〕*n.* 摩托車；機車
bike〔baɪk〕*n.* 腳踏車（= *bicycle*）；機車；摩托車
（= *motorbike* = *motorcycle*）

motorcycle

【背景說明】

Oral Test 61

4. ***I have no clue***.（我不知道。）

   = I'm clueless.

   = I have no idea.

   = I don't know.

   【clueless〔'klulɪs〕*adj.* 無線索的　***have no idea*** 不知道】

   可說成：I have not even thought about it yet.（我想都沒想過。）

5. ***I usually take it in the summer***.（我通常在夏天休假。）【it 在此指 my vacation time】

   = I use my vacation time during the summer.

   = I often vacation during the summer.【vacation 在此是動詞，作「度假」解】

7. ***I'd say September to November***.（我會說九月到十一月。）

   = In my opinion, the autumn is best.

   = From my experience, I'd say the fall is best.

   【***in my opinion*** 依我之見；我認為　autumn〔'ɔtəm〕*n.* 秋天（= *fall*）】

8. ***What foods do you recommend tourists try?***

   （你會推薦觀光客嘗試什麼食物？）

   = What dishes do you suggest tourists try?

   = What types of food should visitors try?

   【recommend（推薦）和 suggest（建議）是慾望動詞，接受詞後，常省略 should 再接原形動詞。】

Oral Test 62

3. ***Do you use public transit often?***（你會常使用大眾運輸嗎？）
= Do you take public transportation a lot?
【***public transportation*** 大眾運輸　***a lot*** 常常】
也可說成：Do you often ride on the metro?（你常搭乘地鐵嗎？）【metro（ˈmɛtro）*n.* 地鐵】Do you ride on the subway or light rail a lot?（你常搭乘地下鐵或輕軌嗎？）【subway（ˈsʌbˌwe）*n.* 地下鐵　rail（rel）*n.* 鐵軌；軌道　***light rail*** 輕軌】Do you use the railway or buses much?（你常使用鐵路或公車嗎？）
【railway（ˈrelˌwe）*n.* 鐵路　much（mʌtʃ）*adv.* 常常（= *a lot* = *often*）】

7. ***Have you ever carpooled?***（你曾經汽車共乘嗎？）
= Have you ever tried "ride sharing"?
= Ever tried car sharing?
也可說成：Ever carpooled with colleagues or neighbors?（曾經和同事或鄰居汽車共乘嗎？）
【colleague（ˈkɑlig）*n.* 同事（= *co-worker*）】

9. ***I have my own bike.***（我有我自己的摩托車。）
= I own a motorcycle.
= I own a bike.
= I'm a motorcycle owner.
= I have a motorcycle.
bike 可指「腳踏車」(bicycle)，也可指「摩托車」(motorbike；motorcycle)。

Oral Test 63

【問與答一起背】

□ 1. ***What kind of car do you have?***	你有什麼種類的車？
A Ford.	一台福特汽車。
I bought it used.	我是買二手的。
□ 2. ***What's your favorite kind of car?***	你最喜愛什麼種類的車？
The Audi R8.	奧迪 R8。
That's my dream car.	那是我夢想中的車。
□ 3. ***Have you ever been pulled over?***	你曾經被迫靠路邊停車嗎？
No, never.	不，從來沒有。
I'm a careful driver.	我開車很小心。

** ———————————

Ford〔 fɔrd 〕*n.* 福特汽車　　used〔 juzd 〕*adj.* 舊的；二手的
kind〔 kaɪnd 〕*n.* 種類
Audi〔ˈaʊdɪ 〕*n.* 奧迪
dream〔 drim 〕*adj.* 理想的；夢想的
pull over 使靠路邊停車
careful〔ˈkɛrfəl 〕*adj.* 小心的
driver〔ˈdraɪvɚ 〕*n.* 駕駛人

Audi

□ 4. ***Have you ever gotten a speeding ticket?***	你有被開過超速的罰單嗎？
Definitely not.	當然沒有。
I don't speed.	我不會超速。
□ 5. ***Do you have a bicycle?***	你有腳踏車嗎？
Yes, I have a bike.	有，我有一台腳踏車。
I use my bike a lot.	我常使用我的腳踏車。
□ 6. ***Do you know any bike paths around here?***	你知道這附近有任何腳踏車專用道嗎？
I know one by the river.	我知道河邊有一條。
It's called the river path.	它叫作河岸車道。

**

speeding (ˈspidɪŋ) *n.* 超速　ticket (ˈtɪkɪt) *n.* 罰單

definitely (ˈdɛfənɪtlɪ) *adv.* 當然

speed (spid) *v.* 超速行駛

bike (baɪk) *n.* 腳踏車 (= *bicycle*)

bike

a lot 常常　path (pæθ) *n.* 小徑；小路；通道

bike path 腳踏車專用道　***around here*** 在這附近

by (baɪ) *prep.* 在…旁邊　***be called*** 叫作

Advanced

□ 7. ***Can you call me an Uber?***	你能幫我叫優步嗎？
Sure, no problem.	當然，沒問題。
I'll check for nearby Uber drivers.	我會看看附近有沒有優步司機。
□ 8. ***Can you flag down a taxi?***	你能揮手攔下計程車嗎？
OK, I'll find one.	好的，我會找一輛。
Just give me a minute.	只要給我一點時間。
□ 9. ***What's the fare for the metro?***	地鐵的車資是多少？
The fare's a dollar fifty.	車資是 1.5 美元。
You can buy a stored-value card.	你可以買一張儲值卡。

** ___

sure〔ʃur〕*adv.* 當然　***check for*** 查看
nearby〔ˈnɪrˌbaɪ〕*adj.* 附近的
flag〔flæg〕*v.* 打旗號使（車子等）停下
flag down 揮手攔下　minute〔ˈmɪnɪt〕*n.* 分鐘；片刻
fare〔fɛr〕*n.* 車資　metro〔ˈmɛtro〕*n.* 地鐵
store〔stor〕*v.* 儲存　value〔ˈvælju〕*n.* 價值
stored-value card 儲值卡

NT$ 300
4G LTE 儲值卡

stored-value card

Oral Test 64

【問與答一起背】

□ 1. ***What traits do you value?***	你重視什麼特質？
I value honesty.	我重視誠實。
I also appreciate courage.	我也欣賞勇氣。
□ 2. ***What makes you happy?***	什麼會使你快樂？
I adore my friends.	我非常喜愛我的朋友。
But I like solitude, too.	但我也喜歡獨處。
□ 3. ***What would you like to be known for?***	你想要因爲什麼而有名？
I want to be known as a team player.	我想要被認爲是個有團隊精神的人。
I hope to be considered dependable.	我希望被認爲是可靠的。

** ______

trait (tret) *n.* 特質　value ('vælju) *v.* 重視
honesty ('ɑnɪstɪ) *n.* 誠實　appreciate (ə'priʃɪ,et) *v.* 欣賞
courage ('kɝɪdʒ) *n.* 勇氣　adore (ə'dor) *v.* 非常喜愛
solitude ('sɑlə,tjud) *n.* 獨處　***be known for*** 因…(特點)而有名
be known as 被稱爲；被認爲是　team (tim) *n.* 團隊
team player 有團隊精神的人　consider (kən'sɪdɚ) *v.* 認爲
be considered (to be) 被認爲是
dependable (dɪ'pɛndəbḷ) *adj.* 可靠的

□ 4. ***What's your number one priority?***	你最優先的事項是什麼？
To score high on my tests.	我考試要得高分。
To get into an excellent school.	要進入一所很優秀的學校。
□ 5. ***What are your short-term goals?***	你的短期目標是什麼？
I'm trying to lose weight.	我正努力減重。
I want to be healthier.	我想變得更健康。
□ 6. ***What are your long-term goals?***	你的長期目標是什麼？
I'd like to write a book.	我想要寫一本書。
I want to be a best-selling author.	我想成爲暢銷作家。

**

number one 第一的
priority (praɪˈɔrətɪ) *n.* 優先事項；優先考慮的事
score (skɔr) *v.* 得分　***score high*** 得高分
excellent (ˈɛksḷənt) *adj.* 優秀的
short-time (ˈʃɔrtˌtɝm) *adj.* 短期的　goal (gol) *n.* 目標
lose (luz) *v.* 失去；減輕　weight (wet) *n.* 重量
lose weight 減重　healthy (ˈhɛlθɪ) *adj.* 健康的
long-term (ˈlɔŋˌtɝm) *adj.* 長期的
best-selling (ˈbɛstˈsɛlɪŋ) *adj.* 暢銷的　author (ˈɔθɚ) *n.* 作家

□ 7. ***How do you plan to reach your goals?***	你打算如何達成你的目標？
I'll learn as much as I can.	我會儘量學習。
I'll improve step by step.	我會一步一步地改善。
□ 8. ***What are your strengths?***	你的優點是什麼？
I am a determined person.	我是個堅定的人。
I always finish what I start.	我總是會完成開始做的事。
□ 9. ***What are your weaknesses?***	你的弱點是什麼？
Sometimes, I want fast results.	有時候我會想要很快就有成果。
I must be more patient.	我必須更有耐心。

** ____________________

reach〔ritʃ〕*v.* 達到　　***as…as one can*** 儘可能…
improve〔ɪm'pruv〕*v.* 改善；進步
step by step 一步一步地
strength〔strɛŋθ〕*n.* 優點
determined〔dɪ'tɝmɪnd〕*adj.* 堅定的
finish〔'fɪnɪʃ〕*v.* 完成
weakness〔'wiknɪs〕*n.* 缺點　　result〔rɪ'zʌlt〕*n.* 結果；成果
patient〔'peʃənt〕*adj.* 有耐心的

【背景說明】

Oral Test 63

1. *A Ford.*（一台福特汽車。）
   = My car is a Ford.
   = I drive a Ford.
   = I own a Ford.
   = I'm the owner of a Ford.

Ford

I bought it used.（我是買二手的。）
= I bought it second-hand.
= I didn't buy it new.
【second-hand〔ˈsɛkənˌhænd〕*adj.* 二手的（= *used*）】

3. ***Have you ever been pulled over?***（你曾經被迫靠路邊停車嗎？）意思是 Have the police ever stopped you?（警察曾經把你攔下來嗎？）Ever get stopped for a traffic violation?（曾經因爲違反交通規則被攔下來嗎？）（= *Ever had a traffic violation?*）
   【violation〔ˌvaɪəˈleʃən〕*n.* 違反；違反行爲】

5. ***I use my bike a lot.***（我常使用我的腳踏車。）
   = I often use my bike.
   = I often ride my bike.
   = I frequently ride my bike.
   = I'm on my bike a lot.

7. ***I'll check for nearby Uber drivers.***
   （我會看看附近有沒有優步司機。）

   = I'll see if any Uber drivers are nearby.
   = I'll look and see if any Uber drivers are available.
   【available〔əˈveləbl̩〕*adj.* 可獲得的；有空的】

8. ***Can you flag down a taxi?***
（你能揮手攔下計程車嗎？）
= Can you hail a taxi for me?
= Can you get me a taxi?
= Please wave down a cab for me.

hail a taxi

【hail〔hel〕*v.* 呼叫　***wave down*** 招手使…停下來
cab〔kæb〕*n.* 計程車（= *taxi*）】

9. ***What's the fare for the metro?***（地鐵的車資是多少？）
= How much does it cost to ride the metro?
= What is the metro fee?
= What is the typical fare for a metro ride?

【fee〔fi〕*n.* 費用　typical〔'tɪpɪkḷ〕*adj.* 通常的　ride〔raɪd〕*n.* 搭乘】

Oral Test 64

2. ***I adore my friends.***（我非常喜愛我的朋友。）
可說成：I love being with friends.（我喜愛和朋友在一起。）
I cherish my close friends.（我很珍惜我親密的朋友。）

4. ***To score high on my tests.***（我考試要得高分。）可說成：To receive excellent grades is my goal.（得高分是我的目標。）
To be the best student I can be.（我要儘量做一個好學生。）

8. ***What are your strengths?***（你的優點是什麼？）
= What are your strong points?
= What are your best qualities?
= What are your top attributes?

【***strong point*** 優點　quality〔'kwɑlətɪ〕*n.* 特質
top〔tɑp〕*adj.* 最優良的　attribute〔'ætrə,bjut〕*n.* 特性；特質】

Advanced

Oral Test 65

【問與答一起背】

□ 1. ***Where do you want to improve?***	你要改善哪一點？
I want to improve my English.	我想要改善我的英文。
I think it will be important in the future.	我認爲英文在未來會很重要。
□ 2. ***What is one step you can take to improve?***	你能採取什麼步驟來改善？
I can take a class.	我可以上課。
I can also read English articles.	我也可以閱讀英文文章。
□ 3. ***What's the hardest thing you've ever done?***	你曾經做過最困難的事是什麼？
My first job was a big challenge.	我第一份工作是個很大的挑戰。
I had to learn fast on the job.	我工作時必須很快地學習。

** ___________________________

where (hwɛr) *adv.* 哪裡；哪一點　　improve (ɪm'pruv) *v.* 改善
future ('fjutʃɚ) *n.* 未來　　step (stɛp) *n.* 步驟
take (tek) *v.* 採取；上（課）　　***take a class*** 上課
article ('ɑrtɪkl̩) *n.* 文章　　hard (hɑrd) *adj.* 困難的
challenge ('tʃælɪndʒ) *n.* 挑戰　　***on the job*** （忙碌地）工作中

□ 4. ***What's your greatest accomplishment?***	你最大的成就是什麼？
Finishing school with honors.	以優異的成績畢業。
I had to work hard to earn it.	我必須很努力才能獲得。
□ 5. ***What's your most recent accomplishment?***	你最近的成就是什麼？
I finished a project at work.	我在工作上完成一項計劃。
I got a bonus for that.	我因爲那樣得到了獎金。
□ 6. ***What's on your bucket list?***	在你的遺願清單上有什麼？
I want to travel to all seven continents.	我想到所有的七大洲旅行。
Going skydiving is on the list, too.	去高空跳傘也在我的清單上。

** ___

accomplishment (əˈkɑmplɪʃmənt) *n.* 成就
finish school 完成學業；畢業　　honors (ˈɑnəz) *n. pl.* 優異成績
earn (ɝn) *v.* 贏得；獲得　　recent (ˈrisn̩t) *adj.* 最近的
project (ˈprɑdʒɛkt) *n.* 計劃　　bonus (ˈbonəs) *n.* 獎金
bucket (ˈbʌkɪt) *n.* 水桶【***kick the bucket*** 死亡】
bucket list 遺願清單；人生目標清單【一個人在有生之年想要做的事情和想要取得的成就的清單】
continent (ˈkɑntənənt) *n.* 洲
skydive (ˈskaɪˌdaɪv) *v.* 高空跳傘

skydiving

□ 7. ***Where do you want to be in 5 years?***	你希望五年後是什麼情況？
I want to be a team leader.	我想要當一個團隊的領導者。
It's a stepping stone to upper management.	這是邁向高階主管的墊腳石。
□ 8. ***What is the biggest obstacle in your way?***	什麼是妨礙你的最大阻礙？
I have many competitors.	我有很多競爭者。
I have to show why I'm better.	我必須展現爲什麼我比較好。
□ 9. ***What roadblocks are keeping you from success?***	阻止你成功的障礙是什麼？
I just need more time.	我只是需要更多的時間。
I need more work experience.	我需要更多的工作經驗。

** ______________________________

where〔hwɛr〕*adv.* 在什麼情形　　in〔ɪn〕*prep.* 再過
team〔tim〕*n.* 團隊　　leader〔'lidɚ〕*n.* 領導者
stepping stone 跳板；墊腳石
upper〔'ʌpɚ〕*adj.*（地位、等級）較高的；上層的
management〔'mænɪdʒmənt〕*n.* 管理；管理部門
obstacle〔'ɑbstəkḷ〕*n.* 阻礙　　***in one's way*** 妨礙某人
competitor〔kəm'pɛtɪtɚ〕*n.* 競爭者　　show〔ʃo〕*v.* 展現
roadblock〔'rod,blɑk〕*n.* 路障；障礙
keep** sb. **from V-ing 使某人無法…　　success〔sək'sɛs〕*n.* 成功

stepping stone

【背景說明】

Oral Test 65

3. *I had to learn fast on the job.*（我工作時必須很快地學習。）
   = I had to learn fast while I was working.
   = I was required to learn quickly at work.
   = I could not learn slowly.
   = There was no time for training.【require（rɪ'kwaɪr）v. 要求】

4. *Finishing school with honors.*（以優異的成績畢業。）
   在美國，以優異成績畢業，就會發一張獎狀，寫 Honorary Graduate（榮譽畢業生）。

6. *What's on your bucket list?*（在你的遺願清單上有什麼？）
   = What are the things you want to achieve before you die?
   = What are the goals you want to achieve in life?

7. *Where do you want to be in 5 years?*（你希望五年後是什麼情況？）
   = What's your five-year goal?
   = Where do you hope to be in five years?
   = In five years, what do you want to be doing?
   It's a stepping stone to upper management.
   （這是邁向高階主管的墊腳石。）
   = It's a method to get ahead.
   = It's an opportunity to get promoted.【promote（prə'mot）v. 使升遷】
   = It's a way to improve.

9. *What roadblocks are keeping you from success?*
   （阻止你成功的障礙是什麼？）
   = What obstacles are blocking you from success?
   = What's stopping you from succeeding?
   【block（blɑk）v. 阻礙　***stop sb. from*** 使某人無法…】

Advanced

Oral Test 66

【問與答一起背】

□ 1. ***What are your plans for retirement?***	你有什麼退休的計劃？
That's too far away.	那還太遙遠。
I haven't thought about it.	我還沒想過。
□ 2. ***What are your plans for college?***	你大學有什麼計劃？
I plan to major in English.	我打算主修英文。
I plan to live on campus.	我打算住在校園裡。
□ 3. ***What are your plans for dinner?***	你晚餐有什麼計劃？
I'm getting fried rice.	我要買炒飯。
I'm going to have a simple meal.	我要吃簡餐。

fried rice

** ―――――――――――――

retirement〔rɪ'taɪrmәmt〕*n.* 退休　***far away*** 遙遠的
think about 考慮　college〔'kɑlɪdʒ〕*n.* 大學
major〔'medʒɚ〕*v.* 主修 < *in* >　campus〔'kæmpәs〕*n.* 校園
get〔gɛt〕*v.* 買　***fried rice*** 炒飯　have〔hæv〕*v.* 吃
simple〔'sɪmpḷ〕*adj.* 簡單的　meal〔mil〕*n.* 一餐

☐ 4. ***What are your plans for summer vacation?***	你暑假有什麼計劃？
I'll study at a cram school.	我會在補習班讀書。
I might get a part-time job.	我可能會打工。
☐ 5. ***Do you have any plans for the 3-day holiday weekend?***	週末三連休你有什麼計劃？
I'm going to catch up on my sleep.	我要補眠。
I'll definitely go shopping or see a movie.	我一定會去購物或看電影。
☐ 6. ***Do you have a graduation trip planned?***	你們有打算去畢業旅行嗎？
Yes, my class is going to Kenting.	是的，我們班要去墾丁。
I'm sure we'll have a great time.	我確信我們會玩得很愉快。

** ———————————

cram〔 kræm 〕*n.* 塡鴨式的用功 ***cram school*** 補習班
part-time〔'pɑrt'taɪm〕*adj.* 兼差的
3-day holiday weekend 週末三連休（= *3-day weekend*）
catch up on 彌補 ***catch up on** one's **sleep*** 補眠
definitely〔'dɛfənɪtlɪ〕*adv.* 一定 graduation〔ˌgrædʒʊ'eʃən〕*n.* 畢業
Kenting〔'kɛn'tɪŋ〕*n.* 墾丁 ***have a great time*** 玩得很愉快

□ 7. ***Did you plan out your European trip yet?***	你的歐洲之旅已經規劃了嗎？
No, not yet.	不，還沒。
I haven't decided what cities to see yet.	我還沒決定要遊覽什麼城市。
□ 8. ***Did you write a business plan for your idea?***	你的點子有寫成商業計劃嗎？
In fact, I did.	事實上，我寫了。
I have a detailed plan here.	我這裡有個詳細的計劃。
□ 9. ***Did you plan for rain, just in case?***	你有擬定萬一下雨的計劃嗎？
No, I didn't.	不，我沒有。
Thanks for reminding me.	謝謝你提醒我。

** ______________________

plan out 規劃　European〔ˌjurəˈpiən〕*adj.* 歐洲的
yet〔jɛt〕*adv.* 已經　***not yet*** 尚未；還沒
decide〔dɪˈsaɪd〕*v.* 決定　see〔si〕*v.* 遊覽；參觀
idea〔aɪˈdiə〕*n.* 想法；點子　***in fact*** 事實上
detailed〔ˈditeld〕*adj.* 詳細的　***plan for*** 擬定…的計劃
in case 以防萬一　remind〔rɪˈmaɪnd〕*v.* 提醒

Oral Test 67

【問與答一起背】

□ **1.** ***Have you ever tried a diet?***	你曾經嘗試節食嗎？
I tried once.	我試過一次。
I had to lose about 5 kilos.	我必須減大約五公斤。
□ **2.** ***Did the diet work?***	節食有效嗎？
It helped.	有幫助。
But exercise helped more.	但運動的幫助更大。
□ **3.** ***Do you ever skip meals?***	你曾經不吃飯嗎？
Never.	從來不曾。
Regular meals are important.	定時吃三餐很重要。

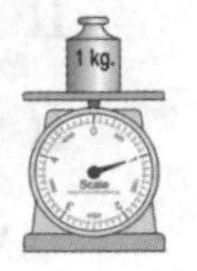

kilo

** ——————————

diet (ˈdaɪət) *n.* 節食　　once (wʌns) *adv.* 一次
lose (luz) *v.* 減輕
kilo (ˈkɪlo) *n.* 公斤（= *kilogram*）
work (wɝk) *v.* 有效
skip (skɪp) *v.* 略過；跳過；不做；不吃
regular (ˈrɛgjələ) *adj.* 規律的；定期的
meal (mil) *n.* 一餐

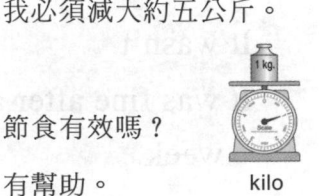

diet

□ 4. ***Have you ever gotten hurt?***	你曾經受過傷嗎？
I once hurt my wrist.	我曾經弄傷我的手腕。
I sprained it playing volleyball.	我打排球時扭傷的。
□ 5. ***Was it serious?***	嚴重嗎？
It wasn't.	不嚴重。
It was fine after about a week.	大約一個禮拜後就好了。
□ 6. ***Have you ever broken anything?***	你曾經有任何部位骨折嗎？
I broke my little toe once.	我曾經小腳趾骨折。
But that wasn't too serious.	但並不是太嚴重。

** ―――――――――――

hurt (hɝt) *v.* 傷害　　once (wʌns) *adv.* 曾經；有一次
wrist (rɪst) *n.* 手腕　　sprain (spren) *v.* 扭傷
volleyball ('vɑlɪ,bɔl) *n.* 排球
serious ('sɪrɪəs) *adj.* 嚴重的
fine (faɪn) *adj.* 好的　　break (brek) *v.* 使骨折
toe (to) *n.* 腳趾

sprain

☐ 7. ***Are you allergic to anything?***	你對任何東西過敏嗎？
I'm allergic to some nuts.	我對一些堅果過敏。
I have to be careful when I eat out.	當我出去吃的時候，我必須小心。
☐ 8. ***Have you ever tried acupuncture?***	你曾經試過針灸嗎？
I tried it once.	我試過一次。
It helped my sore knee.	它對我疼痛的膝蓋有幫助。
☐ 9. ***Have you ever had to stay in a hospital?***	你曾經必須住院嗎？
No, I've never stayed overnight.	不，我從未在醫院過夜。
I've never been there for more than an hour.	我去醫院從未超過一小時。

**

allergic (ə'lɝdʒɪk) *adj.* 過敏的 < *to* >
nut (nʌt) *n.* 堅果 ***eat out*** 去外面吃
acupuncture ('ækju,pʌŋktʃɚ) *n.* 針灸
sore (sor) *adj.* 疼痛的 knee (ni) *n.* 膝蓋
stay (ste) *v.* 暫住 overnight ('ovɚ'naɪt) *adv.* 一整夜地
stay overnight 過夜；住一晚

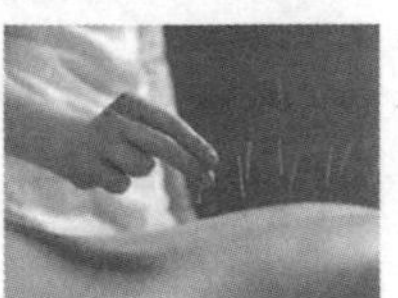
acupuncture

【背景說明】

Oral Test 66

7. ***Did you plan out your European trip yet?***（你的歐洲之旅已經規劃了嗎？）***plan out***（規劃）是 plan 的加強語氣。可說成：Have you decided the itinerary for your European trip?（你的歐洲之旅的行程決定了嗎？）【itinerary〔aɪ'tɪnə,rɛrɪ〕*n.* 旅行日程表】Did you plan out a schedule for your trip yet?（你已經規劃好你的旅遊時間表了嗎？）***I haven't decided what cities to see yet.***（我還沒決定要遊覽什麼城市。）(= *I'm still undecided about which cities to visit.*) 可簡單地說：I still haven't made up my mind.（我還沒決定。）【***make up*** *one's* ***mind*** 下定決心；決定】

9. ***Did you plan for rain, just in case?***（你擬定萬一下雨的計劃嗎？）
= Are you prepared for rain, if it happens?
= Are you ready for rain, if it does?
= If it rains, are you ready?

Oral Test 67

3. ***Do you ever skip meals?***（你曾經不吃飯嗎？）
= Do you ever fail to eat a meal?【***fail to V.*** 未能⋯】
= Do you ever just not eat a meal?

4. ***I sprained it playing volleyball.***（我打排球時扭傷的。）
= I injured it playing volleyball.【injure〔'ɪndʒɚ〕*v.* 使受傷】
= I hurt it in a volleyball game.

6. ***Have you ever broken anything?***（你曾經有任何部位骨折嗎？）
= Have you ever broken a bone?【bone〔bon〕*n.* 骨頭】
= Did you ever break anything on your body?
萬一骨折，第一步是冰敷二十四小時，當消腫後，就要開始熱敷。

Oral Test 68

【問與答一起背】

□ 1. ***What's the most exciting thing you've ever done?***	你曾經做過最刺激的事是什麼？
I flew to Paris, France.	我搭飛機去法國巴黎。
I toured France for 10 days.	我到法國旅行十天。
□ 2. ***Have you ever gotten into trouble?***	你曾經惹上麻煩嗎？
No, not in school.	不，在學校沒有。
But I've been in trouble at home, of course.	但我在家當然有惹過麻煩。
□ 3. ***Have you ever experienced culture shock?***	你曾經經歷過文化衝擊嗎？
Yes, when I went to Europe.	是的，當我去歐洲時。
It was very different.	那眞的非常不同。

**

exciting (ɪk'saɪtɪŋ) *adj.* 刺激的；令人興奮的
ever ('ɛvɚ) *adv.* 曾經　fly (flaɪ) *v.* 搭飛機
Paris ('pærɪs) *n.* 巴黎　France (fræns) *n.* 法國
tour (tʊr) *v.* 到…旅行　***get into trouble*** 惹上麻煩
experience (ɪk'spɪrɪəns) *v.* 經歷　culture ('kʌltʃɚ) *n.* 文化
shock (ʃɑk) *n.* 衝擊　Europe ('jʊrəp) *n.* 歐洲

Paris

□ 4. ***Have you ever won a competition?***	你曾經贏得比賽嗎？
Yes, I entered an art competition.	是的，我參加過美術比賽。
My painting won first place.	我的畫贏得第一名。
□ 5. ***Have you ever read a book or seen a movie that changed your life?***	你曾經讀過或看過改變你一生的一本書或一部電影嗎？
Believe it or not, yes.	信不信由你，有。
The book *The Alchemist* changed my thinking.	《牧羊少年奇幻之旅》這本書改變了我的想法。
□ 6. ***Have you ever been to a theme park?***	你曾經去過主題樂園嗎？
I went to Disneyland in Hong Kong.	我去過香港的迪士尼樂園。
It was so much fun!	非常好玩！

** ─────────────

competition〔ˌkɑmpəˈtɪʃən〕*n.* 競爭；比賽　enter〔ˈɛntɚ〕*v.* 參加
art〔ɑrt〕*n.* 藝術；美術　painting〔ˈpentɪŋ〕*n.* 畫
first place 第一名　change〔tʃendʒ〕*v.* 改變
believe it or not 信不信由你　alchemist〔ˈælkəmɪst〕*n.* 煉金術士
The Alchemist 牧羊少年奇幻之旅【書名】
thinking〔ˈθɪŋkɪŋ〕*n.* 想法　theme〔θim〕*n.* 主題
theme park 主題樂園　Disneyland〔ˈdɪznɪˌlænd〕*n.* 迪士尼樂園
Hong Kong〔ˈhɑŋ ˈkɑŋ〕*n.* 香港　fun〔fʌn〕*n.* 樂趣

□ 7. ***Have you ever been in an accident?***	你曾經發生過車禍嗎？
Yes, a minor one.	是的，小車禍。
Once, another car hit our car.	有一次，別的車撞到我們的車。
□ 8. ***Have you ever given to charity?***	你曾經捐獻給慈善機構嗎？
I've donated money to some charities.	我有捐錢給一些慈善機構。
I also donate my old clothes every year.	我每年也會捐出我的舊衣服。
□ 9. ***Have you ever volunteered for charity?***	你曾經當過慈善機構的義工嗎？
I volunteer at the Animal Shelter.	我在動物收容所當義工。
Working there makes me feel good.	在那裡工作我覺得很好。

**

accident〔ˈæksədənt〕*n.* 意外；車禍
minor〔ˈmaɪnɚ〕*adj.* 較小的；較不重要的
once〔wʌns〕*adv.* 有一次　　hit〔hɪt〕*v.* 撞
charity〔ˈtʃærətɪ〕*n.* 慈善機構；慈善
donate〔ˈdonet〕*v.* 捐贈　　volunteer〔ˌvɑlənˈtɪr〕*v.* 當義工
shelter〔ˈʃɛltɚ〕*n.* 避難所　　***Animal Shelter*** 動物收容所

【背景說明】

Oral Test 68

1. ***I toured France for 10 days.***（我到法國旅行十天。）
   = I traveled around France for ten days.
   = I went all over France for ten days.

6. ***It was so much fun!***（非常好玩！）
   = It was a ball!
   = It was a blast!
   = It was so enjoyable!
   = It was a riot!
   = I had a ball!
   = I had a great time!

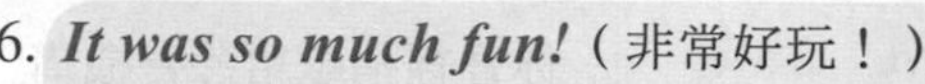

It was so much fun!

【ball〔bɔl〕*n.* 極美好的時光
blast〔blæst〕*n.* 熱鬧的一刻；狂歡的聚會
riot〔ˈraɪət〕*n.* 暴動；狂歡；喧鬧　***have a ball*** 過得快樂無比；盡情作樂　***have a great time*** 玩得很愉快】

8. ***Have you ever given to charity?***（你曾經捐獻給慈善機構嗎？）
   = Ever give money to a charitable organization?
   【charitable〔ˈtʃærətəbl̩〕*adj.* 慈善的
   organization〔ˌɔrgənəˈzeʃən〕*n.* 組織；機構】

9. ***Have you ever volunteered for charity?***
   （你曾經當過慈善機構的義工嗎？）
   = Have you ever offered to help a charity group?
   = Have you ever helped a charity for free?
   = Ever offer to help a charity organization?
   （= *Did you ever offer…?*）
   【offer〔ˈɔfɚ〕*v.* 提議　***for free*** 免費地】

Oral Test 69

【問與答一起背】

□ 1. ***How do you deal with stress?***	你如何應付壓力？
I exercise.	我會運動。
I run or go for a walk.	我會跑步或去散步。
□ 2. ***What is the best advice you have ever received?***	你曾經獲得的最好的勸告是什麼？
It's always best to be honest.	誠實一定是最好的。
Never lie, cheat, or steal.	絕不說謊、欺騙，或偷竊。
□ 3. ***Are you married?***	你已經結婚了嗎？
No, I'm not married.	不，我還沒結婚。
I am still single.	我仍然單身。

**

deal with 應付；處理　stress (strɛs) *n.* 壓力
exercise ('ɛksə,saɪz) *v.* 運動　***go for a walk*** 去散步
advice (əd'vaɪs) *n.* 勸告；建議
ever ('ɛvə) *adv.* 曾經　receive (rɪ'siv) *v.* 得到
honest ('ɑnɪst) *adj.* 誠實的　lie (laɪ) *v.* 說謊
cheat (tʃit) *v.* 欺騙；作弊　steal (stil) *v.* 偷
married ('mærɪd) *adj.* 已婚的　single ('sɪŋgl̩) *adj.* 單身的

☐ 4. ***Are you single?***	你單身嗎？
I'm not married yet.	我還沒結婚。
But I'm in a relationship.	但我有交往的對象。
☐ 5. ***Do you have any children?***	你有小孩嗎？
No, I have no children.	不，我沒有小孩。
I haven't married yet.	我還沒有結婚。
☐ 6. ***What age do you want to get married?***	你想要幾歲結婚？
Around age thirty.	大約三十歲。
I want to establish my career first.	我想要先建立自己的事業。

** ______________________

not…yet 尚未；還沒

relationship (rɪ'leʃən,ʃɪp) *n.* 戀愛關係

be in a relationship 與人交往

get married 結婚　　around (ə'raʊnd) *adv.* 大約

establish (ə'stæblɪʃ) *v.* 建立

career (kə'rɪr) *n.* 事業

□ 7. ***What's your biggest fear?***	你最害怕什麼？
My biggest fear is getting sick.	我最怕生病。
Illness makes me feel helpless.	生病會使我覺得很無助。
□ 8. ***What are some good ways to make money?***	有什麼賺錢的好方法？
Find a job you love.	找個你喜愛的工作。
Work as hard as you can.	儘可能努力工作。
□ 9. ***What topics are taboo in your culture?***	在你們的文化中，什麼話題是禁忌？
Religion, politics, and salary, too.	宗教、政治，以及薪水。
These topics can offend people.	這些話題可能會冒犯人。

** ——————————

fear〔fɪr〕*n.* 恐懼　sick〔sɪk〕*adj.* 生病的
illness〔ˈɪlnɪs〕*n.* 疾病；生病　helpless〔ˈhɛlplɪs〕*adj.* 無助的
way〔we〕*n.* 方法　***make money*** 賺錢
as…as one can 儘可能…　topic〔ˈtɑpɪk〕*n.* 主題；話題
taboo〔təˈbu〕*n.* 禁忌　culture〔ˈkʌltʃɚ〕*n.* 文化
religion〔rɪˈlɪdʒən〕*n.* 宗教　politics〔ˈpɑlə,tɪks〕*n.* 政治
salary〔ˈsælərɪ〕*n.* 薪水　offend〔əˈfɛnd〕*v.* 冒犯

【背景說明】

Oral Test 69

4. ***I'm in a relationship***. (我有交往的對象。)

= I'm seeing someone now.
= I'm going steady with someone now.
= I have a special friend now.
= I'm dating someone now.

【see (si) *v.* 與…結交；和…約會　steady (ˈstɛdɪ) *adj.* 穩定的
go steady with 與…固定交往　date (det) *v.* 和…約會】

6. ***Around age thirty***. (大約三十歲。)

= Around the age of thirty.

9. ***What topics are taboo in your culture?***

(在你們的文化中，什麼話題是禁忌？)

= What conversation topics are not welcome in your country?
= What issues are not acceptable to discuss?
= What things are forbidden to talk about?
= What is a topic people consider rude to discuss?

【issue (ˈɪʃjʊ) *n.* 議題　acceptable (əkˈsɛptəbḷ) *adj.* 可接受的
forbid (fɔrˈbɪd) *v.* 禁止　consider (kənˈsɪdɚ) *v.* 認爲
rude (rud) *adj.* 無禮的】

Advanced

Oral Test 70

【問與答一起背】

□ **1.** ***What's the emergency number in your country?***

在你的國家，緊急電話是幾號？

It's 1-1-9.

是 119。

In the US, it's 9-1-1.

在美國，是 911。

□ **2.** ***Who do you call in an emergency?***

在緊急情況你會打給誰？

I call 1-1-9.

我會打 119。

That's the number for all emergency services.

那是所有緊急服務的電話。

□ **3.** ***When should you call an ambulance?***

你何時應該叫救護車？

In an emergency situation.

在緊急情況時。

Call if someone is unresponsive.

如果有人叫不醒，就要叫救護車。

** ——————————————

emergency (ɪ'mɝdʒənsɪ) *adj.* 緊急的 *n.* 緊急情況

number ('nʌmbɚ) *n.* 號碼；電話號碼

service ('sɝvɪs) *n.* 服務

ambulance ('æmbjələns) *n.* 救護車

situation (ˌsɪtʃʊ'eʃən) *n.* 情況

unresponsive (ˌʌnrɪ'spɑnsɪv) *adj.* 無回應的；沒有知覺的

□ 4. ***How do you call the police?***	你會如何報警？
Dial 110.	撥打 110。
But you can also call 119.	但也可以打 119。
□ 5. ***Who do you call for help?***	你會打電話向誰求救？
I call the emergency hotline—119.	我會打緊急熱線——119。
I call my family if I can.	如果可以，我會打給我的家人。
□ 6. ***Who's your emergency contact?***	誰是你的緊急連絡人？
My mother.	我媽媽。
She's the one to call if I need help.	如果我需要協助，就打給她。

** ———

police〔pə'lis〕*n.* 警察；警方　　dial〔'daɪəl〕*v.* 撥（號）
hotline〔'hɑt,laɪn〕*n.* 熱線
family〔'fæməlɪ〕*n.* 家人
contact〔'kɑntækt〕*n.* 連絡；連絡人
emergency contact 緊急連絡人

□ 7. ***Do you know first aid?***	你會急救嗎？
I know first aid.	我會急救。
I took a course last year.	我去年有上課。
□ 8. ***Are you first aid certified?***	你有急救證照嗎？
Yes, I'm certified.	是的，我有證照。
I'm trained in first aid.	我受過急救訓練。
□ 9. ***Where can I take a first aid course?***	我可以去哪裡上急救課？
You can find a course online.	你可以在網路上找到課程。
Many community centers offer classes.	很多社區中心有提供課程。

** ——————————

aid〔ed〕*n.* 幫助；救援　***first aid*** 急救

take〔tek〕*v.* 上（課）　course〔kors〕*n.* 課程

certified〔ˈsɝtəˌfaɪd〕*adj.* 有執照的　train〔tren〕*v.* 訓練

online〔ˈɑnˌlaɪn〕*adv.* 在線上；在網路上

community〔kəˈmjunətɪ〕*n.* 社區

center〔ˈsɛntɚ〕*n.* 中心　offer〔ˈɔfɚ〕*v.* 提供

Advanced

【背景說明】

Oral Test 70

3. ***Call if someone is unresponsive.***
   （如果有人叫不醒，就要叫救護車。）
   = Call if the victim is unconscious.
   = Call if the victim won't wake up.
   【victim〔ˈvɪktɪm〕*n.* 受害者；患者
   unconscious〔ʌnˈkɑnʃəs〕*adj.* 無意識的　***wake up*** 醒來】

ambulance

4. ***You can also call 119.***（你也可以打 119。）
   = You can also dial 119.
   = You can also contact 119.【contact〔ˈkɑntækt〕*v.* 連絡】

6. ***Who's your emergency contact?***（誰是你的緊急連絡人？）
   = Who is your contact person in an emergency situation?
   = Who should we call first if you have an emergency?

7. ***Do you know first aid?***（你會急救嗎？）
   = Do you know how to give medical care?
   = Are you trained in giving medical aid?
   = Have you taken a first aid class?
   【medical〔ˈmɛdɪkḷ〕*adj.* 醫學的；醫療的　care〔kɛr〕*n.* 照顧
   medical care 醫療　aid〔ed〕*n.* 幫助】

8. ***Are you first aid certified?***（你有急救證照嗎？）
   = Do you have a first aid license?
   = Have you passed a first aid test?
   【license〔ˈlaɪsṇs〕*n.* 執照　pass〔pæst〕*v.* 通過】

Oral Test 71

【問與答一起背】

□ 1. ***Do you know CPR?***	你會 CPR 嗎？
I don't know CPR.	我不會 CPR。
I can't perform CPR.	我不會做 CPR。
□ 2. ***Can you treat an injury?***	你會治療傷口嗎？
I can treat minor injuries.	我會治療輕微的傷口。
I can disinfect a wound.	我會消毒傷口。
□ 3. ***Do you own a first aid kit?***	你有急救箱嗎？
I keep two.	我有兩個。
One in my home, one in my car.	一個在我家，一個在我的車上。

**

CPR 心肺復甦術（= *cardiopulmonary resuscitation*）

【是一種救助心搏驟停病患的急救措施，通過人工保持腦功能直到自然呼吸和血液循環恢復】

perform〔pə'fɔrm〕*v.* 執行；做

treat〔trit〕*v.* 治療　　injury〔'ɪndʒərɪ〕*n.* 傷

disinfect〔,dɪsɪn'fɛkt〕*v.* 將…消毒　　wound〔wund〕*n.* 傷口

own〔on〕*v.* 擁有　　kit〔kɪt〕*n.* 成套工具；工具箱

first aid kit 急救箱　　keep〔kip〕*v.* 保有

□ 4. ***Where's the closest defibrillator?***	最近的電擊器在哪裡？
It's in the hallway.	在走廊。
There is one downstairs.	有一個在樓下。
□ 5. ***Where's the closest fire extinguisher?***	最近的滅火器在哪裡？
I'm not sure.	我不確定。
Let me go check.	讓我去看一下。
□ 6. ***Have you ever had to call 1-1-9?***	你曾經必須打 119 嗎？
Thankfully, no, never.	不，幸好從來不曾有過。
I hope I never have to.	我希望我絕不會需要。

** ______________________

close〔klos〕*adj.* 接近的
defibrillator〔dɪ'fɪbrɪ,letɚ〕*n.* 電擊器
hallway〔'hɔl,we〕*n.* 走廊
downstairs〔'daʊn'stɛrz〕*adv.* 在樓下
extinguisher〔ɪk'stɪŋgwɪʃɚ〕*n.* 滅火器
fire extinguisher 滅火器
check〔tʃɛk〕*v.* 查看　ever〔'ɛvɚ〕*adv.* 曾經
thankfully〔'θæŋkfəlɪ〕*adv.* 幸好

defibrillator

extinguisher

☐ 7. ***Does your home have a smoke detector?***	你們家有煙霧偵測器嗎？
Of course we do.	當然，我們有。
My house has several smoke detectors.	我的家有好幾個煙霧偵測器。
☐ 8. ***Does your home have a sprinkler system?***	你們家有灑水系統嗎？
No, it doesn't.	不，沒有。
We need to install one.	我們需要安裝一台。
☐ 9. ***Do you have a home security system?***	你們有家庭保全系統嗎？
Yes, we bought home security.	是的，我們有買家庭保全系統。
We have cameras inside and outside.	我們室內和室外都有攝影機。

** ———————

smoke〔smok〕*n.* 煙　detector〔dɪ'tɛktɚ〕*n.* 偵測器
of course 當然　sprinkler〔'sprɪŋklɚ〕*n.* 灑水器
system〔'sɪstəm〕*n.* 系統　install〔ɪn'stɔl〕*v.* 安裝
security〔sɪ'kjurətɪ〕*adj.* 安全的；安全保障的
home security system 家庭保全系統
camera〔'kæmərə〕*n.* 攝影機
inside〔'ɪn'saɪd〕*adv.* 在屋內　outside〔'aut'saɪd〕*adv.* 在外面

smoke detector

【背景說明】

Oral Test 71

1. ***Do you know CPR?***（你會 CPR 嗎？）

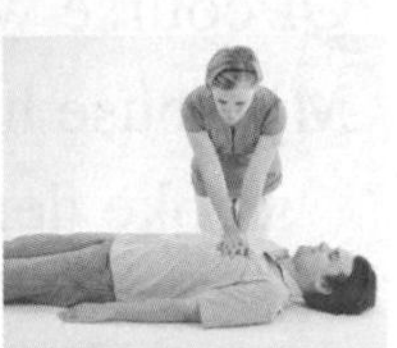

CPR

= Do you know how to give CPR?
= Are you trained in CPR?
= Are you able to administer CPR?
= Can you perform CPR?
【***be able to V.*** 能夠⋯　administer〔əd'mɪnɪstɚ〕*v.* 施行】

2. ***I can disinfect a wound.***（我會消毒傷口。）

= I'm able to clean a wound.
= I can clean and apply medicine to a wound.
【clean〔klin〕*v.* 消毒；洗淨；治療（傷口）　apply〔ə'plaɪ〕*v.* 塗；抹】

5. ***Let me go check.***（讓我去看一下。）

= Let me go look and see.【***look and see*** 看一下】
= Let me go look around.【***look around*** 到處看看】
= Let me go find out.【***find out*** 查明眞相】
在口語中，go 後面的 to 或 and 常省略。

9. ***We bought home security.***（我們有買家庭保全系統。）

= We have home security.
= We purchased home security cameras.
= We bought security video monitors.

security video monitor

【purchase〔'pɝtʃəs〕*v.* 購買（= *buy*）
video〔'vɪdɪ,o〕*adj.* 錄影的；電視影像的
monitor〔'mɑnətɚ〕*n.* 顯示器　***video monitor*** 監視器】

Oral Test 72

【問與答一起背】

□ 1. ***Who are you living with?***	你和誰一起住？
I live by myself.	我自己住。
I have my own place.	我有自己的住處。
□ 2. ***When did you move out?***	你何時搬出去的？
I just moved out.	我剛搬出去。
I moved out of my parents' home last week.	我上星期搬出我父母的家。
□ 3. ***When did you move in?***	你何時搬進來的？
I moved in six days ago.	我六天前搬進來。
I'm still getting settled.	我還沒有安定下來。

** ———

***by** oneself* 獨自
place〔 ples 〕*n.* 地方；住處
move〔 muv 〕*v.* 搬家
move out 搬出去　　just〔 dʒʌst 〕*adv.* 剛剛
move in 搬進來
settle〔ˈsɛtl̩〕*v.* 定居；安頓下來；適應；習慣

□ **4.** ***How did you find the place?***	你是如何找到住的地方？
I found it online.	我在網路上找的。
There were many places to choose from.	有很多地方可以選。
□ **5.** ***How do you like it so far?***	到目前為止你還喜歡嗎？
I love it so far.	到目前為止我很喜愛。
It's just right for me.	它很適合我。
□ **6.** ***How many rooms are there?***	有多少個房間？
There are four rooms.	有四個房間。
Two bedrooms, a living room, and a kitchen.	兩間臥室、一間客廳，還有廚房。

**

online〔ˈɑnˌlaɪn〕*adv.* 在線上；在網路上
choose〔tʃuz〕*v.* 選擇　***choose from*** 從中選擇
so far 到目前為止　***just right*** 正好；正合適
bedroom〔ˈbɛdˌrum〕*n.* 臥室
living room 客廳
kitchen〔ˈkɪtʃɪn〕*n.* 廚房

living room

☐ 7. ***Have you finished unpacking?***	你已經都把包裹打開了嗎？
I'm not finished yet.	我還沒完成。
I'm still unpacking.	我還在打開包裹。
☐ 8. ***Is living alone lonely?***	自己住會寂寞嗎？
It's not easy.	這並不容易。
It takes time to get used to it.	這需要時間適應。
☐ 9. ***Do you want a roommate?***	你想要一位室友嗎？
Yes, I'm looking for one.	是的，我正在找一位室友。
I hope I can find a responsible person.	我希望我能找到一個負責任的人。

** ________________

unpack

finish〔ˈfɪnɪʃ〕*v.* 完成；做完

unpack〔ʌnˈpæk〕*v.* 打開包裹

not…yet 尚未；還沒

alone〔əˈlon〕*adv.* 獨自　　lonely〔ˈlonlɪ〕*adj.* 寂寞的

take〔tek〕*v.* 需要　　***get used to*** 漸漸習慣於；適應

roommate〔ˈrumˌmet〕*n.* 室友　　***look for*** 尋找

responsible〔rɪˈspɑnsəbḷ〕*adj.* 負責任的

Advanced

Oral Test 73

【問與答一起背】

□ 1. ***Did you buy or are you renting?***	你是買的還是租的？
I'm renting it.	我是租的。
The rent is reasonable.	房租很合理。
□ 2. ***Do you pay rent?***	你有付房租嗎？
Yes, I do.	是的，我有。
I pay every month.	我每個月付房租。
□ 3. ***Did you put down a deposit?***	你有付押金嗎？
Yes, I did.	是的，我有。
Two months' rent.	兩個月的房租。

** ——————————

rent〔rɛnt〕*v.* 租　*n.* 房租；租金
reasonable〔ˈriznəbl̩〕*adj.* 合理的
pay〔pe〕*v.* 付　***put down*** 付（定金）
deposit〔dɪˈpɑzɪt〕*n.* 押金；定金

□ 4. ***What floor do you live on?***	你住幾樓？
The third floor.	三樓。
But there is an elevator.	不過有電梯。
□ 5. ***Is your building old or new?***	你們的大樓是舊的還是新的？
It's kind of old.	有點舊。
It's about 20 years old.	大約二十年了。
□ 6. ***How far is your home from your work?***	你的家離你工作的地點多遠？
It's very close.	非常近。
It's only fifteen minutes away.	只有十五分鐘的距離。

** ———

floor〔flor〕*n.* 樓層

elevator〔ˈɛlə,vetɚ〕*n.* 電梯；升降梯

building〔ˈbɪldɪŋ〕*n.* 建築物；大樓

kind of 有點（= *a little*）　　work〔wɝk〕*n.* 工作地點

close〔klos〕*adj.* 接近的

away〔əˈwe〕*adv.* 離…有一定距離；離…有一定時間

□ 7. ***Do you like your landlord or landlady?***	你喜歡你的房東或女房東嗎？
Yes, I like my landlady.	是的，我喜歡我的女房東。
Mrs. Ping is sweet.	平太太很親切。
□ 8. ***How is security?***	安全性如何？
It's pretty good.	非常好。
We have a doorman.	我們有管理員。
□ 9. ***How's the neighborhood?***	鄰近地區如何？
It's pretty quiet.	非常安靜。
It's pretty safe.	非常安全。

** ________________________

landlord〔ˈlænd,lɔrd〕*n.* 房東
landlady〔ˈlænd,ledɪ〕*n.* 女房東
sweet〔swit〕*adj.* 親切的；和藹的
security〔sɪˈkjurətɪ〕*n.* 安全
pretty〔ˈprɪtɪ〕*adv.* 相當；非常
doorman〔ˈdor,mæn〕*n.*（旅館、公寓大樓的）大門警衛
neighborhood〔ˈnebə,hud〕*n.* 鄰近地區
quiet〔ˈkwaɪət〕*adj.* 安靜的　safe〔sef〕*adj.* 安全的

doorman

Advanced

Oral Test 74

【問與答一起背】

□ 1. ***Have you ever moved?***	你曾經搬過家嗎？
Yes, once.	是的，搬過一次。
My family moved ten years ago.	我們家十年前搬過。
□ 2. ***Where did you move from?***	你們是從哪裡搬來的？
We moved from New York.	我們是從紐約搬來的。
It was hard to leave.	要離開很困難。
□ 3. ***Where did you move to?***	你們搬去哪裡？
We moved to California.	我們搬到加州。
It was a big change.	那是很大的改變。

** ──────────

ever〔ˈɛvɚ〕*adv.* 曾經　　move〔muv〕*v.* 搬家

once〔wʌns〕*adv.* 一次

New York〔nju ˈjɔrk〕*n.* 紐約

hard〔hɑrd〕*adj.* 困難的　　leave〔liv〕*v.* 離開

California〔ˌkæləˈfɔrnjə〕*n.* 加州

change〔tʃendʒ〕*n. v.* 改變

□ 4. ***Why did you move?***	你們爲什麼搬家？
Because of my father's work.	因爲我父親的工作。
We didn't have a choice.	我們沒有選擇。
□ 5. ***How old were you?***	你當時幾歲？
I was seven years old.	我當時七歲。
We adapted pretty quickly.	我們很快就適應了。
□ 6. ***Did you want to move?***	你想要搬家嗎？
I really didn't want to move.	我眞的不想搬家。
I didn't want to leave my friends.	我不想離開我的朋友。

** ___

because of 因爲
choice〔 tʃɔɪs 〕*n.* 選擇
adapt〔 ə'dæpt 〕*v.* 適應
pretty〔'prɪtɪ 〕*adv.* 相當；非常

choice

□ **7.** ***What was it like to change schools?***	轉學是什麼樣的情況？
It was hard at first.	起初很辛苦。
But soon I liked the new school.	不過我很快就喜歡新的學校。
□ **8.** ***Was it easy for you to adjust?***	你很容易就適應了嗎？
Not at first.	起初不是。
But then I got used to it.	不過後來我就習慣了。
□ **9.** ***Where do you live now?***	你現在住在哪裡？
Now I live in California.	現在我住在加州。
I still live in Los Angeles.	我仍然住在洛杉磯。

** ———————————

change schools 轉學（= *transfer schools*）

hard〔hɑrd〕*adj.* 困難的；辛苦的　　***at first*** 起初

adjust〔əˈdʒʌst〕*v.* 適應

get used to 逐漸習慣於

Los Angeles〔lɔs ˈændʒələs〕*n.* 洛杉磯

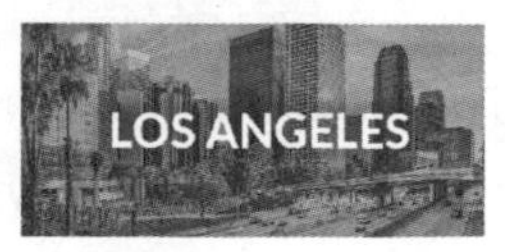

【背景說明】

Oral Test 72

3. ***I'm still getting settled***.（我還沒有安定下來。）
   = I'm still getting adjusted.
   = I'm still getting used to things.
   = I'm not settled yet.
   【adjust〔ə'dʒʌst〕*v.* 適應；使適應】

5. ***It's just right for me***.（它很適合我。）
   = It's perfect for me.
   = It's just what I like.
   = It's exactly what I hoped for.
   = It couldn't be better.（好極了。）
   【perfect〔'pɜfɪkt〕*adj.* 完美的　exactly〔ɪg'zætlɪ〕*adv.* 正是　***hope for*** 希望；期待】

8. ***It takes time to get used to it***.（這需要時間適應。）
   = It takes time to get used to.
   = It takes time to adjust.
   = It doesn't happen overnight.
   【overnight〔'ovə'naɪt〕*adv.* 一夜之間；突然】

Oral Test 73

1. ***Did you buy or are you renting?***（你是買的還是租的？）
   = Are you the owner or a tenant?
   = Are you renting it or do you own it?
   【owner〔'onə〕*n.* 擁有者　tenant〔'tɛnənt〕*n.* 房客】

3. ***Did you put down a deposit?***（你有付押金嗎？）
= Did you give a deposit?
= Did they require a deposit?
= Did you have to give a deposit?
【require〔rɪˈkwaɪr〕*v.* 要求】

5. It's ***kind of*** old.（有點舊。）
= It's ***sort of*** old.
= It's ***somewhat*** old.
= It's ***a little bit*** old.
= It seems old.
= It looks old.【***sort of*** 有點
somewhat〔ˈsʌm,hwɑt〕*adv.* 有點　***a little bit*** 有一點】

6. ***How far is your home from your work?***
（你的家離你工作的地點多遠？）
= How far is your place from your workplace?
= What's the distance from your home to your job?
= How long does it take from your place to work?
【place〔ples〕*n.* 住所　workplace〔ˈwɜk,ples〕*n.* 工作場所
distance〔ˈdɪstəns〕*n.* 距離】

這句話邏輯上不像中文，「你家」跟「工作」離多遠？所以，我們要背句子，才不會說出中式英文。

It's only fifteen minutes away.（只有十五分鐘的距離。）
= It only takes 15 minutes.
= It's just fifteen minutes to get there.
= It's just a quarter of an hour away.
【quarter〔ˈkwɔrtɚ〕*n.* 四分之一　***a quarter of an hour*** 十五分鐘】

美國人喜歡用 away，簡單又清楚，表示「從這裡」(from here)。

A: How far is it?（多遠？）

B: It's ten minutes ***away***.（離這裡十分鐘。）【時間】

It's one mile ***away***.（離這裡一英里。）【距離】

It's a short walk ***away***.（離這裡走路很近。）

It's three red lights ***away***.（離這裡三個紅綠燈。）

It's just 2 bus stops ***away***.（離這裡只有兩個公車站。）

【***red light*** 紅燈　***bus stop*** 公車站】

8. ***How is security?***（安全性如何？）

= How is the security?

= Is it secure?

= Is it safe?

= Does it seem safe?

= Do you feel it's safe?

= Is the security OK?【secure（sɪ'kjur）*adj.* 安全的】

Oral Test 74

5. ***We adapted pretty quickly***.（我們很快就適應了。）

= We adjusted fast.

= We got used to things very quickly.

7. ***What was it like to change schools?***（轉學是什麼樣的情況？）

= How was it to change schools?

= Was it easy or difficult to switch schools?

= Was it difficult changing schools?

= Was it hard to attend a new school?

【switch（swɪtʃ）*v.* 改變；調換　attend（ə'tɛnd）*v.* 上（學）】

Oral Test 75

【問與答一起背】

□ 1. ***Are you afraid of getting older?***	你害怕變老嗎？
Actually, no.	其實不會。
Growing older is part of life.	變老是人生的一部份。
□ 2. ***Where do you see yourself in 5 years?***	你預料自己五年後會是什麼情況？
I see myself happier.	我想我會比較快樂。
I'll be more confident, too.	我也會更有自信。
□ 3. ***Where do you see yourself in 10 years?***	你預料自己十年後會是什麼情況？
I see myself making good money.	我想我會賺很多錢。
I see myself becoming successful.	我想我會變得很成功。

** ______________

be afraid of 害怕　actually〔ˈæktʃuəlɪ〕*adv.* 實際上
grow〔gro〕*v.* 變得（= *become*）
where〔hwɛr〕*adv.* 在哪裡；處於何種情況
see〔si〕*v.* 想像；預料　in〔ɪn〕*prep.* 再過
confident〔ˈkɑnfədənt〕*adj.* 有自信的　make〔mek〕*v.* 賺（錢）
good〔gʊd〕*adj.* 相當多的　successful〔səkˈsɛsfəl〕*adj.* 成功的

□ **4.** ***Where do you see yourself at your parents' age?***	你預料自己在父母的年紀時，會是什麼情況？
Maybe I'll have a family, too.	也許我也會有自己的家庭。
I can see myself starting a family.	我可以想像自己建立了一個家庭。
□ **5.** ***Where do you see yourself at 70?***	你預料自己七十歲會是什麼情況？
I plan to be retired.	我打算退休。
I hope I'll be healthy.	我希望我會很健康。
□ **6.** ***What age do you want to live to be?***	你想要活到幾歲？
I want to live to 100.	我想要活到一百歲。
I think it's possible.	我認爲這是有可能的。

** ————————————

maybe ('mebɪ) *adv.* 也許　start (stɑrt) *v.* 使產生；創辦
start a family 建立一個家庭　plan (plæn) *v.* 計劃；打算
retired (rɪ'taɪrd) *adj.* 退休的　healthy ('hɛlθɪ) *adj.* 健康的
live to 100 活到一百歲　possible ('pɑsəbḷ) *adj.* 可能的

□ 7. ***At what age do you want to retire?***	你想要幾歲退休？
I plan to retire at around 65.	我打算大約六十五歲退休。
Maybe earlier if all goes well!	如果一切順利，也許會比較早！
□ 8. ***Have you started planning your retirement?***	你已經開始做退休規劃了嗎？
Actually, yes, I have.	事實上，是的，我已經開始了。
I'm saving money for retirement.	我正在存退休金。
□ 9. ***Some say that youth is a state of mind. Do you agree?***	有些人說年輕是一種心態。你同意嗎？
I agree with that.	我同意。
I think you are what you think.	我認爲你的心態決定一切。

**

retire (rɪ'taɪr) *v.* 退休

around (ə'raʊnd) *adv.* 大約　***go well*** 進展順利

retirement (rɪ'taɪrmənt) *n.* 退休

save (sev) *v.* 存（錢）　youth (juθ) *n.* 年輕

state (stet) *n.* 狀態　mind (maɪnd) *n.* 心；精神

state of mind 心態　agree (ə'gri) *v.* 同意

save

Advanced

Oral Test 76

【問與答一起背】

□ 1. ***What's your idea of a perfect gift?***	你認爲什麼是完美的禮物？
I like gift cards.	我喜歡禮品卡。
They are useful to anyone.	它們對任何人而言都很有用。
□ 2. ***What's the best gift you've ever received?***	你曾經收過最好的禮物是什麼？
My parents got me a laptop.	我的父母買給我一台筆電。
It's a sturdy computer.	它是很堅固耐用的電腦。
□ 3. ***Is there a tradition of gift-giving in your country?***	你們國家有送禮物的傳統嗎？
We have many gift-giving traditions.	我們有很多送禮物的傳統。
For example, giving red money envelopes.	例如，給紅包。

red money envelopes

** ——————————

idea〔aɪ'diə〕*n.* 概念；想法　gift〔gɪft〕*n.* 禮物
perfect〔'pɝfɪkt〕*adj.* 完美的　***gift card*** 禮品卡
useful〔'jusfəl〕*adj.* 有用的　ever〔'ɛvɚ〕*adv.* 曾經
get *sb. sth.* 爲某人買某物　laptop〔'læp,tɑp〕*n.* 筆記型電腦
sturdy〔'stɝdɪ〕*adj.* 堅固的；耐用的　tradition〔trə'dɪʃən〕*n.* 傳統
envelope〔'ɛvə,lop〕*n.* 信封　***red money envelope*** 紅包

□ 4. ***What's a common graduation gift?*** 常見的畢業禮物是什麼？

Money is a popular gift. 錢是很受歡迎的禮物。

We give it in red envelopes. 我們會把錢放在紅包裡送人。

□ 5. ***What do students give teachers?*** 學生會給老師什麼？

Students give teachers sweets. 學生會給老師甜食。

Some students give drawings. 有些學生會送圖畫。

□ 6. ***What's a gift you would want now?*** 你現在會想要什麼禮物？

I want a plane ticket. 我想要機票。

I'd like money to travel. 我想要旅費。

** ——————————

common〔ˈkɑmən〕*adj.* 常見的

graduation〔ˌgrædʒʊˈeʃən〕*n.* 畢業

popular〔ˈpɑpjələ˞〕*adj.* 受歡迎的

red envelope 紅包　sweets〔swits〕*n. pl.* 甜點

drawing〔ˈdrɔɪŋ〕*n.* 圖畫　plane〔plen〕*n.* 飛機

plane ticket 機票　travel〔ˈtrævl̩〕*v.* 旅行

graduation

□ 7. ***How do you thank your parents?***	你會如何感謝你的父母？
I make them a card.	我會爲他們做卡片。
I'll help out at home.	我在家會幫忙。
□ 8. ***How do you thank friends?***	你會如何感謝朋友？
I might do them a favor.	我可能會幫他們的忙。
I might treat them to a meal.	我可能會請他們吃飯。
□ 9. ***How do you express thanks?***	你會如何表示感謝？
I give a thoughtful thank you.	我會很週到地說謝謝。
Maybe I'll buy a gift.	也許我會買個禮物。

** ________________

card〔kɑrd〕*n.* 卡片　***help out*** 幫忙
favor〔ˈfevɚ〕*n.* 恩惠　***do sb. a favor*** 幫某人一個忙
treat〔trit〕*v.* 招待　meal〔mil〕*n.* 一餐
treat sb. to a meal 請某人吃飯　express〔ɪkˈsprɛs〕*v.* 表達
thanks〔θæŋks〕*n.pl.* 感謝　give〔gɪv〕*v.* 說
thoughtful〔ˈθɔtfəl〕*adj.* 體貼的；考慮週到的
maybe〔ˈmebɪ〕*adv.* 也許

gift

【背景說明】

Oral Test 75

2. ***Where do you see yourself in 5 years?***
（你預料自己五年後會是什麼情況？）
= Where do you imagine you will be in five years?
= What do you think your situation will be like five years from now?
【imagine〔ɪ'mædʒɪn〕v. 想像】

I see myself happier.（我想我會比較快樂。）
= I imagine myself happier.
= I feel I'll be doing better.
= I'm confident I'll be happier.
【do〔du〕v. 表現；進展】

3. ***I see myself making good money.***
（我想我會賺很多錢。）
= I think I'll be making more money.
= I feel my salary will be higher.
= I picture myself making a lot of money.
【salary〔'sælərɪ〕n. 薪水　picture〔'pɪktʃɚ〕v. 想像】

making good money

5. ***I plan to be retired.***（我打算退休。）
= I plan to retire.
= I expect to be retired.
retire（退休）是動詞，retired（退休的）是形容詞。

6. ***I want to live to 100.***（我想要活到一百歲。）
= I'd like to live till one hundred years old.
= I hope I'll live to 100.

7. ***I plan to retire at around 65.***（我打算大約六十五歲退休。）

= I plan to retire at around 65 years old.

= I plan to be retired at around 65.

Maybe earlier if all goes well!（如果一切順利，也許會比較早！）

= I might retire earlier if everything turns out right!

【***turn out*** 結果（是）　right（raɪt）*adj.* 完滿的；妥善的】

9. ***I think you are what you think.***（我認為你的心態決定一切。）

= Your thoughts determine who you are.

= Your attitude greatly influences you.

【determine（dɪ'tɝmɪn）*v.* 決定　attitude（'ætə,tjud）*n.* 態度　influence（'ɪnfluəns）*v.* 影響】

Oral Test 76

1. ***I like gift cards.***（我喜歡禮品卡。）在台灣還沒有 ***gift card***（禮品卡），只有「禮券」（gift certificate）。在美國，***gift card*** 非常普遍，可以在很多商店買東西，美國人喜歡送 ***gift card*** 當作禮物。

7. ***I'll help out at home.***（我在家會幫忙。）

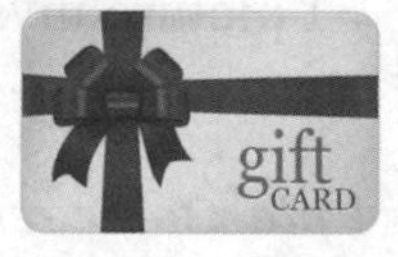

= I'll help at home.

= I'll help them at home.

= I'll do things to help them.

= I'll do work around the house.【***around the house*** 在家】

9. ***I give a thoughtful thank you.***（我會很週到地說謝謝。）可說成：I'll write a sincere thank-you card.（我會寫一張真誠的感謝卡。）【sincere（sɪn'sɪr）*adj.* 眞誠的　***thank-you card*** 感謝卡】

Advanced

Oral Test 77

【問與答一起背】

□ 1. ***Are you good at saving money?***	你擅長存錢嗎？
I suppose I'm pretty good.	我想我很擅長。
I'm frugal and cautious.	我很節儉又謹慎。
□ 2. ***How do you save money?***	你如何存錢？
I have a budget.	我有預算。
I keep track of my spending.	我會記錄我的花費。
□ 3. ***What do you like to spend money on?***	你喜歡把錢花在什麼上面？
I like to buy books.	我喜歡買書。
I also enjoy good meals!	我也喜歡好的餐點！

**

be good at 擅長　　save〔 sev 〕*v.* 存（錢）
suppose〔 sə'poz 〕*v.* 猜想；以爲
pretty〔'prɪtɪ 〕*adv.* 相當；非常　　frugal〔'frugḷ 〕*adj.* 節儉的
cautious〔'kɔʃəs 〕*adj.* 謹愼的；小心的
budget〔'bʌdʒɪt 〕*n.* 預算　　track〔 træk 〕*n.* 痕跡；足跡
keep track of 記錄　　spending〔'spɛndɪŋ 〕*n.* 開銷；花費；支出
enjoy〔 ɪn'dʒɔɪ 〕*v.* 享受；喜歡　　meal〔 mil 〕*n.* 一餐

□ 4. ***Where do you keep your money?***	你都把錢存放在哪裡？
I keep it in the bank.	我把錢存在銀行。
I have a savings account at the bank.	我在銀行有儲蓄存款帳戶。
□ 5. ***What bank do you use?***	你往來的是什麼銀行？
I use Citibank.	我和花旗銀行往來。
I have an account there.	我在那裡有帳戶。
□ 6. ***Do you have a credit card?***	你有信用卡嗎？
No, not yet.	不，還沒。
I use my parents' card.	我用我父母的卡。

** ———————————

keep〔kip〕*v.* 保存　　bank〔bæŋk〕*n.* 銀行

savings〔'sevɪŋz〕*n. pl.* 儲蓄；儲金

account〔ə'kaʊnt〕*n.* 帳戶

savings account 儲蓄存款帳戶【checking account 活期存款帳戶】

Citibank〔'sɪtɪ,bæŋk〕*n.* 花旗銀行

credit〔'krɛdɪt〕*n.* 信用

credit card 信用卡　　***not yet*** 尚未；還沒

credit card

□ **7.** ***Do you prefer to pay with cash or a credit card?***	你比較喜歡用現金支付還是用信用卡？
I prefer credit.	我比較喜歡用信用卡。
I'd rather use a credit card.	我寧願用信用卡。
□ **8.** ***Do you have a bank account?***	你有銀行帳戶嗎？
Yes, I have a checking account.	是的，我有活期存款帳戶。
I also have a savings account.	我也有儲蓄存款帳戶。
□ **9.** ***Are you saving up for anything?***	你有在爲了什麼而存錢嗎？
Actually, yes, I am.	事實上，是的，我有。
I'm saving up for the new iPhone.	我正在爲了新的 iPhone 而存錢。

** ______________________

prefer〔prɪ'fɝ〕*v.* 比較喜歡
pay〔pe〕*v.* 支付
cash〔kæʃ〕*n.* 現金 ***would rather*** 寧願
save〔sev〕*v.* 存錢 ***save up*** 儲蓄；存錢
actually〔'æktʃuəlɪ〕*adv.* 實際上

cash

【背景說明】

Oral Test 77

2. ***I keep track of my spending***.（我會記錄我的花費。）
   = I write down all my expenses.
   = I record all my expenses in an account book.
   【expense〔ɪk'spɛns〕*n.* 花費　***account book*** 帳本】

5. ***What bank do you use?***（你往來的是什麼銀行？）
   = What's your bank?
   = Which bank is your bank?
   I use Citibank.（我和花旗銀行往來。）可說成：Citibank is my bank.（花旗銀行是我的銀行。）I have a Citibank account.（我有花旗銀行帳戶。）I'm a customer of Citibank.（我是花旗銀行的客戶。）

7. ***Do you prefer to pay with cash or a credit card?***
   （你比較喜歡用現金支付還是用信用卡？）
   = Do you prefer to pay in cash or by credit card?
   = Do you prefer cash or plastic?
   = Do you like to buy things with cash or by credit card?
   【plastic〔'plæstɪk〕*n.* 塑膠；信用卡】
   I prefer credit.（我比較喜歡用信用卡。）
   = I prefer to pay ***with a credit card***.
   = I prefer to pay ***by credit card***.
   = I like to buy things with a credit card.
   = I prefer using plastic.

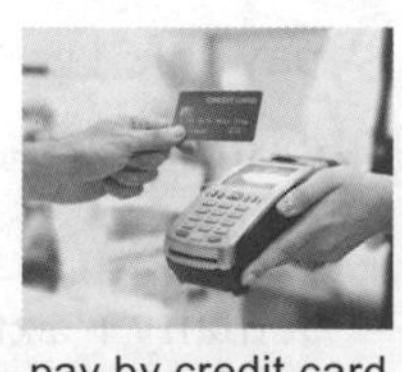
pay by credit card

Advanced

Oral Test 78

【問與答一起背】

□ 1. ***What was your first job?***	你的第一份工作是什麼？
I worked at Starbucks Coffee.	我在星巴克咖啡工作。
It was a good first job.	它是很好的第一份工作。
□ 2. ***Did you work part-time or full-time?***	你是做兼職或是全職的工作？
I worked part-time.	我做兼職的工作。
I was still a student then.	我那時還是個學生。
□ 3. ***What were your work hours?***	你工作的時間是幾點到幾點？
I worked on weekends.	我週末工作。
I worked from 5 to 10 pm.	我從下午五點工作到晚上十點。

** ___________________________

Starbucks (ˈstɑr,bʌks) *n.* 星巴克
part-time (ˈpɑrtˈtaɪm) *adv.* 兼職地
full-time (,fʊlˈtaɪm) *adv.* 全職地
hours (aʊrz) *n. pl.* 時間
weekend (ˈwikˈɛnd) *v.* 週末 ***on weekends*** 在週末
pm (ˈpiˈɛm) *adv.* 下午 (= *p.m.*)

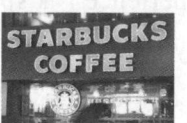

□ 4. ***Did you like your job?***	你喜歡你的工作嗎？
I liked it.	我喜歡。
I got a lot of experience.	我得到很多經驗。
□ 5. ***What did you like about your job?***	你喜歡你的工作的什麼？
The pay was good.	薪水很不錯。
And I met lots of people.	而且我認識了很多人。
□ 6. ***Did you get along with your boss?***	你跟你的老闆相處融洽嗎？
Yes, I did.	是的，我是。
I got along with my manager.	我和我的經理處得很好。

** ______________________

experience (ɪk'spɪrɪəns) *n.* 經驗
pay (pe) *n.* 薪水
meet (mit) *v.* 認識
get along with 與…和睦相處
boss (bɔs) *n.* 老闆　manager ('mænɪdʒə) *n.* 經理

manager

□ 7. ***Did you like your co-workers?***	你喜歡你的同事嗎？
I liked my colleagues.	我喜歡我的同事。
My co-workers were friendly.	我的同事很友善。
□ 8. ***How did you balance work and school?***	你如何在工作與學業之間取得平衡？
I learned how to manage my time.	我學習如何管理我的時間。
I had to give up a few fun things.	我必須放棄一些有趣的事。
□ 9. ***What made you apply for that job?***	什麼原因使你去應徵那份工作？
I needed money for college.	我需要錢唸大學。
I also wanted some independence.	我也想要獨立一點。

**

colleague

co-worker〔'ko,wɝkɚ〕*n.* 同事
colleague〔'kɑlig〕*n.* 同事
friendly〔'frɛndlɪ〕*adj.* 友善的
balance〔'bæləns〕*v.* 平衡
school〔skul〕*n.* 學業　　manage〔'mænɪdʒ〕*v.* 管理
give up 放棄　　fun〔fʌn〕*adj.* 有趣的
apply for 申請；應徵　　college〔'kɑlɪdʒ〕*n.* 大學
independence〔,ɪndɪ'pɛndəns〕*n.* 獨立

Oral Test 79

【問與答一起背】

□ 1. ***May I ask what you do?***	我可以問你是做什麼的嗎？
I work in sales.	我在業務部門工作。
I'm a sales manager.	我是業務經理。
□ 2. ***How do you like it?***	你喜不喜歡它？
I like my job.	我喜歡我的工作。
It's interesting and the pay is good.	它很有趣，而且薪水很不錯。
□ 3. ***Do you like to work? Why?***	你喜歡工作嗎？爲什麼？
Yes and no.	有時喜歡，有時不喜歡。
But I need the paychecks.	但我需要薪水。

** ─────────────

sales〔selz〕*n.* 銷售業務；銷售部門　*adj.* 銷售的
manager〔ˈmænɪdʒɚ〕*n.* 經理　***sales manager*** 業務經理
interesting〔ˈɪntrɪstɪŋ〕*adj.* 有趣的
pay〔pe〕*n.* 薪水　paycheck〔ˈpeˌtʃɛk〕*n.* 薪水支票

□ 4. ***What exactly do you do?***	你究竟是做什麼的？
I sell computers.	我賣電腦。
I like helping customers find the best one for them.	我喜歡幫助顧客找到最適合他們的電腦。
□ 5. ***What other fields are you interested in?***	你對什麼其他的領域有興趣？
I like I.T.	我喜歡 I.T.。
That's information technology.	也就是資訊科技。
□ 6. ***Was this your first career choice?***	這是你最想選擇的職業嗎？
No, it wasn't.	不，它不是。
I wanted to be an engineer.	我本來想當工程師。

** ———

exactly (ɪɡ'zæktlɪ) *adv.* 究竟
computer (kəm'pjutɚ) *n.* 電腦
customer ('kʌstəmɚ) *n.* 顧客　field (fild) *n.* 領域
be interested in 對…有興趣　***I.T.*** 資訊科技
information (ˌɪnfɚ'meʃən) *n.* 資訊
technology (tɛk'nɑlədʒ) *n.* 科技
career (kə'rɪr) *n.* 職業　choice (tʃɔɪs) *n.* 選擇
engineer (ˌɛndʒə'nɪr) *n.* 工程師

I.T.

□ 7. ***What is your company's name?***	你們公司叫什麼名字？
We're called U.T.	我們叫作 U.T.。
It stands for United Technology.	U.T. 代表聯合科技。
□ 8. ***How many are there in your company?***	你們公司有多少人？
We have 25 employees.	我們有 25 個員工。
Most have been there since the beginning.	大部份員工都是從一開始就在的。
□ 9. ***How long have you worked there?***	你在那裡工作多久了？
For six years.	六年了。
I'm just about ready for a change.	我差不多準備要做個改變了。

** ______

company〔ˈkʌmpənɪ〕*n.* 公司　　***stand for*** 代表
united〔juˈnaɪtɪd〕*adj.* 聯合的　　employee〔ˌɛmplɔɪˈi〕*n.* 員工
beginning〔bɪˈgɪnɪŋ〕*n.* 開始　　***just about*** 差不多；幾乎
ready〔ˈrɛdɪ〕*adj.* 準備好的
change〔tʃendʒ〕*n.* 改變；變化；換地方；換環境

Oral Test 80

【問與答一起背】

□ 1. ***Have you ever worked overseas?***	你曾經在國外工作嗎？
Not yet.	還沒。
But I hope to do so soon.	但是我希望不久能這麼做。
□ 2. ***Is this your first job?***	這是你的第一份工作嗎？
Actually, it is.	事實上，它是。
And I think it's a good first step.	而且我認爲這是很好的第一步。
□ 3. ***How's your boss?***	你的老闆如何？
He's experienced and fair.	他很有經驗又公平。
I like working with him.	我喜歡和他一起工作。

** ——————————

overseas (ˈovəˈsiz) *adv.* 在海外　　***not yet*** 尚未；還沒
actually (ˈæktʃuəlɪ) *adv.* 實際上　　step (stɛp) *n.* 步；步驟
boss (bɔs) *n.* 老闆
experienced (ɪkˈspɪrɪənst) *adj.* 有經驗的
fair (fɛr) *adj.* 公平的

fair

□ 4. ***Do you travel a lot for your job?***	你會因爲工作而常常旅行嗎？
Yes, I do.	是的，我會。
I'm on the road a lot.	我常常到處奔波。
□ 5. ***How old is your company?***	你的公司成立多久了？
It's ten years old.	已經十年了。
It's grown a lot in that time.	它在這段時間內成長很多。
□ 6. ***Do you plan to retire with your company?***	你打算在你的公司做到退休嗎？
I hope so.	但願如此。
It depends on the future.	這要看未來的情況而定。

** ______________________

a lot 常常（= *much* = *often*）

on the road 在路上；在旅途中；到處奔波以招攬生意

grow〔gro〕*v.* 成長　　retire〔rɪ'taɪr〕*v.* 退休

depend on 視…而定　　future〔'fjutʃɚ〕*n.* 未來

□ 7. ***Are the benefits pretty good?***	福利很好嗎？
Yes, I get good benefits.	是的，我有很好的福利。
I can't complain.	我沒什麼好抱怨的。
□ 8. ***Is your company growing?***	你的公司正在成長嗎？
At the moment, yes.	目前是的。
Things are looking good.	情況看起來很好。
□ 9. ***Do you often work overtime?***	你常會加班嗎？
I often do.	我常加班。
Overtime is part of my job.	加班是我工作的一部份。

** ———————————

benefits (ˈbɛnə,fɪts) *n. pl.* 利益；福利
pretty (ˈprɪtɪ) *adv.* 相當；非常
complain (kəmˈplen) *v.* 抱怨　***at the moment*** 目前
things (θɪŋz) *n. pl.* 情況　look (lʊk) *v.* 看起來
overtime (ˈovɚˈtaɪm) *adv.* 超時地　*n.* 加班
work overtime 加班

work overtime

【背景說明】

Oral Test 78

3. ***What were your work hours?***（你工作時間是幾點到幾點？）
   = What were your ***working hours***?
   = What was your ***work time***?
   = What was your ***working time***?
   = What time did you work?
   = What hours did you work?

8. ***How did you balance work and school?***
   （你如何在工作與學業之間取得平衡？）
   = How did you handle both work and school?
   = How did you manage both schoolwork and the job?
   【handle〔ˈhændḷ〕*v.* 應付；處理　manage〔ˈmænɪdʒ〕*v.* 管理；處理
   schoolwork〔ˈskul,wɝk〕*n.* 學業】

9. ***I also wanted some independence.***（我也想要獨立一點。）
   = I also wanted to be a little more independent.
   = I also wanted to be a little bit more independent.
   【independent〔,ɪndɪˈpɛndənt〕*adj.* 獨立的】

Oral Test 79

1. ***I work in sales.***（我在業務部門工作。）
   = I work in the sales department.
   = My job is sales.

= My job is in sales.

= I'm in the sales division.

= I do sales.

= I'm in sales.

【department (dɪ'pɑrtmənt) *n.* 部門　division (də'vɪʒən) *n.* 部門】

2. ***How do you like it?***（你喜不喜歡它？）

= Do you enjoy it?

= How do you feel about it?

= You enjoy it?

= Is it OK?

3. ***Yes and no.***（有時喜歡，有時不喜歡。）

= Sometimes yes, and sometimes no.

= On some days yes, and on some days no.

= My answer is both yes and no.

I need the paychecks.（我需要薪水。）美國人付薪水多用支票。

= I need the money.

= I need the income.

= I need the salary.

= I do it for the money.

paycheck

【income ('ɪn,kʌm) *n.* 收入　salary ('sælərɪ) *n.* 薪水】

6. ***Was this your first career choice?***（這是你最想選擇的職業嗎？）

= Was this the job you always hoped for?

= Was this the job you always wanted?

= Was this job part of the career you hoped for?

【***hope for*** 希望；期待】

8. ***How many are there in your company?***（你們公司有多少人？）

= How many workers or employees are there in your company?

= How many (*people*) work in your company?

= How many (*people*) are employed there?

【employee〔ˌɛmplɔɪˈi〕*n.* 員工　employ〔ɪmˈplɔɪ〕*v.* 雇用】

9. ***I'm just about ready for a change.***

（我差不多準備要做個改變了。）

= I'm considering a change.

= I'm thinking about switching jobs.

= I might change my job soon.

= It's almost time for me to change my work.

【consider〔kənˈsɪdɚ〕*v.* 考慮　***think about*** 考慮

switch〔swɪtʃ〕*v.* 改變；調換】

switch

Oral Test 80

4. ***I'm on the road a lot.***（我常常到處奔波。）

= I travel a lot.

= I'm often traveling.

= Traveling is a big part of my job.

= I fly a lot.【fly〔flaɪ〕*v.* 飛行；搭飛機】

= I'm out of the office a lot.

= I do a lot of business on the road.

現在 ***be on the road*** 不一定是指在陸地上旅行，也可指搭飛機。

6. ***Do you plan to retire with your company?***
(你打算在你的公司做到退休嗎？)
= Will you stay with your company till retirement?
= Do you plan to stick with your job till you retire?
= Think you'll remain at your current job till retirement?
(= *Do you think you'll…?*)
【retirement (rɪ'taɪrmənt) *n.* 退休　***stick with*** 堅持
remain (rɪ'men) *v.* 停留　current ('kɝənt) *adj.* 現在的】

7. ***I can't complain***. (我沒什麼好抱怨的。)
= I have no complaints.
= I'm satisfied.
= I'm content.
= I feel good about it.
【complaint (kəm'plent) *n.* 抱怨
satisfied ('sætɪs,faɪd) *adj.* 滿足的；滿意的
content (kən'tɛnt) *adj.* 滿足的　***feel good about*** 對…感到滿意】

8. ***Things are looking good***. (情況看起來很好。)
= Everything is fine.
= The current situation is good.
= To me, everything looks OK.
= Things are good.
= The situation now looks good.
【current ('kɝənt) *adj.* 現在的】

Advanced Oral Tests

※ 請掃瞄 QR 碼，聽完題目後，練習回答兩句。

Oral Test 55

☐ 1. Do you enjoy shopping?

____

____

☐ 2. Where do you like to shop for clothes?

____

____

☐ 3. Do you like outlet stores or the mall?

____

____

☐ 4. In your city, where is a good place to go shopping?

____

____

☐ 5. How do you feel about online shopping?

____

____

☐ 6. Do you prefer to shop online or in person?

____

____

☐ 7. What products do you prefer to shop online for?

____

____

☐ 8. What products do you prefer to shop in stores for?

____

____

☐ 9. What is your favorite e-commerce site?

____

____

Oral Test 56

☐ 1. Do you have any favorite brands?

____

____

☐ 2. What style of clothes do you like?

____

____

☐ 3. Do you dress for style or comfort?

____

____

☐ 4. Do you follow fashion trends?

____

____

☐ 5. I like your jacket. Where did you get it?

____

____

☐ 6. I like your shoes. How much were they?

____

____

☐ 7. Nice watch. Is it waterproof ?

____

____

☐ 8. How often do you shop at street markets?

____

____

☐ 9. Do you like to haggle for a lower price?

____

____

Oral Test 57

☐ 1. Do you enjoy flying?

____

____

☐ 2. Do you fly often?

____

____

☐ 3. Which airline do you fly with most?

____

____

☐ 4. Why do you prefer them?

____

____

☐ 5. Ever fly business class?

____

____

☐ 6. Ever fly first class?

____

____

☐ 7. How do you normally check in?

____

____

☐ 8. How much luggage do you bring?

____

____

☐ 9. Have you ever missed your flight?

____

____

Oral Test 58

☐ 1. Do you prefer the aisle or window seat?

____

____

☐ 2. Do you have any plane tips?

____

____

☐ 3. How do you pass the time?

____

____

☐ 4. Do you ever chat with strangers on the plane?

____

____

☐ 5. Do you like airline food?

____

____

☐ 6. Are you afraid of flying?

____

____

☐ 7. Any funny stories about flying?

____

____

☐ 8. What's the longest flight you've ever taken?

☐ 9. Ever had a scary, bumpy flight?

Oral Test 59

☐ 1. Do you like to travel?

☐ 2. Why do you like to travel?

☐ 3. How often do you travel?

☐ 4. Have you ever been abroad?

☐ 5. What country do you most want to visit?

☐ 6. What is your dream vacation?

☐ 7. What do you want to do there?

☐ 8. Why do you usually travel?

☐ 9. Where do you like to go on vacation?

Oral Test 60

☐ 1. What kind of places would you like to go?

☐ 2. Have you ever been camping?

☐ 3. Have you ever taken a cruise?

☐ 4. Ever been to Europe?

☐ 5. Do you ever use English while traveling?

☐ 6. Do you have any good travel stories?

☐ 7. Where did you spend your last vacation?

☐ 8. What did you do?

☐ 9. Do you prefer traveling alone or with a group?

Oral Test 61

☐ 1. What's the most amazing place you have been to?

☐ 2. What do you like to do when traveling?

☐ 3. Do you know any travel tips?

☐ 4. Where are you going for your next trip?

☐ 5. How much vacation time do you get a year?

____

____

☐ 6. Where are the best places to visit in your country?

____

____

☐ 7. What are the best months to visit your country?

____

____

☐ 8. What foods do you recommend tourists try?

____

____

☐ 9. If you could go anywhere, where would you go?

____

____

Oral Test 62

☐ 1. Do you have a passport?

____

____

☐ 2. What do you think of public transportation?

____

____

☐ 3. Do you use public transit often?

____

____

☐ 4. Do you have good public transportation where you live?

____

____

☐ 5. Have you ever used Uber?

____

____

☐ 6. Do you prefer Uber or taxis?

____

____

☐ 7. Have you ever carpooled?

____

____

☐ 8. Have you ever seen an accident?

____

____

☐ 9. Can you ride a motorcycle?

____

____

Oral Test 63

☐ 1. What kind of car do you have?

____

____

☐ 2. What's your favorite kind of car?

____

____

☐ 3. Have you ever been pulled over?

____

____

☐ 4. Have you ever gotten a speeding ticket?

____

____

☐ 5. Do you have a bicycle?

____

____

☐ 6. Do you know any bike paths around here?

____

____

☐ 7. Can you call me an Uber?

____

____

☐ 8. Can you flag down a taxi?

____

____

☐ 9. What's the fare for the metro?

____

____

Oral Test 64

☐ 1. What traits do you value?

____

____

☐ 2. What makes you happy?

____

____

☐ 3. What would you like to be known for?

____

____

☐ 4. What's your number one priority?

____

____

☐ 5. What are your short-term goals?

____

____

☐ 6. What are your long-term goals?

____

____

☐ 7. How do you plan to reach your goals?

____

____

☐ 8. What are your strengths?

____

____

☐ 9. What are your weaknesses?

____

____

Oral Test 65

☐ 1. Where do you want to improve?

____

____

☐ 2. What is one step you can take to improve?

____

____

☐ 3. What's the hardest thing you've ever done?

____

____

☐ 4. What's your greatest accomplishment?

____

____

☐ 5. What's your most recent accomplishment?

____

____

☐ 6. What's on your bucket list?

☐ 7. Where do you want to be in 5 years?

☐ 8. What is the biggest obstacle in your way?

☐ 9. What roadblocks are keeping you from success?

Oral Test 66

☐ 1. What are your plans for retirement?

☐ 2. What are your plans for college?

☐ 3. What are your plans for dinner?

☐ 4. What are your plans for summer vacation?

☐ 5. Do you have any plans for the 3-day holiday weekend?

☐ 6. Do you have a graduation trip planned?

☐ 7. Did you plan out your European trip yet?

☐ 8. Did you write a business plan for your idea?

☐ 9. Did you plan for rain, just in case?

____

____

Oral Test 67

☐ 1. Have you ever tried a diet?

____

____

☐ 2. Did the diet work?

____

____

☐ 3. Do you ever skip meals?

____

____

☐ 4. Have you ever gotten hurt?

____

____

☐ 5. Was it serious?

____

____

☐ 6. Have you ever broken anything?

____

____

☐ 7. Are you allergic to anything?

____

____

☐ 8. Have you ever tried acupuncture?

____

____

☐ 9. Have you ever had to stay in a hospital?

____

____

Oral Test 68

☐ 1. What's the most exciting thing you've ever done?

____

____

☐ 2. Have you ever gotten into trouble?

____

____

☐ 3. Have you ever experienced culture shock?

____

____

☐ 4. Have you ever won a competition?

☐ 5. Have you ever read a book or seen a movie that changed your life?

☐ 6. Have you ever been to a theme park?

☐ 7. Have you ever been in an accident?

☐ 8. Have you ever given to charity?

☐ 9. Have you ever volunteered for charity?

Oral Test 69

☐ 1. How do you deal with stress?

☐ 2. What is the best advice you have ever received?

☐ 3. Are you married?

☐ 4. Are you single?

☐ 5. Do you have any children?

☐ 6. What age do you want to get married?

☐ 7. What's your biggest fear?

☐ 8. What are some good ways to make money?

☐ 9. What topics are taboo in your culture?

Oral Test 70

☐ 1. What's the emergency number in your country?

☐ 2. Who do you call in an emergency?

☐ 3. When should you call an ambulance?

☐ 4. How do you call the police?

☐ 5. Who do you call for help?

☐ 6. Who's your emergency contact?

☐ 7. Do you know first aid?

☐ 8. Are you first aid certified?

☐ 9. Where can I take a first aid course?

Oral Test 71

☐ 1. Do you know CPR?

☐ 2. Can you treat an injury?

☐ 3. Do you own a first aid kit?

☐ 4. Where's the closest defibrillator?

☐ 5. Where's the closest fire extinguisher?

☐ 6. Have you ever had to call 1-1-9?

☐ 7. Does your home have a smoke detector?

☐ 8. Does your home have a sprinkler system?

☐ 9. Do you have a home security system?

Oral Test 72

☐ 1. Who are you living with?

☐ 2. When did you move out?

☐ 3. When did you move in?

☐ 4. How did you find the place?

☐ 5. How do you like it so far?

☐ 6. How many rooms are there?

☐ 7. Have you finished unpacking?

____

____

☐ 8. Is living alone lonely?

____

____

☐ 9. Do you want a roommate?

____

____

Oral Test 73

☐ 1. Did you buy or are you renting?

____

____

☐ 2. Do you pay rent?

____

____

☐ 3. Did you put down a deposit?

____

____

☐ 4. What floor do you live on?

____

____

☐ 5. Is your building old or new?

____

____

☐ 6. How far is your home from your work?

____

____

☐ 7. Do you like your landlord or landlady?

____

____

☐ 8. How is security?

____

____

☐ 9. How's the neighborhood?

____

____

Oral Test 74

☐ 1. Have you ever moved?

☐ 2. Where did you move from?

☐ 3. Where did you move to?

☐ 4. Why did you move?

☐ 5. How old were you?

☐ 6. Did you want to move?

☐ 7. What was it like to change schools?

☐ 8. Was it easy for you to adjust?

☐ 9. Where do you live now?

Oral Test 75

☐ 1. Are you afraid of getting older?

☐ 2. Where do you see yourself in 5 years?

☐ 3. Where do you see yourself in 10 years?

☐ 4. Where do you see yourself at your parents' age?

☐ 5. Where do you see yourself at 70?

☐ 6. What age do you want to live to be?

☐ 7. At what age do you want to retire?

☐ 8. Have you started planning your retirement?

☐ 9. Some say that youth is a state of mind. Do you agree?

Oral Test 76

☐ 1. What's your idea of a perfect gift?

☐ 2. What's the best gift you've ever received?

☐ 3. Is there a tradition of gift-giving in your country?

☐ 4. What's a common graduation gift?

☐ 5. What do students give teachers?

☐ 6. What's a gift you would want now?

☐ 7. How do you thank your parents?

☐ 8. How do you thank friends?

☐ 9. How do you express thanks?

____

____

Oral Test 77

☐ 1. Are you good at saving money?

____

____

☐ 2. How do you save money?

____

____

☐ 3. What do you like to spend money on?

____

____

☐ 4. Where do you keep your money?

____

____

☐ 5. What bank do you use?

____

____

☐ 6. Do you have a credit card?

____

____

☐ 7. Do you prefer to pay with cash or a credit card?

____

____

☐ 8. Do you have a bank account?

____

____

☐ 9. Are you saving up for anything?

____

____

Oral Test 78

☐ 1. What was your first job?

____

____

☐ 2. Did you work part-time or full-time?

____

____

☐ 3. What were your work hours?

____

____

☐ 4. Did you like your job?

____

____

☐ 5. What did you like about your job?

____

____

☐ 6. Did you get along with your boss?

____

____

☐ 7. Did you like your co-workers?

____

____

☐ 8. How did you balance work and school?

____

____

☐ 9. What made you apply for that job?

____

____

Oral Test 79

☐ 1. May I ask what you do?

____

____

☐ 2. How do you like it?

____

____

☐ 3. Do you like to work? Why?

____

____

☐ 4. What exactly do you do?

____

____

☐ 5. What other fields are you interested in?

____

____

☐ 6. Was this your first career choice?

____

____

□ 7. What is your company's name?

____

____

□ 8. How many are there in your company?

____

____

□ 9. How long have you worked there?

____

____

Oral Test 80

□ 1. Have you ever worked overseas?

____

____

□ 2. Is this your first job?

____

____

□ 3. How's your boss?

____

____

□ 4. Do you travel a lot for your job?

____

____

□ 5. How old is your company?

____

____

□ 6. Do you plan to retire with your company?

____

____

□ 7. Are the benefits pretty good?

____

____

□ 8. Is your company growing?

____

____

□ 9. Do you often work overtime?

____

____

英語口試——優級

Superior

英語口試「優級」Oral Test 81~90

1. 「優級」的句子最長，而且最難，不容易背到變成直覺。
2. 要把「初級」、「中級」、「中高級」，和「高級」背到滾瓜爛熟，再背「優級」。
3. 把這些問與答當成課本讀即可。
4. Superior Oral Tests的錄音QR碼只有唸問題，保留足夠的時間讓你練習回答。

Oral Test 81

Superior

【問與答一起背】

☐ 1. ***What is the biggest animal?***	體型最大的動物是什麼？
The elephant.	大象。
An elephant is 3m tall and weighs 5 tons.	大象有三公尺高，五公噸重。
☐ 2. ***What is the fastest animal?***	速度最快的動物是什麼？
The cheetah.	獵豹。
Its dash is as fast as 120 km/h.	牠衝刺的速度，最快可達時速 120 公里。
☐ 3. ***What is the biggest mammal in the ocean?***	海洋中最大型的哺乳類動物是什麼？
The blue whale.	藍鯨。
It is 33m long and 181 tons.	牠身長33公尺，重 181 公噸。

** ——————————

weigh〔 we 〕*v.* 重…　　***m*** 公尺（= meter〔ˈmitɚ〕）
ton〔 tʌn 〕*n.* 公噸　　cheetah〔ˈtʃitə〕*n.* 獵豹
dash〔 dæʃ 〕*n.* 猛衝
km 公里（= kilometer〔ˈkɪləˌmitɚ, kəˈlɑmətɚ〕）
km/h 時速…公里（= *kilometer per hour*）
mammal〔ˈmæml̩〕*n.* 哺乳類動物　　ocean〔ˈoʃən〕*n.* 海洋
whale〔 hwel 〕*n.* 鯨魚　　***blue whale*** 藍鯨

cheetah

□ 4. ***What is the tallest animal?*** 最高的動物是什麼？

The giraffe. 長頸鹿。

It is around 5m tall. 大約五公尺高。

□ 5. ***What is the biggest bird?*** 最大的鳥是什麼？

The ostrich. 駝鳥。

It is 2.5m tall and 150kg. 高 2.5 公尺，重 150 公斤。

□ 6. ***What is the smallest bird?*** 最小的鳥是什麼？

The hummingbird. 蜂鳥。

The smallest one weighs 1.8 grams. 最小的蜂鳥重 1.8 公克。

Superior

**

giraffe〔dʒəˈræf〕*n.* 長頸鹿
around〔əˈraʊnd〕*adv.* 大約
ostrich〔ˈɔstrɪtʃ〕*n.* 駝鳥
kg 公斤（= kilgoram〔ˈkɪlə,græm〕）
hummingbird〔ˈhʌmɪŋ,bɝd〕*n.* 蜂鳥
gram〔græm〕*n.* 公克

giraffe

ostrich

□ 7. ***What is the biggest reptile?***	最大的爬蟲類動物是什麼？
The saltwater crocodile.	鹽水鱷魚。
It is 10m long and 2,000kg.	牠身長 10 公尺，重 2,000 公斤。
□ 8. ***What is the biggest tortoise?***	最大的陸龜是什麼？
The Galapagos Giant Tortoise.	加拉巴象龜。
It is 1.5m long and 175kg.	長 1.5 公尺，重 175 公斤。
□ 9. ***What is the biggest snake?***	最大的蛇是什麼？
The green anaconda.	綠森蚺。
It is around 8m long.	大約八公尺長。

** ——————————

reptile (ˈrɛptḷ, ˈrɛp,taɪl) *n.* 爬蟲類動物

crocodile

saltwater (ˈsɔlt,wɔtɚ) *adj.* 鹽水的

crocodile (ˈkrɑkə,daɪl) *n.* 鱷魚

tortoise (ˈtɔrtəs) *n.* 陸龜【turtle (ˈtɝtḷ) *n.* 海龜】

Galapagos (gəˈlɑpəgəs) *n.* 加拉巴象龜

giant (ˈdʒaɪənt) *adj.* 巨大的　　snake (snek) *n.* 蛇

anaconda (,ænəˈkɑndə) *n.* 森蚺【產於巴西等之原始森林的無毒大蟒蛇】

Oral Test 82

【問與答一起背】

Mt. Everest

□ 1. ***What is the highest mountain in the world?***	全世界最高的山是什麼山？
Mt. Everest.	聖母峰。
Its altitude is 8,848 meters.	它的高度是 8,848 公尺。
□ 2. ***What is the longest river in the world?***	全世界最長的河是什麼河？
The Nile.	尼羅河。
It is 6,650km long.	它有 6,650 公里長。
□ 3. ***What is the largest desert in the world?***	全世界最大的沙漠是什麼沙漠？
The Sahara Desert.	撒哈拉沙漠。
It is 9.4 million km^2.	它有 940 萬平方公里。

** ______________________

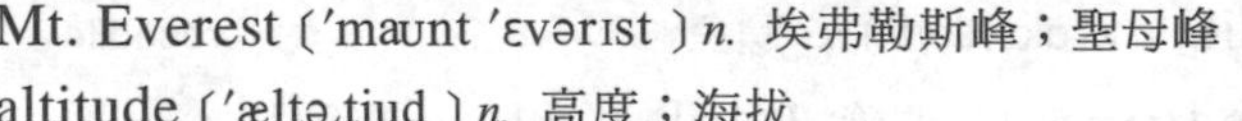

Mt. Everest (ˈmaʊnt ˈɛvərɪst) *n.* 埃弗勒斯峰；聖母峰

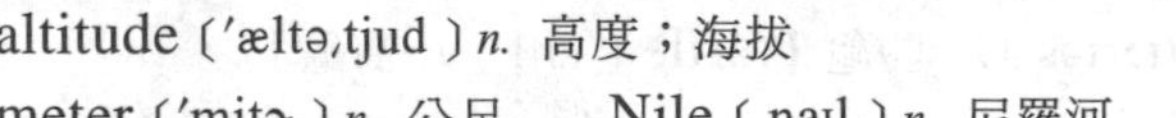

altitude (ˈæltə,tjud) *n.* 高度；海拔
meter (ˈmitɚ) *n.* 公尺　　Nile (naɪl) *n.* 尼羅河
desert (ˈdɛzɚt) *n.* 沙漠
Sahara (səˈhɛrə) *n.* 撒哈拉沙漠
km² 平方公里 (= *square kilometer*)
【square (skwɛr) *adj.* 平方的】

Sahara Desert

□ 4. ***What is the largest ocean in the world?***	全世界最大的海洋是什麼洋？
The Pacific Ocean.	太平洋。
The area of the Pacific Ocean is 161.8 million km^2.	太平洋的面積是一億六千一百八十萬平方公里。
□ 5. ***What is the largest lake in the world?***	全世界最大的湖是什麼湖？
The Caspian Sea.	裏海。
It is 371 million km^2.	它有三億七千一百萬平方公里。
□ 6. ***What is the biggest waterfall?***	最大的瀑布是什麼瀑布？
The Niagara Falls.	尼加拉瀑布。
Its average flow rate is 2,400 m^3/s.	它的平均流量是每秒 2,400 立方公尺。

Superior

** ___

pacific (pəˈsɪfɪt) *adj.* 和平的；太平的
the Pacific Ocean 太平洋　area (ˈɛrɪə) *n.* 面積
lake (lek) *n.* 湖　Caspian Sea (ˈkæspɪən ˈsi) *n.* 裏海
waterfall (ˈwɔtəˌfɔl) *n.* 瀑布
Niagara Falls (naɪˈægrə ˈfɔlz) *n.* 尼加拉大瀑布
average (ˈævərɪdʒ) *adj.* 平均的
flow (flo) *n.* 流；流動
rate (ret) *n.* 比率；速度　***flow rate*** 流量
m^3/s 每秒…立方公尺（= *cubic meter per second*）

Niagara Falls

Superior

□ 7. ***Who is the first man who walked on the moon?***	誰是第一個登陸月球的人？
Neil Alden Armstrong.	尼爾・奧爾登・阿姆斯壯。
He walked on the moon in 1969.	他在 1969 年登陸月球。
□ 8. ***What is the brightest star in the night sky?***	在夜空中最亮的星是什麼星？
Venus.	金星。
It is named after the Roman goddess of love and beauty.	它是以羅馬愛與美的女神的名字命名的。
□ 9. ***What is the biggest planet in the solar system?***	太陽系中最大的行星是什麼星？
Jupiter.	木星。
It is 2.5 times the total mass of the other planets in the solar system.	它的質量是太陽系其他行星總質量的 2.5 倍。

Neil Alden Armstrong

** ___

Neil Alden Armstrong〔ˈnil ˈældn̩ ˈɑrmstrɑŋ〕*n.* 尼爾・奧爾登・阿姆斯壯【美國太空人】
Venus〔ˈvinəs〕*n.* 金星；維納斯
be named after 以…的名字命名
Roman〔ˈromən〕*adj.* 羅馬的　goddess〔ˈgɑdɪs〕*n.* 女神
beauty〔ˈbjutɪ〕*n.* 美　planet〔ˈplænɪt〕*n.* 行星
solar〔ˈsolɚ〕*adj.* 太陽的　***solar system*** 太陽系
Jupiter〔ˈdʒupɪtɚ〕*n.* 木星　time〔taɪm〕*n.* 倍
total〔ˈtotl̩〕*adj.* 全部的；總計的　mass〔mæs〕*n.* 質量

Oral Test 83

【問與答一起背】

□ 1. ***What is the tallest building in the world?***
全世界最高的建築物是什麼？
The Burj Khalifa. 哈里發塔。
It is in Dubai and it is 828m tall.
它位於杜拜，高 828 公尺。

Burj Khalifa

** Burj Khalifa〔'burdʒ hɑ'lifə〕*n.* 哈里發塔
Dubai〔djʊ'baɪ〕*n.* 杜拜

□ 2. ***What is the biggest stadium in the world?***
全世界最大的體育館是什麼體育館？
The Pyongyang Arena in North Korea.
北韓的平壤體育館。

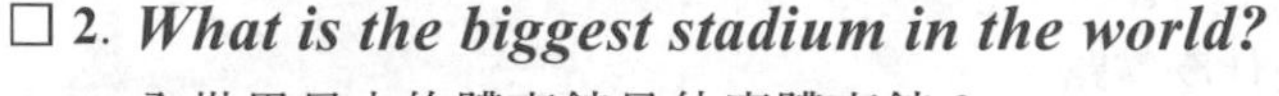

Its area is 207 thousand m^2.
它的面積是二十萬七千平方公尺。

Pyongyang Arena

** stadium〔'stedɪəm〕*n.* 體育館
Pyongyang〔'pjɔŋ'jæŋ, pjʌŋ'jɑŋ〕*n.* 平壤　area〔'ɛrɪə〕*n.* 面積
arena〔ə'rinə〕*n.* 競技場；圓形運動場

□ 3. ***What is the biggest zoo in the world?***
全世界最大的動物園是什麼動物園？
It is Zoo Berlin in Germany.
是德國的柏林動物園。
It is also the oldest and was opened in 1744. 它也是最古老的，於 1744 年開放。

Zoo Berlin

** zoo〔zu〕*n.* 動物園　Berlin〔bɜ'lɪn〕*n.* 柏林
Germany〔'dʒɜmənɪ〕*n.* 德國

Superior

Superior

□ 4. ***What is the railway of the highest altitude?***

緯度最高的鐵路是什麼鐵路？

The Qinghai-Tibet Railway in China. 中國的青藏鐵路。

It is 5,072m above sea level.

它的海拔有 5,072 公尺。

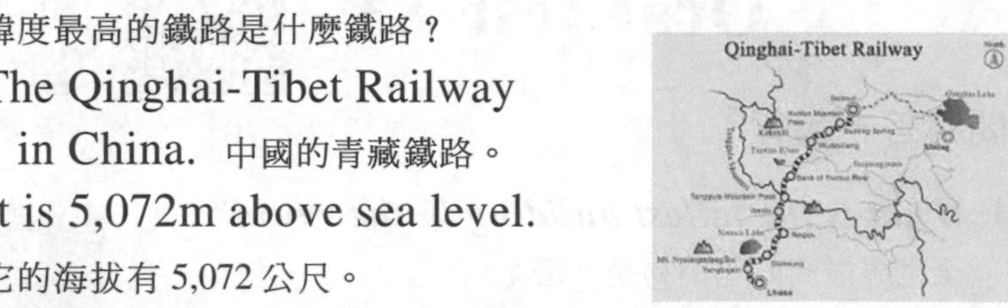

** railway (ˈrel,we) *n.* 鐵路
altitude (ˈæltə,tjud) *n.* 高度；海拔
Qinghai (ˈtʃɪŋˈhaɪ) *n.* 青海　　Tibet (tɪˈbɛt) *n.* 西藏
sea level 海平面　　***above sea level*** 海拔

□ 5. ***What is the longest railway?***

最長的鐵路是什麼鐵路？

The Trans-Siberian Railway in Russia.

俄羅斯的西伯利亞鐵路。

It is 9,288km long. 它是 9,288 公里長。

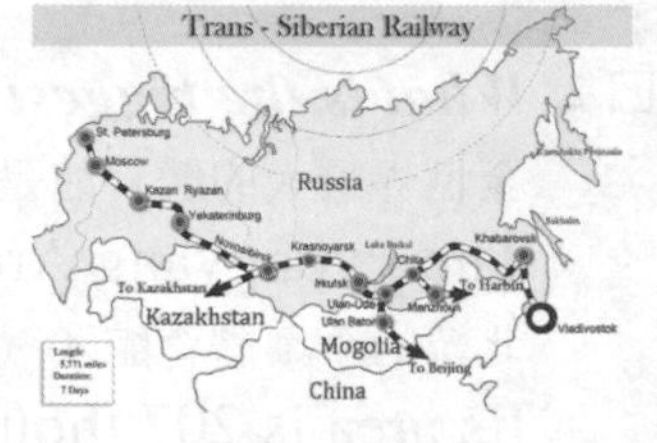

** trans 表「橫越」。　　Siberian (saɪˈbɪrɪən) *adj.* 西伯利亞的
Russia (ˈrʌʃə) *n.* 俄羅斯

□ 6. ***What is the fastest railway train?***

速度最快的火車是什麼火車？

The TGV of France.

法國的高速列車。

It is as fast as 574.8 km/h.

它的時速高達 574.8 公里。

TGV of France

** ***TGV*** 法國高速列車 (= *Train á Grande Vitesse*)
as fas as 和…一樣快　　***km/h*** 時速…公里 (= *kilometer per hour*)

□ 7. ***What is the best-selling book of all time?***

有史以來最暢銷的書是什麼書？

The Bible. 聖經。

More than 5 billion copies have been sold and distributed. 已經出售和發行超過 50 億本。

** best-selling (ˈbɛstˈsɛlɪŋ) *adj.* 最暢銷的 ***of all time*** 有史以來
Bible (ˈbaɪbl̩) *n.* 聖經 billion (ˈbɪljən) *n.* 十億
copy (ˈkɑpɪ) *n.* (一) 本 distribute (dɪˈstrɪbjʊt) *v.* 發行

□ 8. ***What is the most popular movie?***

最受歡迎的電影是什麼電影？

Avengers: Endgame.

復仇者聯盟：終局之戰。

It has surpassed *Avatar* and *Titanic*.

它已經超越阿凡達和鐵達尼號。

** avenger (əˈvɛndʒɚ) *n.* 復仇者 surpass (sɚˈpæs) *v.* 超越
Avatar (ˌævəˈtɑr) *n.* 阿凡達 Titanic (taɪˈtænɪk) *n.* 鐵達尼號

□ 9. ***What is the longest-running Broadway musical?***

上演最久的百老匯音樂劇是哪一部？

The Lion King. 獅子王。

It has been on stage since November 13th, 1997.

它自從 1997 年 11 月 13 日以來就一直上演。

** run (rʌn) *v.* 上演 longest-running *adj.* 上演最久的
Broadway (ˈbrɔdˌwe) *n.* 百老匯
musical (ˈmjuzɪkl̩) *n.* 音樂劇 stage (stedʒ) *n.* 舞台

Oral Test 84

Superior

【問與答一起背】

□ **1.** ***What are the largest countries in the world?***

全世界最大的國家是哪幾國？

Russia, Canada, and the United States.

俄羅斯、加拿大，和美國。

Together they occupy roughly a quarter of Earth's landmass. 它們總共約佔全球土地面積的四分之一。

** Russia〔ˈrʌʃə〕*n.* 俄羅斯　together〔təˈgɛðɚ〕*adv.* 一起；總共
occupy〔ˈɑkjə,paɪ〕*v.* 佔據　roughly〔ˈrʌflɪ〕*adv.* 大約
quarter〔ˈkwɔrtɚ〕*n.* 四分之一　earth〔ɝθ〕*n.* 地球
landmass〔ˈlænd,mæs〕*n.* 大陸；陸地板塊

□ **2.** ***What are the smallest countries in the world?***

全世界最小的國家是哪幾國？

Vatican City, Monaco, and Nauru.

梵蒂岡、摩納哥，和諾魯。

Nauru is an island country in the southwestern Pacific Ocean.

諾魯是位於西南太平洋的島國。

Vatican City

** Vatican City〔ˈvætɪkən ˈsɪtɪ〕*n.* 梵蒂岡
Monaco〔ˈmɑnə,ko〕*n.* 摩納哥
Nauru〔nɑˈuru〕*n.* 諾魯
island〔ˈaɪlənd〕*n.* 島
southwestern〔ˈsaʊθ,wɛstɚn〕*adj.* 西南方的
Pacific Ocean〔pəˈsɪfɪk ˈoʃən〕*n.* 太平洋

□ 3. ***What are the largest and the smallest continents in the world?*** 全世界最大和最小的洲是哪一個？

The largest continent is Asia. 最大的洲是亞洲。

The smallest continent is Australia. 最小的洲是澳洲。

** continent〔ˈkɑntənənt〕*n.* 洲；大陸
Asia〔ˈeʃə, ˈeʒə〕*n.* 亞洲　　Australia〔ɔˈstreljə〕*n.* 澳洲

*　　*　　*

□ 4. ***What are the Seven Wonders of the Ancient World?***

古代的世界七大奇觀有哪些？

The Great Pyramid of Giza, the Colossus of Rhodes, the Hanging Gardens of Babylon, and the Lighthouse of Alexandria.

埃及吉薩金字塔、羅德斯島的太陽神銅像、巴比倫的空中花園，以及亞歷山卓的燈塔。

Also, the Mausoleum at Halicarnassus, the Statue of Zeus at Olympia, and the Temple of Artemis at Ephesus.

還有哈利卡納索斯的摩索拉斯陵墓、奧林匹亞的宙斯像，和以弗所的阿特蜜絲神殿。

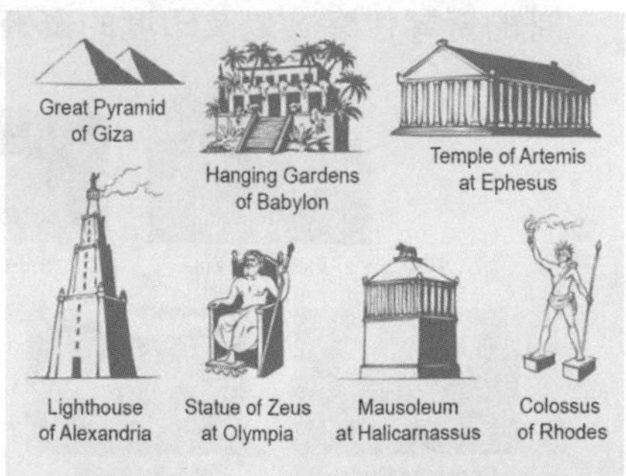

Seven Wonders of the Ancient World

** wonder〔ˈwʌndɚ〕*n.* 奇觀；奇蹟　　ancient〔ˈenʃənt〕*adj.* 古代的
pyramid〔ˈpɪrəmɪd〕*n.* 金字塔　　Giza〔ˈgizə〕*n.* 吉薩
colossus〔kəˈlɑsəs〕*n.* 巨像　　Rhodes〔rodz〕*n.* 羅德斯島
hanging〔ˈhæŋɪŋ〕*adj.* 懸掛的；位於高處的
hanging garden 空中花園　　Babylon〔ˈbæblən〕*n.* 巴比倫
lighthouse〔ˈlaɪtˌhaʊs〕*n.* 燈塔
Alexandria〔ˌælɪgˈzændrɪə〕*n.* 亞歷山卓港　　also〔ˈɔlso〕*adv.* 而且
mausoleum〔ˌmɔsəˈliəm〕*n.* 大陵寢；皇陵
Halicarnassus〔ˌhælɪkɑrˈnæsəs〕*n.* 哈利卡納索斯
statue〔ˈstætʃʊ〕*n.* 雕像　　Zeus〔zus〕*n.* 宙斯
Olympia〔oˈlɪmpɪə〕*n.* 奧林匹亞　　temple〔ˈtɛmpl̩〕*n.* 廟；神殿
Artemis〔ˈɑrtəmɪs〕*n.* 阿特蜜絲　　Ephesus〔ˈɛfɪsəs〕*n.* 以弗所

Superior

□ 5. ***What are the Seven Wonders of the Modern World?***
現代的世界七大奇觀有哪些？

The Great Wall of China, the city of Petra in Jordan, the Colosseum in Italy, and the Christ the Redeemer statue in Brazil. 中國的萬里長城、約旦的佩特拉、義大利的羅馬競技場，以及巴西里約熱內盧的基督像。

Also, Machu Picchu in Peru, Chichen Itza in Mexico, and the Taj Mahal in India. 還有祕魯的馬丘比亞、墨西哥的奇琴伊察，以及印度的泰姬瑪哈陵。

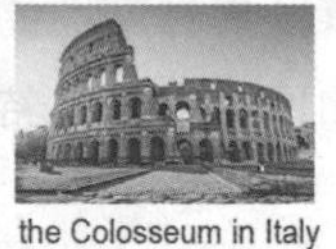

the Great Wall　　Petra　　the Colosseum in Italy

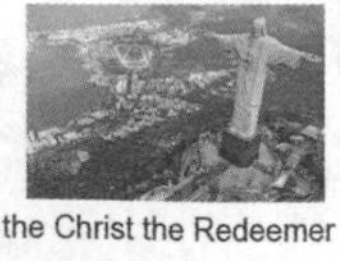

the Christ the Redeemer　　Machu Picchu　　Chichen Itza　　the Taj Mahal

Seven Wonders of the Modern World

** modern〔ˈmadɚn〕*adj.* 現代的　　***the Great Wall*** 萬里長城
Petra〔ˈpitrə, ˈpɛtrə〕*n.* 佩特拉　Jordan〔ˈdʒɔrdn̩〕*n.* 約旦王國
Colosseum〔ˌkaləˈsiəm〕*n.* 古羅馬的圓形大競技場
Christ〔kraɪst〕*n.* 基督
Redeemer〔rɪˈdimɚ〕*n.* 贖罪者；救主；基督
Brazil〔brəˈzɪl〕*n.* 巴西
Machu Picchu〔ˈmatʃu ˈpitʃu〕*n.* 馬丘比丘
Peru〔pəˈru〕*n.* 祕魯
Chichen Itza〔tʃɪˈtʃɛn iˈtsa〕*n.* 奇琴伊察
Mexico〔ˈmɛksɪˌko〕*n.* 墨西哥
Taj Mahal〔ˈtadʒ məˈhal〕*n.* 泰姬瑪哈陵
India〔ˈɪndɪə〕*n.* 印度

□ 6. ***What is the Nobel Prize?*** 諾貝爾獎是什麼？

The will of the Swedish chemist Alfred Nobel established the five Nobel prizes in 1895.

瑞典的化學家阿弗雷德‧諾貝爾的遺囑，於 1895 年設立了五個諾貝爾獎。

Alfred Nobel

The prizes are regarded as the most prestigious awards available in their respective fields.

這些獎被認爲是在其各自領域中，能獲得的最有聲望的獎。

** Nobel Prize〔noˈbɛl ˈpraɪz〕*n.* 諾貝爾獎
will〔wɪl〕*n.* 遺囑　　Swedish〔ˈswidɪʃ〕*adj.* 瑞典的
chemist〔ˈkɛmɪst〕*n.* 化學家
Alfred Nobel〔ˈælfrɪd noˈbɛl〕*n.* 阿弗雷德‧諾貝爾
establish〔əˈstæblɪʃ〕*v.* 設立；創辦　　regard〔rɪˈgard〕*v.* 認爲
prestigious〔prɛsˈtɪdʒəs〕*adj.* 有聲望的

award〔ə'wɔrd〕*n.* 獎　　available〔ə'veləbl̩〕*adj.* 可獲得的
respective〔rɪ'spɛktɪv〕*adj.* 各自的　　field〔fild〕*n.* 領域

*　　*　　*

☐ 7. ***What are the Academy Awards?***

什麼是奧斯卡金像獎？

They are also known as the Oscars.

它們也被稱爲奧斯卡獎。

They are awards for artistic and technical merit in the film industry.

這些獎是頒給在電影業的藝術及技術方面有功勞的人。

** academy〔ə'kædəmɪ〕*n.* 學院【奧斯卡獎是由美國電影藝術與科學學院所頒發】　***Academy Awards*** 奧斯卡金像獎
be known as 被稱爲　　Oscar〔'ɔskɚ, 'ɑskɚ〕*n.* 奧斯卡
the Oscars 奧斯卡獎　　artistic〔ɑr'tɪstɪk〕*adj.* 藝術的
technical〔'tɛknɪkl̩〕*adj.* 技術的
merit〔'mɛrɪt〕*n.* 功勞；功績　　film〔fɪlm〕*n.* 電影
industry〔'ɪndəstrɪ〕*n.* 產業；…業

☐ 8. ***What are the King and Queen of Fruits?***

水果之王和水果之后是什麼？

The King of Fruits refers to the durian.

水果之王是指榴槤。

The Queen of Fruits is the mangosteen.

水果之后是山竹。

** ***refer to*** 是指　　durian〔'dʊrɪən〕*n.* 榴槤
mangosteen〔'mæŋgə,stin〕*n.* 山竹

Superior

□ 9. ***What are superfoods?*** 超級食物是什麼？

Superfoods can help ward off heart disease, cancer, cholesterol, and more.

超級食物有助於防止心臟病、癌症、膽固醇，和其他疾病。

They are beans, blueberries, broccoli, oats, oranges, pumpkin, salmon, soy, spinach, tea, tomatoes, turkey, walnuts, and yogurt.

它們是豆類、藍莓、綠花椰菜、燕麥、柳橙、南瓜、鮭魚、大豆、菠菜、茶、蕃茄、火雞肉、胡桃，和優格。

** superfood (ˈsupɚˌfud) *n.* 超級食物 ***ward off*** 避開；防止
heart disease 心臟病 cancer (ˈkænsɚ) *n.* 癌症
cholesterol (kəˈlɛstəˌrol) *n.* 膽固醇 bean (bin) *n.* 豆子
blueberry (ˈbluˌbɛrɪ) *n.* 藍莓 broccoli (ˈbrɑkəlɪ) *n.* 綠花椰菜
oat (ot) *n.* 燕麥 orange (ˈɔrɪndʒ) *n.* 柳橙
pumpkin (ˈpʌmpkɪn) *n.* 南瓜 salmon (ˈsæmən) *n.* 鮭魚
soy (sɔɪ) *n.* 大豆 spinach (ˈspɪnɪdʒ) *n.* 菠菜
tomato (təˈmeto) *n.* 蕃茄 turkey (ˈtɝkɪ) *n.* 火雞（肉）
walnut (ˈwɔlnət) *n.* 胡桃 yogurt (ˈjogɚt) *n.* 優格

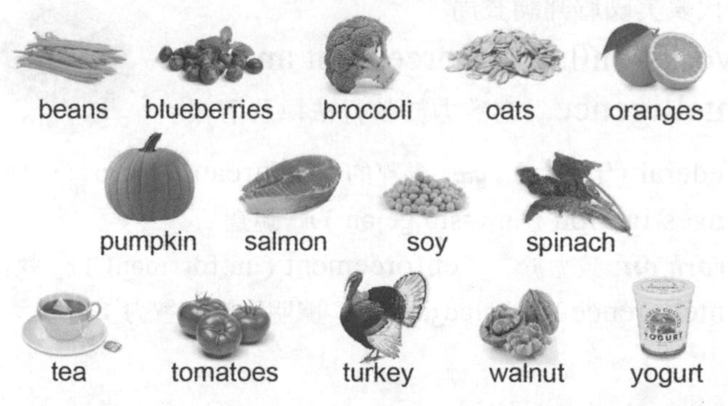

Superior

Oral Test 85

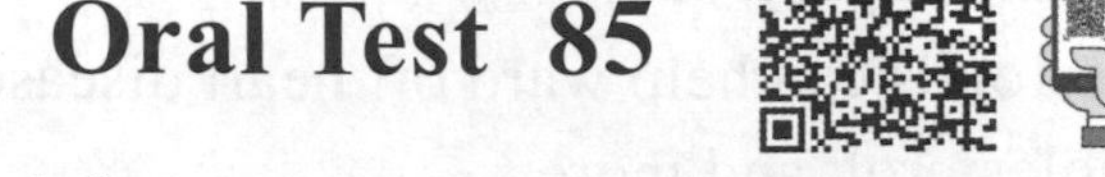

【問與答一起背】

☐ 1. ***What is IQ?*** IQ是什麼？

It stands for Intelligence Quotient. 它代表智力商數。

Humans' average IQ is 100. 人類的平均智商是100。

** ***stand for*** 代表 intelligence〔ɪn'tɛlədʒəns〕*n.* 智力
quotient〔'kwoʃənt〕*n.* 商數 average〔'ævərɪdʒ〕*n.* 平均值

☐ 2. ***What is EQ?*** EQ是什麼？

It stands for Emotional Quotient. 它代表情緒商數。

It is an index of how well people control their emotions.
它是人類情緒控制力的指數。

** emotional〔ɪ'moʃənḷ〕*adj.* 情緒的
index〔'ɪndɛks〕*n.* 指數；指標 emotion〔ɪ'moʃən〕*n.* 情緒

☐ 3. ***What is the FBI?*** FBI是什麼？

FBI stands for the Federal Bureau of Investigation.
FBI代表美國聯邦調查局。

It works on law enforcement and intelligence. 它致力於執行法律及情報。

FBI

** federal〔'fɛdərəl〕*adj.* 聯邦的 bureau〔'bjʊro〕*n.* 局
investigation〔ɪn,vɛstə'geʃən〕*n.* 調查
work on 致力於 enforcement〔ɪn'forsmənt〕*n.* 執行
intelligence〔ɪn'tɛlədʒəns〕*n.* 聰明才智；智力；情報

* * *

□ 4. ***What is the CIA?*** CIA 是什麼？

It is the Central Intelligence Agency.

它是美國中央情報局。

CIA

It works on intelligence collection.

它致力於情報的收集。

** central〔ˈsɛntrəl〕*adj.* 中央的　agency〔ˈedʒənsɪ〕*n.* 局
collection〔kəˈlɛkʃən〕*n.* 收集

□ 5. ***What is 5G?*** 5G 是什麼？

It is the 5th generation of mobile networks.

它是第五代的行動通訊網路。

It is characterized by a high transmission rate and large-scale device connectivity.

它的特色是高傳送速率及大規模裝置連接。

** generation〔ˌdʒɛnəˈreʃən〕*n.* 世代
mobile〔ˈmobḷ〕*adj.* 機動的
network〔ˈnɛtˌwɝk〕*n.* 網路
characterize〔ˈkærɪktəˌraɪz〕*v.* 以…爲特色
be characterized by 特色是
transmission〔trænsˈmɪʃən〕*n.* 傳送
rate〔ret〕*n.* 速率　scale〔skel〕*n.* 規模
large-scale *adj.* 大規模的
device〔dɪˈvaɪs〕*n.* 裝置
connectivity〔ˌkənɛkˈtɪvətɪ〕*n.* 連接

Superior

□ 6. ***What is A.I.?*** A.I. 是什麼？

It stands for artificial intelligence. 它代表人工智慧。

It simulates human intelligence with computer programs. 它是用電腦程式來模擬人類的智慧。

** artificial 〔ˌɑrtəˈfɪʃəl〕*adj.* 人工的
simulate 〔ˈsɪmjəˌlet〕*v.* 模擬
program 〔ˈprogræm〕*n.* 程式

*　　*　　*

□ 7. ***What is a 3D printer?***

3D 印表機是什麼？

3D printer

It is a type of industrial robot.
它是一種工業機器人。

It builds a three-dimensional object from a computer-aided design model.
它會用電腦輔助設計模型創造出立體的東西。

** printer 〔ˈprɪntɚ〕*n.* 印表機　type 〔taɪp〕*n.* 類型
industrial 〔ɪnˈdʌstrɪəl〕*adj.* 工業的
robot 〔ˈrobət〕*n.* 機器人　build 〔bɪld〕*v.* 建造
three-dimensional 〔ˈθri dəˈmɛnʃənḷ〕*adj.* 3D 的；立體的
object 〔ˈɑbdʒɪkt〕*n.* 物體；東西　aid 〔ed〕*v.* 幫助
design 〔dɪˈzaɪn〕*n.* 設計　model 〔ˈmɑdḷ〕*n.* 模型

□ 8. ***What is big data?*** 大數據是什麼？

It is a way of analyzing and extracting information.
它是一種分析並選用資訊的方式。

It deals with data sets that are too complex for database management tools to process.

它能處理資料庫管理工具無法處理的太複雜的資料集。

** data〔'detə〕*n. pl.* 資料　***big data*** 大數據
analyze〔'ænḷ,aɪz〕*v.* 分析
extract〔ɪk'strækt〕*v.* 抽取；選用
information〔,ɪnfə'meʃən〕*n.* 資訊
deal with 處理　***data set*** 資料集
complex〔kəm'plɛks, 'kɑmplɛks〕*adj.* 複雜的
database〔'detə,bes〕*n.* 資料庫
management〔'mænɪdʒmənt〕*n.* 管理
tool〔tul〕*n.* 工具　process〔'prɑsɛs〕*v.* 處理

□ 9. ***What is bitcoin?***

比特幣是什麼？

bitcoin

It is a cryptocurrency.

它是一種加密虛擬貨幣。

It is a decentralized digital currency without a central bank.

它是一種沒有中央銀行，去中央化的數位貨幣。

** bitcoin〔'bɪt,kɔɪn〕*n.* 比特幣
crypto〔'krɪpto〕*adj.* 神祕難解的
currency〔'kɝənsɪ〕*n.* 貨幣
cryptocurrency〔,krɪpto'kɝənsɪ〕*n.* 加密虛擬貨幣
decentralized〔di'sɛntrəl,aɪzd〕*adj.* 去中央化的
digital〔'dɪdʒɪtḷ〕*adj.* 數位的　***central bank*** 中央銀行

Oral Test 86

【問與答一起背】

□ 1. ***Who is Thomas Edison?***

Thomas Edison

湯瑪士‧愛迪生是什麼人？

He has been described as America's greatest inventor.

大家都說他是美國最偉大的發明家。

He said, "Genius is one percent inspiration and ninety-nine percent perspiration."

他說：「天才是百分之一的靈感，百分之九十九的努力。」

** Thomas Edison (ˈtɑməs ˈɛdəsn̩) *n.* 湯瑪士‧愛迪生
describe (dɪˈskraɪb) *v.* 描述；形容；說成 < *as* >
great (gret) *adj.* 偉大的；很棒的
inventor (ɪnˈvɛntɚ) *n.* 發明家　　genius (ˈdʒinjəs) *n.* 天才
percent (pɚˈsɛnt) *adj.* 百分之…的
inspiration (ˌɪnspəˈreʃən) *n.* 靈感
perspiration (ˌpɚspəˈreʃən) *n.* 流汗；努力

□ 2. ***Who is Dale Carnegie?***

Dale Carnegie

戴爾‧卡內基是什麼人？

He was an American specialist in interpersonal relationships.

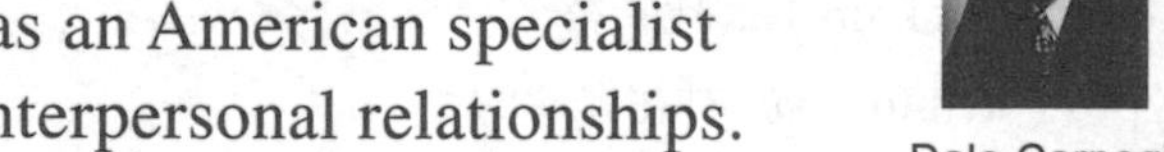

他是一位美國的人際關係專家。

He wrote *How to Win Friends and Influence People*, a very popular book.

他寫了《人性的弱點》這本非常受歡迎的書。

** Dale Carnegie (ˈdel kɑrˈnegɪ , ˈdel ˈkɑrnəgɪ) *n.* 戴爾・卡內基
specialist (ˈspɛʃəlɪst) *n.* 專家
interpersonal (ˌɪntəˈpɝsn̩l) *adj.* 人與人之間的
interpersonal relationships 人際關係
win (wɪn) *v.* 贏得；獲得　　influence (ˈɪnfluəns) *v.* 影響
How to Win Friends and Influence People 如何贏得朋友與影響他人；人性的弱點【書名】

□ 3. ***Who is William Shakespeare?***

William Shakespeare

威廉・莎士比亞是什麼人？

He is regarded as the greatest English poet and playwright.

他被認爲是最偉大的英國詩人及劇作家。

His most famous tragedies are *Hamlet*, *King Lear*, *Macbeth*, and *Othello*.

他最有名的悲劇是「哈姆雷特」、「李爾王」、「馬克白」，和「奧賽羅」。

** William Shakespeare (ˈwɪljəm ˈʃekˌspɪr) *n.* 威廉・莎士比亞
regard (rɪˈgɑrd) *v.* 認爲　***be regarded as*** 被認爲是
English (ˈɪŋglɪʃ) *adj.* 英國的　　poet (ˈpo・ɪt) *n.* 詩人
playwright (ˈpleˌraɪt) *n.* 劇作家
famous (ˈfeməs) *adj.* 有名的　　tragedy (ˈtrædʒədɪ) *n.* 悲劇
Hamlet (ˈhæmlɪt) *n.* 哈姆雷特
King Lear (ˈkɪŋ ˈlɪr) *n.* 李爾王
Macbeth (məkˈbɛθ) *n.* 馬克白　　Othello (oˈθɛlo) *n.* 奧賽羅

*　　*　　*

Superior

Superior

□ 4. ***Who is Michael Jackson?***

Michael Jackson

麥可‧傑克森是什麼人？

He is regarded as one of the greatest entertainers of the 20th century.

他被認為是二十世紀最偉大的藝人之一。

His album "Thriller" is the best-seller of all time. 他的專輯「戰慄」是有史以來最暢銷的。

Thriller

** Michael Jackson〔ˈmaɪkḷ ˈdʒæksṇ〕*n.* 麥可‧傑克森
entertainer〔ˌɛntəˈtenɚ〕*n.* 藝人
century〔ˈsɛntʃərɪ〕*n.* 世紀　album〔ˈælbəm〕*n.* 專輯
thriller〔ˈθrɪlɚ〕*n.* 使人毛骨悚然的東西；恐怖小說或電影
best-seller〔ˈbɛstˈsɛlɚ〕*n.* 暢銷書或唱片　***of all time*** 有史以來

□ 5. ***Who is Michael Jordan?*** 麥可‧喬登是什麼人？

Michael Jordan

He won six NBA championships.

他贏得六次 NBA 冠軍。

He is called "the King of Basketball."

他被稱為「籃球大帝」。

** Michael Jordan〔ˈmaɪkḷ ˈdʒɔrdṇ〕*n.* 麥可‧喬登
NBA 美國職業籃球聯賽（= *National Basketball Association*）
championship〔ˈtʃæmpɪənˌʃɪp〕*n.* 冠軍（資格）

□ 6. ***Who is Steve Jobs?***

Steve Jobs

史蒂夫‧賈伯斯是什麼人？

He was the chairman, CEO, and co-founder of Apple Inc.

他是蘋果公司的總裁、執行長，及共同創辦人。

He said, "Stay hungry. Stay foolish."
他說：「要求知若渴，虛心若愚。」

** Steve Jobs〔'stiv 'dʒɑbs〕*n.* 史蒂夫•賈伯斯
chairman〔'tʃɛrmən〕*n.* 主席；總裁
CEO 執行長（= *Chief Executive Officer*）
co-founder〔'ko'faʊndɚ〕*n.* 共同創辦人
Inc. 股份有限公司（= *Incorporated*）
Apple Inc. 蘋果公司　stay〔ste〕*v.* 保持
hungry〔'hʌŋgrɪ〕*adj.* 飢餓的；渴望的
foolish〔'fulɪʃ〕*adj.* 愚蠢的；顯得愚蠢的

*　*　*

□ 7. ***Who is Warren Buffett?***
華倫•巴菲特是什麼人？

Warren Buffett

He is considered the most successful investor in the world.
他被認爲是全世界最成功的投資者。
He is called the "god of stocks." 他被稱爲「股票之神」。

** Warren Buffett〔'wɔrən 'bʌfɪt〕*n.* 華倫•巴菲特
consider〔kən'sɪdɚ〕*v.* 認爲　***be considered (to be)*** 被認爲是
investor〔ɪn'vɛstɚ〕*n.* 投資者　stock〔stɑk〕*n.* 股票

□ 8. ***Who is Steven Spielberg?***
史蒂芬•史匹柏是什麼人？

Steven Spielberg

He is an American director, producer, and screenwriter.
他是一位美國的導演、製片，及電影編劇。

Superior

Three of Spielberg's films—*Jaws*, *E.T. the Extra-Terrestrial*, and *Jurassic Park*—achieved box office records. 史匹柏有三部電影——「大白鯊」、「E.T. 外星人」，和「侏羅紀公園」——創下票房記錄。

** Steven Spielberg〔ˈstivən ˈspilbɝg〕*n.* 史蒂芬•史匹柏
director〔dəˈrɛktɚ〕*n.* 導演
producer〔prəˈdjusɚ〕*n.* 製作人；製片
screenwriter〔ˈskrin,raɪtɚ〕*n.* 電影編劇　film〔fɪlm〕*n.* 電影
jaws〔dʒɔz〕*n. pl.* 嘴巴　***Jaws*** 大白鯊【電影名】
extra-terrestrial〔,ɛkstrətəˈrɛstrəl〕*n.* 外星人
(= *extraterrestrial* = *E.T.*)
Jurassic〔dʒʊˈræsɪk〕*adj.* 侏羅紀的　achieve〔əˈtʃiv〕*v.* 達到
box office 票房　record〔ˈrɛkɚd〕*n.* 紀錄

□ 9. ***Who is Ang Lee?*** 李安是什麼人？

Ang Lee

He is a Taiwanese director, producer, and screenwriter.
他是一位台灣的導演、製片，及電影編劇。

He has won three Academy Awards: Best Foreign Language Film for *Crouching Tiger*, *Hidden Dragon*, and Best Director for *Brokeback Mountain* and *Life of Pi*. 他得過三座奧斯卡獎：「臥虎藏龍」的最佳外語片，以及「斷背山」和「少年 Pi 的奇幻漂流」的最佳導演。

** Ang Lee〔ˈæŋ ˈli〕*n.* 李安　***Academy Awards*** 奧斯卡金像獎
foreign〔ˈfɔrɪn〕*adj.* 外國的
crouch〔kraʊtʃ〕*v.* 蹲伏　hidden〔ˈhɪdn̩〕*adj.* 隱藏的
dragon〔ˈdrægən〕*n.* 龍　***Brokeback Mountain*** 斷背山
pi〔paɪ〕*n.* 希臘字母第十六個字母（π）；圓周率

Oral Test 87

【問與答一起背】

☐ 1. ***Who is Mark Twain?***

Mark Twain

馬克•吐溫是什麼人？

An American writer and humorist.

一位美國的作家和幽默大師。

He wrote *The Adventures of Tom Sawyer* (1876).

他寫了在 1876 年出版的《湯姆歷險記》。

** Mark Twain〔ˈmɑrk ˈtwen〕*n.* 馬克•吐溫
writer〔ˈraɪtɚ〕*n.* 作者；作家
humorist〔ˈhjumərɪst〕*n.* 幽默家；幽默作家
adventure〔ədˈvɛntʃɚ〕*n.* 冒險
Tom Sawyer〔ˈtɑm ˈsɔjɚ〕*n.* 湯姆•莎耶
The Adventures of Tom Sawyer 湯姆歷險記【書名】

☐ 2. ***Who is Mark Zuckerberg?***

馬克•佐克伯是什麼人？

Mark Zuckerberg

He is a technology entrepreneur.

他是一位科技企業家。

He is the CEO of Facebook.

他是臉書的執行長。

** Mark Zuckerberg〔ˈmɑrk ˈtsʊkɚbɝg〕*n.* 馬克•佐克伯
technology〔tɛkˈnɑlədʒɪ〕*n.* 科技
entrepreneur〔ˌɑntrəprəˈnɝ〕*n.* 企業家
CEO 執行長（= *Chief Executive Officer*）
Facebook〔ˈfesˌbʊk〕*n.* 臉書

□ 3. ***Who is Mother Teresa?*** 德蕾莎修女是什麼人？

Mother Teresa

She was a Roman Catholic nun and missionary.

她是一位羅馬天主教的修女及傳教士。

She received a number of honors, including the 1979 Nobel Peace Prize.

她得過一些獎，包括 1979 年的諾貝爾和平獎。

** Mother Teresa〔ˈmʌðɚ təˈrisə〕*n.* 德蕾莎修女
Roman〔ˈromən〕*adj.* 羅馬的
Catholic〔ˈkæθəlɪk〕*adj.* 天主教的　nun〔nʌn〕*n.* 修女；尼姑
missionary〔ˈmɪʃən,ɛrɪ〕*n.* 傳教士
receive〔rɪˈsiv〕*v.* 收到；得到　***a number of*** 幾個；許多
honor〔ˈɑnɚ〕*n.* 獎；獎勵　including〔ɪnˈkludɪŋ〕*prep.* 包括
Nobel〔noˈbɛl〕*n.* 諾貝爾
peace〔pis〕*n.* 和平　prize〔praɪz〕*n.* 獎

*　*　*

□ 4. ***Who is Mahatma Gandhi?*** 聖雄甘地是什麼人？

Mahatma Gandhi

He was an Indian lawyer and anti-colonial nationalist.

他是一位印度的律師及反殖民的國家主義者。

He employed nonviolent resistance to lead the successful campaign for India's independence from British rule.

他使用非暴力抵抗的方式，帶領印度成功脫離英國統治而獨立。

** mahatma〔məˈhɑtmə〕*n.*（印度的）大聖者；聖雄
Gandhi〔ˈgɑndi〕*n.* 甘地（1869-1948，印度民族運動領袖）
Indian〔ˈɪndɪən〕*adj.* 印度的
lawyer〔ˈlɔjɚ〕*n.* 律師　anti〔ˈæntɪ〕反…

colonial〔kə'lonɪəl〕*adj.* 殖民的
nationalist〔'næʃənḷɪst〕*n.* 國家主義者
employ〔ɪm'plɔɪ〕*v.* 運用；使用
nonviolent〔,nɑn'vaɪələnt〕*adj.* 非暴力的
resistance〔rɪ'zɪstəns〕*n.* 抵抗　lead〔'lid〕*v.* 領導
campaign〔kæm'pen〕*n.* 運動　India〔'ɪndɪə〕*n.* 印度
independence〔,ɪndɪ'pɛndəns〕*n.* 獨立
British〔'brɪtɪʃ〕*adj.* 英國的　rule〔rul〕*n.* 統治

□ 5. ***Who is Isaac Newton?*** 艾薩克•牛頓是什麼人？

Isaac Newton

He was an English mathematician, physicist, and astronomer.
他是一位英國的數學家、物理學家，及天文學家。
He is one of the most influential scientists of all time, and a key figure in the scientific revolution.
他是有史以來最具影響力的科學家之一，也是科學革命的重要人物。

** Isaac Newton〔'aɪzək 'njutṇ〕*n.* 艾薩克•牛頓
mathematician〔,mæθəmə'tɪʃən〕*n.* 數學家
physicist〔'fɪzəsɪst〕*n.* 物理學家
astronomer〔ə'strɑnəmɚ〕*n.* 天文學家
influential〔,ɪnflu'ɛnʃəl〕*adj.* 有影響力的　key〔ki〕*adj.* 重要的
figure〔'fɪgjɚ〕*n.* 人物　scientific〔,saɪən'tɪfɪk〕*adj.* 科學的
revolution〔,rɛvə'luʃən〕*n.* 革命

□ 6. ***Who is Albert Einstein?***
阿爾伯特•愛因斯坦是什麼人？

Albert Einstein

He was a German-born theoretical physicist who developed the theory of relativity. 他是一位德裔理論物理學家，研發出相對論。

Superior

He is best known for his mass-energy equivalence formula $E = mc^2$.

他最有名的，就是他的質能等價公式 $E = mc^2$。

** Albert Einstein〔'ælbɚt 'aɪnstaɪn〕*n.* 阿爾伯特‧愛因斯坦
German-born〔'dʒɝmən,bɔrn〕*adj.* 德裔的
theoretical〔,θiə'rɛtɪkl̩〕*adj.* 理論的
develop〔dɪ'vɛləp〕*v.* 發展；研發　theory〔'θiərɪ〕*n.* 理論
relativity〔,rɛlə'tɪvətɪ〕*n.* 相對性；相對論
be best known for 最有名的是　mass〔mæs〕*n.* 質量
energy〔'ɛnɚdʒɪ〕*n.* 能量　equivalence〔ɪ'kwɪvələns〕*n.* 相等
formula〔'fɔrmjələ〕*n.* 公式
mass-energy equivalence formula 質能等價公式
$E = mc^2$ 唸成：E equals MC squared。

* * *

□ 7. ***Who is Wolfgang Amadeus Mozart?***

Mozart

沃夫岡‧阿瑪迪斯‧莫札特是什麼人？

He was a prolific Austrian composer.

他是一位多產的奧地利作曲家。

His influence on Western music is profound.

他對西方音樂的影響很深遠。

** Wolfgang Amadeus Mozart〔'wʊlf,gæŋ ,ɑmə'deəs 'mozɑrt〕*n.* 沃夫岡‧阿瑪迪斯‧莫札特
prolific〔prə'lɪfɪk〕*adj.*（作家、樂團等）多產的
Austrian〔'ɔstrɪən〕*adj.* 奧地利的
composer〔kəm'pozɚ〕*n.* 作曲家
influence〔'ɪnflʊəns〕*n.* 影響 < *on* >
Western〔'wɛstɚn〕*adj.* 西方的；歐美的
profound〔prə'faʊnd〕*adj.* 很深的

Superior

□ **8. *Who is Audrey Hepburn?***

奧黛麗•赫本是什麼人？

Audrey Hepburn

She was an Academy-Award winning British actress and a fashion icon in the 20th century.

她是一位得過奧斯卡獎的英國女演員，也是二十世紀的時尚指標。

She is considered one of the most beautiful and elegant women in the world then and now.

不管是當時還是現在，她都被公認爲全世界最美麗而且優雅的女人之一。

** Audrey Hepburn〔'ɔdrɪ 'hɛpbɝn〕*n.* 奧黛麗•赫本
Academy-Award winning 得到奧斯卡獎的
actress〔'æktrɪs〕*n.* 女演員　fashion〔'fæʃən〕*n.* 流行；時尚
icon〔'aɪkən〕*n.* 指標（= *indicator*）；偶像
century〔'sɛntʃərɪ〕*n.* 世紀　consider〔kən'sɪdɚ〕*v.* 認爲
elegant〔'ɛləgənt〕*adj.* 優雅的
then and now 那時和現在；時時刻刻

□ **9. *Who is Tom Cruise?*** 湯姆•克魯斯是什麼人？

Tom Cruise

An American actor and film producer.

一位美國的演員及電影製片。

He is one of the best-paid actors in the world and one of the highest-grossing box-office stars of all time.

他是全世界片酬最高的男演員之一，也是有史以來票房收入最高的明星之一。

** Tom Cruise〔'tɑm 'kruz〕*n.* 湯姆•克魯斯
actor〔'æktɚ〕*n.* 演員　best-paid〔'bɛst,ped〕*adj.* 薪水最高的
gross〔gros〕*v.* 總共賺得；獲得…總收入
box-office〔'bɑks,ɔfɪs〕*adj.* 票房的　star〔stɑr〕*n.* 明星

Superior

Oral Test 88

【問與答一起背】

□ 1. ***What is the capital city of the U.S.?***

美國的首都是哪裡？

Washington, D.C.

The capital city of the United States of America is Washington, D.C.

美國的首都是華盛頓哥倫比亞特區。

It is located on the East Coast of the United States.

它位於美國的東岸。

** capital〔ˈkæpətḷ〕*n.* 首都　*adj.* 首都的　***capital city*** 首都
the United States of America 美國（= *the U.S.A.* = *the United States* = *the U.S.* = *America*）
Washington, D.C.〔ˈwɑʃɪŋtn̩ ˈdiˈsi〕*n.* 華盛頓哥倫比亞特區；華府
be located on 位於　east〔ist〕*adj.* 東方的
coast〔kost〕*n.* 海岸

□ 2. ***What is the capital city of Canada?***

加拿大的首都是哪裡？

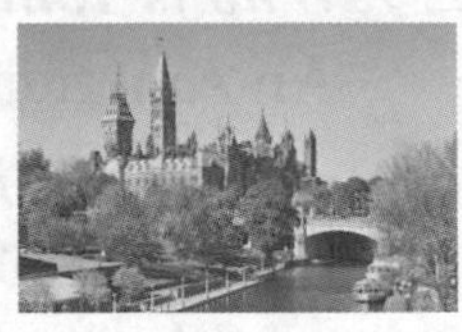
Ottawa

The capital of Canada is Ottawa in the province of Ontario.

加拿大的首都是位於安大略省的渥太華。

Ottawa is the fourth most populous city in the country.

渥太華是該國人口第四多的城市。

** Canada〔ˈkænədə〕*n.* 加拿大　Ottawa〔ˈɑtəwə〕*n.* 渥太華
province〔ˈprɑvɪns〕*n.* 省　Ontario〔ɑnˈtærɪˌo〕*n.* 安大略省
populous〔ˈpɑpjələs〕*adj.* 人口衆多的；人口稠密的

Superior

□ 3. ***What is the capital city of Brazil?***
巴西的首都是哪裡？
Brasilia has been the capital of Brazil since 1960.

Brasilia

自 1960 年起，巴西利亞就是巴西的首都。
It is a relatively new city. 它是個相當新的城市。

** Brazil (brəˈzɪl) *n.* 巴西　Brasilia (brəˈzɪljə) *n.* 巴西利亞
relatively (ˈrɛlətɪvlɪ) *adv.* 相對地；相當地

*　*　*

□ 4. ***What is the capital city of Australia?***
澳洲的首都是哪裡？
Canberra is Australia's capital and the largest inland city.

Canberra

坎培拉是澳洲的首都，也是最大的內陸城市。
The city is located between Australia's largest cities, Melbourne and Sydney, and 150km from the Pacific Ocean. 坎培拉位於澳洲最大的城市墨爾本和雪梨之間，離太平洋 150 公里遠。

** Australia (ɔˈstreljə) *n.* 澳洲　Canberra (ˈkænbərə) *n.* 坎培拉
inland (ˈɪnlənd) *adj.* 內陸的
be located between A and B 位於 A 和 B 之間
Melbourne (ˈmɛlbɜn) *n.* 墨爾本
Sydney (ˈsɪdnɪ) *n.* 雪梨　***the Pacific Ocean*** 太平洋

□ 5. ***What is the capital city of New Zealand?*** 紐西蘭的首都是哪裡？
The capital city of New Zealand is Wellington. 紐西蘭的首都是威靈頓。

Wellington

It is a port city located at the southern tip of the North Island of New Zealand.
它是位於紐西蘭北島南端的一個港市。

** New Zealand 〔 nju'zilənd 〕*n.* 紐西蘭
Wellington 〔'wɛlɪŋtən 〕*n.* 威靈頓
port 〔 port 〕*n.* 港口 southern 〔'sʌðən 〕*adj.* 南方的
tip 〔 tɪp 〕*n.* 尖端 ***North Island*** 北島

□ 6. ***What is the capital city of Germany?***
德國的首都是哪裡？

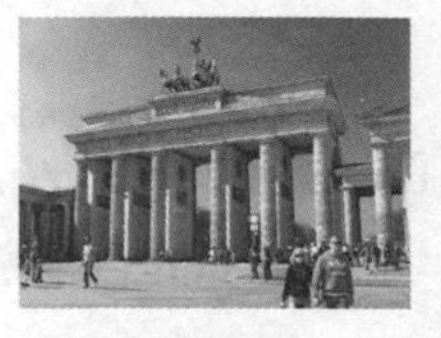
Berlin

Berlin is Germany's capital and is the largest city in the country.
柏林是德國的首都，也是最大的城市。
Berlin is one of the most frequented cities in the European Union, attracting millions of visitors annually. 柏林是歐盟當中，人們最常去的城市之一，每年都吸引數百萬名遊客。

** Germany 〔'dʒɝmənɪ 〕*n.* 德國 Berlin 〔 bɝ'lɪn 〕*n.* 柏林
frequent 〔 frɪ'kwɛnt 〕*v.* 常去
European 〔ˌjʊrə'piən 〕*adj.* 歐洲的 union 〔'junjən 〕*n.* 聯盟
European Union 歐盟（= *E.U.*） attract 〔 ə'trækt 〕*v.* 吸引
millions of 數百萬的 annually 〔'ænjuəlɪ 〕*adv.* 每年

* * *

□ 7. ***What is the capital city of Norway?***
挪威的首都是哪裡？

Oslo

Oslo is the capital city of Norway.
奧斯陸是挪威的首都。

Superior

Its population is 2 million and 761 thousand.

它的人口有 276 萬 1 千人。

** Norway〔ˈnɔrwe〕*n.* 挪威　　Oslo〔ˈɑzlo , ˈɑslo〕*n.* 奧斯陸
population〔ˌpɑpjəˈleʃən〕*n.* 人口

☐ 8. ***What is the capital city of Denmark?***

Copenhagen

丹麥的首都是哪裡？

Copenhagen is the capital and largest city in Denmark.

哥本哈根是丹麥的首都，也是最大城。

Its residents have been ranked as the happiest people in the world.

它的居民被評爲全世界最幸福的人。

** Denmark〔ˈdɛnmɑrk〕*n.* 丹麥
Copenhagen〔ˌkopənˈhegən〕*n.* 哥本哈根
resident〔ˈrɛzədənt〕*n.* 居民
rank〔ræŋk〕*v.* 將…評價爲 < *as* >

☐ 9. ***What is the capital city of Sweden?***

Stockholm

瑞典的首都是哪裡？

The Swedish capital is Stockholm.

瑞典的首都是斯德哥爾摩。

2.3 million residents live in the Stockholm metropolitan area.

有 230 萬個居民住在斯德哥爾摩的都會區。

** Sweden〔ˈswidn̩〕*n.* 瑞典　　Swedish〔ˈswidɪʃ〕*adj.* 瑞典的
Stockholm〔ˈstɑkˌhom〕*n.* 斯德哥爾摩
metropolitan〔ˌmɛtrəˈpɑlətn̩〕*adj.* 大都市的
area〔ˈɛrɪə〕*n.* 地區

Oral Test 89

【問與答一起背】

□ **1.** ***What is the capital city of the United Kingdom?***

英國的首都是哪裡？

The capital city of the UK is London.

London

英國的首都是倫敦。

It is situated on the River Thames.

它位於泰晤士河畔。

** capital〔ˈkæpətḷ〕*adj.* 首都的　*n.* 首都　***capital city*** 首都

the United Kingdom 英國（= *the U.K.* = *Britain*）

London〔ˈlʌndən〕*n.* 倫敦　situate〔ˈsɪtʃʊˌet〕*v.* 使位於

Thames〔tɛmz〕*n.* 泰晤士河

be situated on the River Thames 位於泰晤士河畔

□ **2.** ***What is the capital city of France?***

Paris

法國的首都是哪裡？

Paris is the capital city of France.

巴黎是法國的首都。

The city has an approximate area of 41 square miles.

這個城市的面積大約 41 平方英里。

** France〔fræns〕*n.* 法國　Paris〔ˈpærɪs〕*n.* 巴黎

approximate〔əˈprɑksəmɪt〕*adj.* 大約的

area〔ˈɛrɪə〕*n.* 面積　square〔skwɛr〕*adj.* 平方的

☐ 3. ***What is the capital city of the Netherlands?***

荷蘭的首都是哪裡？

Amsterdam

Amsterdam is the capital of the Netherlands.

阿姆斯特丹是荷蘭的首都。

The port city is also home to manufacturing industries, such as diamond cutting, metallurgy, and clothing.

這個港市也是製造業的所在地，像是鑽石切割、冶金，以及服裝。

** the Netherlands〔ðəˈnɛðələndz〕*n.* 荷蘭（= *Holland*〔ˈhɑlənd〕）
Amsterdam〔ˈæmstəˌdæm〕*n.* 阿姆斯特丹
port〔port〕*n.* 港口　***be home to*** 是…的所在地
manufacture〔ˌmænjəˈfæktʃɚ〕*v.* 製造
industry〔ˈɪndəstrɪ〕*n.* 工業；行業；…業
manufacturing industry 製造業　***such as*** 像是
diamond〔ˈdaɪmənd〕*n.* 鑽石
metallurgy〔ˈmɛtəˌlɝdʒɪ〕*n.* 冶金術　clothing〔ˈkloðɪŋ〕*n.* 衣服

*　*　*

☐ 4. ***What is the capital city of Belgium?***

比利時的首都是哪裡？

Brussels

The capital of Belgium is Brussels.

比利時的首都是布魯塞爾。

This city also serves as the administrative center of the European Union.

這個城市也是歐盟的行政中心。

** Belgium〔ˈbɛldʒɪəm〕*n.* 比利時
Brussels〔ˈbrʌsl̩z〕*n.* 布魯賽爾　***serve as*** 充當；當作
administrative〔ədˈmɪnəˌstretɪv〕*adj.* 行政的

□ 5. ***What is the capital city of Switzerland?***

瑞士的首都是哪裡？

Bern

Bern is the capital of Switzerland.

伯恩是瑞士的首都。

It is located on the Swiss Plateau.

它位於瑞士高原。

** Switzerland (ˈswɪtsəˈlənd) *n.* 瑞士
Bern (bɜn) *n.* 伯恩 ***be located on*** 位於
Swiss (swɪs) *adj.* 瑞士的 plateau (plæˈto) *n.* 高原

□ 6. ***What is the capital city of Austria?***

奧地利的首都是哪裡？

Vienna

Vienna is the capital city of Austria.

維也納是奧地利的首都。

It is also the largest city in the country with a population of 1.8 million people.

它也是該國最大的城市，人口有 180 萬。

** Austria (ˈɔstrɪə) *n.* 奧地利 Vienna (vɪˈɛnə) *n.* 維也納
population (ˌpɑpjəˈleʃən) *n.* 人口
million (ˈmɪljən) *n.* 百萬

* * *

□ 7. ***What is the capital city of Italy?***

義大利的首都是哪裡？

Rome

Rome is the largest city and the capital of Italy.

羅馬是義大利最大的城市，也是首都。

It is the third most visited city in the European Union, after Paris and London, and receives about 10 million visitors annually.
它是歐盟最多人造訪的城市第三名，僅次於巴黎和倫敦，而且每年要接待大約一千萬名遊客。

** Italy〔ˈɪtḷɪ〕*n.* 義大利　　Rome〔rom〕*n.* 羅馬
receive〔rɪˈsiv〕*v.* 接待　　annually〔ˈænjuəlɪ〕*adv.* 每年

□ **8.** ***What is the capital city of Spain?***

Madrid

西班牙的首都是哪裡？
Madrid is the capital of Spain.
馬德里是西班牙的首都。
It is the third-largest city in the European Union. 它是歐盟的第三大城市。

** Spain〔spen〕*n.* 西班牙　　Madrid〔məˈdrɪd〕*n.* 馬德里

□ **9.** ***What is the capital city of Portugal?***

Lisbon

葡萄牙的首都是哪裡？
Lisbon is the capital of Portugal.
里斯本是葡萄牙的首都。
The city is located along the Atlantic Coast. 這個城市位於大西洋沿岸。

** Portugal〔ˈportʃəgḷ〕*n.* 葡萄牙
Lisbon〔ˈlɪzbən〕*n.* 里斯本
along〔əˈlɔŋ〕*prep.* 沿著；在…附近
Atlantic〔ætˈlæntɪk〕*adj.* 大西洋的　　coast〔kost〕*n.* 海岸

Oral Test 90

Superior

【問與答一起背】

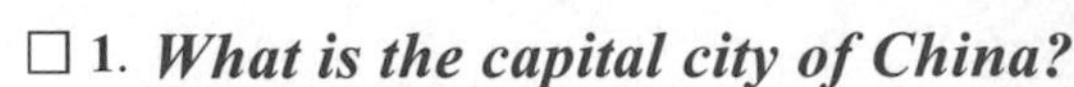

☐ 1. ***What is the capital city of China?***

Beijing

中國的首都是哪裡？

Beijing is the capital city, but Shanghai is the largest city in China.

北京是首都，但上海是中國最大的城市。

Beijing is among the most populated capital cities in the world.

北京是全世界人口最稠密的首都之一。

** capital (ˈkæpətḷ) *adj.* 首都的 *n.* 首都 ***capital city*** 首都
Beijing (ˈbeˈdʒɪŋ) *n.* 北京 Shanghai (ˈʃɑŋˈhaɪ) *n.* 上海
populate (ˈpɑpjəˌlet) *v.* 使人居住於

☐ 2. ***What is the capital city of Japan?***

Tokyo

日本的首都是哪裡？

Tokyo is the capital city of Japan.

東京是日本的首都。

Tokyo's metropolitan region also has the largest population in the world with about 40 million residents.

東京的市區也有全世界最多的人口，大約四千萬個居民。

** Japan (dʒəˈpæn) *n.* 日本 Tokyo (ˈtokɪˌo) *n.* 東京
metropolitan (ˌmɛtrəˈpɑlətn̩) *adj.* 大都市的

region〔'ridʒən〕*n.* 地區　population〔,pɑpjə'leʃən〕*n.* 人口
a large population 衆多的人口　resident〔'rɛzədənt〕*n.* 居民

☐ 3. ***What is the capital city of South Korea?***
南韓的首都是哪裡？
Seoul is the capital city of South Korea. 首爾是南韓的首都。
It is located along the Han River.
它位於漢江沿岸。

Seoul

** South Korea〔'sauθ kə'riə〕*n.* 南韓
Seoul〔sol〕*n.* 首爾　***be located*** 位於
along〔ə'lɔŋ〕*prep.* 沿著；在…附近　***the Han River*** 漢江

*　*　*

☐ 4. ***What is the capital city of Thailand?***
泰國的首都是哪裡？
Bangkok is the capital of Thailand and the largest city in the country.
曼谷是泰國的首都，也是泰國最大的城市。
It is called "the City of Angels."
它被稱爲「天使之城」。

Bangkok

** Thailand〔'taɪlənd〕*n.* 泰國
Bangkok〔'bæŋkɑk〕*n.* 曼谷　angel〔'endʒəl〕*n.* 天使

☐ 5. ***What is the capital city of Vietnam?***
越南的首都是哪裡？
Hanoi is the capital city of Vietnam.
河內是越南的首都。

Hanoi

Hanoi is located about 1,760 km north of Ho Chi Minh City, which is the largest city in Vietnam.

河內位於越南的最大城胡志明市北方 1,760 公里處。

** Vietnam 〔ˌviɛtˈnɑm〕*n.* 越南　　Hanoi〔hæˈnɔɪ〕*n.* 河內
north of 在…的北方　　***Ho Chi Minh City*** 胡志明市

□ 6. ***What is the capital city of the Philippines?***

菲律賓的首都是哪裡？

Manila is the nation's capital.

馬尼拉是該國的首都。

Manila

It has immense historical and cultural significance for the people of the Philippines.

對於菲律賓人而言，它有極大的歷史和文化的重要性。

** the Philippines〔ðə ˈfɪləˌpinz〕*n. pl.* 菲律賓群島；菲律賓共和國
Manila〔məˈnɪlə〕*n.* 馬尼拉
immense〔ɪˈmɛns〕*adj.* 巨大的
historical〔hɪsˈtɔrɪkl̩〕*adj.* 歷史的
cultural〔ˈkʌltʃərəl〕*adj.* 文化的
significance〔sɪgˈnɪfəkəns〕*n.* 重要性

*　　*　　*

□ 7. ***What is the capital city of Malaysia?***

馬來西亞的首都是哪裡？

Kuala Lumpur is the capital city of Malaysia.

吉隆坡是馬來西亞的首都。

Kuala Lumpur

It is the largest city in the country.
它是該國最大的城市。

** Malaysia〔məˈleʃə〕*n.* 馬來西亞
Kuala Lumpur〔ˌkwɑlə ˈlumpur〕*n.* 吉隆坡

☐ **8. *What is the capital city of India?***

New Delhi

印度的首都是哪裡？
The capital city of India is New Delhi. 印度的首都是新德里。
It is located in the north-central part of India. 它位於印度的中北部。

** India〔ˈɪndɪə〕*n.* 印度　New Delhi〔nju ˈdɛlɪ〕*n.* 新德里
north-central part 中北部

☐ **9. *What is the capital city of Turkey?***

Ankara

土耳其的首都是哪裡？
Ankara is the capital city of Turkey. 安卡拉是土耳其的首都。
Ankara became the capital in 1923, replacing Istanbul after the Ottoman Empire came to an end. 在鄂圖曼帝國結束之後，安卡拉於 1923 年取代伊斯坦堡，成爲首都。

** Turkey〔ˈtɝkɪ〕*n.* 土耳其　Ankara〔ˈæŋkərə〕*n.* 安卡拉
replace〔rɪˈples〕*v.* 取代　Istanbul〔ˌɪstænˈbul〕*n.* 伊斯坦堡
Ottoman〔ˈɑtəmən〕*adj.* 奧圖曼帝國的
empire〔ˈɛmpaɪr〕*n.* 帝國　***come to an end*** 結束

Superior Oral Tests

※ 請掃瞄 QR 碼，聽完題目後，練習回答兩句。

Oral Test 81

☐ 1. What is the biggest animal?

☐ 2. What is the fastest animal?

☐ 3. What is the biggest mammal in the ocean?

☐ 4. What is the tallest animal?

☐ 5. What is the biggest bird?

☐ 6. What is the smallest bird?

☐ 7. What is the biggest reptile?

☐ 8. What is the biggest tortoise?

☐ 9. What is the biggest snake?

Oral Test 82

☐ 1. What is the highest mountain in the world?

☐ 2. What is the longest river in the world?

☐ 3. What is the largest desert in the world?

☐ 4. What is the largest ocean in the world?

☐ 5. What is the largest lake in the world?

☐ 6. What is the biggest waterfall?

☐ 7. Who is the first man who walked on the moon?

☐ 8. What is the brightest star in the night sky?

☐ 9. What is the biggest planet in the solar system?

Oral Test 83

☐ 1. What is the tallest building in the world?

☐ 2. What is the biggest stadium in the world?

☐ 3. What is the biggest zoo in the world?

☐ 4. What is the railway of the highest altitude?

☐ 5. What is the longest railway?

☐ 6. What is the fastest railway train?

☐ 7. What is the best-selling book of all time?

☐ 8. What is the most popular movie?

☐ 9. What is the longest-running Broadway musical?

Oral Test 84

☐ 1. What are the largest countries in the world?

☐ 2. What are the smallest countries in the world?

☐ 3. What are the largest and the smallest continents in the world?

☐ 4. What are the Seven Wonders of the Ancient World?

☐ 5. What are the Seven Wonders of the Modern World?

☐ 6. What is the Nobel Prize?

☐ 7. What are the Academy Awards?

☐ 8. What are the King and Queen of Fruits?

☐ 9. What are superfoods?

Oral Test 85

☐ 1. What is IQ?

☐ 2. What is EQ?

☐ 3. What is the FBI?

☐ 4. What is the CIA?

☐ 5. What is 5G?

☐ 6. What is A.I.?

☐ 7. What is a 3D printer?

☐ 8. What is big data?

☐ 9. What is bitcoin?

Oral Test 86

☐ 1. Who is Thomas Edison?

☐ 2. Who is Dale Carnegie?

☐ 3. Who is William Shakespeare?

☐ 4. Who is Michael Jackson?

☐ 5. Who is Michael Jordan?

☐ 6. Who is Steve Jobs?

☐ 7. Who is Warren Buffett?

☐ 8. Who is Steven Spielberg?

☐ 9. Who is Ang Lee?

Oral Test 87

☐ 1. Who is Mark Twain?

☐ 2. Who is Mark Zuckerberg?

☐ 3. Who is Mother Teresa?

☐ 4. Who is Mahatma Gandhi?

☐ 5. Who is Isaac Newton?

☐ 6. Who is Albert Einstein?

☐ 7. Who is Wolfgang Amadeus Mozart?

☐ 8. Who is Audrey Hepburn?

☐ 9. Who is Tom Cruise?

Oral Test 88

☐ 1. What is the capital city of the U.S.?

☐ 2. What is the capital city of Canada?

☐ 3. What is the capital city of Brazil?

☐ 4. What is the capital city of Australia?

☐ 5. What is the capital city of New Zealand?

☐ 6. What is the capital city of Germany?

☐ 7. What is the capital city of Norway?

☐ 8. What is the capital city of Denmark?

____

____

☐ 9. What is the capital city of Sweden?

____

____

Oral Test 89

☐ 1. What is the capital city of the United Kingdom?

____

____

☐ 2. What is the capital city of France?

____

____

☐ 3. What is the capital city of the Netherlands?

____

____

☐ 4. What is the capital city of Belgium?

____

____

☐ 5. What is the capital city of Switzerland?

____

____

☐ 6. What is the capital city of Austria?

____

____

☐ 7. What is the capital city of Italy?

____

____

☐ 8. What is the capital city of Spain?

____

____

☐ 9. What is the capital city of Portugal?

____

____

Oral Test 90

☐ 1. What is the capital city of China?

____

____

☐ 2. What is the capital city of Japan?

____

____

☐ 3. What is the capital city of South Korea?

____

____

☐ 4. What is the capital city of Thailand?

____

____

☐ 5. What is the capital city of Vietnam?

____

____

☐ 6. What is the capital city of the Philippines?

____

____

☐ 7. What is the capital city of Malaysia?

____

____

☐ 8. What is the capital city of India?

____

____

☐ 9. What is the capital city of Turkey?

____

____

INDEX・索引

Index

Index

Index

Index

Index

Index

Index

Index

Index

Index

Index

Index

Index

Index

Index

Index

Index

Index

Index

Index

心得筆記欄

英語口試寶典

A Treasury of English Oral Tests

附錄音 QR 碼　售價：480 元

主　　　編 / 劉　毅
發　行　所 / 學習出版有限公司　　　☎ (02) 2704-5525
郵 撥 帳 號 / 05127272 學習出版社帳戶
登　記　證 / 局版台業 *2179* 號
印　刷　所 / 裕強彩色印刷有限公司
台 北 門 市 / 台北市許昌街 10 號 2F　　☎ (02) 2331-4060
台灣總經銷 / 紅螞蟻圖書有限公司　　☎ (02) 2795-3656
本公司網址　www.learnbook.com.tw
電 子 郵 件　learnbook@learnbook.com.tw

2020 年 1 月 1 日初版

4713269383437

練習、練習、再練習，
熟能生巧。

Less talk, less mistakes.
Less speech, less offense.
Less food, less sickness.

* * *

少說，少錯。
少說，少禍。
少吃，少病。

Less desire, less anxiety.
Less money, less stress.
Less love, less hurt.

* * *

慾望少，焦慮少。
錢少，壓力少。
少愛，少受傷害。

Less fat, less sweat.
Less waste, less worry.
Less fame, less expensive.

* * *

不胖，不流汗。

不浪費，不擔憂。

名氣越小，越不貴。